To Mohame

CW00815935

THE MORTAL MAZE
a novel by Ian D. Richardson

In journalism, there has always been a tension
between getting it first
and getting it right

AMERICAN COLUMNIST AND PULITZER PRIZE WINNER,
ELLEN GOODMAN

Best wishes,
Ian Richardson
Sept 2015

PROOF COPY (contains some
small errors)

First edition. Published September 14, 2015
by Preddon Lee Limited
26 Ascott Avenue, London W5 5QB. UK
http://www.preddonlee.com/
http://www.themortalmaze.com/
© Ian D. Richardson 2014

Cover design: Rachel Lawston, London, UK
Story editor: Jan Woolf, London, UK
Final draft editor and page design: Rosemary Batson

ISBN: 978-0-9571401-9-6

CHAPTERS

Also by this author:

God's Triangle

The true story of scandal and establishment cover-up in
Australia and East Bengal
http://www.godstriangle.com/

ACKNOWLEDGEMENTS

My thanks to all the family, friends and colleagues who have supported and contributed to the writing of *The Mortal Maze* and the associated screenplay.

Particular thanks must go to Penny Berry for her encouragement and expert advice about cultural, language and regional details, to Jan Woolf for editing the book, to Pippa Gwilliam for her proofing and her assessment of the initial draft, to Rachel Lawston for the cover design, and Sally Glover for building the website.

Further thanks to Graeme Turpie, John Trevenen, Sue Flemons, Ruth Wheatman, Lorraine Batson and Warwick Millar for test reading the developed manuscript.

CHAPTER 1

Jackson Dunbar – Jacko to his colleagues and friends – surveys the scene before him with some disappointment. He has been in Armibar, capital of Central Arabia, for a month now and he still hasn't been able to get a report on the BBC's *Ten O'Clock News*.

It is a frustrating time for an ambitious TV correspondent. Twice he has been to demonstrations in this shabby street, pock-marked by bullets from a long-past battle, and in a part of the city well away from the eyes of most citizens. On both occasions, a promised dramatic event failed to make the grade, except for a few short clips on the World News channel.

Jackson's young Australian cameraman, Pete Fox, is busy filming about 100 Arab men chanting and waving placards calling for the destruction of Britain, America and Israel. They are mostly in grubby traditional outfits, the ankle-length thawb or dishdash, and headwear, the keffiyeh. Women wearing black hijabs stand in the doorways ululating and clapping.

It is very routine stuff, unlikely to have any impact, and Jackson wonders why the demonstration is being held in such an out-of-the-way run-down street with its dusty pot-holed roads, broken pavements and heaps of stinking uncollected rubbish. Police and soldiers in their cheap crumpled uniforms are there in substantial numbers as they always are for demonstrations, but even they are looking upon the protest in a manner that suggests they wish they were back in their barracks playing cards or football.

Pete, in his late twenties and with an accent and choice of clothes that make clear his Down Under origins, comes over to Jackson: "Do you want to do a piece-to-camera, mate?"

Jackson takes another look around him and shakes his head. "It's another no-no. Let's pack it in and get back to the bureau."

Pete is unsure. "I think I'll stick around a bit while they're still here," nodding towards the CNN and Al-Jazeera crews and newsagency reporters.

"Please yourself, but my expenses need urgent attention," Jackson says with a grin.

1

He goes to the BBC's silver Range Rover 4x4 parked nearby and gets in beside the staff driver, Yassin Azizi, an easy-going young Arab with a bushy dark moustache, wearing smart western clothes and smoking a cigarette.

Five minutes later the car is moving down an avenue alongside the Armibar Central Plaza, a busy and prosperous air conditioned shopping mall with life going on as though the city is at total peace with itself. It is a world and a culture away from where they have just been. Many of the women are confidently wearing fashionable Western clothes and proudly flaunting expensive designer handbags. Were it not for the many men bustling about in their neat white thawbs and patterned keffiyehs, it could be any flourishing business centre in the developed world.

Jackson spots a modern glass-fronted bank and tells Yassin to pull over at the ATM. He inserts his card and taps in the PIN. The card is rejected. Jackson angrily bangs the machine with his fist and walks back to the car, watched with resignation by Yassin.

"Bloody banks!" mutters Jackson.

Yassin anticipates what will happen next and already has his wallet out by the time Jackson gets back into the passenger seat. He hands over a $50 note.

"Thanks," says Jackson, embarrassed that this is not the first time. "I'll give it back when I get my exes." Yassin sighs but says nothing.

The car resumes the journey back to the bureau. Jackson's mobile phone rings. He sees on the screen that Pete is calling. "Hi Pete!" There is no answer and the line goes dead. "Bloody phones," declares Jackson.

The car continues on its way, both men remaining silent. Then, as they turn into the street lined with modern brick office blocks where the bureau is situated, they spot the thirties-something Anglo-Arab office manager, Samira Lang, at the front door. She simultaneously sees the car and runs out onto the roadway, waving her hands furiously. Jackson winds down his window. "Go back, go back," Samira shouts. Jackson's mobile rings. It is Pete again.

"What's the problem, Pete?" Jackson listens briefly, then, "Okay. We're on our way back now." There is a Hollywood-style squealing of tyres as Yassin does a fierce U-turn and speeds back down the road.

Ten minutes later, Jackson is back at the scene of the demonstration. It could not be more shockingly different than when they left it such a short time ago. It is a blood bath. Wounded and dead Arabs, both military and civilian, both male and female, are lying in pools of blood on the road and in doorways. Soldiers are tensely lined up, rifles raised and firing shots into the air, to keep back a gathering crowd. There are sirens as police and military cars and ambulances arrive. Some of the injured demonstrators are already in the back of private utility trucks that charge away with headlights and horns blazing.

Jackson sees Pete filming from a doorway and runs to him. Pete has blood running down his face. "What the fuck happened?"

Pete replies while continuing filming. "The demo was infiltrated by militants just before you left."

"Did you see them?" Jackson demands.

"I guess I did."

"Well, why the fuck didn't you tell me?"

"How the hell was I to know they were carrying hidden guns and grenades?! They just looked like regular demonstrators who'd turned up late. Anyway, mate, don't blame me for your own failings. You shouldn't have pissed off before you knew the story was really over. You should know how sensitive everything is in this city."

Jackson accepts that Pete is right and that is how the acerbic bureau chief, Mack Galbraith, will also see it. He knows he has to do something fast and drastic to salvage the situation. "C'mon. Let's not get into an argument, Pete, I need to know what you filmed?"

"Most of it, mate."

"Thank Christ!" Jackson mutters.

Pete pauses to wipe the blood from his face before adding caustically: "And thanks for asking how I am!"

"Sorry, Pete. What happened?"

"A ricochet off the wall just above me when the troops opened fire on a guy who had appeared at a window with his gun. It's only a graze. I'll be okay. But the guy at the window copped it."

"Glad you weren't badly hurt."

Having expressed his concern, even belatedly, Jackson is anxious to get back to the story. He nods towards the *CNN* and *Al Jazeera* crews as they speed away. "How much did they get?"

"All of it, mate, and both Jane and Omar were in the middle of doing their pieces-to-camera when it all blew up."

"Oh shit, shit, shit! Mack is going to tear my balls off over this."

Desperation is taking hold of Jackson. "Look mate, I've really got to do a piece-to-camera."

"That's going to look a bit lame at this stage, Jacko."

"No it won't. Run into that derelict building over there, filming as you go, then turn the camera on me as I run in after you."

Pete hesitates. Jackson panics as he sees his promising career coming apart before his eyes. "Do it, will you! Just do as I say!"

The row begins to attract bystanders, now that most of the wounded and bodies have been taken away. Pete is embarrassed and runs without enthusiasm into the derelict building as instructed. Jackson pauses then races after Pete as though competing in a 100-metre sprint. Once inside, he crouches down, catches his breath and begins pouring out words to the camera:

> *What started out today as a peaceful protest has turned violent. It...*

Jackson suddenly flinches and anxiously looks around before resuming his report.

> *Er. It isn't quite clear why the protest turned into such a savage confrontation, but there are many dead and wounded. This bloody event is sure to place additional pressure on the Central Arabian Government, which has been facing serious allegations of corruption and a weakness towards what is seen as the imperial ambitions of Israel and Western governments.*

Jackson flinches again, looks around anxiously, pauses a few seconds, then casually stands up and dusts himself down. "That should do the trick, Pete. Let's get this back to the office."

As they return to the 4x4, Jackson fails to notice a small heap of human excrement just inside the entrance to the building. He steps right into it. He screws up his face and wipes his shoe clean on a tuft of grass. "You could be in the shit in more than one way," laughs Pete.

******

At the BBC bureau, MacDonald "Mack" Galbraith angrily paces about his untidy office. He is 50 and a caricature of an old-fashioned world-weary Glaswegian hack. He puffs furiously on a cigarette and his clothes need the attention of an iron. As he mostly confines himself to doing reports for radio and online, his appearance doesn't really matter. The ash tray on Mack's untidy desk is overflowing, his book shelves lack any apparent order and the large wall map of the Middle East is faded and torn with Post-it stickers and scribbles all over it.

Mack goes to the door to the main work area and shouts at Samira: "Where the fuck is that numptie?"

Samira attempts to calm him: "He'll be here in a few minutes. He says he's got a great piece-to-camera."

"He'd better or I'll have him cut off at the knees," Mack shouts as he returns to his desk, lights another cigarette from a smoking butt and glares at three TV monitors fixed to the wall. They are permanently tuned to BBC World News, CNN and Al Jazeera.

Meanwhile, Yassin is swerving through the traffic, horn tooting and headlights flashing. Jackson is in the front seat and turns to Pete who is in the back studying the piece-to-camera on the camera monitor. "It'll work fine if you add some shooting and bullet pings to the sound track," he declares.

Pete frowns. "I'm not going to fake it, Jacko."

"Jeez! We're not really faking it. It's what would have happened if I'd been there. Anyway, you must've done it all the time in Australia."

"There are witnesses to what you – we – did, Jacko. And besides, we're working for the British Broadcasting Corporation, not some two-bit commercial outfit in Australia!"

"Don't get pompous with me, Pete!"

Pete fiddles with the camera, then turns back to Jackson. "I've deleted your piece. Debate over!"

Jackson sinks back into his seat, crushed. "Shit!"

Back at the bureau, Mack's fury knows no bounds as he watches the TV monitors and sees that *CNN* and *Al Jazeera* are already on air with their version of the story. He lights another cigarette even though his previous one is only half smoked. He pours himself a large whisky from a bottle in a drawer in his desk.

******

Jackson and Pete come crashing through the entrance door and go into the main open-plan work area. Farouk Ahmed, the bureau's Arab technician, is setting up a camera on the platform in the corner of the room used as a TV broadcast area.

Mack comes to his office door. "About fucking time, too," he shouts and points to the TV monitors showing *CNN* and *Al Jazeera's* coverage of the story. Jackson flinches and turns to Samira: "Quick! Get me the latest Reuters."

"A 'please' would be nice, Jacko," she curtly replies.

"I don't have time for 'pleases', Samira. Just get me the Reuters stuff. I need it now, now, now!"

Samira sighs and prints the latest Reuter reports from her computer while Pete lines up his film. Jackson closes his eyes and does deep breathing to calm himself. He grabs a brush from his desk and tidies his dark wavy hair as he moves in front of the studio camera. Farouk turns on the TV lights and attaches a clip microphone to Jackson's shirt. Samira goes to Jackson and dabs make-up on his forehead to take away the shine.

The TV monitors beside the camera come to life and show the *BBC World News* studio with presenter Margaret Mathieson talking to a studio guest.

"Are you there, London?" Jackson calls out.

"Yes, we're here," says a disembodied male voice on a speaker, "we'll come to you in a couple of minutes as soon as this interview is wound up."

Jackson nods and is handed a couple of sheets of Reuters by Samira.

"Thanks," he says with a weak apologetic smile.

Mack's fury grows as he paces about his office watching *CNN* and *Al Jazeera* doing their reports. He turns up the sound on the CNN monitor as reporter Jane Kubinski delivers her piece-to-camera:

> *The gun battle started without warning after the relatively peaceful and routine demonstration was infiltrated by ...*

There is a rapid burst of gunfire and Jane crouches down and looks around her. She looks up to a window where a man in Arab dress is waving a white flag. He is shot dead and slumps forward, half hanging out the window. Jane hesitates then resumes her report with a trembling voice:

> *As I was saying, the demonstration was infiltrated by a group of men who seem to have hidden hand grenades under their thawbs, their traditional ankle-length garment. Without warning, they began attacking soldiers and police who were monitoring the demonstration. The soldiers retaliated with indiscriminate gunfire and ...*

Mack kills the sound and turns up the *Al Jazeera* report in Arabic. Their correspondent, Omar Abbas, is seen running to take shelter while simultaneously trying to explain what is happening. At that moment, Mack sees *BBC World News* presenter Margaret Mathieson end the studio interview and turn to the camera. He brings up the sound:

> *We are just getting reports from the troubled country of Central Arabia that there has been a violent demonstration resulting in many dead and wounded. Our correspondent, Jackson Dunbar, was there and is in our studio in the capital, Armibar ... Hello Jackson, tell us what happened ...*

Jackson appears on screen and talks in a confident manner that belies his turbulent emotional state:

> *Well, Margaret, no-one could have predicted the slaughter I witnessed a short while ago. Although the Central Arabian regime is very much on the defensive these days, demonstrations take place frequently and are hardly worth reporting because they seem directionless and unlikely to change anything. I've been to several of these demonstrations since arriving in Armibar a month ago and they have never been newsworthy. The regime mostly ignores them.*

Mack shouts at the monitor: "Jings, Jacko! Just tell us what fucking happened!"

At that point, Margaret, jumps in with an edge to her voice:

> *Yes, we understand that Jackson, but can you tell us what actually went wrong today?*

Jackson correctly takes this as a polite reprimand.

> *Yes, of course, Margaret... It seems that the demonstration was infiltrated by a group of jihadists armed with grenades. Without warning, they began hurling the grenades at the soldiers who were keeping a watch on the demonstration. And here's what happened: This film was taken by my colleague Peter Fox and contains scenes that some viewers may find distressing.*

Farouk plays in Pete's uncut film. It is not one for the faint-hearted. There are graphic and bloody scenes of killing and wounding with screams from the victims and the watching women and children. No commentary is needed.

Mack comes out of his office to join Jackson, Pete, Samira and Farouk who are watching the film. "This is strong stuff, Pete. We'd better remove some of the blood and guts before we re-run it." He pats Pete on the shoulder and belatedly notices the gash on his forehead: "What happened?"

"It's nothing. Just a routine part of a crazy Aussie cameraman's day in a warzone," he grins.

Farouk shouts to Jackson: "Thirty seconds to go." Jackson resumes his place in front of the camera. Mack turns to him and asks about the piece-to-camera. "Sorry," Jackson replies, "we had a problem with it. Sorry." "Fuck", exclaims Mack. He does a hand movement as though firing a revolver at Jackson. "We'll talk about this later Mr Rising Bloody TV Star Who Never Misses a Story!"

Mack goes back into his office, slamming the door behind him with such force that the glass is in danger of shattering. He flops down at his desk, lights up another cigarette and checks the TV monitors. His phone rings and he pushes the speaker button. "Mack Galbraith," he answers distractedly.

"Hi Mack. It's Mary Dunstan on the foreign desk."

"Yes, Mary."

"Powerful stuff from Jacko! A shame, though, that CNN and Al Jazeera beat us to air with it. Anyway, we're setting aside 10 minutes for a package in tonight's *Ten O'Clock*. We'll need it early so that we can sort out the graphics and other stuff."

"Righto. Will see to that."

"Good, Mack. We're getting advice from Foreign Office insiders that Central Arabia is going to be the next big story in the Middle East. Do you agree?"

"Could well be. People here are getting worried that they'll be going the way of Egypt, Iraq and Libya."

"Right, Mack. We'll look forward to getting lots more good stuff from Jacko."

Mary hangs up. Mack gives a sigh and gets up to give Jackson his instructions. Jackson is slumped at his desk, shaken by the dramatic events of the past hour and upset that he has been scooped by his rivals. He cheers up a little on being told that he will be starring in the *Ten*.

Mack decides that now is not the time or the place to give Jackson a serious bollocking. "Just do your best with Pete's great stuff while I think up some excuses for London."

Jackson is repentant: "I'm really sorry, Mack. Really, really sorry. It won't happen again."

"I hope not. I need to rely 100% on everyone in this bureau," Mack says, as he returns to his office, lighting up another cigarette and gulping down the remains of his whisky.

CHAPTER 2

It is late at night by the time Jackson finishes his commitments to London and gets back to his apartment in Armibar's central residential district. It has a functional open plan living area with a kitchenette. Arabic and English newspapers and magazines are scattered about. A few unwashed dishes lie in water in the kitchen sink. There is a medium-sized TV set, plus a computer, a stereo music unit, a sofa, two armchairs and some kitchen stools. A landline telephone, notebooks and assorted gadgets are scattered on the kitchen bench. An electronic keyboard is on a stand in the corner of the room close to a shelf full of assorted books. Pop group and modern art posters decorate the walls. It is untidy, but thanks to a maid coming in every few days, it is clean.

Jackson turns on *BBC World News* and watches some of Pete's film being repeated. He takes a bottle of whisky from a cupboard and pours himself a large drink, pauses, then pours himself an even larger one. The stresses of the past 12 hours or so are taking their toll.

Jackson switches on his laptop and goes to an American gambling site called *Towering Treasures Inc*. It says: *Funds Required.* His mobile phone rings and his mind is still on the gambling site as he takes the call.

The call is from his mother in London. "Oh, hello, Mother. Did you see my piece on the *Ten*?" He is annoyed by his mother's response: "Yes, yes, yes! I know Dad always wore a tie, but I've told you before, Mother, it's different now." There is more chat from his mother and he begins to shout: "For Christ's sake! Is that the best you can say, that I looked untidy? And stop calling me Roger!" Jackson angrily snaps shut the phone, ending the call without so much as a 'good bye'. He gulps down his whisky and goes to the bathroom to turn on the shower.

******

Next morning: Jackson is running late and Samira, Jackson, Pete and Farouk are already in Mack's office as the morning editorial conference with Foreign News in London begins. They are all worn out.

Mary Dunstan is again making the call from London and can be heard on Mack's phone speaker: "Right. Let's talk about today. We need a good strong follow-up with an assessment of whether Central Arabia is beginning to come apart at the seams and whether anyone should give a damn. We'll be getting onto bankers and big business reps over here to see if they're worried about the huge investments they've made in the country. In addition, Jackson will need to provide fresh packages for the lunchtime, Six and Ten bulletins. We're assuming that you, Mack, will be doing all the radio and online stuff."

"Not a problem, Mary," Mack replies, exuding confidence that he hopes isn't misplaced.

"Great," says Mary, "now let's consider your staffing situation. If this story continues to grow, as some people expect, you might need back-up. Someone from the World Affairs Team could be flown in."

Mack and the team exchange alarmed looks. "Oh no, Mary, we'll be fine. The last thing we need at the moment is some know-nothing from London trampling all over our story."

"Well, it's not my decision, but we don't want a repeat of what happened yesterday. There is some disenchantment on the top floor about how we were beaten by the opposition. More importantly, we were the only one not to have an action piece-to-camera."

Pete, wearing a Bondi Beach surfer T-shirt, hastily chips in: "Jacko did do a strong piece, Mary, but it must have been corrupted when I banged my camera taking cover from the shooting. You tell those pricks on the top floor to get stuffed if they raise it again. They bloody weren't here dodging the bullets. Some of those useless bastards in designer suits and clubland ties haven't covered anything more dangerous than a church fete in their entire bloody careers."

Mack and Jackson are taken aback by the ferocity of Pete's intervention. "No, I understand that, Pete," says Mary. "I'll vigorously defend you guys when I go upstairs for the morning briefing. Shit happens. It just wasn't your lucky day – losing the piece-to-camera and having that puncture."

Everyone but Mack is baffled by this last remark. What puncture? Mack hastily responds: "Yes, Mary, as I said last night, you can be unlucky sometimes."

"Understood, Mack. Just one other thing before I go: Reuter is reporting that a little known group called *Soldiers for Allah* is claiming responsibility for the riot. Ever heard of them?"

"Nope," replies Mack. "Sounds like a made-up name. These days any wanker can put stuff up on the internet claiming to be this, that or the other."

"Okay, Mack. All the best for today. We'll talk again later."

Mary hangs up and there is a sigh of relief around the room. Mack brings the meeting to an end. "Well, we got away with it this time, thanks to our 'puncture' and Pete's intervention. Perhaps one day, Pete, you and Jacko will tell me what really happened with that piece-to-camera." Pete smirks. Jackson looks away, still embarrassed.

"By the way," adds Mack, "I got this email overnight from some ponce in Health and Safety wanting assurances that you were both wearing flak jackets yesterday. I wrote back that if I ever caught you without your flak jackets I would personally tie you both to a tree in a public square and give you 100 lashes with a stick of wet rhubarb."

They all laugh and their mood lifts. Mack dismisses Jackson and Pete with a gentle wave of his hand. Yesterday is best forgotten. Today is another day.

******

Two days have passed and all is well. Jackson has made his peace with Mack and his professional reputation has been restored as he delivers well-crafted and perceptive packages for all television outlets, including the *Ten* and *Newsnight*. While he knows that appearing on *BBC World News* means his reports are seen by tens of millions around the globe, he gets a special kick from being on the

Ten and the other major outlets back home. There is nothing like knowing that his friends and his mother are seeing him on screen doing a big story.

Jackson has a lunch appointment at the *Hotel Armibar* in one of the better parts of the city. He waits in the guest bar and feeds American dollar coins into a poker machine. He strikes it lucky and his body tingles with excitement as a payout of $100 crashes into the winnings tray.

"So, your lucky day!" declares an English public schoolboy voice from behind him.

Jackson turns to see Thomas Fulham standing there. Thomas is roughly the same age as him – about 35 – and is wearing an expensive suit and tie in contrast to Jackson's usual on-screen wear of open-necked smart casual.

"Looks as though the drinks are on you," observes Thomas.

"Looks like it," says Jackson with a grin as he scoops up the coins and drops them into a large empty ash tray on a nearby table.

He and Thomas shake hands. "Nice to catch up with you again, Tommy."

Jackson motions Thomas to a seat at the table and calls over a waiter. "What's your poison?" he asks Thomas.

"A G&T would be welcome, dear chap."

Jackson turns to the waiter: "A double gin-and-tonic for my friend here and a Coke with ice and lemon for me."

Thomas raises an eyebrow at the Coke order. "How things have changed!"

"Booze and broadcasting don't mix, you know," Jackson responds.

Jackson and Thomas study each other awkwardly for several seconds before Jackson breaks the silence: "Well then, how come you are in this God-forsaken place, Tommy? It doesn't seem your scene."

"Um, I'd prefer to be called Thomas, dear chap. You know, now that I'm in the diplomatic service."

"Ah yes. Well, you always were a bit of a pompous bastard, Thomas," Jackson said, deliberately stressing "Thomas". "I'll tell you what. I'll stop calling you Tommy if you'll stop addressing me as 'dear chap'."

Thomas accepts this with a faint smile and a shrug: "Fair enough, Jacko, or should that be Jackson?"

"I'm quite comfortable with Jacko among friends and colleagues."

"Right then, 'Jacko' it is," says Thomas.

The waiter returns with the drinks and Jackson pays him from his winnings.

"So, back to my question, Thomas, how and why are you here?"

Thomas hands Jackson a business card. Jackson studies it and breaks into a smile: "Thomas J. Fulham, Commercial Attaché, Embassy of the United Kingdom, Armibar! That's a turn-up. I don't recall you ever knowing much about commerce. You were more of a rugger bugger with an interest in military matters."

"You're overlooking the fact that my family was very successful in business, which is where the family money comes from."

"I didn't know that," Jackson admits, "but I still don't see why someone with your posh connections hasn't been sent to one of the better postings in Europe or North America, or even Australia."

"It's because of my Arabic. And no matter how shitty the country, there are always commercial opportunities to be exploited and protected. I'm here to make sure Britain gets its fair share."

"Well, Thomas, in that respect you haven't changed one bit."

They laugh and sip their drinks. Thomas picks up the local Arabic-language newspaper, *The Voice*, lying on an adjacent table and points to the main front page story: "You know this is total horse manure, of course."

"Probably," agrees Jackson, "but at least it gives us some sort of view of the regime's thinking."

They are interrupted by the approach of an elegant woman in her mid-thirties, blonde and wearing a stylish trouser suit. She has a loose-fitting headscarf over her hair. She carries a Harrods shopping bag and is greeted by Thomas: "Flip, darling! This is a pleasant surprise."

Flip, more formally known by her proper name, Felicity, smiles awkwardly at both Thomas and Jackson and takes a seat at the table. She puts her bag down beside her. "Well," says Thomas with a sweep of his hand towards Felicity and Jackson, "I believe you know each other."

"Yes. Hello, Roger," she says softly.

"Oh, it's Jackson these days, darling," interrupts Thomas with a sarcastic edge to his voice.

"Oh yes. So I've noticed from the television," she agrees.

"Hello, Felicity," says Jackson, "nice to see you again. It's been many years."

"Yes 15 years, at least."

Jackson smiles, but cannot entirely obscure a certain tension in his voice: "Yes, 15 at least," he confirms.

Thomas points to Felicity's shopping bag: "So what have you been spending our money on?

She is about to reply, but Thomas's phone rings. He looks at the screen and announces: "I must take this."

He gets up and walks over to a balcony at the bar, out of hearing. Jackson notes, without paying too much attention, that Thomas has a limp.

Jackson and Felicity lean towards each other, their voices lowered.

"Christ, I didn't expect to see you here!" Jackson declares.

"Nor did I expect to see you," she admitted, "but I go to whatever country Thomas is posted to. As for being here today, Thomas often meets his contacts in this bar, so I just popped in on the off-chance. I was passing anyway."

Jackson breaks into a warm smile: "Well, it's good to see you again."

"And you, too," says Felicity, a little edgily.

There is a pause in the conversation with Felicity keeping a watchful eye on Thomas on the balcony. Jackson leans forward again: "What does Thomas know?"

"Oh, nothing much," she reassures him, "he knows we were university friends and attended some of the same lectures, but that's about it. He was too tied up with his Arabic studies and his boozy dining club chums to hear anything more than that."

"Good. We'd best leave it at that," says Jackson. There is a pause, then he adds: "I was surprised when I heard on the grapevine that you had ended up with Thomas."

"Ended up? That's so, so insulting, Roger!"

Jackson is instantly apologetic: "Oh God! I didn't intend it to come out like that. But you know what I mean. Thomas never struck me as your sort."

"Thomas is okay. Don't be fooled by the 'Hooray Henry' exterior. He's very intelligent and we have a comfortable life."

"So it wasn't entirely for love?"

"Leave it, will you, Jackson!" she says crossly.

Felicity watches Thomas end his phone call and changes the subject. "So, what's this 'Jackson' business? What's wrong with Roger?"

"Oh, Roger was too confusing, you know," says Jackson, "and it wasn't much fun having Dad and me with the same name and both being reasonably well-known journalists. Anyway, Jackson Dunbar has a certain ring of authority to it, don't you think?"

Felicity raises an eyebrow: "It's more memorable, perhaps."

"Well, I can't change it back now," Jackson says with a shrug.

Thomas rejoins them and gulps down the rest of his G&T. "Something urgent has come up, dear chap, er Jacko, so we'll have to do lunch another time. Better still, come around for dinner one evening soon. We can take the opportunity to swap some thoughts on the future of this crappy little country. I'll leave it to Flip to organise."

Thomas gives his wife a cursory kiss and hurries away, leaving her and Jackson sitting there, not knowing quite what to say or do.

"Well, um, <u>would</u> you like to come around for dinner?" asks Felicity tentatively.

"Mmm. That would be good," he replies as he consults his phone diary. "Next Tuesday is a day off, if that suits you."

"Good. Next Tuesday it is. Give me your business card and I'll email you a confirmation with our address."

Jackson gets a card from his wallet and hands it over. "Are you quite sure it'll be okay?"

"Yes, yes, of course," she replies, a little snitchily, "the past is the past. Anyway, we'll be moving in the same small social circle here, so we can hardly avoid seeing each other. And it would be nice for you to meet our kids."

"Oh, you've got kids? How many?"

"Two. One of each, both primary school age."

"Okay. Well, I'll get to meet them next Tuesday."

Felicity looks at her watch. "Well, Roger – sorry <u>Jacko</u> – I must go. Pity that your lunch appointment with Thomas didn't happen. I'm afraid that you'll find him not very reliable on that front."

She stands up to leave and Jacko points to the shopping bag that she had brought. "Don't forget that!"

"Oh yes, I was going to show you this when we were interrupted by Thomas's call."

Felicity gently removes a vase from the bag and carefully hands it to Jackson. It is about 30cms high, elegantly shaped, obviously quite old and decorated with Arabic images and text. Jackson flicks it with a finger and it resonates with a satisfying sound. It is a quality item. "My word, that must have cost you a few dollars!"

"Oh no. It's a gift from a grateful parent."

"How come?"

"I'm a volunteer at the Fouad Rehabilitation Centre."

"Oh, I've heard of that. It's not far from our bureau. We might do a feature on it one day." He studies the vase more closely. "It's lovely. I'm sure you're worth it."

Felicity and Jackson exchange air kisses as she leaves. He notes that she is wearing the same distinctive perfume that he remembered from their university days. He did once know what it was called.

Jackson calls the waiter and orders a sandwich. The waiter enquires if he wants another Coke. He agrees, then changes his mind and orders a beer.

Jackson goes to the poker machine and begins feeding his winnings into it. At the same time, he makes a call on his mobile: "Hi, William. It's Jackson Dunbar. Any chance you could fix me up with an off-the-record chat with Sir Gordon?"

******

Jackson is wearing a sober suit and tie as he arrives by taxi at the British Embassy. It's a large Edwardian brick building with a high iron railing fence. He is frisked by an armed British military guard at the entrance gate and escorted into Reception. The young receptionist immediately recognises him. "Good morning, Mr Dunbar. I'm Katherine. I believe you have an appointment with His Excellency. I'll see if he's ready to receive you."

The receptionist dials an internal number. "Oh hello, Jane. Mr Dunbar of the BBC is here for his meeting with Sir Gordon. I'll get someone to escort him up."

She puts the phone down, pushes a button on the desk to summon a guard and turns back to Jackson. "A security officer will be along in a minute or two," then adds, "Congratulations on your reports on the riots the other day. It must have been very dangerous."

Jackson feigns modesty: "It was okay. In our job one learns how to look after oneself."

"Yes, I'm sure, Mr Dunbar. But congratulations all the same."

******

A uniformed security guard escorts Jackson through a maze of corridors to a lift that takes them to an upper floor where he is met by the embassy press attaché, William Crawford. William ushers him into a vast, ridiculously-grand ambassadorial suite. Sir Gordon Shortwood, a man in his late fifties with an air of British public school entitlement, gets up from behind his large carved wooden desk and shakes hands with Jackson. He wears a dark three-piece suit more suited to a Gentlemen's Club in London than the Middle East.

William takes a seat to one side of the room and discreetly switches on a hand-held audio note-taker.

"Nice to meet you in the flesh, Mr Dunbar" says Sir Gordon, "please take a seat." He waves Jackson towards one of several large leather-bound chairs.

"I have, of course, been watching your reports with great interest. A nasty situation you found yourself in the other day, I see!"

"Yes, a bit tricky, Your Excellency."

"Oh, no need for 'Your Excellency'. Sir Gordon will suffice on these private occasions."

"Thank you, Sir Gordon. And please call me Jackson."

"Yes. Well, Jackson, how can I help?"

"As you know, I'm new on this patch, so I thought it would be useful if we could get acquainted and I could draw on your wisdom as a highly-regarded diplomat with considerable experience of the machinations in the Central Arabian regime."

"Very nice of you to say so, Jackson. Yes, the truth is that I'm one of the better informed ambassadors in this region," he says, unconsciously puffing out his chest.

Jackson takes a notebook from his pocket. His mobile phone rings. He glances at the screen, then turns off the phone. The interview begins.

CHAPTER 3

Back at the bureau, Mack wonders where Jackson is. "He's not planning to come in until after lunch," Samira tells him. "Who says?" asks an irritated Mack. "Who runs this bloody bureau? Him or me?"

"I tried phoning him," she responds, "but he must be in a black spot. Do you want me to try again?"

"Don't bother," shrugs Mack, "just as long he gets here soon. *Newsnight* wants to clarify something in that package he did for them."

"I'll tell him as soon as he gets in," says Samira.

******

Jackson's off-the-record chat with Sir Gordon Shortwood comes to an end. The ambassador escorts him to the door of his suite. "Well, as I've said, there's no doubt in my mind that eventually this regime will implode because of corruption, cronyism and incompetence. But for the time being, al-Qaeda and their jihadist conspirators are much more concerned with attacking Christian Europe and America. This place is of no interest to them."

"That's most useful guidance, Sir Gordon. I appreciate you sparing the time to brief me," says Jackson. "Your background knowledge is immensely useful to a newcomer such as myself."

Sir Gordon is suitably flattered: "Well, young man, I hope that I've been able to put you on the right track. May your posting to Armibar be both successful and enjoyable."

Sir Gordon and Jackson shake hands and the security guard reappears to escort Jackson from the building. They are walking along a long corridor when Jackson spots Thomas in shirt sleeves down a side corridor, punching a number into a door security code.

"Hey, Thomas!" Jackson calls out, but Thomas doesn't hear and disappears through the doorway. Jackson runs down to the door, but is pursued by the security guard. "Sir, Sir! Please come back immediately. You're in a restricted area." Jackson sees a sign "Authorised Personnel Only". The guard firmly takes him by the arm and they return to the main corridor.

"What's down there?" Jackson asks. "No idea, sir," lies the guard, "it's a separate division of the embassy."

Back at reception, Jackson thanks the guard and goes to the receptionist. "Hello again, Katherine. Could you raise Thomas Fulham for me, please?"

She looks surprised. "Er, why would you need to see him? He doesn't do interviews with the press."

"Oh, we know each other and I was just going to say hello."

"I'm very sorry, Mr Dunbar, but Mr Fulham isn't able to see anyone without an appointment."

"Really? It was just going to be a quick word about some, er, commercial matters," he lies.

"Oh, well. You need to talk to Mr O'Brien about that."

"Not Mr Fulham?"

"No, Mr O'Brien would be best."

"Well, it's Mr Fulham I was hoping to see."

"I'm terribly sorry, Mr Dunbar, but I have strict instructions about this. If you wish, I'll pass on a message to him that you called. I'm sure he will make contact with you as soon as he is able."

Jackson gives up. "Well, thanks anyway," he says as he heads for the exit.

Jackson is increasingly suspicious about the reaction of the receptionist. Once outside the embassy, he gets Thomas's business card from his wallet and phones the number on his mobile. It is promptly answered: "It's Jacko, Thomas. What game are you playing?" He listens to Thomas's reply, then demands: "Yeah. Well, I think you'd better come clean with me." He listens again, responds with a curt "right!" and pockets his phone.

******

Jackson crosses the road from the British Embassy and goes into a coffee shop. He orders two Arabic coffees and water and sits down at a discreet corner table. As the drinks are brought to him, he is joined by Thomas who takes a seat but doesn't speak until the waiter has moved away.

"Look, dear chap, er Jacko, it's very sensitive. I couldn't just come right out and say what the situation really is. You're a man of the world. You must know that."

"I shouldn't really be surprised," admits Jackson, "the commercial attaché crap just didn't fit."

"The opposition intelligence people probably aren't fooled either. It's all a kind of game, you know, but with very serious intent."

"What does Felicity feel about this?"

"Oh God!" exclaims Thomas, "I haven't told Flip. It would be too much pressure for her. Too unsettling. To use a cliché, 'ignorance is bliss'."

Jackson shrugs his shoulders in a non-committal way and sips his coffee. Thomas looks around to check that he can't be overheard and leans forward to Jackson: "Now that you've guessed what I'm really doing here, I'd like you to do me a little favour."

Jackson is suspicious. "What sort of 'little favour'?"

"Nothing much. It won't involve you in anything other than showing me the full uncut video from that riot the other day."

Jackson is still suspicious. Thomas tries to reassure him: "It won't be a problem for you. Honest! I just need a quick look, then that's it."

"Okay," says Jackson, "I'll make an excuse to stay on at the bureau after the others have packed it in for the day, but don't think I'll make a habit of this!"

"Thanks. I owe you."

******

Jackson takes a taxi to the bureau and as he arrives, he removes his tie, rolls it up and puts it in his jacket pocket. He strolls upstairs to the office to be greeted by an irritated Mack. "Thanks for coming in today, Jacko," he says sarcastically.

Jackson doesn't understand: "What's the problem, Mack? I left you a *Post It* note before I finished up last night." He points to a yellow bit of paper among the mess on Mack's desk. "See. There it is!"

"Oh yes," grumps Mack, "well, next time put your notes where I can't miss them!"

"Will do," Jackson replies, then adopts a faux casual tone: "Oh, by the way, I had a chat with the ambassador this morning."

"Who? The British ambassador?"

"Yes."

"What were you doing talking to Stumpy Shortwood? That's my job as the Chief of Bureau."

"Oh, it was just by accident," lies Jackson, "I was passing by the embassy and popped in to say 'hello' to William Crawford at the press office. He introduced me to Sir Gordon."

"Did Stumpy tell you anything useful?"

Jackson shakes his head. "No, nothing really. Pompous old fart, I thought."

"He is that," agrees Mack, "but just remember relations with Stumpy are my responsibility."

"Okay. Understood."

Later, after the rest of the bureau has left for the day, Jackson logs onto the *Towering Treasures Inc* gambling website. He loses money fast and is cursing under his breath. There is a knock on the door and Thomas is there as arranged. Jackson hastily shuts down the gambling site. He and Thomas go to one of the video editing machines. "Right," says Jackson, "Here's what you're after. What bits do you want to see?"

"I'm not sure," replies Thomas, "but let's start with the period just before the violence erupts."

Jackson spools through to the requested section. There is some desultory chanting and banner-waving, then a group of about half-a-dozen men in full Arab dress with masks covering the lower part of their faces appear from a side street and discreetly join the protest.

"Stop it there," says Thomas, "these are the jihadis, I'm sure. Let's see it again."

Jackson pushes the slow motion button and he and Thomas watch intently as the infiltrators work their way to the front of the crowd. One particular Arab appears to be issuing instructions. His mask slips from his face for a few seconds and Pete has instinctively zoomed in on it. Thomas becomes excited: "Hey! Stop it there! Oh yes! That's him alright!"

"That's who?" enquires Jackson.

"Don't know yet, but he pops up from time to time, stirring the shit for all it's worth."

"He's not one of the dead, then?"

"Hell no! Too cunning to get killed. Run the video a bit further and I bet we see him slip away just before the action gets under way."

Jackson spools through the video and it confirms Thomas's forecast. Just seconds before the grenades are thrown, the mystery man can be seen disappearing into a side street.

"Right, Jacko, let's go back to that close-up your cameraman got."

Jackson spools the recording back and freeze-frames the close-up. Thomas is ecstatic. "Brilliant! Give me a print of that."

"Hang on," shouts Jackson, "that's not part of the deal. You said you just wanted to see the video, not take copies of any of it."

"Sorry, mate, I really must have a print. It's far and away the best shot we have ever seen of this nasty piece of goods. We must have it."

Jackson sighs and sends a grab of the frame to a colour printer. Thomas snatches the print and studies it with unrestrained glee. "Fantastic! Just fantastic!"

Jackson studies the close-up and frowns: "There's something vaguely familiar about him."

"In what way?"

"Don't know. Just vaguely familiar."

"Think hard."

"Maybe I might have seen him lurking in the background at some of the other demos recently." He jokes: "See one and you've seen 'em all."

"Yeah, that's true," agrees Thomas with a laugh, "but if you do remember anything, let me know."

They shake hands as Thomas prepares to leave with his prized print. "I owe you, Jacko, and on this topic, let me give you a tip that you're wasting your time with Stumpy Shortwood. He's just a pompous not-of-this-age jobsworth diplomat at the end of his career. On the other hand, I see and hear things that could be really useful to you."

"What's the *quid pro quo*?" Jackson asks suspiciously.

"Nothing, dear b... Nothing that would cause you problems. We just discreetly scratch each other's back a little and everyone's a winner."

"That's a tricky road to go down, Thomas."

"Oh, c'mon, Jacko. Lighten up."

They shake hands again and Thomas leaves. Jackson takes a second print of the grab and puts it in a drawer in his desk. He reopens the gambling page. He is about to resume playing, but pauses, then logs off with a sigh. It pleases him to know that he has done that, as he has already lost too much money – money that he can't afford. He shuts down his computer, checks that the video player and other equipment has been switched off, turns out the lights and leaves, pulling the door behind him.

******

Jackson returns to his flat, switches on the TV, sticks a ready-made pasta meal in the microwave, pours himself a beer and boots up his computer. He types "gambling" into the browser and selects the *Gateway to Greenbacks* site that offers free registration and the enticement of a $US50 as start-up money.

The microwave pings and Jackson takes out the pasta. He chooses a plate and a fork from among the dirty dishes in a pool of sludge in the sink, and gives them a quick rinse under the tap. The pasta is emptied onto the plate and he takes it back to the computer.

Jackson studies the computer screen, knowing that he has already lost money gambling that day. He rationalises his desire to register with this site by convincing himself that he will stop if he loses the "free" $50. He discovers that he cannot claim the $50 without first paying in $100 of his own money. He decides to go ahead anyway and gets out his credit card. He types in his number and other details, but it is rejected. He gets out his debit card. He begins typing in its details, but common sense prevails and he shuts down the page.

Jackson switches on a wildlife documentary on the TV as he eats his meal and sips his beer. He returns the empty plate and fork to the sink sludge, and opens a battered address book beside the phone. He dials a number under something called the *Zing Zing Club*.

"Hi, it's Jackson. Is Zareena available tonight?" He listens to the reply. "Okay. That'll be fine. Just time to have a shower." He listens again. "Terrific. Um, just one other thing. I didn't get a chance to go to the bank today, so don't have much cash on me. Okay if it goes on my tab?" Listens again. "Oh, c'mon. You know you'll get your money. I've never let you down, have I?" He listens again. "Okay, okay! Just a straight massage tonight, and I will definitely settle up with Zareena next time."

Jackson hangs up the phone with a troubled sigh, pours himself another beer and turns on the shower. He knows that he has to get a grip on his life, but tonight, he will settle for a massage from the lovely Zareena.

******

Next morning Jackson turns up at the bureau and finds himself immediately summoned into Mack's office.

"I saw Stumpy Shortwood at an American Embassy reception last night," says Mack, lighting his umpteenth cigarette of the morning.

"Oh," responds Jackson, trying not to be defensive, "did he give you a story?"

"No, but it soon became clear that it was a cock 'n' bull yarn about how you met him!"

"Well, I <u>was</u> taken to meet him by William Crawford."

"Yes, but you know that's less than half the truth." Mack waves a finger in Jackson's face. "Let me make it very clear to you, laddie, I'm the fucking boss here and I will not tolerate colleagues who go behind my back. Do you understand that, Jacko? Do you fucking understand?!"

"Well, I just thought you wouldn't mind," Jackson replies without conviction.

Mack becomes even angrier, his Glaswegian accent getting broader by the second. "I do fucking mind. I really do. We're supposed to be a team here. I admire ambition, but not at my expense, or at the expense of the rest of the team. Don't you forget that you've a whole career ahead of you and I can make or break it. Do you fucking understand, laddie?!"

"Yes. Sorry Mack. Really sorry."

Jackson is shaken by the ferocity of the dressing down. He hates to admit it, but he knows that Mack is right, although he regards the intensity as an over-reaction.

The rest of the team come in for the morning editorial meeting. Once again, it is Mary on the line from London. Mack puts her on his speaker: "Right, Mack, what's on offer today?"

"Nothing huge, Mary. There've been some fairly minor incidents we've been covering for World Service, but nothing outstanding. A few minor explosions and some routine arrests, but I sense the tension is growing. The British ambassador has agreed to do an on-the-record TV and radio interview today on what he sees is the cause of the growing tensions here."

"Mmm. Stumpy Shortwood? Not a very exciting bloke, as I understand it."

"True, Mary, but he has long experience of this patch, and I reckon that with a bit of prodding I can get something lively from him. It's important, too, that we keep him on side."

"Okay. Let's see how it goes. Probably won't make the *Ten*, but *Newsnight* and *World News* might pick it up if he reveals anything substantial."

"Fair enough, Mary. Talk to you tomorrow."

Mack ends the call and turns to Pete, who is wearing a T-shirt displaying two cartoon kangaroos wearing boxing gloves and having a fight. "For Christ's sake, Pete, change into something more appropriate for the ambassador!"

Pete grins. "Well, I've got this great shirt with Kylie Minogue looking fabulously sexy. I'm sure Stumpy will lust over that."

"Hah, bloody hah," retorts Mack, in no mood for jokes. He turns to Jackson: "What's on your plate today?"

"I need to catch up with my expenses first of all, and I want to check out some rumours that al-Qaeda is taking an increasing interest in Central Arabia."

"Okay, it's possible, I guess, but nothing has come my way to suggest that it's the case. They're too tied up elsewhere. As for your expenses, laddie, I know you're always a bit short of the readies, but don't make them too much of a work of fiction, eh!" he says with a knowing smile.

******

An hour later, Jackson finishes his expenses and hands them to Samira. It is her job to check them before presenting them to Mack for his signature. Samira takes a quick look . "Mmm. Just $450 this time – and you've even got a few receipts. Congratulations!"

Jackson accepts the teasing. "I mustn't push my luck, you know. But I'd like you to put them through as quickly as you can."

"I'll do what I can," agrees Samira, "but I don't understand why you're always short. You're on good money – a darned sight better than I am."

"I've got a lot of commitments," he says, trying to come up with a plausible explanation. "I bought a flat in London, not realising that the market was about to slip, and the mortgage and other things have been eating into my earnings."

Samira accepts this as the truth. "That's bad luck. I know a few people who've got caught like that."

"And there was another problem," said Jackson, unable to stop enhancing his tale of woe, "I had a tenant who trashed the place and did a runner, leaving me with huge bills."

"Yes, bad luck," Samira repeats, "my parents also had serious financial problems when they were ripped off after they fled to

England from Iraq. You have my sympathy. I'll get Mack to sign them as soon as he gets a moment."

Jackson is embarrassed and disgusted with himself that he has fraudulently generated Samira's sympathy.

CHAPTER 4

Mack comes out of his office, wearing a jacket and tie. Both are typically crumpled, but he knows that Pete won't make him look too bad in the short periods he will be in shot. He calls to Pete, who is at a desk with his camera kit. "Right, let's go and see what Stumpy has to say!"

Yassin, who has been reading from a pile of Arabic and English magazines he keeps in the corner of the room, stands up to drive them to their destination. Mack instructs Yassin to fuss about as Pete's lighting assistant when they get to the embassy. Then, as an after-thought, he turns to Farouk, who is in the middle of editing a video. "Leave that for now, Farouk, and come with us. It doesn't matter what you do, just look as though it's important. It'll flatter old Stumpy rotten if we turn up with a four-man team."

Mack notes that Pete is now wearing a plain blue open-necked shirt and a fresh pair of jeans. "Well, that's better. I suppose it's too much to ask if you have a tie?"

"Not one that would meet with your approval," Pete grins.

"Oh well," says Mack with a sigh, "it's better than your usual Bondi Beach cast-offs. I'll explain to His Excellency that you are colonial Australian and know no better." Pete laughs.

The team leaves and Jackson returns to his desk. He takes the print of the grab from the riot video from his drawer, studies it for a while and remains baffled why it unsettles him. He gives up thinking about it and returns it to the drawer.

The bureau phone rings and Samira takes the call. "BBC Armibar. Samira Lang speaking." She listens. "Yes, Mr Dunbar is here. Who will I say is calling?" She listens. "Well, I will see if I can interrupt him."

Samira calls to Jackson. "There's some guy with a posh voice wants to speak to you. He won't give his name. He says he's an old university friend."

Jackson picks up the call on his desk phone. It is Thomas, but he doesn't let on to Samira. "Fancy hearing from you, er, Bill. What are you doing in this town?" He listens. "Well, it would be nice to catch up with you. There's a coffee shop across the road from the British Embassy. Do you know where that is?" He listens. "Fine. We can meet there in about half an hour." Jackson hangs up and turns to Samira. "I better go and see this guy. He's here for only a short period. If I'm not back when Mack returns, tell him that I'm checking out the al-Qaeda angle.

Samira tuts. "Why do you always feel compelled to talk bullshit, Jacko? I'll just tell him the truth – that an old mate has turned up in town and you've gone to have a coffee with him."

Jackson shrugs. "Whatever. I'll be on my mobile if I'm needed."

******

Fifteen minutes later, Jackson gets out of a taxi and goes into the coffee shop across from the British Embassy. Thomas is waiting for him at a discreet corner table. He is sipping a coffee and has a second one awaiting Jackson.

Jackson takes a seat: "Well, what have you got for me?"

Thomas produces the grab from the riot video: "I thought you might like to know that this nasty bag of excrement has quite a track record. My colleagues in London recognised him straight away. He appeared from nowhere a few months ago, but has already been linked to al-Qaeda operations in several countries."

"So, who the hell is he?"

"We can't put a name to him yet, but he seems to understand Western ways better than most. We reckon he is probably a convert."

"Mmm. Could be. Converts are often the worst."

"Yes, no doubt about that, Jacko."

Jackson studies the photo: "What's he doing here, do you reckon?"

"Can't be sure, but there is more Western investment here than most people realise, now that so much of the Middle East seems to want to go back to the dark ages. Hence, this place could be the newest target for those twisted buggers who want to destroy our society."

Jackson agrees and sips his coffee as he reflects on what might happen now. "I don't suppose your people have any idea where he's hiding?"

"Well, if we did, I wouldn't be sitting here chatting to you," says Thomas with a smile, "but we do know where he was until yesterday."

"Christ! How did you find that out?"

"Look, Jacko, we're not as incompetent as you guys think. We just missed the bastard by a whisker."

"Had he been tipped off, or something?"

"No, nothing like that. He'd just popped down the street to buy some cigarettes a few minutes before the raiding party arrived. As he returned, he spotted our armoured vehicles and scarpered. Extraordinary good luck for him; extraordinary bad luck for us."

Jackson now sees a story in the making: "Can I use any of this?"

"You can not only use it, here's the address you'll need."

Thomas hands Jackson a slip of paper. Jackson immediately recognises the address: "Shit! That's just down the street from the apartments where Pete and I live."

"I know," says Thomas with a smirk, "your neighbourhood obviously isn't as classy as you think."

"Obviously not," agrees Jackson, "but it's still a surprise that he would have been holed up in our residential area."

"Not really, Jacko, less likely to be noticed in a well-to-do area than a slum. It also reinforces other information that he's quite comfortable among the educated middle classes and not some half-arsed petty criminal who's been radicalised while in prison."

Jackson is now most intrigued and thanks Thomas for the tip-off.

"Just a little thank you for the help you gave me the other day. Just make bloody sure that it can't be traced back to me."

Thomas finishes his coffee and heads for the exit. Jackson studies the address for a minute or two, wondering how best to act on this information. He comes to a decision and phones Pete who, he learns, has finished the Stumpy Shortwood interview and has gone back to his apartment.

"I'll be there in 10 minutes," Jackson tells Pete, "we have another job to do."

When Jackson turns up at the apartments, he finds Pete in a poor mood: "Jeez, Jacko! What's this all about? I thought I'd finished for the day."

"Stop complaining, this could be a terrific story."

"Does Mack know about it?"

"Not yet. It might not come to anything and, anyway, he won't want to be interrupted while he's editing the Shortwood interview."

******

It is late evening on the same day and Mack is relaxing in his apartment above the bureau. It has been a good day and London was reasonably pleased with what he extracted from Stumpy. He and wife Joan are enjoying an old episode of *Dad's Army* on the TV. She has a glass of wine, while he smokes a cigar and has his usual whisky. Like Mack, Joan is Glaswegian and about the same age, but better preserved. Despite Mack's notoriously-grumpy behaviour, she remains immensely fond of him and enjoys the variety of life abroad. She and Mack met when he was a young Glasgow *Daily Herald* reporter sent to interview her about the first of several historical novels she has written over the years. They were unable to have children, but rationalised that this was probably a good thing for a couple with unsettled professional careers.

Dad's Army comes to an amusing end and Joan announces that she is off to bed.

"Righto, Hen," says Mack, "Won't be long. I just want to see where they run my Shortwood interview." He turns to World News as the *Newsnight* signature is played and goes to the drinks cabinet to pour himself a final nightcap.

Mack has his back to the TV as he casually pours his drink and adds a smidgen of mineral water. His serenity abruptly switches to disbelief, then rage, as he hears a headline declaring that "the BBC has learned that a leading al-Qaeda activist has turned up

34

unexpectedly in the troubled Middle Eastern state of Central Arabia. We have the full story from our correspondent Jackson Dunbar in Armibar". Mack spills his drink down the front of his shirt as he swings around to look at the screen.

"Good God!" Mack shouts as he watches a montage of images flash across the screen. He sits down, his jaw having dropped, literally. He is temporarily speechless. He instinctively reaches for the phone to dial Jackson, but realises that before he relieves Jackson of his testicles, figuratively speaking, he needs to see the story. His torment is exacerbated by having to watch presenter Bill Smythe make a leisurely tour of the other stories that will be appearing later in the show.

At last Jackson is introduced and appears on the screen with a pre-recorded piece-to-camera in which he stands outside an apartment block in the street where he lives:

> *Less than 48 hours ago, a man seen as potentially one of the most dangerous al-Qaeda terrorists in the Middle East was living quietly in this street and in this ordinary-looking apartment block. He is now believed to have moved to another safe house. We don't know where, but we can exclusively reveal what he looks like, as we filmed him a few days ago, directing a group of men armed with guns and grenades who infiltrated an initially-peaceful demonstration in this city.*

The report cuts to a clip from the riot film, freezing on the close-up of the terrorist. Jackson continues his report over the freeze frame:

> *I have not yet been able to establish who this person is, but intelligence sources are convinced that he is a high-ranking member of al-Qaeda and that he has been involved in major terrorist acts in several countries.*

Jackson appears back on the screen:

> *I spoke to several people living in this apartment block. They don't wish to appear on screen but confirmed to me that the man had been living unobtrusively in the block*

until a day or so ago when a raid was carried out by a team of unknown persons, believed to be American or British military people. I am told that the raid was unsuccessful because the terrorist had gone out to buy some cigarettes from a local shop and was able to escape when he returned to see the raiding party entering his building.

Mack has heard enough – more than enough -- and as Jackson continues his report, he picks up the phone and stabs the fast-dial button for Jackson's home number. He gets the answering machine, so he tries the mobile number, but again no answer.

"Fuck, fuck, fuck!" rages Mack. Joan reappears in the room in her nightdress, startled by her husband's outburst.

"What's wrong, Mack? What's wrong?"

"Look at that!" he replies, pointing to the TV.

"Look at what? It's just Jacko."

"It's not 'just Jacko'. That little shit has gone and dumped me in it."

At this point, the cameras cut back to Bill Smythe:

Well, Jackson Dunbar's report will surely come as a shock to Britain's ambassador in Armibar, Sir Gordon Shortwood, as earlier in the day he told our chief correspondent, Mack Galbraith, that he was confident there was no outside involvement in Central Arabia's recent troubles.

Stumpy Shortwood appears on the screen beaming with arrogant confidence:

There's absolutely no doubt that the root causes of the troubles here is deeply-embedded corruption and a power struggle within the regime. Some ministers are anxious to align themselves more with the West while others want the country to remain 100% Arab and Muslim.

Mack hurls his whisky glass at the TV. It misses and shatters the glass front to Joan's prized crystal cabinet.

"Oh, for God's sake, Mack, look what you've done!" Joan shouts. She goes to the cabinet and finds that a Chinese figurine is broken. She holds it up for Mack to see: "That was given to me by Granny McPherson!"

"Oh jings, Hen, I'm really sorry, but Jacko has really over-reached himself this time."

Mack tries Jackson's phone again, but all he gets is an answering machine announcement. He rings Pete's mobile and this time it is answered. Mack doesn't bother with opening pleasantries: "What do you know about this al-Qaeda package that just been aired?" he demands.

"Yeah, I filmed it for Jacko late this afternoon. Good story, boss."

"Why wasn't I told about it?"

"Buggered if I know, Mack. That's Jacko's job!"

"Look laddie, don't get arsey with me! Even if you don't see it as your job, you must have known that it dumped all over everything in my interview with Stumpy Shortwood. Weren't you listening to what he said?"

"Not really. I was too busy getting the filming right and, anyway, he's such a boring bastard."

"Well, what about Farouk? Didn't he spot the contradictions when he edited Jacko's package?"

"Dunno, Mack. He probably thought it was none of his business."

By now, Mack is not just angry but mightily frustrated: "I've been trying to get hold of Jacko. Do you know where he is?"

"Sorry, not the faintest. He borrowed a hundred bucks from me and said he was going out for the rest of the evening."

"I'm seriously pissed off by all of you," roars Mack, as though that wasn't already blindingly obvious, "and I want to see you all in my office at 8.30 before I have to talk to London."

******

There is a good reason why Mack has been unable to contact Jackson. He is in a rather shady part of town with very poor mobile signal cover. Not that Jackson is inclined to answer any calls at the moment. He is in an illegal gambling den, engaged in a game of poker that requires his total attention. He is competing at a round table with half a dozen Arabs, some in traditional dress while others are in smart casual Western outfits.

The den is run by a small, tidy hard-eyed man with a neatly-trimmed short beard. He is about 40 and always wears expensive white suits without ties. He calls himself Archibald, but no-one believes that is his real name. His Arabic suggests he is Moroccan, but he speaks English with an accent that appears to have been acquired by watching old black-and-white movies made in Britain in the 1940s. "Archibald" is never seen anywhere without two heavily-built and armed clean-shaven Arab guards, wearing traditional dress and a thug's trademark oversize sun glasses.

Jackson is on a winning streak and has converted the $100 borrowed from Pete into a bundle totalling at least five thousand dollars. His heart pounds with the excitement and his skin has a pleasant tingling that comes with addiction. Suddenly, he scoops up his money and stands up, declaring that he wants to take a break. The Arab players protest that he isn't giving them a chance to win back at least some of their losses. "Don't worry," he announces in Arabic, "I'll be back soon to relieve you of even more of your precious dollars."

The Arabs continue to protest, but Jackson brushes aside their complaints. He counts out a thousand dollars and puts it on the table as an assurance that he will be back. "I shall return – just as soon as I've fulfilled a little engagement next door," he says with a wink. The Arabs laugh knowingly and their grumbles subside.

A few minutes later, Jackson is next door, still in an ebullient mood. He walks into a discreetly-lit room decorated with erotic paintings and photographs never likely to have the distinction of being displayed in an art gallery. Arabic music plays softly in the background. He is greeted by an Arab woman aged about 50, wearing smart western dress and sitting at a small desk. She addresses him in precise English and in the traditional Arab way, as

"Mr Jackson", rather than "Mr Dunbar": "Welcome back, Mr Jackson. Nice to see you again. Are you here to settle your account, or to be entertained, or both?"

"Good evening, Leila. I'm here to do both. Is Zareena in tonight?"

"She was about to leave, but I am sure she will be delighted to stay on a little longer for her favourite client."

"That's good. She's my favourite too," he says with a genuine smile.

Leila picks up the phone on her desk and dials an internal number: "Zareena. Your friend from the television is here and will be along in a minute." She turns to Jackson with her hand out: "First, let's deal with the little matter of your debt."

Jackson takes a bundle of dollar notes from his pocket and begins to count them out: "Here you are… $150 for last week, $25 for the massage the other night, $75 for tonight, and $150 on account."

Leila nods approvingly and points to a hallway: "Off you go, Mr Jackson. She's in the usual room."

******

Next morning, Mack waits impatiently in his office, still steamed up about last night's *Newsnight* package. Pete and Farouk are there, but there is no sign of Jackson. Mack stubs out a cigarette, having first used it to light another. He is about to phone his errant correspondent when Jackson appears breathlessly at the door and looking less than cheerful. "Sorry, Mack, I got your message, but was held up in the traffic," he lies.

"You've always got some excuse," says Mack sarcastically, "and I have to say you don't look too bright."

"I'll be okay, just had a disturbed night, that's all," Jackson replies, not able to admit that on his return visit to the gambling den, he had lost all but a few measly dollars of his earlier winnings. It is true he had a disturbed night, but that was largely due to anger at his turn of bad luck in the gambling den.

"Right then," says Mack, declaring the *ad hoc* meeting open, "would someone, perhaps starting with Jacko, do me the honour of telling me what happened yesterday. In other words, why was I not told about the al-Qaeda development?"

Jackson makes a defensive apology: "Sorry, Mack, but we were working right up to the wire on this one. We didn't finish the edit until a couple of minutes before transmission. No-one told me what Stumpy Shortwood had said, so there was no special reason to bother you so late at night."

Mack is furiously unimpressed: "Look, laddie, I repeat that we are supposed to be working as a team in this bureau. You knew the story was a big one and you should've given me a quick call to let me know about it. Anyway, where the hell were you last night? I tried to call both your numbers and got no answer."

"I went to see a friend who was briefly in town. I had my mobile on, so I guess I must have been in a black spot."

"Well, you are certainly in my black spot, laddie. I am seriously beginning to wonder about you."

Samira appears at the door: "Sorry to interrupt, Mack, but Sir Gordon Shortwood wants an urgent word."

"Oh jings!" says Mack, slapping his forehead in frustration, "put him through."

Mack picks up the phone on his desk: "Good morning, Sir Gordon, it's Mack Galbraith." Mack listens to Sir Gordon and flinches at what he hears. "Well, Sir Gordon, I understand that you're very upset, and I'm sure that in the end, your theories about the situation here will be proved to be the correct ones. There was absolutely no intention on my part to have your views undermined, but in this business, things can move very fast and we are sometimes not as well co-ordinated as we should be." Mack listens. "Yes, well... I'm just about to have our morning editorial conference with London and I will pass on your displeasure at the way they handled the story. And yes, Mr Dunbar and I will see you at the embassy at 10 o'clock to discuss this further." He listens again. "Well, you have our sincerest apologies, Sir Gordon. All will be explained when we see you. Goodbye."

Mack puts the phone down and stabs a finger in Jackson's direction: "Now look what you've done!"

Samira pokes her head in the door again: "London's on the line, Mack."

Mack puts the call on the phone speaker: "Good morning, London."

"Morning, Mack, it's Harry Kingston here on the Foreign Desk. Let me begin by congratulating all of you on the coverage last night. Terrific piece from Jacko and much amusement here at how Mack let Shortwood prove to the world that he's a stupid old fart who knows bugger all. Great stuff. There are suggestions here that Stumpy will be retired or moved to a post where his views won't matter."

Mack is both surprised and relieved by Harry's comments. Jackson's immediate reaction is that he has been let off the hook.

Harry continues: "Well, as for a follow-up, how do you see it, guys?"

Jackson decides it is diplomatic to let Mack do the talking: "Well, Jacko and I have to see Stumpy shortly to smooth things down as best we can, then we'll see what else we can learn about this mysterious terrorist and why al-Qaeda has decided to target Central Arabia. This country is the last major domino still standing in this part of the region, and my educated guess is that they want to see this one toppled, so they can then focus their attention on Saudi Arabia and its neighbours."

"Yes, could be, Mack. Perhaps you could do us something along those lines while Jacko follows up his links."

"Will do, Harry. I'll also see if I can have lunch with the American Ambassador, who seems a sharper operator than Stumpy. Anyway, that's it from here for now. We'll no doubt talk later. Bye."

The call ends and Mack lights a cigarette while he ponders the conversation that has just taken place. He turns to Jackson, again stabbing his finger at him. "We may be heroes today in London, laddie, but you're not my hero. In the end, this is what matters for your career. From now on we operate as a team with a capital T. Do you understand that? Team with a capital T!"

Jackson nods acceptance.

Mack and Jackson turn up at the British Embassy at 10am on the dot. They are taken up to the ambassadorial suite by a guard and met by William Crawford and Sir Gordon who is in a thunderous mood. The ambassador remains seated, makes no offer to shake hands and leaves them standing like two naughty boys before the headmaster. William takes a seat to one side and starts recording the conversation.

Mack begins by repeating his apologies, but he is cut short by Sir Gordon: "You chaps deliberately set me up, didn't you!"

"No, no, that's not true Sir Gordon," protests Mack, "it was just a most unfortunate collision of circumstances beyond our control."

"Unfortunate is hardly the word for it. You were suggesting that Her Majesty's representative in Armibar didn't have a clue what was going on. Outrageous! Sadly typical of what I've come to expect of journalists from your lot."

Jackson leaps to the defence: "Sorry, Your Excellency. I assumed that someone in your position would be in possession of the same information that I was given."

"No, I did not have that information," he shouts. "You know why? Because it's total nonsense. That Arab chappie could be anyone. Any low-level jumped-up jihadist. Let me repeat, there's no substance to your story and I've personally informed the Foreign Minister of that fact. He's chewing the carpet and will be making personal representations to your Director-General.

"With respect, Your Excellency," Jackson responds with forced civility, "I now have evidence to support the accuracy of the story."

"Would it be too much to ask that you tell me your source, young man?"

Jackson shakes his head. "You know I can't do that, Your Excellency."

Sir Gordon stands up, fit to have a seizure. "In that case, there's no point in continuing this discussion. Let me assure you that I won't forget this." He dismisses them with a wave and they are escorted from the suite by William Crawford.

As the trio wind their way back along the corridors to Reception, William confirms that Jackson's story is probably right. "Don't be too fussed by the old man's tantrum," he tells Mack and Jackson. "Once he gets an idea fixed in his head, nothing will change it, no matter what the evidence is. Don't hesitate to remain in touch with me, but keep it discreet."

They reach Reception and William shakes hands with Mack and Jackson and bids them a cheery farewell. As they leave the building, Mack turns to Jackson: "I hope you've learned something from this experience, laddie." Jackson nods agreement. "Right then," announces Mack, "I'll let you get back to the bureau while I have lunch with the American ambassador and pick his brains."

CHAPTER 5

Jackson arrives back at the bureau, grateful that his row with Mack seems to be over the worst. As he settles down at his desk, Samira arrives back from the bank with the staff expenses money. She counts it out and clips it to the expenses sheets.

"The 'fraud sheets' are back, chaps," she announces with a broad smile, "so come and get your money."

Farouk and Yassin go to her and each get $75 while Pete collects $150. Jackson is still at his desk, staring intently as the computer screen. Samira goes to him with his money. "Here you are, Jacko," she says with a certain look of expectation on her face. "Thanks," he says, breaking away from his computer screen. He picks up the money and frowns. "Hey! Is this all?" Samira smirks agreement. He then checks his several expenses sheets and sees that some large items have been crossed out. "Hey, what's Mack playing at?" he demands. Samira shrugs: "There's a clear lesson for you there, Jacko. Don't go pissing off the Chief of Bureau."

Jackson groans, knowing that there is nothing he can do about it, especially as several of the lunch and taxi claims were entirely fictitious. Yassin and Pete are both amused by what has happened and rub it in by approaching Jackson with their hands out, a reminder that he owes them money. He gives Yassin his $50 and Pete has his $100 returned.

"Cheer up, Jacko," declares Pete, "you've still got a couple of hundred bucks there, more than enough to buy us all a nice coffee instead of the dreadful instant stuff we have in the kitchen."

Jackson sees the funny side and laughs. He agrees to go to the coffee shop next door and buy a round.

******

The street is unusually quiet as he comes out into it. He half notices a large black Mercedes saloon parked nearby. A tall bearded Arab man in a thawb alights from the back seat and walks briskly towards him. "Hello," the Arab says in accented English, "are you Mr Jackson Dunbar?"

"Yes," confirms Jackson, instantly cautious. "How can I help?"

"My friends would like a word with you," he says, pointing towards the Mercedes. Jackson goes over and sees two Arab men in the front seat. One points an automatic handgun at him: "No fuss please, Mr Dunbar, just get in the back." Jackson fleetingly considers trying to make a run for it, but judges that he has no choice but to do as he is told. He gets into the back seat, his mind and heart racing.

The man who intercepted him on the footpath gets in beside him and the car pulls away. He is ordered to lie down on the seat and a blanket is placed over him so that no-one can see him and he, in turn, cannot see the route the car is taking. He hears one of the men make a phone call to report in Arabic that they have Jackson in their possession and should be able to deliver him in half an hour. Jackson knows from his Hostile Environment Training that there is nothing he can do except try not to antagonise his captors.

Jackson can tell from the number of potholes the car is hitting that he is being driven through a poor area. After about 15 minutes, he notes that they are now travelling along a better stretch of road.

******

Jackson's bureau colleagues are getting irritated about his failure to return with the coffees. Samira dials his mobile number. It rings and Jackson tries to see who is calling, but the man sitting beside him snatches the phone away. He looks at the screen and demands: "Who is Samira? Your girlfriend?" Jackson explains that she is the bureau manager. His captor turns the phone off and puts it in his pocket.

After what seems an eternity – certainly more than the predicted half-an-hour – the car slows, makes a sharp turn and travels along what sounds to be a gravel driveway. The car pulls up and Jackson, still covered by the blanket, is guided from the car and taken indoors. He looks down at his feet and sees a patterned marble floor. Finally, he is ushered into a room and the blanket is removed.

He is in a plushly-furnished room with the blinds drawn. Clearly, he is not in a slum. He is ordered to wait quietly in a chair upholstered in thick fabric decorated with Arabic patterns. He does as he is told.

Back at the bureau, Samira is worried and goes looking for Jackson. The owner of the coffee shop tells her that he saw Jackson talking to some men and getting into a car. She urgently phones Mack, who is at the American Embassy waiting to be taken upstairs to lunch with the ambassador.

Mack's reaction to the news that Jackson is missing is at first dismissive, until he is told about the men in the car. He apologises profusely to the ambassador, claiming that there is a crisis with a news story and that he has been ordered back to the bureau immediately.

******

Jackson is now a little calmer. He studies his surroundings and mentally runs through all the possibilities that could lie ahead of him and how he might best react. Nothing, however, prepares him for what happens next. A door opens and an Arab man in a thawb and keffiyeh strides in. Jackson's pulse races as he realises that he is in the presence of the terrorist featured in his reports.

The man takes a seat and studies Jackson in silence, enjoying the mixture of astonishment and fear that flickers across his captive's face. Jackson breaks the silence, addressing the man in Arabic. "Why have you brought me here? What do you want?"

Jackson is taken aback when the man responds in English with an educated London accent: "My friend, let's talk in our mother tongue. I'm English and my Arabic is not very good."

Jackson is astonished. "So who exactly are you?"

"Roger, my friend, you don't recognise me?"

"Only from the film my cameraman shot of the riot. And where did you get 'Roger' from?"

The terrorist is enjoying himself: "You really don't know who I am, do you!"

Jackson shakes his head and the man reaches for a folder and takes from it a colour snapshot of two scrawny youths posing in front of a very traditional red brick British school. They have their arms around each other's shoulders. Jackson is gobsmacked. "Who gave you this?"

"You did, my friend. <u>You</u> did."

The penny suddenly drops for Jackson: "Shit! It's me and Binnie – Ahmed Faisel Bin Hassan."

"Yes, my friend Roger, it's me, Binnie or Ahmed, grown up, no longer the skinny kid, and now with this bushy beard."

As Jackson absorbs the stunning revelation, a servant comes in and serves them with water and Arabic coffee.

"How's your granny? Granny Dunbar?" asks Ahmed.

"Er, died a few years ago, I'm very sorry to say."

"Sad. I liked her a lot. And what of your father? I haven't seen him in the papers recently."

"His style of journalism went out of fashion, and he's dead too."

"Sorry about that. I didn't know your dad."

"Nor did I really," responds Jackson with some residual bitter memories.

The two men study each other in silence, with Jackson still astonished by the extraordinary circumstances he finds himself in.

"Well?" enquires Ahmed finally, "have you nothing else to say?"

"Yes. My overwhelming question is why are you mixed up in this evil shit, Binnie? It makes no sense. You were a great school friend from a hard-working and respectable refugee family."

"Hard-working, respectable – and all dead."

"Hell! What happened?"

"As you probably know, we all moved back to Iraq after I left school. We needed to look after my grandparents who were getting very frail. I got a job and married a nice local girl and everything was more or less okay until the Bush-Blair invasion. I was at work one day when American marines smashed their way into the house and slaughtered everyone – my wife, my baby, my parents and my grandparents. The marines said they were tipped off that we were terrorists, but I think they just killed for the fun of it. They walked away laughing and were never called to account."

"Oh shit!"

"Yes, Roger, 'oh shit', as you say. My mission in life is now clear."

Jackson is shocked: "What mission? To kill the innocent along with the guilty?"

"My family was innocent and never did anyone any harm, but no-one cared when they died. No-one!"

"I'm sure that's not true, Binnie, but sometimes terrible things happen in war."

"It is true, Roger. You and your granny were the only ones who treated me with respect when I was at that bloody school in London."

Ahmed picks up the folder and takes from it a battered A4 group photograph from his school days. He holds it up for Jackson to see. Ahmed is the sole non-European boy in the photograph. A crude target has been drawn on his chest with a gun pointing at it. Scribbled in large letters across the top of the photograph are the words "You're dead, you stinking wog!" Ahmed puts the photograph back in the folder. "There were many more like that, Roger. Very nasty. Very upsetting."

Jackson shakes his head in shame. "I'm shocked, Binnie, but that still doesn't justify terrorism."

"It's not terrorism, my friend; it's war: Iraq, Chad, Gaza, Yemen, Aghanistan, Pakistan. You name the country. It's war."

"But, Binnie, you must realise that you can't survive this war. Sooner or later you will be hunted down and killed – or martyred as you probably prefer to put it."

"I'm not into that martyr stuff, Roger. I'm simply a soldier of Allah with a duty to avenge the wiping out of my family and all the others who have died unjustly at the hands of the West and the Israelis. If and when I die, I don't assume that I'll go to Paradise. The chances of a cluster of eager virgins awaiting me are as likely as the claim that Jesus Christ was the result of a virgin birth, or that your God parted the Red Sea for Moses." Jackson and Ahmed both briefly giggle at this, bringing back memories of the mischievous fun they had together teasing the bumbling religious education teacher at their school.

"So," asks Jackson, "who are *Soldiers of Allah*? Are they your mob?"

"Yes, my 'mob', as you so disparagingly put it. "It draws its inspiration from Osama Bin Laden, but that's all. We are not al-Qaeda or anyone else. We're entirely independent. I have a small cell of people I trust 100%. Because of that, we'll never be infiltrated by our enemies."

"Well, if I may suggest it, Binnie, your website is crap. I saw it yesterday and assumed that it was created by some kid with little or nothing to do with his life. If you want the media and the world at large to view you as a serious organisation, you need to get it fixed."

"Thank you, Roger, I will arrange that."

Jackson sips his coffee then puts a delicate question to Ahmed: "Your mission… Would it extend to killing me? You know, killing your old school friend?"

Ahmed gives a "maybe, maybe not" gesture, and looks away, embarrassed. Finally, he turns back to Jackson. "I'm about to send you back to your office," he announces. "You can reveal my name, if you wish, as it will become known sooner or later, but it goes without saying that you must not reveal clues that might lead to my being traced. Is that understood?"

"I don't see that I have a choice – even if I had the faintest idea where this house is."

"Good. Then I'll reward you with occasional tip-offs and maybe even a scoop interview for your beloved BBC."

"How will I be able to contact you?"

"You can't. I'll contact you when I feel it's necessary."

Ahmed extends his hand and it is shaken uncertainly by Jackson.

"Goodbye, for now, my friend," says Ahmed.

Jackson nods an acknowledgement. He turns to follow his captors from the room, but Ahmed has an afterthought: "Hey, I nearly forgot to ask what happened with *Plink Plonk*?"

Jackson laughs. "Best forgotten, I think. It was just the usual teenage fantasy."

"So, you didn't make it onto *Top of the Pops*?"

"No, we didn't even get to make a record. To be honest, we were rubbish."

"I have to agree with that, my friend," agrees Ahmed with a smile.

Ahmed shakes Jackson's hand a second time.

"I really wish you wouldn't do this stuff, Binnie," implores Jackson, weighed down by sadness at the thought of what will lie ahead for his friend and his potential victims.

"I also wish that things were different, but the die is cast, to use a well-worn cliché."

They shake hands again and Jackson is led from the room.

******

Jackson is being returned to the bureau in the same car and by the same men who had snatched him off the street. Again, he is made to lie down on the seat, covered by a blanket. On arrival, the blanket is pulled from him and he is pushed from the car. He trips and crashes heavily onto the pavement. The passenger in the car throws Jackson's phone after him, but he fails to catch it. It hits the ground hard and splinters. Jackson retrieves the bits and picks himself up as the car accelerates away.

Jackson's brain is in a swirl as he goes up the stairs and braces himself for a likely volcanic reaction by Mack on his reappearance. Samira is the first to spot him and is both relieved and furious. "Oh my God! What happened to you? We've been so worried."

Pete looks up from an editing suite and can't resist a tactless joke. "Yeah, mate. And where are our fucking coffees?"

Jackson doesn't respond as he watches Mack getting up from his desk and heading towards him. "Where the fuck have you been? And look at the state of you!"

Jackson hasn't dusted himself down after his fall and he has a nasty graze on his face and there is blood on his hands: "I got lifted, Mack."

"Who by?"

"Um, some Arabs who wanted to talk to me."

"Did they beat you up?"

"No. They just wanted to talk to me."

"Well, what's all this?" Mack asks, pointing at the blood on Jackson's face and hands.

"I tripped when they pushed me out of their car". Samira comes over with the bureau's First Aid kit and uses medical wipes to remove the blood from his face and his hands. "And by the way," Jackson adds, "I'm going to need a new mobile." He takes the broken one from his pocket and puts the bits on his desk for Mack to see. Mack is more concerned about the story than Jackson's phone. "What did these guys want to talk to you about?"

"The guy who featured in my report the other night wanted to explain his reasons for engaging in war against us."

"Same old bullshit, no doubt, and hardly worth reporting."

Jackson disagrees. "What he told me is definitely worth reporting – and I do have his name."

Mack is now interested again. "Oh, that's better!"

"His name is Ahmed Faisel Bin Hassan and he's a Londoner."

"Are you sure?"

"Very sure."

"Sure enough to name him on air?"

"Yes. We can name him with confidence."

Mack is sceptical: "You may have the confidence, but I've got to convince London. We can't get this wrong. You could've been told any old name and we could end up in deep shit libelling some innocent chap who's had his identity stolen."

"Trust me, Mack. I'm 100% sure. I have his age and I even know where he used to live in London."

"How the hell do you learn this? Did he show you a passport or have some other proof of identity?

"He didn't need to," says Jackson.

Jackson worries that he has already revealed too much. He stalls for time. "Just give me a break, Mack. I'm shattered. Let me go home to freshen up, then we can resume this conversation when I come back."

"Fuck that, laddie! This is a news organisation, not a social club. Just sit down at your desk and get cracking on a full account of what happened and how we should sell the story to London. Meanwhile, I'll tip off the legal department so they can give some thought to how far we can go with this yarn."

Mack heads back to his office with the parting words: "And don't go overboard with the heroics. Just remember. This story is about Ahmed Whatshisname, not about you."

Mack sits down at his desk, lights up a cigarette and picks up the phone.

Jackson turns to Samira: "Christ! Mack's all heart, isn't he! When those buggers snatched me I thought I was done for, or at least would be chained up in a cage somewhere."

Samira puts a sympathetic arm around his shoulder. "Mack means you no harm. You've had a frightening experience, but this is small beer to what he went through last year. He was seized by local gangsters who were upset about a story he wrote exposing their corrupt links to a highly-placed politician."

"Really? I didn't know that."

"Yes, they put him through two mock executions and said he wouldn't be released without a huge ransom being paid. He managed to escape when his overnight guard got pissed and fell asleep. He phoned the SAS team at the British Embassy and they dealt with the gangsters in the way they felt was appropriate, if you get my meaning."

"Shit! Why wasn't it on the news?"

"Mack's an old-fashioned hack. He hates 'celebrity journalism'. He thinks journalists should <u>report</u> stories, not <u>be</u> the story. He reckons that if they choose to put themselves at risk, they shouldn't whinge if things sometimes go wrong. Mack just lights another ciggie, pours himself a large whisky and gets on with the job."

It is a steadying message for Jacko. He starts writing his report and Samira makes him a strong coffee.

Half an hour later, Jacko is in Mack's office with the requested report. Mack studies it calmly, most of his anger dissipated. He is not even smoking.

"This is interesting, Jacko, but mostly for what it <u>doesn't</u> tell me. I've just had a chat with the solicitors in London and they caution us against naming this guy without strong supporting evidence."

"Can't I just name him and say that I'm not at liberty to say how I know this?"

"Mmm. You could, but it's bloody risky and the London bosses get twitchy, wanting to be sure their backs are covered."

Mack stares into the middle distance and silently chews over the options. He comes to a decision. "Right, I'm going to trust you on this. I'll tell London that you've given me the full story and that I am absolutely confident we can go with it. If our bosses want to know more, I will invoke 'security reasons' and insist the sources cannot go beyond me."

"Thanks, Mack."

"Let's go with the story as you suggest, using the footage you have of Ahmed and where he's said to have been living. Describe how the meeting took place, without over-dramatising it. I'll do a separate package making an educated guess why the jihadists are suddenly taking an interest in this country."

"Thanks again, Mack," says Jackson as he gets up to return to his desk. He calls to Farouk to dig out Pete's video taken of the riot and of the house where Ahmed had been living. The traumas of the past few hours are temporarily swept aside as he begins planning his report.

Mack wins the day with London and the reports are given prominence on the evening news bulletins and *Newsnight*. The phones ring incessantly as journalists from around the world seek more information and beg to be let into the secret of how Jackson obtained Ahmed's name and background. Some offer substantial financial rewards. He rejects them all, despite the seductiveness of the sums being mentioned and threats of stories accusing him of making it all up.

Jackson packs up for the day and catches a taxi to his apartment. He is desperate for a shower, a stiff drink and a good night's sleep, but he finds Thomas waiting for him outside in a British Embassy Bentley with darkened windows. Thomas gets out of the limousine and furiously demands to know why Jackson didn't tip him off before the broadcast. "Some mate you are!" he shouts at Jackson.

"Knock it off, Thomas! I'm not obliged to tell you. And anyway, you now have the information, so what's it matter?"

"It matters because he's probably fled the country as a result of the publicity."

Jackson shakes his head. "Pretty unlikely. I think you'll find he's here to stay for as long as it takes to carry out his mission, whatever that might be, or he's killed."

"What makes you so sure?"

"I'm sure. Just believe me."

Thomas calms down. "I hope you're right. We really need to catch this bastard before he kills too many people."

"Well that's for you to do. It's for me to report the truth as best I can. Just leave me be. I need to get some rest. It's been a very hard day."

"Righto. We'll have a chance to talk about this again tomorrow. I believe you're due to have dinner with us."

"Yes. See you then."

"Oh, and by the way, Jacko, you will be interested to learn that Stumpy Shortwood is most unamused by your revelations. He says he is going to demand that you be recalled to London."

Jackson gives a sigh of resignation.

Thomas laughs. "Don't worry, dear boy. I think he'll be leaving Armibar before you do!"

CHAPTER 6

The bureau phones are still ringing every few minutes as the team gathers for the morning editorial meeting. Everyone is tired but exhilarated by yesterday's scoop.

Mack dials the Foreign Desk and Mary Dunstan is again on duty. "Morning guys," she declares cheerfully over the phone speaker, "nice little story you got yesterday. Congratulations."

"Thanks, Mary," chorus Mack and Jackson.

"Unless you've got anything more to reveal today, the emphasis of the story will be back here while we ferret around for some Foreign Office reaction and talk to Ahmed Bin Hassan's old school and the people who now live at his old address. We'll also be..." Mary has been interrupted by someone at her end. Muffled speech can be heard through her hand placed over the phone mouthpiece. A short while later she comes back on the line. "Er, chaps, Amanda Murphy wants a word."

Mack and Jacko quietly groan. Amanda is from the Director-General's office and is not someone to be messed with. "Morning all," she declares, falsely cheerful and with a dollop of menace in her voice, "I hope you are all in top form after yesterday's exertions?"

"Yes, thank you, everything is fine here, Amanda."

"Good, good. Now, about this story of yours!"

"What about it?" enquires Mack defensively.

"Nothing to worry about, I'm sure, but the DG wants to be certain this isn't going to lead to more uncomfortable issues on top of all the other things he has to deal with. I mean, the *Daily Mail* and the *Daily Telegraph* are already running stories implying that it's a 'beat up' with little or no substance."

"That's no surprise," replies Jackson, "they first tried to bribe me for more information, then when that failed, they warned they'd trash me."

"Even so, Jackson, disturbing complaints are beginning to pour in. The papers have tracked down the only school in London that had an Ahmed Faisel Bin Hassan as a student. The headmaster is

The Mortal Maze

furious. He said the man shown in your report is most definitely not the one who attended his establishment. It's a posh private school with many powerful friends and the head is particularly aggrieved about your man's allegations of racism. The school now relies heavily on attracting wealthy students from the Middle East and the allegations have been financially damaging. The chairman of the school board, Sir Henry Daniels-Smith, is breathing fire and threatening to issue writs."

"It's definitely the right guy. I'm super sure of that!" snaps Jackson, still reluctant to admit his link to Ahmed and grateful that no-one has yet spotted his own connection to the school.

Amanda presses on: "Another thing: there are suspicions – and I put it no higher than suspicions – about where you said this Ahmed chappie lived in London. The right-wing media think it's just too convenient that all the houses in that street were torn down and replaced by an apartment block and a supermarket about 15 years ago. So, you know, there's no-one around who can remember who lived in those houses."

"I don't bloody care what's happened to that street, that's where he used to live," Jackson explodes.

"Don't get snippy with me, Jackson, we have broadcast your report in good faith without either you or Mack being able to prove that the chap you met – if you really did meet him – had not stolen some innocent person's identity and spun you a string of lies."

Jackson begins shouting. "Stop making the outrageous suggestion that I fake stuff!"

Pete Fox, who has been watching the exchange with some amusement, smiles to himself on hearing Jackson's last statement. Thinking back to Jackson's faked piece-to-camera after the riot, he begins to share Amanda's doubts.

Mack tries to calm the exchange. "Look, Amanda, tell the DG I fully understand his concerns. I'm completely confident in our story. I'm sorry that we can't tell you more about the background, but there is a 'security issue' here, which I'm sure the DG will understand."

"Yes, Mack, I'll tell him that, but I have to warn you all that you won't get off lightly if this story unravels. Do you understand?"

"I understand."

Mary comes back on the line. "Well, that's seems to be all that needs to be said for now. We'll talk later." She hangs up and Mack turns to Jackson. "Blimey, this story had better not turn to custard or I'll be at the head of the queue to rip your balls off."

"I think we should toss a coin for that privilege," adds Pete with an edge to his voice.

As the meeting breaks up, Samira takes yet another phone call. She mouths to Jackson that it is his mother. He sighs and pauses before deciding to answer it. He does so without warmth. "Yes, Mother." He listens. "Yes, I know my mobile isn't working. I'm getting it replaced. Anyway, why are you phoning?" He listens. "Yes, of course my report is true. It wouldn't have been broadcast otherwise." He listens. "Oh for God's sake, Mother, I've told you before that you should not read the bloody *Daily Mail*! It's crap and has a very clear anti-BBC agenda." He listens. "Yes, yes, I know that the *Mail* isn't always wrong and you like it for its Fashion and Health sections, but it's wrong in this instance. If you don't stop going on about this, I'll hang up on you again." He listens for a few moments, then angrily ends the call and mutters to himself "bloody woman!"

Samira is offended. "That's a shocking way to behave, Jacko."

"Just be grateful she isn't your mother, Samira!"

"She can't be as bad as you make out. I really don't like you when you talk to her in such a disrespectful way."

"Sometimes I don't like myself very much," he admits, "but I don't think that has anything to do with my mother."

Jackson points to his wrecked mobile. "More importantly, I need you to get me another one of these before the day is out."

"Can't you see I'm busy! Get it yourself! The phone shop is just a few doors away." Jackson turns to Yassin who is sitting in the corner reading an English girlie magazine. "Do me a favour mate and get me a replacement phone. Samira will give you the money."

Samira rolls her eyes in annoyance and gets some dollar notes from her petty cash drawer.

******

That evening, Jackson arrives by taxi at an imposing gated apartment block favoured by diplomats in Armibar. He is carrying a bunch of flowers. There is a guard box outside the building's entrance. Sitting inside is a man wearing an unspecific military uniform and carrying a stubby automatic gun. Jackson shows his press pass and the guard presses a button opening the gate. Jackson enters, checks a board listing the tenants, then unhurriedly goes up the stairs, deep in thought.

Throughout the day, when not thinking about his unsettling adventure with school friend Binnie, he has been anxiously speculating the course his dinner might take with Felicity and Thomas Fulham. He hopes there will be no difficult moments. He and Felicity had been an item for nearly a year when they were at Oxford. He knew that if he had been better behaved, the two of them might still be together. He tries not to think of her being in bed with Thomas, a person he is never likely to admire.

Although he and Thomas studied Arabic together at university, they were never tempted to be more than casual acquaintances and he had never expected that they would, years later, find themselves posted to the same country. Jackson couldn't help jealously wondering if the inventive sexual activities he and Felicity enjoyed are matched in any way when she is intimate with Thomas.

Jackson reaches the second floor and quickly finds the Fulham's flat. He rings the door bell and stands with the flowers held behind his back. The door is opened by Felicity. She is wearing a very elegant knee-length dress that Jackson guesses came from a fashionable designer shop in London or Paris. He notes that she has made a special effort with her make-up and swept-up hair style. She looks magnificent -- even better than he remembers her from their university days.

"Ah, so you were able to make it okay," she says with a warm smile.

"Yes. Mack's on call tonight, so it's an evening off for me."

"Thomas is running a little late but should be here any minute."

Felicity ushers Jackson into the dining room with the table already set for a meal. He produces his flowers with a flourish and she responds with delight. "Thank you! They're lovely." She holds them up to smell the perfume, then breaks into laughter. "Oh, they're imitation!"

"Of course," he confirms, "where the hell would I get real ones in this God-forsaken city!"

"Too true. Anyway, they're very nice. I've got just the place for them."

Felicity goes to a sideboard and skilfully arranges them in the vase she showed him the other day. "There you are! Perfect! And I won't ever have to water them."

They both laugh. There follows an awkward pause, broken by Jackson. "Well then, don't I get a welcome kiss?"

"Oh yes," she replies with a tinge of embarrassment. She lightly embraces him. Jackson goes to kiss her on the lips, but she neatly offers him one cheek, then the other. He pulls her close to him and kisses her on the neck. Again he recognises the perfume. He prolongs the embrace, enjoying the warmth of a body that he remembers so vividly.

Felicity gently pushes him away and raises an affectionate eyebrow that signals that he has overstepped the boundary that must now exist between them. "Erm, make yourself at home while I check that the children are out of the bath and dressed for bed," she tells him, slightly flustered by their physical encounter.

She leaves the room and Jackson sees an upright piano in the corner of the tastefully furnished room. He goes to it, lifts the keyboard lid and plays some trills and random chords to check the tuning.

Felicity returns to the room and says the children will join them shortly. "Do you still play the piano?" she asks.

"Sometimes, when I'm in the mood," he replies.

"Good. I'd like the kids to learn to play."

Felicity's two children burst noisily into the room. They are wearing Disney pyjamas. They shyly run to their mother who gives them a hug and does the introductions. "Children, this is Uncle Jackson. You know, the man you sometimes see on the television news." They give him a smile of recognition. "And Jackson, this is Sam, who is seven and Sophie, who is five."

"Hello," says Jackson, offering his hand which is timidly shaken by each child, "it's very nice to meet you."

Jackson is instantly at ease with the children and points to the cartoon characters on their pyjamas. "And who are those?" he asks, affecting not to know.

"Donald and Minnie," replies Sophie.

"Ah, yes. Mr Donald Duck and Miss Minnie Mouse. I remember now."

"Can you read us a story, Uncle Jackson?" asks Sam.

"Oh I think I can," agrees Jackson, "what would you like?"

Sam goes to a pile of books on a coffee table beside a sofa and selects one. "This is our favourite." He holds up *Hairy Maclary from Donaldson's Dairy*.

"Oh yes," exclaims Jackson, "I just love *Hairy Maclary*. I used to read it when I was a little boy… Yes, let's read that."

He sits on the sofa and the two children squat on the floor in front of him, watched with interest and affection by Felicity. The children are delighted when Jackson recites some lines without even opening the book. "Bottomley Potts covered in spots, Hercules Morse as big as a horse."

The front door opens and Thomas comes in. He sees Jackson with the children. "Ah, I see Jacko has already made himself part of the family!" he says with just a hint of envy in his voice.

Sam and Sophie run to him and he gives them a hug. Felicity goes over to Thomas and they exchange a cursory kiss on the lips. Jackson gets up from the sofa and shakes hands with Thomas.

"Sorry I'm a bit late," says Thomas, "but it's been another busy day in the embassy's Commerce Division." He gives Jackson a discreet hint of a wink at this lie.

The children tug at Jackson's clothes. "Can we read now, please, Uncle Jackson?"

"Oh yes," replies Jackson, but Thomas interrupts and tells the children that it is their bed time. "Uncle Jackson will read to you some other time. We don't want Mummy's dinner for our guest going cold."

"Oh please Daddy. Just a few pages," they implore. Thomas is firm and insists that they must go to bed. "C'mon kids, let's not have a fuss. Daddy will tuck you in and you can read to yourselves in bed for 10 minutes."

Thomas takes the protesting children to their bedrooms. Felicity goes to the kitchen and returns seconds later with a tray of starters. "Seafood still okay for you?" she enquires. Jackson smiles his agreement. Felicity lowers her voice. "And for the main course, I have your favourite dish, Welsh leg of lamb, flown in fresh by the embassy caterers." Jackson smiles broadly. "You remembered. Wonderful!"

Felicity makes final adjustments to the table setting, lights a couple of candles, distributes the starters and dims the room lights.

Jackson's attention is captured by a selection of family photographs on a framed wall display. One is of Felicity in her wedding dress, standing arm-in-arm with Thomas looking very smart and proud in a British Army officer's dress uniform. Another shows Thomas in battle fatigues and armed with an automatic rifle. "Where's this?" he asks pointing to the second photograph. "Afghanistan," she replies. "Mmm," says Jackson with a sly smile, "so you've married a trained killer." Felicity is offended. "Hey! That's not funny!" Jackson realises he has over-stepped the mark. "Sorry, sorry. Poor joke in very bad taste." She accepts his apology with a resigned shrug and points to a chair at one end of the dining table. "You can sit there, if you would."

Jackson goes to the seat as Thomas returns carrying two bottles of wine. "Are you drinking tonight, Jacko?"

"Oh, I think I can risk a small red, seeing I'm not on duty."

61

"Good, good," says Thomas, pouring a red for Jackson and himself and a white for Felicity.

Thomas and Felicity take their seats and raise their glasses to Jackson. "Greetings and welcome, Jacko," says Thomas. "Yes," agrees Felicity, "nice to have you here." They clink their glasses and prepare to eat, but are startled by a brilliant flash of light that illuminates the room in much the same way as a bolt of lightning.

"Shit! What was that?" exclaims Thomas, spilling his drink. Further words are drowned out by the roar of an explosion followed by the air concussion that blows back the curtains on the open window and causes the candles on the table to flicker.

Both Jackson and Thomas leap up from the table and run to the window. They get there in time to see a huge ball of fire rising into the sky a kilometre or so away.

Sam and Sophie come running into the room, frightened by the noise. Felicity puts comforting arms around them. "Don't worry, children, it's just an accident. Nothing for you to worry about." They are not convinced and burst into tears.

Jackson grabs his new mobile phone and dials Pete Fox. The call is instantly answered. "Did you hear that, Pete?" He listens. "Christ! You mean that big mosque we drove past the other day?" He listens again. "Right. I'm not far away so I'll meet you there."

Jackson turns to Felicity and Thomas. "Really sorry about this; I've got to go."

"I'll come with you," announces Thomas as they both head for the door.

As they emerge into the street, crowds have turned out to see what is going on. Jackson waves down a passing taxi and he and Thomas leap into it. "Take us as close as you can to the explosion," Jackson tells the driver in Arabic. The driver shakes his head furiously. "No, no, too dangerous!"

Jackson turns to Thomas. "Got any American dollars?"

Thomas gets his wallet out. Jackson grabs it and removes two $25 notes. He waves the money at the driver and shouts: "$25 now and $25 when you get us to the mosque!" The taxi driver takes the first $25 and accelerates towards the explosion, flashing his lights and furiously tooting his horn as they weave through the traffic, most of which seems to be fleeing the explosion.

Thomas returns the wallet to his pocket and frowns at Jackson. "You're a bit fast and loose with other people's money, aren't you!" Jackson grins. "Oh, I'm sure you'll be able to put it on your most generous expenses. Something like 'fee to informant' probably." Thomas does not demur.

The taxi turns a corner and a wall of flames can be seen a block or two ahead. The driver pulls up, anxious not to go any further. "Closer, closer!" shouts Jackson in Arabic. The taxi travels 200 metres further along the street and pulls up again. The driver is too frightened to go further. Jackson accepts this and hands over the second $25. He and Thomas run towards the blaze.

CHAPTER 7

Mack snoozes in his comfy chair in his apartment. The television is on with the sound down. Joan comes in and stirs him. "Did you hear that?"

"No," he mutters, "what was it?"

"A boom. You know, like a bomb going off."

"Mmm. It can't be anything much if it didn't wake me." He closes his eyes and resumes his snooze.

Back at the scene of the explosion, Jackson realises that he is witnessing a major incident, even bigger than he had first expected. The front of the mosque has been blown in and the dome has collapsed. The mosque and neighbouring buildings are ablaze. There are many dead or injured. Screams come from the wounded and from those who are discovering family and friends among the casualties.

Jackson spots Pete Fox busily filming in the swirling smoke. He is wearing his flak jacket with the word "Press" in English and Arabic. Jackson runs to him. "Boy, this is a big 'un. Can we get Yassin to bring the satellite link down here?" Pete shakes his head. I phoned him on my way here before I knew how big this was. He's just arrived, but without the satellite gear." Pete points to the Range Rover parked about 50 metres away in the semi-darkness.

"What about Mack?" asks Jackson, "does he know?"

"The mobile phone tower beside the mosque has been wrecked and I can't get a signal. But he must have heard the bomb go off."

Jackson looks at his mobile phone screen and he, too, can't find a signal.

The CNN and Al-Jazeera crews have turned up and Jackson is anxious to avoid being scooped. "Quick. Let's do a piece-to-camera. Yassin can run it back to the bureau for transmission from there."

Pete points to a spot among the debris. "Just stand over there so that I can shoot you with the flames and ambulances in the background."

Pete hands the microphone to Jackson who hastily gets himself into position. He begins his report:

> *After several days of relative peace in Armibar, this has happened. Behind me is the city's largest mosque now lying in ruins. There are many dead and wounded and...*

Jackson's report is interrupted by a burst of automatic gunfire and he and Pete dive to the ground. Jackson does his best to keep talking to the camera:

> *As you will have heard, there's shooting and I think it's best we move to a safer spot.*

They run crouching towards the BBC car, but as they do, a young bearded man in traditional Arab clothes and with a rucksack on his back appears from the darkness shouting "Allahu Akbah! Allahu Akbar!"

Pete sees him and dives to the ground, instinctively holding his camera aloft to avoid it being damaged and allowing his body to take the blow. His experience as a rugby player in Sydney has come in useful.

Pete shouts a warning to Jackson, but it is drowned out by the chattering of automatic gunfire directed from the darkness at the young man. He is hit several times, but he is able to trigger an explosive device in his rucksack as he falls backwards to the ground. Jackson is about five metres away and is sent crashing to the ground, splattered with blood and body parts.

Pete sits up in shock and surveys the scene. All that remains of the bomber are his leg stumps and head scattered on the ground a few metres away. He vomits.

Jackson's mind is in turmoil as he slowly sits up and tries to comprehend what has just happened. His ears are ringing from the blast. There is pandemonium. He looks around and sees the face of the suicide bomber blankly staring at him with what he wildly imagines is hatred. His vision becomes blurred and when he wipes his eyes, he realises that his face is covered in blood and other unknown matter.

Pete gets up and runs to him. "Jeez, mate! Are you hurt?"

"I don't think so," he mumbles, "nothing serious anyway."

Pete flinches. "Oh God, mate. You're covered in his blood and guts." Jackson is nauseated but somehow manages to stop himself throwing up.

Yassin and the CNN and Al-Jazeera crews come over to see what's going on. "Oh my God, Jacko," exclaims Jane Kubinski, "are you okay?"

"Well, it depends what you mean by okay, Jane," looking at his blood-covered slimy hands in disgust.

"Yassin should get you and Pete back to the bureau as quickly as possible. The three of us can pool our stuff so that we're all on an equal footing with the bulletins."

"Agreed," confirms Omar Abbas, "let's work on this together."

"Thanks guys," mutters Jackson before turning away and vomiting.

Pete takes the memory card from his camera and hands it to Omar. "Here's what I shot. You can use the piece-to-camera if you think it won't cause viewers to chuck up on their lounge room carpets."

Yassin goes back to his car and gets a plastic sheet from the boot and lays it over the back seat. Jackson eases himself onto the seat, trying not to touch anything as he does so.

Pete returns and gets in the front seat with Yassin. "Let's go, mate. And keep the windows open. Jacko is seriously on the nose."

As Yassin accelerates away, Pete tries to phone Mack, but he still can't find a signal. He turns to Jackson, sitting stunned in the back. "Christ only knows what the suicide guy had for his last meal, but it smells like a seriously dodgy curry!" Pete, never one to miss cracking a joke whatever the circumstances, adds: "Look on the bright side, Jacko. At least you didn't have to fake this piece-to-camera!" Yassin laughs, but Jackson is in no mood for humour.

Back at the Galbraith's apartment, Mack is urgently shaken awake by Joan. "Mack, Mack! Wake up. Quick. Something big has happened." He sits up with a start as she turns up the volume on the

TV to hear the BBC presenter reading from notes that have just been placed in front of him:

> *...it isn't yet clear just how serious the explosion at the mosque was, but initial reports and some early social media film posted on Twitter suggest that it is a major incident. We have a team on the scene and are expecting to get a report from Armibar any moment now. Meanwhile, we have unconfirmed reports that the number of dead and injured is…*

Mack is incredulous. "Fuck, fuck, fuck! How come I wasn't called about this!?"

"I did tell you earlier that I'd heard what could have been an explosion," responds Joan. "You should have made a check to see if there was anything in it."

Mack, now wide awake, runs from the room and heads downstairs to the bureau. He finds it empty and in darkness. He turns on the television sets and sees all three of them are showing scrappy reports about the explosion. "Fuck, fuck, fuck," he keeps muttering to himself. He picks up the phone and dials Jackson, but can't get a response.

Outside in the street, the BBC car arrives back from the scene of the explosion. Pete orders Jackson to remain in the back seat while he runs upstairs to alert Mack. He bursts into the bureau and is met by a volley of abuse. "What the fuck's going on?!" Mack demands. "Why didn't someone phone me?"

"Shut up, will you!" shouts Pete, who runs to the broom cupboard and takes from it two large buckets. "Help me fill these!" Mack can't understand why. "Just do it, mate," shouts Pete, "then come with me."

A couple of minutes later Mack and Pete emerge into the street with the buckets of water. Jackson now stands shaking uncontrollably alongside the BBC car. Pete orders him to remove his shirt, trousers, shoes and socks and to move onto the roadway, away from the vehicle. Jackson meekly does as instructed, despite this leaving him exposed in a public street in his underpants. A small crowd of curious Arab men gather in the darkness, watching this extraordinary behaviour with a mixture of astonishment and amusement.

"Brace yourself, mate," warns Pete, who then hurls his bucket of water over his colleague. As Jackson stands spluttering and protesting at the indignity, Pete brusquely orders him to turn around, then does the same with the second bucket of water. "Right," Peter informs Jackson, "now you smell a bit better. Shake yourself off a bit and we'll go inside." For once, Mack is speechless.

Yassin, his face contorted with revulsion, takes the plastic sheet from the back of the 4x4 and uses it to wrap Jackson's soiled clothes. He places the lot in one of the few street bins in the area.

Back inside the bureau, Pete grabs a couple of tea towels from the kitchen. He hands them to Jackson who dries himself off and gets a spare set of clothes from his wardrobe. He begins shaking again as he gets dressed, then flops down at his desk, unable to discipline the swirling images of what has taken place.

Mack lights up a cigarette and attempts to re-assert his authority. "Right, Jacko and Pete, I have three immediate questions: "What the hell happened? How the hell are we going to cover the story? And why did you bampots not phone me?"

Pete replies. "The answer to Question Three is that there was no mobile signal." Pete then points to the television screens. "As for the first two questions, the answer is right there, boss." Mack turns to see all three networks have graphic film of the mosque explosion. Then, as though on Pete's cue, the BBC runs Jackson's piece-to-camera. Mack is transfixed by the jerky, powerful images that end with a white-out as the suicide bomber blows himself up. "Jings!" is all he can say.

They watch the rest of the images in silence for a few minutes, then Mack's decades of crisis management begins to kick in. "Right," he says, "that's wonderful stuff guys, but we have to keep the ball rolling. And London will, no doubt, want to know why I didn't cover the story, seeing that they know I was on call."

"No worries on that score, Mack," asserts Pete, "you'll come out of this smelling as sweet as a pod of fresh green peas. You'll tell them the truth that Jacko and I just happened to be close by to the bombing. They don't need to know that you weren't aware of the story. Just tell them you instructed us to cover it while you co-ordinated everything from the bureau. As for the coverage, you'll explain that your Duty of Care required you to ensure that your staff were safe and well, which is why a deal was struck with CNN and Al-Jazeera to pool all three lots of film and for us to return immediately to the bureau. You now take over coverage of the story while I return Jacko home for a well-deserved drink. As I said, 'no worries'!"

Mack is humbled by this sensible and sudden role reversal -- a junior staff member telling the boss how to respond to a crisis. Pete's scenario makes a lot of sense. He accepts it as a case of one honest friend advising another in a time of unexpected difficulty.

The bureau phone rings. It is Samira. She has just seen the television news and wants to know if Jackson and Pete are okay. Mack assures her that they unharmed, but it would be helpful if she came in to help Mack and Farouk with the rest of the coverage.

The phone rings again. Mack takes it and finds that it is Jackson's mother. "Oh, hello Lady Dunbar. Yes, there's something wrong with the mobile phones tonight, but I'll hand you over to him." Jackson shakes his head furiously, adamant that he won't take the call. "Oh, sorry Lady Dunbar," says Mack, "I see Jackson is in the middle of , er, a live radio report and can't be interrupted. I'm sure he'll call you when he gets a moment. Meantime, there's no need to worry. Your boy wasn't injured; just a bit shaken. It probably looked worse on the screen than it really was." He listens. "Yes, I'll make sure that your message is passed on. Bye." He hangs up. "Thanks, Mack," says Jackson, "there is only so much strife I can cope with at the moment."

Mack takes another phone call. "Yes, who shall I say is calling?" He turns to Jackson. "Someone called Felicity for you?" Jackson picks up the call at his desk. "Hi, there," doing his best to sound upbeat. "Don't worry. I'm okay, apart from a few bruises and a ruined set of clothes." He listens. "Sorry the dinner was all messed up." He listens. "What about Thomas? Did he get back okay?" He listens. "Are the kids okay? Not too upset, I hope. Tell them I'll read them *Hairy Maclary* when I see them next." He listens. "Right. Well, I'd better go. I'll give you a call in a day or so." He hangs up and finds that Mack has put a large whisky on his desk. "Drink up," says Mack, "you've earned it."

CHAPTER 8

Jackson and Pete arrive by taxi outside their apartment block. "Do you want to come in for a steadying nightcap?" Jackson asks his colleague.

"No, I'd better go to my own pad. I'm stuffed and rather sore and I need to ring the family in Sydney to tell them I'm okay."

"Righto. See you in the morning."

"Yeah. Okay."

They enter the building, nod to the night concierge and press the call button for a lift to take them up to their apartments. As they wait, Pete reflects on the night's events. "It's a bit of a mystery, Jacko, isn't it?"

"What is?"

"You know, mate, how you weren't killed and I wasn't injured or worse."

"Well, I wouldn't have wanted to be any closer to that guy, if that's what you mean."

"No, I don't mean that, Jacko. Don't suicide bombers usually pack their explosive with nails and stuff? If that had been the case, you'd be on a mortuary slab right now, looking like a dead porcupine. And so would I, probably."

"Oh Christ, Pete, haven't I got enough on my mind tonight without you coming up with that graphic stuff! Let's be grateful we're still alive and able to spend the night in our own beds."

"Yeah. Sorry mate," says Pete as the lift arrives to take them upstairs.

On reaching his front door, Jackson's hands begin shaking and he has difficulty opening the lock. He twice drops the keys before he manages to insert the correct one to gain entry. He switches on the lights and goes straight to an almost-full whisky bottle on the bench. He pours himself a large one, gulps it down, then immediately replenishes the glass. He doesn't feel like eating, but knows he must. He empties a tin of baked beans into a bowl and puts it in the microwave. While the beans heat up, he finds some bread to toast.

The red message light is flashing on Jackson's answering machine and he sees there have been 10 calls, all in the past half hour or so. He presses Play. There are no messages, just a click as each call is terminated prematurely.

The microwave dings and he pours the baked beans onto the toast without bothering to butter it. He eats without enthusiasm and takes another gulp of whisky to steady his shattered nerves.

The phone rings and he studies it for a few moments, not wanting to take the call, but curious to know who has been trying repeatedly to get in touch. He presses the speaker button on the phone and answers in poor humour. "Yes. Jackson Dunbar!"

"It wasn't us," says a male voice without preamble, "it wasn't us!"

Jackson is suddenly attentive: "Who's that?"

"It's Roger's old school friend," says the voice, which Jackson now recognises.

"Ahmed! Binnie!"

"Yes, my friend. I saw your report, but it wasn't us. We don't target mosques."

"Oh really," responds Jackson, his voice heavily laced with sarcasm, "so who else would have done that?"

"Ask MI6, the CIA, Mossad, or the government. Ask them, my friend!"

"What about that fucking suicide bomber who nearly killed me?"

"Trust me, Roger. It wasn't us."

Jackson reaches for a notepad and pen and prepares to question Ahmed further, but there is a click as the call ends. He thumps the table with frustration and pours another whisky, his baked beans forgotten. He phones the bureau and the call is answered by Samira.

"Is everything alright, Jacko?"

"Yes, as alright as anyone can be after being blown up."

"You don't sound good. Have you been drinking?"

"Just a soothing tot or two of Scotland's finest."

Samira is worried. "Look, I'll be finished here soon. Would you like me to come over for a bit of company and a chat? You know, to talk things over. I could stay for the night in your spare bed."

"Thanks, my dear, but I'm going to hit the sack shortly. I'll be fine in the morning, apart from a bit of bruising."

"If you're sure?"

"Yes, I'm sure, but first I urgently need to speak to Mack."

"Sorry, but he's about to do a live interview any second now. Can't it wait until the morning?"

"Well, just tell him not to put too much stress on the al-Qaeda angle. It might be someone else."

"That doesn't sound very likely. Are you certain?"

"I'm pretty sure. Just run and tell him that now, please!"

"I'll do that, Jacko, but you'd better not drink any more." She hangs up.

Jackson goes to the bathroom and runs a hot bath while he undresses. He examines himself in a full-length mirror and is hugely relieved to see that his body is unmarked by the explosion. He has brought with him the whisky bottle, still half full. He eases himself into the hot water and takes another drink, straight from the bottle. He is beyond caring that this is a stupid thing to be doing.

As the bath and the alcohol ease his body's tension, Jackson allows himself to be fully submerged in the hot water. In his drunken state, he idly wonders what it would be like to drown. He holds his breath for what seems like a couple of minutes, but in reality is much briefer, before bursting out of the water, gasping for air. He takes another gulp from the whisky bottle.

Hours pass and Jackson realises that he has been lying unconscious and chilled in what is now a cold bath. He reaches for the whisky bottle, but it is empty. He struggles to get out of the bath and can only do so by rolling himself with great difficulty over the side and onto the floor. He lies on his back staring at the ceiling for a while before slowly rolling over and crawling on all fours through the kitchen towards the bedroom, leaving a trail of water puddles. He grasps a tea towel from a kitchen rail and tries with only modest success to dry himself. He attempts to pull himself upright, using the kitchen rail, but it comes adrift and he crashes back onto the floor.

Four more hours go by and he is woken by a persistent ringing of his front door bell. He is still lying naked on the kitchen floor. As he attempts to stand up, the doorbell stops ringing, followed seconds later by a call on his landline phone. He yanks the cable and catches the phone as it falls towards him. "Yes," he mumbles into the handset. It is Pete standing outside Jackson's flat and wanting to know if he is ready to go to the bureau. "Not just yet," his voice barely audible.

Pete recognises there is a problem and demands to be let into the flat. "Give me a minute," replies Jackson as he drags himself unsteadily to his feet with the aid of a chair. He goes to the bathroom, splashes water on his face, pulls the plug on the cold water in the bath and returns to the kitchen, where he bins the empty whisky bottle.

The doorbell rings again. Jackson puts on a dressing gown from behind the bedroom door and lets Pete in. "Christ, Jacko!" exclaims Pete, "you look like a heap of pig shit."

"Thanks for the flattery," responds Jackson caustically, "I feel like shit, but there's no need to tell me so."

Pete puts down his camera kit and goes to the kitchen area. "Have a shave and get dressed, mate, and I'll make some coffee and get you something to eat." Jackson mumbles his agreement and staggers to the bathroom.

Pete fills the electric kettle and rummages around in the cupboards for a jar of instant coffee. He opens the bread box and finds a few slices of stale bread that have yet to go mouldy and sticks them in the toaster. He opens the refrigerator and finds butter and jam to put on the table. He opens a container of milk, but it fails the sniff test and he pours the contents down the kitchen sink.

Jackson returns sheepishly to the room as Pete puts the coffee and toast on the table. He sits down feeling very sorry for himself, and more than a little ashamed. "Thanks, Pete. Sorry about all this. Not very professional is it!"

Pete is sympathetic. "Don't feel bad about it, Jacko. This is your first really big test as a correspondent. Being lifted the other day by those blokes was small cherries compared with being blown up. We choose to put ourselves at risk and when it gets nasty we have to learn to shut our minds down in some respects. This crazy business is not for Nervous Nellies."

Jackson eats some toast and jam and washes down a couple of paracetamol. He lets his colleague continue to do the talking.

"There's another thing to keep in mind, mate. What happened to us last night wasn't personal. They weren't out to get us as individuals. We just happened to be in the wrong place when that nutter blew himself up. We could easily have been a block away and it would've been just another interesting element to the story. It's when it gets personal that you've reason to be nervous."

Jackson is now irritated by this lecture. "Stop it, Pete! What would you know? When you were in Australia you probably never covered anything more dangerous than road accidents and house fires and crap politicians and third-rate celebrities mouthing off at press conferences."

Now it is Pete's turn to get angry. "Bullshit!" He pulls up his T-shirt and points to a scar to the side of his chest.

"Hell," exclaims Jackson. "That looks nasty."

"I got it when a gang boss and his biker mates ambushed me after I filmed them doing a big drug exchange in Sydney. The fuckers intended to kill me so there'd be no witnesses. They grabbed my camera and made their escape, thinking that I was dead, but the bullet missed my heart by a centimetre or so and I survived."

"Bloody hell!"

"Yep, not good. I spent a couple of months in hospital under police guard."

"Why the guards? Where you considered a suspect?"

"The gang didn't know that I had taken the memory card from the camera and put it in my pocket. It was used as evidence at the trial and the lot of them were sent to the slammer for 20 years."

"Well, that was a good outcome," Jackson enthused.

"Up to a point, mate. The gang boss took out a contract on me from behind his cell bars. The New South Wales Police advised me to go abroad for the foreseeable future. And here I am!"

"Blimey! Shouldn't you have moved somewhere a little quieter than here?"

"Of course," agrees Pete with a smile, "but that would be very boring for someone born to live dangerously."

They both laugh and Pete tells Jackson to finish his toast and coffee and get ready to go to the bureau.

******

Jackson and Pete arrive at the bureau just as everyone is gathering in Mack's office for the morning editorial conference. Samira is pleased to see them and gives them both a comradely hug. "I appreciated your offer last night," Jackson tells her, "but you don't need to be concerned. Pete and I reckon we'll be okay."

"Yes, I'm sure you will, but I was worried when I saw what happened. If you do want to talk things through, I'm available."

"Thanks, Samira," says Pete.

Both Jackson and Pete have done their best to look presentable, but this is only partly successful. They gingerly ease themselves into their seats. Jackson's thumping headache is easing, thanks to the paracetamol, but he cannot entirely hide his hangover and the trauma that led to it.

Mack lights up a cigarette from a packet that is already half empty and studies Jackson and Pete for a few moments. "Morning, lads. You both look a bit delicate, if you don't mind me saying so."

"I think I might have had a whisky or two more than was wise," Jackson admits, "but give me a few hours and I'll be okay."

Mack nods sympathetically. "What about you, Pete?"

"Oh, I'm okay, boss, apart from being a bit sore from when I hit the ground. I'll be set for any filming you want today."

"Good. You'll be pleased to know that your film, particularly the piece-to-camera, has been much in demand around the world and our competitors have offered another pooling arrangement today to allow you a bit of a rest. By the way, how did you come to be so handy for the explosion?" asks Mack as something of an afterthought.

"Oh, I was having dinner a few blocks away with some university friends who are in town," says Jackson, blurring the full truth, "and I had no more than a mouthful of the starter when it all happened."

"It was worse for me," announces Pete, "I was preparing to have a most enjoyable time with a fine Aussie lady of my acquaintance. It was trousers-down and action stations when all hell broke loose at the other end of the street. *Coitus interruptus* big time."

Mack is amused. "I'm sorry to hear that both of you had your evening spoiled so spectacularly – particularly you, Pete. I admire your dedication to your chosen career, never going anywhere without your camera, even with a good shag in prospect."

Mack's phone rings, and as expected, it is the Foreign Desk in London. He puts the call on his speaker phone. "Morning London."

"Hi Mack, it's Harry Kingston. We hope that Jacko and Pete are okay."

"Yes, we're okay," Jackson and Pete reply in chorus.

"Good," says Harry, "the pooling arrangement with CNN and Al-Jazeera worked to everyone's benefit, but we hope that coverage from your end will soon return to normal. More thought needs to be given to sending you some backup. Frederick Wynter is wondering whether the story is important enough for his attention.

Mack is now bolt upright in his seat. "We don't want fucking 'Wet' Wynter trampling all over our patch and offering our audience nothing more than shallow platitudes!" he shouts.

"Understood," acknowledges Harry, "but you may find it's either him or Sally Singer."

"What a choice!" says Mack, slumping back into his seat, reaching for another cigarette.

Harry knows that the presence of "bigfoot correspondents" descending on a major story is always a sensitive matter, with local correspondents feeling, often with justification, that they are being pushed aside with no added value to the reporting. "Well, just let's see how the situation plays out," he says. "Those two are pretty much a law unto themselves."

There are murmured voices in the background in London and Harry announces that he has just been joined by Amanda Murphy from the DG's office.

"Hello to everyone in Armibar," says Amanda without warmth. "Before we move on to the business of the day, let me say that the comments I have just heard about Frederick Wynter and Sally Singer are unfair and unwelcome. Both are highly regarded members of the newsgathering team and their views on international affairs are respected by a great many of our listeners and viewers. I would remind you that we are 'one BBC' and this sort of professional rivalry is not productive. I urge you to accept that Mr Wynter and Ms Singer are an important part of the 'BBC brand'.

Mack's response is laced with ill-disguised sarcasm. "Yes, Amanda, they are both highly respected in certain sections of the population at large, but the corporation also has a professional responsibility to provide a depth and richness of insight that only a correspondent based on a patch can provide. I, myself, do not see us as a 'brand'. It is, as our founder, good Lord Reith, would agree from his grave, a public service broadcaster with the emphasis on 'service', not on 'celebrity'.

"This is obviously a conversation for another time, Mack," Amanda responds acidly, "but meantime, I have been asked by the Director-General to pass on his praise for the dedication and courage shown by Jackson Dunbar and his cameraman Peter Fox. The DG has issued a statement to the press to that effect. He also asks that I convey to you the need not to put yourselves unnecessarily in harm's way. It was noted that Mr Dunbar was not wearing the regulation flak jacket when he filmed his piece-to-camera last night."

This is too much for Mack. "Stop it Amanda! Just bugger off back to your posh office and get on with whatever you overpaid, over-important bureaucrats seem to do each day – shuffling bits of paper around your desk, attending pointless meetings and lunches and messing about with the lives of the people who do the real work – the broadcasters."

Amanda is deeply offended. "I am choosing to ignore your intemperate remarks, Mr Galbraith. I will put them down to the stresses you have obviously undergone in recent days. On this occasion, I will not convey to the DG or others on the board of management just how rude you have been. Please do not show such disrespect on future occasions, otherwise there will be consequences."

Mack terminates the call.

"Great stuff, boss," says Pete, holding up his hands like a sportsman who's just scored, "I really enjoyed that." And so, it seemed, did all the others in the room.

"Well, she really gets on my tits, that woman," says Mack, "but she'll probably see that I pay dearly for this insubordination at a time of her choosing. When I calm down I'll call Harry back and sort out today's coverage."

The editorial meeting breaks up, but Jackson and Pete are asked to stay behind. Mack wants to be assured that they have not suffered any long-term physical or mental consequences from yesterday's event. "Would you guys like the day off? I've got all the pooled stuff for a package and Farouk is okay with a camera if I need extra film."

"I think I'd prefer to keep working, if you don't mind," says Jackson, "I don't see much point us just sitting around doing bugger all and thinking too much about yesterday."

"I agree, boss," says Pete.

"Well, don't go pushing yourselves to the brink."

"We'll be fine, Mack," Jackson assures him, with nodded agreement from Pete.

"Good. There's one thing I wanted to ask you, Jacko. Why did you want me to back off the al-Qaeda angle last night? It seemed solid enough, but I did as you said and left a question mark over the possibility."

"I can't go on record with this, but I had a very brief call from Ahmed Bin Hassan denying it was his lot. He hung up before I could get any more information, but he could have been telling the truth. If it were al-Qaeda or one of their affiliates or imitators, we should have heard from them by now. More importantly, Pete and I are wondering why the suicide bomber didn't have his rucksack packed with nails and ball bearings and so forth."

"Mmm. Good point," muses Mack, "and there's another issue we should keep in mind for the future. It looks as though the reason you couldn't use your mobiles was because the only public network – the one owned by a corrupt business associate of President Hasani -- was switched off for several hours last night. I'd better order some more portable satellite phones from London, so we don't get caught next time there's a crisis."

Jackson and Pete nod their agreement.

Jackson's mobile rings. It's Thomas Fulham wanting to talk. Jackson gets Mack's permission to go for a short coffee break with his "university friend".

CHAPTER 9

Jackson and Thomas sit at their usual table in the café across from the British Embassy. Thomas is anxious to know how Jackson is but, in truth, his main concern is that had Jackson been killed he would have lost a most useful and developing contact. He tells Jackson that he had witnessed what happened with the suicide bomber, but from a safe distance. "Sorry that I didn't go to your aid, but I could see that you already had help, and to be honest, it shook me up a bit."

"Not really a surprise, I guess. It was a nasty thing to witness."

"It wasn't only that. It just brought back memories of the Taliban bomb that nearly blew off my leg in Afghanistan."

Thomas discreetly pulls up his left trouser leg and shows Jackson a deep scar running the length of his calf.

Jackson winces. "So that's why you walk with a bit of a limp."

"Yes, and it's why I was invalided out of the marines and transferred to military intelligence." Thomas rolls down his trouser leg. "I convinced myself that there was nothing to be gained last night by sticking around the mosque. I went back home to make sure Sam and Sophie were settled down in bed and to finish the dinner Flip cooked for us."

Arabic coffees and water are brought to their table and Thomas turns the conversation to speculation about what was behind the attack on the mosque. "No doubt it was your contact, Ahmed Faisel Bin Hassan."

"Not sure about that, Thomas."

"Why not? That'd be the most obvious way to do it if he's trying to make a name for himself and his so-called *Soldiers of Allah* group."

"That's my point, Thomas. So why haven't they laid claim to it? There's been nothing given to the media and their new website says nothing. And there's another oddity about last night's attack. Why did that suicide bomber not have a proper belt packed with stuff that would have killed me?"

"I don't know the answer, but you shouldn't assume that just because a group doesn't claim responsibility for something it doesn't mean they didn't do it. There are sometimes internal reasons for not making a claim – or even denying it. I can think of at least one incident in Afghanistan where an operation was carried out without the approval of the leadership, so it was never admitted and the bombers were quietly taken aside and shot."

"That may be so, Thomas, but take a tip from me. Don't waste time on the al-Qaeda angle."

Thomas is suspicious. "Are you keeping something back from me?"

Jackson shakes his head. "I'm just letting you have the benefit of my instincts, based mainly on the meeting with Binnie when he had me lifted."

"Binnie?" asks Thomas.

Jackson is flustered at his slip. "Sorry. I mean Bin Hassan. I'm so tired I can't think straight."

Thomas thinks it may be more than a slip of the tongue and makes a mental note.

Jackson turns the conversation around to what Thomas and his intelligence colleagues have learned about the mosque bombing.

"Not much, to be honest," Thomas replies, "but we're being hounded by HQ in London to give the matter priority. Anything you can help us out with will be gratefully received -- and suitably rewarded, of course."

"Well, I've already told you that I think you should be looking elsewhere for the culprits. Ask yourself why the *Soldiers of Allah* would attack a mosque? My assessment is that they are anti-western and not involved or interested in stirring up conflict between the various permutations of Islam. I'm going to sniff around the possibility that the Israelis are involved. I think you should do the same."

"Yes, but there are limits to how much digging around I can do with them. Anything involving them is hugely sensitive, hugely political. The Israelis and the West have conflicting interests in this country. While we want it to remain stable, for political and commercial reasons, the Israelis like to keep their neighbours on edge. They want to be the only stable country in the region because that allows them to continue to dominate it."

"I have the same problem with London if any story involves the Israelis," says Jackson. "If we broadcast anything the Israelis don't like they're banging on the DG's door before you can say 'anti-Zionist scum'. I'd need rock solid evidence and let's face it, that's unlikely to come my way."

Jackson checks his watch. "I've got to get back to the bureau," he says, gulping down his coffee, despite it being tepid and hardly drinkable. "Give my regards to Felicity and tell the kids that I will read to them when I see them next."

"Yes, I will get Felicity to make another attempt at having you around for dinner."

"Good. I'll leave you to pay for the coffee. Sorry, but I don't have any cash on me."

Thomas takes a sip from his coffee, screws up his face, and decides to leave the rest of it. He puts an American dollar note under the saucer and follows Jackson from the café.

******

Back at the bureau, Mack and Farouk are at the editing desk assembling their package for the evening bulletins. Pete is cleaning his beloved camera, Samira is working at her computer and Yassin is at his usual spot in a corner, smoking and flicking through some English-language sports magazines.

Smoke from Yassin's cigarette drifts across Samira's desk, causing her to frown. "Do you have to smoke those shocking French cigarettes? Between you and Mack, this place stinks."

"Mr Mack says it's okay," he shrugs.

"Yes, well he would, wouldn't he," she groans.

Jackson arrives back and goes to his desk to check his emails. "Anything new?" he asks of no-one in particular.

"Yes indeed," declares Mack, "Pete's just come back with some new film of the mosque. We've got something to show you."

"Oh?"

"First of all let's look at Pete's film of your piece-to-camera last night."

Pete puts his camera down and joins them at the editing desk. He plays the final seconds of the film in slow motion. "Right, Jacko. Watch carefully how the guy goes down as he's raked with bullets. He topples backwards, probably because of the weight of the rucksack, which explodes as it hits the ground."

"Yes, I see that. But what's your point?"

"The point is, mate, that if he had fallen forward, you would definitely be dead meat now. And I'll show you why."

Pete cues up a section of the video he shot today when he returned to the mosque. "See that fucking great hole in the ground? Well, that was caused by the rucksack exploding downwards, instead of into the crowd." He spools through to a close-up of the hole. "And see all the silver bits glinting in the sun? Well, they're the nails and ball bearings that were supposed to kill everyone within a range of 20 or 30 metres."

Jackson now gets the point and goes cold as he considers how close he came to being killed. He sits down, gasping for breath and on the edge of a panic attack. Samira hurries over and puts a consoling arm around his shoulders. He begins to cry. She reaches for tissues from his desk and wipes his tears. As she does, she begins to weep.

"Oh, bugger me, guys," exclaims Pete, "don't go all weepy on me. Just think what lucky bunnies we are. We should be celebrating. We should be buying tickets in the lottery. With our luck, we're certain to win the big prize."

Pete's bravado fails him and he finds that he, too, is wiping away tears. Mack pats Jackson on the shoulder and as tears well up in his eyes, he retreats to his office where he won't be seen. Both Farouk and Yassin look away in embarrassment at this flood of emotion by the Westerners.

Mack phones the nearby coffee shop and orders a delivery of best Arabic coffee for everyone. By the time it turns up about 15 minutes later, emotional equilibrium of sorts has been restored and he calls everyone into his office for an editorial meeting.

He turns first to Pete. "Righto, laddie. What did you learn when you went filming at the mosque this morning?"

"Apart from what I discovered about the close shave that Jacko and I had, not a lot. The mosque will have to be rebuilt, that's for sure. And so will several of the neighbouring buildings. The initial bomb was loaded in a horse and cart that pulled up right outside the main entrance. There is still some confusion about the number of dead and wounded, but we're well into double figures, I reckon."

"Who are the mosque people blaming?" Mack asks.

"Oh just about everyone – the Israelis, the Americans, the British and any Muslim group with a different interpretation of the Koran. The usual thing."

Mack turns to Jackson. "What do you reckon?"

"As I think it is unlikely to have been the *Soldiers of Allah*, I reckon it was most likely the Israelis, using one of their proxy groups, so they have deniability."

"Don't even go there, Jacko! I'm in enough trouble with London without making accusations against the Israelis – accusations, I assume, we won't be able to substantiate."

"No, it's an educated guess."

"Yeah, well, I'll get onto my mates at the American Embassy. I doubt the CIA would have been involved as the Americans have too many business and military interests here and they would want those protected. But they may know something. Meantime, London wants us to give them as much as we can about *Soldiers of Allah*, in case it does turn out to be an outfit that everyone has to take seriously. I'll stall them until tomorrow on that one because I reckon Jacko and Pete should pack it for the rest of the day. Yassin can drive you home."

Jackson and Pete make no attempt to disagree.

"Go back to the apartment," Mack urges them both, "have a hot bath and watch a bit of crap television to unwind. I suggest, though, that Jacko keeps off the booze."

Jackson nods agreement with a wan smile and shuts down his computer. Pete packs his camera in its travelling case and he and Jackson leave with Yassin.

******

As Yassin drives them to their apartments, Pete dials a number on his mobile. It is promptly answered. "Hi there, Kelly. It's Pete. Look, sorry about the other night. An unfortunate time to be interrupted, eh!" He listens. "Yeah, well it was a bit unpleasant. I was okay, but my mate had a shitty time, literally. Umm. Look, are you around this evening? I could really do with some warm and sympathetic company." He listens. "Great! I'll go home and have a shower so I can be smelling nice and fresh for you." He listens. "Oh, crikey, that sounds even better! I'll be there before you can get your knickers off. Bye."

Pete flips shut his mobile and turns to Jackson and Yassin with a broad grin. "Well, guys, my situation has just taken a turn for the better. An 'assisted shower' has just come on offer. If Yassin would just make a short detour to Independence Avenue, that would be much appreciated."

Yassin grins and knows where to go, having delivered Pete to that address before. He drops him off outside a gated block of modern apartments, mostly occupied by foreigners working tax free in Armibar. "You lucky bastard!" mutters Jackson as Pete alights and waves them a triumphant goodbye.

A short time later, Yassin delivers Jackson to his apartment block. By now, Jackson feels like a deflated balloon and as with Pete, fancies some warm female company. He makes a phone call to Leila at the *Zing Zing Club*. He learns that his favourite girl, Zareena, will be available in a couple of hours, so he has a hot bath – this time without any accompanying whisky – and changes into shorts and T-shirt.

Jackson now feels marginally better, switches on the TV and flicks through the dozens of satellite channels without finding anything that appeals. He makes a mug of instant coffee and boots up his computer. He is pre-occupied by yesterday's brush with death and Pete's joking observation that it would be an auspicious time to buy a ticket in the lottery. He prefers the instant gratification of his favourite gambling website, but there is a familiar problem – he has reached his credit limit. He checks a couple of other sites, but they all tell him the same story. He tries a top-up from his four credit cards, but they too have hit the spending ceilings, despite them totalling close on $20,000. He knows it is a waste of time trying his bank account because that has reached the limit of his overdraft and his next month's salary isn't due for several more days.

Although it should now be blindingly obvious to Jackson that his gambling is destroying his finances and his emotional well-being, he isn't yet ready to stop. He remains convinced, as gambling addicts so often are, that given a fair wind, his fortunes will take a sharp turn for the better. It is only a matter of time before he will not only clear his debts, but be put back into substantial profit. Then, he tells himself, he will give up gambling altogether. For now, though, he needs access to some ready cash to "invest" and to tide him over until his salary goes into his account.

Jackson checks his contacts list, pushes the speaker button on his landline phone and dials an international number. It is promptly answered by a man with an educated southern English accent. "Good afternoon, this is Briteson and Associates of London. Adam Gower speaking. How can I help?"

"Good afternoon to you, Adam. It's Jackson Dunbar here."

"Oh yes, Mr Dunbar. How are you? I see from the television last night that you had a very lucky escape, wherever it is you are in the Middle East. Must have been a shocking experience for you."

"I'm fine. It probably looked worse on television than it really was."

"I'm pleased about that, Mr Dunbar. And how can I help you today?"

"Adam, I'm about to make a small, er, investment and need to lay my hands on about a couple of thousand dollars fairly urgently. I'm wondering about selling some more of my shares."

"Well, let me see how you're placed. Give me a minute or two to go into your account."

"Right. I'll hang on."

Jackson's call is put on hold and he is forced to listen to electronically-generated background music that would disgrace a string quartet in a first rehearsal. Eventually the music ceases and Adam comes back on the line.

"Mmm. Well, Mr Dunbar, I see that your share portfolio has been run down over the past six months or so. There isn't a lot left, I'm afraid. However, your Shaft Mining Limited shares are currently holding up well, so if you sold those, you'll probably get the dollar equivalent of about £1,500. Would that do?"

"Yes, Adam, let's sell those. And as the banks are still open, I would appreciate an advance of £500 into my main operating account today."

"Umm. Well, we don't really like doing that, but as it's you, I sure we can arrange it."

"Good. That'll be much appreciated."

"Our pleasure as always, Mr Dunbar. And as you are in contact today, could I say that my colleagues and I are wondering whether these, er, investments you've been making recently are giving you the right sort of returns. Our chief financial adviser, Wilfred Travers, would be happy to talk to you. It is none of our business of course how you wish to--."

Adam is abruptly interrupted by Jackson. "You're right, it's none of your business. I'd just be grateful if you could just arrange that money transfer, as requested."

"Of course, Mr Dunbar. Sorry if I've been a bit out of--."

Jackson terminates the call and mutters "cheeky bugger" under his breath.

Jackson brews a fresh mug of coffee and makes a cheese and pickle sandwich from fresh bread left earlier in the day by his part-time maid. He remembers that he forgot to ring his mother back. He again pushes the speaker button. He can't remember her number, despite it being unchanged for at least a decade, and has to look it up in his contacts list. She answers promptly. "Good afternoon. Lady Dunbar speaking." She speaks with an acquired upper class accent and a rasp that suggests she is a heavy smoker.

"Hello, Mother. It's Jackson. Sorry I didn't call you back sooner, but we've been very busy."

"Yes, you've always got some excuse for not returning my calls," she replies caustically.

"Oh c'mon, Mother. That's not fair. You must have known it was a difficult time for us."

"Well, I'm pleased you weren't hurt, darling, but to be honest, I don't know why you agreed to go to such a terrible place. Why can't you be sent somewhere nice like Paris or Rome or Washington? Even to Sydney, if it it's just for a short while? It's no wonder that no decent woman wants to marry you. Sir Roger was sometimes offered postings to uncivilised places, but he always refused them because he knew they would make me unhappy."

"As I've told you repeatedly, I'm not Dad. And why do you always refer to him as "Sir Roger", even in the family? I know he was a knight and all that, but people in the media don't wave around their titles, except on very formal occasions. And don't you think it's time you dropped the "Lady Dunbar" bit? After all, you're Anne Dunbar and a "lady" only because of Dad's title."

"That's very offensive, Roger. I earned the title as much as your father. Without my social networking skills, he wouldn't have had such an extensive pool of significant people to interview or write about."

"Well, you know as well as I do that he wasn't into hard-hitting bite-your-ankles journalism. He only got his knighthood because he sucked up to so many of the so-called great and so-called good."

"How dare you, Roger!" she shouts.

Jackson's doorbell rings. "Look, Mother, I'm not going to continue this pointless conversation. Someone has just turned up for an interview, so I must go. Bye."

Jackson ends the call and goes to the door. It is Zareena. She is about 25 and tall with a neat figure, dark hair and olive skin. She is expensively and carefully dressed in a Western outfit that would not be out of place in high social circles just about anywhere. Although born in Armibar, she speaks perfect English with just a hint of a local accent.

Zareena and Jackson exchange friendly air kisses and she takes a seat on the sofa.

"A drink?" Jackson asks her.

"Just the usual fruit juice, if you have any."

"Sure. I've got apple or orange."

"Either, perhaps with a little ice."

Jackson goes to the refrigerator, takes out two juice containers and checks their use-by date. He decides that the apple juice is the least likely to have gone off. He pours two glasses and adds some ice.

Zareena points to the electronic keyboard in the corner of the room. "Can you play that?"

"Of course."

"What sort of music?"

"Oh, pretty much anything, I guess. I once played in a pop band, but I really enjoy Bach organ music. Sometimes when I need to get things out of my system, I prefer to blast away at something by The Rolling Stones. *Start Me Up* is a favourite, but it just depends on how I feel."

"Can you sing?"

"Sort of, but it's best if I'm drowned out by lots of loud instruments," he laughs.

"I'd like to learn the piano," says Zareena, "and perhaps one day I will."

Jackson sits down beside Zareena with the drinks and they clink their glasses in greeting.

She points to his juice. "Aren't you having anything stronger?"

"Not after last night," he says with a shrug, "I overdid it with the whisky."

She nods. "I saw what happened yesterday. You're lucky to be alive."

"That's probably why I got so drunk."

"You must take care. Things aren't good in this country. As soon as I finish my business and English literature studies, I'm going to leave."

"Where will you go?"

"Anywhere that'll take me – preferably a country where I can use my English and my Arabic. Maybe I could get a job with the BBC. What do you think?"

"I hadn't thought of that," admits Jackson with a smile, "but it's not out of the question, you know. Social and racial diversity are buzz words of this age and you're getting a good education."

Zareena finishes her drink and changes the subject. "Well, my friend, that's for the future. What would you like to do tonight? Straight sex?"

"Let's start with a massage," he replies, "and see how it goes from there."

"Well, Leila says we owe you two hours. Is that okay?"

"Yes. Of course."

They go into Jackson's bedroom. Both undress. Zareena applies perfumed oil to his body and the massage begins. As it proceeds, Jackson realises just how tense the past 24 hours have made him. Zareena works her usual soothing magic, but there is one thing different from his previous encounters with her – an erection doesn't seem in prospect.

Zareena pauses and looks down at him with a sympathetic smile. "Well, your little friend looks very tired tonight. I think we should just let him have a little rest. I am sure he'll be more enthusiastic next time."

"Yesterday's events have hit me much harder than I thought."

"Well, don't be embarrassed. Let's have a nice shower together then a relaxing meal at your favourite restaurant."

Soon after, Jackson, now in his usual smart casual clothes, is feeling more like his old self as he escorts Zareena into *The Cedar Tree*, a pleasant Arabic restaurant a few doors from his apartment. The head waiter and owner, Jamil, knows them both. They exchange greetings in Arabic and are shown to a quiet table to one side of the dimly-lit room. For the next hour, they eat a light meal of seafood, olives, humous and pitta bread dipped in oil and talk as friends rather than as prostitute and client. The topics range from the political situation in the Middle East, to the future of the European Union, and to their own families in Armibar and London. It comes to an end only when Zareena tells him she must leave for another customer a few blocks away. Jackson is disappointed.

"Don't worry," she tells him, "it's my last for the night – just a nice lonely old man who wants a 'jerk off' – so it shouldn't take me long. If you like, I'll come back to your place for the night. I won't charge and Leila needn't know." Jackson sighs. He likes the idea of her returning for the night, but would prefer not to hear of Zareena's other clients or what she is required to do for them.

When the time comes to pay the bill, Jackson asks that it be added to his account. "Very sorry, Jamil, but I accidentally left my wallet at the office," he lies.

"That's alright, Mr Jackson," replies Jamil, "but may I respectfully ask in all kindness that you settle up before too long as we are just a small family restaurant struggling to make a living in these difficult times."

"Yes, of course, Jamil, I'll pop by in the next day or so."

As Jackson and Zareena leave, she turns to him. "Tut, tut, Jackson. You've been gambling again and lost your money!"

Jackson just shrugs and Zareena waves down a taxi to take her to the next client.

CHAPTER 10

Zareena returns to Jackson's apartment as promised and they literally sleep together. Both wake early and Jackson is refreshed. Zareena, now without make-up and wearing casual clothes for a day at Armibar University, treats him to percolated coffee and a full English breakfast – something she learned to do several years ago when she worked for a year as a waitress and assistant cook in a "24-hour Breakfast" café in London's West End.

They both have spare time before Jackson needs to be in the bureau and Zareena has her first lecture of the day. As they eat, Jackson is curious to know more about her.

"Is Zareena your real name?"

She laughs. "Of course not. That would be stupid, and before you ask, I won't be giving you the real one."

"You're a very intelligent woman," he observes, "so why do you need to sell your body?"

"Money, of course," she replies. "My mother, the only one left in my family, is not well. When I finally can get out of this wretched country, I want to be able to take her with me. It's as simple as that."

"Yes, but isn't it dangerous sometimes? You know, just going off and having sex with anyone who is willing to pay?"

"But I don't just have sex with just anyone. Leila's club is very upmarket and she's very careful who she does business with. At the slightest hint of trouble or inappropriate demands, the clients get banned, and if needs be, dealt with by her 'heavies'. Also, I d on't take return bookings with anyone I really don't like. So, you see, the risk is minimal."

"I suppose I must have passed Leila's vetting," he laughs, "but isn't there a special man in your life?"

"Umm. No." There is a pause for a moment, then Zareena continues. "Do you realise that I'm 'bi'?"

"Bi?"

"Yes. You know, bi, bi-sexual, or as you English sometimes put it, I 'bat for both teams'."

"That must present you with relationship problems."

"I don't see why. It's just that if I ever wanted to settle down, it would probably be with a woman. Less complicated than with a man, I feel. As you can imagine, same-sex relationships are very difficult to have here, which is another reason why I have to move abroad to a more liberal society."

Zareena turns the questioning back on Jackson. "So, why does a handsome young man like you need to pay for sex. Don't you have any girlfriends who'll satisfy your needs for nothing?"

"Not as many as you might imagine, and the relationships usually get rather complicated. Mostly my fault, I have to admit."

"That's a shame, Jacko."

"You and I seem to have something in common: we both have difficulty with heterosexual relationships."

"Seems like it," she agrees with a smile.

"Do you enjoy your sex with me, Zareena?"

She laughs. "What sort of naive question is that? The important question is 'do I give you sexual satisfaction'?"

"Of course, otherwise I wouldn't be asking for you every time."

"Good. Well, that's it then, isn't it! You get your satisfaction and I get your money. It's a business deal, Jackson, but in your case, a pleasant one that suits both parties."

Jackson is amused by Zareena's frankness and decides that he should not press her further. Anyway, Yassin is due about now to take him and Pete to the bureau. He offers to drop Zareena off at the university, but she doesn't want to be seen to be arriving in a 4x4 plastered with BBC and Press signs. He agrees, on reflection, that it would be best if they weren't seen together, at least not by her university friends or his colleagues.

They arrange to leave the building separately, Zareena departing first. Jackson waits for a minute, then catches the lift to the foyer.

Pete is waiting downstairs for him, wearing a "I'm a wave rider from Surfer's Paradise" T-shirt and carrying his camera.

"Hey, Jacko, did you see that tasty sheila leaving just now?"

"What 'tasty sheila'?"

"You know, the tall dark-haired good-looking one in the jeans and sweat shirt?"

"Nope. Didn't see her."

"Well, I think she came from your floor, so it might be worth checking her out."

"Oh, she was probably just visiting one of the other tenants."

Yassin is waiting downstairs as arranged. Jackson gets in the front seat and Pete in the back. As the car accelerates, Jackson notes that despite his outwardly-chirpy manner, Pete looks very ragged.

"Long night, was it, Pete?"

"No, not really. My lady friend and I did the business, had a drink and a bit of a chat and then I went home early."

"So why are you looking as though you've been through a spin drier?"

"I kept having terrible nightmares. Suicide bombers kept running at me and blowing themselves up. I felt like my feet were nailed to the ground, and I kept being covered in blood and guts. It was just like watching a horror video on a loop."

"Mmm. Not nice, but at least it was just a nightmare and not for real."

"It sure felt fucking real, mate! Anyway, how was your night?"

"Oh, it was okay. I slept well. I think I got everything out of my system earlier in the day."

"Lucky you," says Pete.

******

Mack, Farouk and Samira are already at the bureau when Jackson, Pete and Yassin arrive. The morning editorial conference is over and Mack and Farouk are editing a TV package while Samira is checking budget spreadsheets on her computer.

"Morning, boys," says Mack, full of good cheer as he turns to study Jackson and Pete. "Well, Jacko, you look much improved this morning, so that's good. But I can't say the same for our Aussie mate. You look well done in, Pete! Are you okay?"

"Yeah, I'm good," he replies without conviction. "Just overdid it a bit last night with my lady friend, if you get my drift."

"Understood, young man. I hope she was grateful for all the attention you gave her."

"It was mutually appreciated, I believe," he says with a weak grin, being careful to avoid eye contact with Jackson.

"By the way," asks Mack as an afterthought, "what does this friend of yours do when she's not shagging you?"

"She's the personal assistant to one of the British bank chiefs here."

"Will she be able to give you any inside information?"

"Only in a very general sense, boss, but she tells me the bank is getting a bit nervous about the way things are going here."

"Well, let us know if this nervousness shows signs of turning into panic. Meanwhile, today should be quiet for you on the filming front. London wants Jacko and me to spend a bit of time sniffing around the traps for any insider guidance on the situation here."

Samira remembers something. "Oh, Jacko, I nearly forgot. Your beloved mother phoned just before you arrived."

"Hell! What'd she want?"

"She said to tell you that she'd sent you some nice new shirts and trousers to replace those ruined in the bombing. Oh, and there'll also be a selection of half a dozen silk ties for you to wear."

"Bloody hell!"

Samira breaks into a broad grin. "Only kidding. The shirts and trousers are true, but I made up the bit about the ties."

"You stirrer!" he shouts, throwing a screwed up sheet of paper at her. She laughs and so does he.

Mack comes out of his office and announces that he has been invited to a briefing lunch with the American ambassador, Andrew Costello. He turns to Samira. "Fancy a free lunch, young lady?"

"What today?"

"Yes, today. With the ambassador."

"Why would he want me to go along?"

"Oh, you caught his attention at that cocktail party you went to a couple of weeks ago."

Samira is surprised. "I'm a bit busy, but I could go, I suppose. Always good to have an 'in' with a senior diplomat. If Yassin will drop me home I'll change into a dress and tart myself up a little."

"Yes, a pretty dress would be good."

Samira understands the sexual sub-text, then says, "But what about you?"

"What about me?"

"Look at you! I'm not going out for lunch with any old scruff!" she laughs.

"I'm okay," he insists.

"No you're not! Go upstairs and get Joan to tidy you up. You'll need a properly-ironed shirt and trousers, a clean tie and a nice jacket without any cigarette ash on it."

Mack looks in the TV studio mirror and agrees that he isn't looking his smartest. "You're a bossy thing," he tells Samira with a grin as he departs upstairs for the sartorial attentions of his wife.

******

A waiter wearing a white jacket, plain white shirt and black bow tie escorts Mack and Samira to a table set for four in the executive dining room at the American Embassy in Armibar. Mack is now as tidy and smart as he is ever likely to be and Samira is wearing a stylish flower-patterned dress and high heels. The neck-line is just low enough to attract male interest without being overly inviting. Unusually, she is wearing make-up.

The waiter sits them down, tells them they will be joined shortly by the ambassador, and offers them a drink.

"Orange juice would be fine for me," replies Samira. "And a Jim Beam on ice would do me nicely," says Mack.

The waiter goes over to the bar to prepare their drinks and Mack and Samira soak up the sight and atmosphere of their expensively-furnished surroundings.

"Boy, the American diplomats really know how to live," observes Mack, "imagine what it must have cost to ship in all this antique furniture from God-knows where."

Samira, who has never been beyond the reception desk at the American Embassy before, agrees. She points to a large dark wood display cabinet full of fine China and assorted ornaments. "My mother's family in Lebanon had something like that once. Several centuries old and very beautiful. It had to be sold to help raise money for the family to escape to Britain."

"Oh, yes. I remember the Lebanon connection now. Your family was Christian, wasn't it?"

"Token Christians. They didn't attend church except on special family occasions."

"Why did your family leave Lebanon?"

"Not really sure. Something to do with a Christian militia group accusing my father of something or other. I was never told the details and knew it was pointless to ask."

Their conversation is interrupted as their drinks are delivered by the waiter and a door swings open to admit Ambassador Andrew Costello. He is about 50, tall, slim and tanned and has a full head of dark hair with flecks of grey. He is wearing a neatly-pressed dark suit and tie and his accent is best described as East Coast neutral. He looks as though he has been chosen by central casting.

Mack and Samira stand to greet him. The ambassador and Mack vigorously shake hands. "Nice to see you again, Mack," enthuses the ambassador. "And you, too," replies Mack.

The ambassador's eye rest on Samira. "Well now, how nice to see the delightful Samira Lang again!"

Samira steps forward and proffers her hand. "Pleased to meet you again, Mr Ambassador."

He encases Samira's hand in both of his and takes half a step back to admire her.

"Wonderful of you to come, Samira, and there's no need to be formal over this lunch. Please call me Andrew."

"Thank you… Andrew."

They take their seats. Andrew nods towards the spare table setting and explains that they will be joined shortly by the embassy press attaché, Randolph Abrahams.

******

Pete, Farouk and Yassin have gone to the bombed mosque to get film of the demolition and temporary repairs, leaving Jackson alone at the bureau. He takes the opportunity to check his online bank account. The £500 advance on his shares is there. He transfers $300 to his account with the *Towering Treasures Inc* gambling website and is about to begin playing when his colleagues arrive back from the mosque. He quickly shuts down the screen.

"Anything new?" he asks Pete a little too hastily.

"Well, it's going to be a long while before that mosque is operating again. Farouk had a chat to a few of his mates there and learned that another 15 more bodies -- 10 men and five youths -- were found under rubble being cleared by the bulldozers."

"Can we go with that, Farouk?" asks Jackson.

"Sure," replies Farouk in his broken English, "definitely 100 deaths, at least."

"Okay, let London know when you send your rushes to them. If they need a package, I'll knock it out later. I have to go out now."

Jackson leaves, walks along the street to an ATM and draws out $100. He counts out $80, carefully folds it and puts in a trouser pocket. The other $20 goes into his wallet.

******

Lunch is going well at the American Embassy. Randolph Abraham – "Randy" to most of his associates – has joined them. He is a tall mixed-race man in his early forties and sees his primary task as keeping his rather unpredictable boss out of trouble.

The main course of fine imported American fillet steaks and a local salad is being washed down by the three men with a vintage Southern States red. Samira sticks to her juice.

Ambassador Costello is entranced by Samira, who has been primed by Mack to ask some of the trickier questions in the hope that the answers will be franker than the ones offered to him.

"So how many CIA people are stationed here in Armibar?" asks Samira cheekily.

Ambassador Costello is taken aback by her directness and turns to Mack. "My word, your young lady is not backward in coming forward, eh!"

Mack grins. "Well, you must admit that it's an important issue because it would indicate how seriously your government takes its presence here in Central Arabia."

"That's true. Officially, of course, we don't have any CIA people here, just a military attaché in a passive liaison role and a representative of the arms manufacturers."

"But that can't be true," asserts Samira.

He laughs. "Of course it isn't true!"

"So, how many people do you have here?"

Randy Abrahams jumps in before the ambassador has a chance to answer. "I'm afraid, Miss Lang, that's a question that can't be answered for national security reasons. I'm sure you understand."

The ambassador is undeterred, seeking to impress Samira. "Randy is quite right, young lady, but I think that as we're speaking off-the-record, no harm will be done in telling you that it's more than 40 and less than 60." Then he adds with a leery grin: "But if you ever suggest that this information came from this embassy I'll deny it and never invite you to another lunch!"

Randy is worried that too much information is being disclosed. "I'm sure Miss Lang is an entirely trustworthy young woman, but there are some matters that should not be revealed to the press."

"I understand," sympathises Samira, "but there is just one other general point, off-the-record, of course. Who effectively controls the activities of the CIA here – you or the Pentagon?"

"Oh well, that's a delicate issue, of course," replies the ambassador. "In theory, they have to answer to their masters back home, but I think I can safely say that my views – both political and military – carry a lot of weight here. You may not know it, but President Benson is a cousin, so I have access to the Oval Office. I'm not like your ambassador, Shortwood, who doesn't seem to have a clue what's going on and is, I gather, a bit of a joke with your intelligence people. I'm sure Randy will agree with me when I say that I'm very much in the intelligence loop here and nothing significant goes back to the Pentagon without my nod."

Randy nods loyally. The ambassador leans over to Samira. "By the way, is it true that Stumpy is being replaced by someone more attuned to what's really going on?"

"They seem to be just rumours," replies Samira, "but we've heard that the Foreign Office in London was chewing their carpet over that interview he gave Mack."

"Oh yes, we all fell about laughing over that one, Mack. You really stitched him up like a sack of oats."

Mack nods his thanks, grateful that no-one outside the bureau realises what really happened. The waiter removes the empty plates and asks if anyone would like ice cream or cheese. They all decline both choices. The ambassador suggests a Cuban cigar and Mack is delighted to accept as he is beginning to feel nicotine deprivation, not having had a cigarette for more than an hour. Randy and Samira decline.

Mack takes over the questioning as he and the ambassador light up.

"Who do your people think were behind the mosque bombing?"

The ambassador doesn't have a definite answer. "We don't know for sure, Mack, but it was most probably that splinter group, *Soldiers of Allah*, or whatever they call themselves. We can't see it would be anyone else. But we're a bit mystified that they haven't made a public claim, as you'd normally expect of a group trying to mark out its territory."

He turns to Randy. "Do you agree?"

"Yes, sir, probably *Soldiers of Allah*, but there are some doubts."

"Do you think that terrorists pose a threat to this embassy?" enquires Mack.

"Not a special threat, I wouldn't think. We're very secure here and if the recent riot and the mosque bombing are any indication, they're more interested in blowing each other up. That's fine by us," he adds with a laugh, "but I wouldn't want to be quoted on that."

"I'm sure you're right," agrees Mack with an acquiescing smile.

CHAPTER 11

Jackson is in the *Hotel Armibar* feeding dollars coins into the poker machine with very little to show for it. He hears a voice from behind. "You're wasting your money, you know."

Jackson turns to see Thomas Fulham who has invited him to the hotel to have their postponed lunch. "Oh, it's just a bit of harmless fun from time to time. Just fun," he asserts without conviction.

"Well, I've a busy afternoon ahead," says Thomas, "so we'd better have our lunch."

Thomas leads the way to a large dining room, an unimaginative eating place that would be found in any modern four-star hotel anywhere in the world. About half the tables are occupied, mostly by men, some wearing western suits, others in traditional Arab wear. The few women are wearing fashionable western clothes.

The maître d comes over and Thomas points to a table away from the main groups of diners. They sit down and study the menu while a formally-dressed waiter hovers nearby.

"A glass of wine, Jacko?"

Jackson hesitates. "Um, well I don't suppose it'll matter if I have a small Merlot."

"Good," says Thomas, "and what do you fancy to eat?"

"Oh, I believe the seafood salad here is excellent."

"Yes, it is."

Thomas waves over the waiter and addresses him in English: "The seafood special for both of us, a large glass of Pinot Grigio for me and a small Merlot for my guest. Oh, and a bottle of still mineral water each." He taps his watch and adds: "We don't have much time, so we would like to be served without delay."

The waiter understands and hurries towards the kitchen.

"Right then, Jacko. Any new thoughts on those responsible for the mosque bombing?"

"Nothing more than what I've already told you. Mack is having a lunch at the American Embassy as we speak, so he may come back with something."

"No doubt being given the full treatment by Ambassador Costello."

"Could be," agrees Jackson, "all I know is that he's taken Samira, the bureau manager, with him."

Thomas grins. "Ah, a smart move. Mr Ambassador has a keen eye for a good-looking young woman."

The waiter arrives with the water and two glasses of wine. Thomas waits until he is out of hearing before resuming the conversation.

"It's very interesting to learn how you escaped being killed the other day. My contacts have told me about another interesting aspect. They say that the guy who blew himself up wasn't a committed jihadist. He was some poor kid from a local mental asylum. He was religious, but in a seriously mental sort of way, and was conned into blowing himself up in return for a promise that he would be given a grand palace in Paradise with an endless supply of servants and virgins to meet his every need."

Jackson raises an eyebrow. "Are you sure? Why would the terrorists need to use a certified nutter when there are plenty of uncertified ones around, all desperate to be blasted to Paradise?"

"Ah yes, Jacko, why indeed?" Thomas pauses for dramatic effect. "Now, my old friend, let me tell you something else: my contacts believe that the people behind the mosque attack are in the government."

Jackson is surprised. "Really? Why would they want to do that?"

"You clearly aren't up to speed yet on the make-up of this bunch of shysters," Thomas laughs, "most of the people running this country are Sunnis, while most of the Shia – the disempowered -- are poor."

"But the wrecked mosque is Sunni!" interrupts Jackson.

"Exactly, Jacko! We reckon that someone in the government is trying to set up a situation in which it seems entirely reasonable to blame the Shia for the country's problems – then, of course, they can organise a Shia clear-out. You know, drive them from the country."

103

There's another pause in the conversation as the waiter arrives with the salads.

"Mmm. That food looks good," observes Thomas. Jackson agrees. The waiter goes to serve another table and Thomas and Jackson clink their wine glasses and tuck into the meal. After a pause, Jackson raises a question: "Your theory is an interesting one, but I still don't get it. Why would the government want to rock the boat?"

"Yes, there are some unanswered questions, but our political department reckons that there are people who take the view that dealing with the Shia is necessary for the long-term stability of the country. The attack on the mosques gives the government a perfect excuse to act against them."

"You might be right, but a lot of people died in the attack and most of them would've been Sunnis."

Thomas laughs. "God, you are naïve, Jacko! The people who run this country are ruthless with a capital R. I bet that if we went through all those who died, we wouldn't find a person of any significance. All the government's mates and power-brokers would have been somewhere else."

"Were they tipped off?"

"Hell, no! Cleverer than that. At the time of the mosque attack, there was a huge Independence Day party in the Presidential Palace. It was a 'must attend' event and everyone who was anybody in Armibar was there. The result: the party kept all the government's Sunni friends and allies out of harm's way, without them realising that the mosque attack had been deliberately timed to coincide with the event. Cunning, eh!"

Jackson has to agree that there is a certain plausibility to Thomas's theory. "Mmm. It's a scenario worth investigating. But I can't imagine this Machiavellian intention would meet with the approval of the West, least of all the investors here."

"It most certainly does not. The trouble with the government is that it's too stupid to realise that its scheme would not just drive out the Shia, but also the big companies that keep this country afloat.

All the diplomats here are doing their best to convince the powers-that-be to treat the Shia with more respect, rather than try to drive them away. But the government seems to be dominated by those who have an obsessive religious hostility to the Shia and see them as a potential Third Column. If our diplomats fail to persuade these idiots to change their ways, some other more rigorous methods will have to be employed."

"Such as?" asks Jacko.

"You surely don't expect me to answer that question do you?"

"No harm in asking," replies Jackson with a shrug.

Thomas finishes his salad, checks his watch and gulps down his wine. "I really must get going, but there's something I'd like to suggest that might be useful for both of us."

"Oh yes, what's that?" asks Jackson suspiciously.

"Set up an interview with the Development Minister, Khaled Mohamed."

"Why him? He'll probably just bore me to tears with heaps of bullshit about the wonderful commercial future the country has."

"It wouldn't surprise us if he orchestrated the mosque attack and is hoping to elbow the president aside. He's a Sunni and a seriously corrupt bugger, and nasty with it. Don't underestimate him, Jacko."

"Well, I still don't see why you're so keen for me to interview him. What's in it for you?"

"Christ, Jacko! I'm doing you a favour – a tip-off that you should establish contact with someone who'll become a newsmaker in the near future. You should be grateful. All I ask from you in return is that you somehow weave into the conversation a suggestion that I am a person of influence worth meeting."

"And just how am I supposed to do that?"

"Use a little bit of imagination. It can't be all that hard for someone who's supposed to be very bright!"

"Yeah, all right," Jacko says irritably, "but I can't see why you can't set up a meeting with him yourself."

"His minders won't even pass on my requests for a meeting because they think I'd be of no use to him. It's important that I get a face-to-face with him in his office so I get a sense of what the bugger is up to."

"Okay, I'll look into it the next time we have a quiet news day."

"Try not to leave it too long. The sooner the better, in fact."

"I'll think about it, Thomas. But no promises."

"Oh by the way," adds Thomas as he checks the bill and leaves a $50 note on the plate, "I meant to ask you what the name Binnie means to you?"

Jackson is thrown by this question. "Er, I don't understand."

"It's simple Jacko. The other day you referred to someone called Binnie."

"Oh that! Well, that was just a slip of the tongue. I meant Bin Hassan. I said so at the time, you'll remember. Why have you brought it up now?"

"This morning, there was an unexplained reference to someone with that name in some of the intelligence stuff crossing my desk. It seems more than a coincidence that you should refer to a Binnie."

Jackson tries hard to make light of the matter. "Oh c'mon, Thomas, you intelligence guys see conspiracies everywhere. It was just a slip of the tongue."

Thomas grins. "You might be right. Anyway, must get away. Let me know ASAP if you succeed in setting up an interview with Khaled Mohamed."

******

Mack and Samira arrive back from lunch. Jackson decides to take up Thomas's suggestion and puts in a bid for an interview with Khaled Mohamed. He is told by the minister's office that the bid will be passed on to the minister within the next day or so.

Mack briefs Jackson on lunch with the ambassador and expresses scepticism about the American assessment. Jackson summarises what he has been told by Thomas, without naming him. They agree to make further enquiries before dismissing *Soldiers of Allah* as being the people behind the mosque bombing. Jackson casually mentions that he has heard rumours about the growing importance of Khaled Mohamed and thinks he might be worth interviewing. Mack agrees, but only if nothing more important is going on.

Mack goes upstairs to change back into some more comfortable clothes. Jackson turns to admire Samira, still in the outfit she wore to lunch and still wearing make-up. "Mmm. You look very tasty this afternoon."

She responds with a smile. "Well, thank you, sir, although I am not sure 'tasty' is a word I should accept as a married woman and a feminist."

"Okay then, what about 'elegantly glamorous'?"

"Yes, that's better," she agrees with a grin, "I like that."

"So, tell me. How did you enjoy your posh lunch?"

"The food was very nice and as Mack has already told you, the ambassador was quite forthcoming, even if we think he isn't as clued up as he reckons."

"I hear on the grapevine that he's what might be termed a 'hands on' diplomat when it comes to attractive young females," says Jackson.

"Well, he's certainly an attractive man with film star good looks. I'll accept him lusting over me if it means he reveals more information than he should, but I'll make sure he keeps his hands to himself. I'll have to be very careful not to find myself alone with him."

The phone rings and Samira picks up the call. It is for Jackson. A "Mrs Fulham" wishes to speak to him. Jackson says it is a "business matter" and will take it in Mack's office. He closes the door behind him and winces at the mess on Mack's desk. He pushes aside an assortment of scribbled notes and empties the overflowing ashtray into the bin. He settles down in Mack's chair and pushes the speaker button on the phone.

"Hi, Felicity! How are you?"

"I'm fine, but more importantly, how are you?"

"I'm okay. Still a bit shaken up, but over the worst of it, I think."

"Good. Well, look after yourself, Jacko. Don't go doing anything silly will you."

"Like what?"

"You know what I mean: don't drink too much and don't get involved in gambling."

"You needn't worry about me on either count. I'm getting my act together. Really I am."

"Well, I sincerely hope that's true, Jacko. Anyway, Thomas wants us to have another try at dinner here – without being interrupted this time by terrorists. Let me know when you have an evening free in the next week or so.

"Right. Will do."

There is a pause and Felicity can be heard talking to someone else in the room. She comes back to Jackson. "I've just been joined by a young gentleman who's heard that I am talking to his Uncle Jackson."

She hands the phone over to Sam Fulham. "Hello, Uncle Jackson. Are you coming to see us again soon?"

"Hello, Sam. Yes, I'll see you as soon as I get an evening free."

"Can you tell me some *Hairy Maclary,* please?"

"Now let me think... Oh yes... Bitzer Maloney all skinny and bony, Muffin McLay like a bundle of hay, Bottomley Potts covered in spots, Hercules Morse as big as a horse -- and Hairy Maclary from Donaldson's Dairy."

Jackson has his back to the door and is unaware that Pete and Farouk have returned and come into the office.

"More, Uncle Jackson. More," pleads Sam.

"That's all I can remember for now. We'll read the book together when I come to see you."

"Promise?"

"Yes, it's a promise."

Jackson ends the call and swivels back to face the door. He is embarrassed to see Farouk and Pete there, smirking.

"I'm impressed you're so well read in the Scottish classics," says Pete.

Jackson responds with a good-humoured two fingers. "Not Scottish, you illiterate. The author's from New Zealand."

"Really? I didn't know the bloody Kiwis could even read," Pete jokes.

Mack comes in, having changed into more comfortable clothes. He observes Jackson sitting in his chair. "What's this," he teases, "I leave the office for a few minutes and you try to take over!"

Jackson laughs and points at the mess on the desk. "Well, anyone taking over from you would want to clean up this shit first."

"There's nothing wrong with my desk, Jacko. I know exactly where to find everything. Anyway, if you've finished with it, I'd like it back."

"Sorry. I just came in to take a private call."

Mack sits down at the desk, takes a cigar from his pocket and lights it up. Jackson and the others wince.

"I nicked it while Ambassador Costello was looking the other way," Mack explains. By the way, there's no need for you guys to stick around. I've had word from London that most of their bulletins tonight will be dominated by news that a government minister has been filmed half-naked with a woman who's not his wife. Worse, his lady friend is a prominent member of the Opposition."

"Christ!" declares Jackson. "Who are they?"

"No names yet. It's a tabloid exclusive with the names being saved for tomorrow."

******

On his way back to his apartment, Jackson calls in at *The Cedar Tree* and hands Jamil the $80 he had kept aside in his pocket. "Thank you, Mr Jackson. I'll get your change."

"No, no, Jamil. Keep it. You've been very tolerant when I've been caught short without cash."

Back in his apartment, Jackson checks his bank account online and discovers that his monthly salary has come through. He feels a tingle through his body. He pours himself a whisky and runs a hot bath.

A few hours later, Jackson makes a return to Archibald's gambling den, cashed up with $1000 he drew from an ATM conveniently situated a short distance away. Zareena is with him and is unhappy.

"Are you sure you should be doing this, Jacko?" she asks. "You know you're no good with poker."

"I'm giving up on poker. Too many crooks. Roulette is much better."

"You're deluding yourself. You must know that. There's only one real winner here and that's Archbibald."

Jackson gets angry. "Stop nagging, please! I brought you here as a good luck charm, so stay happy."

Zareena realises she is wasting her breath. Jackson takes his roll of banknotes from a pocket, peels off $100 and gives it to her. "Here's your money in advance, so just stop worrying."

Zareena puts the money in her purse with a sigh and draws up a chair behind Jackson so that she can look over his shoulder. He buys $500 worth of $10 chips and turns to Zareena. "So, what colour do you prefer? Red or black?"

"Black is negative," she replies, "so it has to be red."

"Right, red it is! And should I go for odds or evens?"

"I prefer even numbers."

For the next hour, Jackson's fortunes at the roulette wheel ebb and flow. His mobile rings, but he is so engaged in the spinning wheel that he switches it off without checking to see who is calling.

Zareena makes a further attempt to get him to quit while he still has money left in the kitty, but it just makes him angry. She is fed up. She tells him she will see him another time and leaves.

Without Zareena's restraining presence, Jackson raises his bets and goes for the long odds with the prospect of big returns. Inevitably, after half-an-hour, he finds himself cleaned out. He goes to Archibald who agrees to give him a short-time credit of $500 with an extortionate interest rate of 10% for the first day, increasing by 5% for every subsequent day for up to two weeks.

Any residual self-control is abandoned as Jackson continues to play for high stakes, desperate to get that big win that will allow him to leave with his pockets full and his head held high. Another half-hour passes and he is again cleaned out. Archibald refuses to extend further credit and Jackson regains sufficient control of himself to know that he must go home to bed.

Jackson steps out into the dark and grubby street and goes to the nearby ATM, planning to withdraw enough cash to get a taxi to his apartment. His card is rejected. He has forgotten that he had reached his withdrawal limit for the next 24 hours. He comes out in a cold sweat as he contemplates the prospect of walking home several kilometres away through a slum, notorious for its criminal gangs.

Jackson frantically rummages through his pockets but finds just a few coins – certainly not enough to pay for a taxi back to the apartment. His panic intensifies. About 50 metres from the gambling den he comes across a chauffeured stretch limousine. The driver is asleep behind the wheel. Jackson shakes him awake.

The driver explains that he is employed by one of Archibald's wealthy clients who is likely to be gambling into the early hours. Jackson offers the driver $50 to take him home. The driver wants $75 – triple the normal rate for such a trip – and Jackson has no option but to accept. He explains that he has the money back at his apartment, which is a fact as he always keeps an emergency reserve of about $100 in a tin.

It is no surprise that the chauffeur is reluctant to make an unauthorised journey without seeing the money first. Jackson offers his Rolex watch as collateral. The driver studies it carefully with a pocket torch and agrees to take him, provided that he can have possession of the watch to ensure that Jackson doesn't do a runner on reaching his destination.

The chauffeur speeds through the streets, anxious to get back to his spot near the gambling den before his absence is noticed. Outside his apartment, Jackson tells the driver he will be back in a few minutes with his $75. As he walks to the apartment block entrance, the driver does a sharp u-turn and accelerates away. Jackson watches the vehicle disappear in the darkness and knows that he will never see his Rolex again.

CHAPTER 12

Next morning, Jackson walks the five kilometres to the bureau, calling at an ATM along the way. It confirms that he can't withdraw any money until that evening.

Samira is at her desk in the bureau, concentrating on a spreadsheet. She nods an acknowledgement of his arrival. Jackson sees Mack on the phone, puffing away at a cigarette in his office. Pete, Farouk and Yassin have yet to arrive.

Jackson sits down, staring vacantly into space and making no move to turn on his computer. Samira looks and notices that Jackson is not his usual self.

"Is something wrong, Jacko?"

"Um, no... Er, yes..." He holds up his left hand and points to where his watch would normally be wrapped around his wrist. "I was mugged last night and my Rolex was nicked."

"Oh really! What happened?"

"It was all very fast. I was walking along the street when some guy with a large knife suddenly appeared out of the dark and demanded the watch and all my American dollars."

"That's terrible," Samira sympathises. "Have you told the police?"

"Absolutely no point."

Samira agrees. "The coppers here are useless. Even if they recovered your watch, they'd probably sell it on the black market. What's it worth, do you think?"

"Ten grand at least."

"Ten thousand? How could you possible afford that?"

"I couldn't. It was a 30th birthday present from my grandmother, Granny Dunbar."

"Oh dear," says Samira as she returns to her spreadsheets. Jackson stares into the middle distance for a minute or two then turns back to Samira. "Can you give me an advance on my exes? I need to buy a new watch pronto."

"Can't you just go to the ATM next door and draw out some cash? Our salaries came through yesterday."

Jackson flounders for an excuse. "Er, I can't. I've mislaid my bank card. I was so confused when I tumbled into bed after being robbed last night that I must have dropped it somewhere."

Samira nods sympathetically. "Well, if you don't find it by this evening you'd better report it missing in case it's fallen into the wrong hands." She unlocks a drawer in her desk and takes out her petty cash container. "Here's $100, but I must have it back tomorrow or Mack'll get very cross."

Jackson gratefully takes the money. "I'll choose something a little less attractive to thieves," he promises.

Mack comes out of his office and before he has a chance to comment on Jackson's gloomy appearance, Samira chips in. "Jacko got mugged last night and his Rolex was stolen."

"Huh! Serves you bloody right for wearing such an item in this part of the world," says Mack.

"Thanks for caring," replies Jackson sarcastically.

Mack realises that he has been a bit harsh. "Sorry Jacko. You weren't hurt, I hope."

"No, there was no struggle or anything like that. He was a big guy who appeared to be looking for an excuse to use his knife. I didn't argue."

"Well, I'm glad you're okay. By the way I tried to ring you last night, but got no answer."

"Was it important?"

"No, not specially. But where were you anyway?"

"I must've been in a black spot. I went to see a couple of guys after getting a tip-off that they knew something about the *Soldiers of Allah*."

"And did they?"

"Nope. It was a false lead, and I was on my way back to the flat when I was robbed."

"Mmm. Well, make sure you get a cheaper replacement." Mack points to his own watch. "I got this for 20 quid at a service station in Scotland and it's as good as gold."

Jackson nods agreement, then adds as an afterthought: "Umm. As I was on duty at the time of the mugging, I suppose I can claim the stolen watch on my expenses?"

Mack responds not with words but with raised eyebrows and an expression that make it brutally clear he thinks Jacko is trying it on.

Jackson changes tack. "No, of course not. I'll claim it on my personal property insurance."

"That'd be a good idea," says Mack caustically as he goes back into his office.

Jackson rolls his eyes at Samira, hoping for sympathy, but he doesn't get it.

"Just stop pushing your luck with your expenses," she says. "It's getting very irritating." He shrugs and leaves to buy his replacement watch.

******

Within the hour, Jackson arrives back at the bureau proudly waving his new purchase, a solar-powered Seiko. "Looks almost as good as my Rolex," he announces to Samira.

"How much?" she demands.

"A little under a hundred bucks."

"How little?" she persists.

"It was seventy-five dollars," he admits with an embarrassed smile.

Samira holds her hand out for the change, but Jackson shakes his head. "Oh c'mon. I need the change to buy dinner tonight."

"Okay," she says, "but I really must have all the money back by tomorrow, regardless of whether you've found your bank card."

"Christ, you're a hard woman!"

Samira lets the subject drop and hands Jackson a yellow *Post It* note. "Looks like your bid for an interview with Khaled Mohamed has been accepted. Ring that number and his people will give you a date and time. You should be warned that he's a very boring man and you're unlikely to get an interview worthy of the name."

"Well, let's see, Samira. I have an instinct about this guy. I suspect there's more to him than meets the eye."

"Unlikely, but I'm prepared to be surprised."

Samira goes back to her spreadsheets and Jackson rings the number he has just been given.

******

Next morning, Jackson decides to make a brisk walk to work in the hope that this will invigorate him. The 'brisk' bit lasts just a couple of hundred metres; the rest of it done in the manner and pace of an unwell person, which he is. He has endured another bad night. Despite knocking himself out with a couple of very large whiskies, he had woken a few hours later in a cold sweat about what had happened at the gambling den. Another large whisky had put him back to sleep, but barely an hour later he had a terrifying repeat nightmare about being blown up outside the mosque.

Jackson comes across an ATM and cheers up a little when it confirms that his bank account is active again. He withdraws $150 -- $50 for himself and $100 to replenish Samira's petty cash.

By the time he reaches the bureau, Mack is at his desk reading an Arabic newspaper, making notes and working his way through his fourth cigarette of the morning. Samira is filing documents in a metal cabinet, and Pete and Farouk are monitoring a feed of Middle Eastern videos from the Reuters news agency.

"Morning," mutters Jackson as he hangs his jacket behind the entrance door. There is a similarly-muttered response from Samira, Pete and Farouk as they continue what they were doing.

Jackson takes the ATM withdrawal from his pocket and counts out $100, which he places on Samira's desk. "Your money back, as promised," he tells her as she continues with the filing.

"Oh good," she replies, "You found your bank card?"

"What do you mean?"

"Your bank card! You know, the one you mislaid!"

Jackson has temporarily forgotten his little lie to Samira and flounders for an answer. "Oh yes. Yes, found it. Umm. Yes, I found it when I got back to the apartment last night. It'd just fallen off the bedside table where I put my things before going to bed."

"Oh, good," she says as she finishes the filing and returns to her desk. It is at this point that she observes Jackson's miserable physical and mental state.

"Oh Jacko! What's wrong?"

"Nothing."

"What do you mean, 'nothing'. You look dreadful. You haven't even shaved."

"Well, I don't feel all that special," he admits as he strokes the whiskers on his face and realises that he had forgotten to have his usual pre-breakfast shave.

"Have you been boozing?"

"No, no," he insists, "nothing like that. No more than a small glass of wine with dinner last night." He pats his stomach as he creates yet another plausible lie. "I did think there was something odd about the main course I had at *The Cedar Tree*. Yes, that would be it. I'll have a word with Jamil when I next go there. I've never had problems before, so he should be told."

"My word, Jacko, you have had a rough few days," Samira observes.

"Yes, could be better," he admits.

Mack calls everyone into his office for the morning editorial meeting. He takes one look at Jackson and sighs. "Pissed again, Jacko!"

"No, no! Definitely not!" He pats his stomach. "A bad dose of food poisoning from my local restaurant."

"Well, go home and go to bed. There's nothing much going on and I don't want you throwing up or shitting yourself in the bureau. Give me a call after lunch if you're feeling better and you can do the late shift."

Jackson isn't inclined to argue and gratefully accepts an offer from Yassin to drive him home.

******

Back at the apartment, Jackson puts on a soothing CD and contemplates the fix he has got himself into. Not least is the challenge he faces over the money owed to Archibald.

He makes a strong instant coffee, and without too much thought, picks up a near-empty whisky bottle and pours a hair of the dog into a large glass.

His landline phone rings and he listlessly pushes the speaker button.

"Jackson Dunbar."

"Jacko, it's Thomas."

"Oh, hi Thomas," he says, unable to hide his current state of mind.

"You don't sound too good."

"Yeah, I'm not feeling the best."

"You sound a bit pissed. Isn't it a bit early in the day to be hitting the booze!"

"I am not – repeat not – pissed," he replies with growing anger, "I'm home coping with severe food poisoning."

"Sorry, Jacko. That's a bit of a bugger. I hope you make a quick recovery."

"So do I," says Jackson. "So why are you calling?"

"Well, I believe you're being granted an interview with Khaled Mohamed."

"Hell! How did you know that?"

Thomas laughs. "We just know."

"Well, I don't have a time and date yet, but I believe that he'll see me."

"Excellent. I need to talk to about something. Can I come around to your apartment?"

"When?"

"About half an hour?"

"Hell! Can't you leave it to another time?"

"No, not really. It's important that I see you now, before you do the interview."

"Okay. But make it an hour, so that I can have a shower and get my brain into gear."

"Right. See you in an hour."

The call ends. Jackson sits sipping his coffee, transfixed by the glass of whisky on the bench. He studies it with a mixture of hatred and longing. Eventually common sense is the victor and he empties the glass into the sink, then does the same with the dregs of the whisky bottle.

He opts for a hot bath instead of a shower. As it runs, he has his belated shave. The mirror steams up and he is unconsciously grateful for this. In his present state, the less he looks at himself the better.

Thomas turns up as scheduled, by which time Jackson is feeling the benefit of the bath and a short nap on the sofa. He is also pleased that he was able to resist more hair of the dog. He brews freshly ground coffee in a cafetiere as Thomas takes a seat on the sofa and casts his eye around the room. He spots a Rolling Stones poster on wall. "Ah, Jacko, a Stones man, eh! Have you ever been to one of their gigs?"

"Just one – that terrific gig in Hyde Park some years ago. How do you want your coffee?"

"A dash of milk and a half a spoon of sugar, thanks."

Jackson pours two mugs, puts them on the coffee table in front of the sofa, and gets a plastic container of milk and a bowl of sugar. "I'll leave you to add the milk and sugar," he tells Thomas.

There is an uncomfortable silence as the two men fix their coffees and take test sips. Jackson is the first to speak. "Right, Thomas, what's this about?" his voice heavy with suspicion.

"Hey, lighten up, dear boy, er Jacko. It's something that could be to your great advantage, while at the same time fulfilling a need by my people."

Jackson's suspicion grows. "How would that be?"

"As I've already made clear to you, we believe that Khaled Mohamed is a hidden power behind the throne. It's essential we know what he's up to. For starters we need to know if we're right in suspecting that he was involved in the mosque bombing. That's where you come into the frame. When you do the interview, we need you to put a monitoring device in his office."

Jackson is incredulous. "You must be nuts," he shouts. "Why I would do that, even if I wanted to?"

"Calm down," Thomas demands. "Don't get on your high horse before I've explained it all."

"There's nothing to explain, Thomas. Nothing! I'm bound to be searched when I arrive, so how the hell would they not notice a bug? I'd end up rotting in a Central Arabian prison. At the very least, it would also mean the end of my career with the BBC or anyone else."

"Shut up, for God's sake, and let me finish!"

Jackson agrees and sips his coffee.

"Here's the situation, Jacko: among the equipment you take with you will be what looks like an ordinary nine volt battery – just like you'd buy from any hardware store. But it's not a battery. It's an incredibly powerful surveillance device. You don't need to know all the details, but let me say that even if this device is x-rayed or otherwise scanned, it'll still look like a battery. And even if the minister is paranoid enough to have his office swept for bugs, the kit won't be detected because it automatically shuts down as a sweep begins. It also transmits an encrypted signal that disguises itself as a normal electronic field generated by computers and lots of other bits of household equipment. And before you ask, even if it's found, it'll continue to look like a battery and if someone tries to test it, it'll show 'battery flat'. When the device is no longer required, we send a signal that scrambles its innards. It's brilliant, believe me."

"Most impressive," admits Jackson, "but I'm still not interested. Where am I supposed to hide this, er, bug? And how would I be able to do it when there's almost certainly going to be other people in the room?"

Thomas is exasperated. "Create a diversion of some sort. Surely you're clever enough to come up with something. It's magnetised, so it'll takes just seconds to attach to anything metal."

"I'm still not doing it," says Jackson. "It's too much of a risk and there's nothing in it for me."

"But there is," asserts Thomas, "there's lots in it for you." He gulps down his coffee before continuing. "Your interview with this guy will give you many brownie points with your bosses when he suddenly becomes big news, which I can assure you he will. Next, by placing the device in his office, you will be doing something important in the British national interest which in due course will be rewarded in a discreet way. And finally, there'll be some help with your present financial problems."

"What financial problems?" demands Jackson angrily.

"Oh c'mon, Jacko, don't get shirty with me. It's obvious that you've over-extended yourself in some way and find it difficult to get from one month to the next without running out of cash. We can help you."

Jackson stalls for time to think about this. "Want a coffee top-up?"

"No, I'm fine," replies Thomas.

Jackson finishes his coffee and unhurriedly pours himself a fresh one before resuming the conversation.

"I didn't realise that it was so obvious that I was, er, pressed for cash. Between you and me things are a bit tight at the moment. I over-reached myself on a mortgage on this flat I bought in London at the peak of the market. Frankly, I got ripped off by the estate agent, but that's another story. And I help out my mother from time-to-time with some cash when things get difficult for her."

Thomas nods sympathetically. "Yes, I see. So a bit of cash would be very useful for you, and from our point of view, we would consider it a just and well-earned reward for helping us out."

"What sort of sum did you have in mind?" asks Jackson, attempting to make it a casual enquiry, as though he is having a friendly chat with an amiable bank manager.

"Well, we thought ten thousand US dollars would be appropriate."

"Oh yes. I see," he says, trying not to sound impressed. "Yes, I could use that to pay off part of my mortgage, I suppose. Yes, I could do that."

Jackson's brain is now in a spin as he contemplates the risk to his career and his freedom, counter-balanced by the thought that the unexpected offer could give him a much-needed financial recovery. He again stalls for time by putting milk and sugar into his coffee and giving it a gentle stir.

Thomas watches Jackson intently and knows that a deal is about to be done. Jackson sips his coffee and resumes the conversation.

"I'm wondering about how this might be viewed by outsiders? If such a payment were revealed, would it cause me problems? Would it be better if this were, er, some kind of loan – one that could be paid back once my financial situation improves?"

"That's an excellent thought, Jacko. Let's make it a loan. It'll be a gentlemen's agreement that we'll get the money back as soon as you find that possible."

"Yes, I'd feel more comfortable with a loan."

"It would probably be best if we set up a special bank account for you. You know, one that doesn't raise any questions about where the money has come from. We have a special department that arranges such things."

"Okay, I'll do it. But I want it understood that I won't get involved in anything like this again."

"That's understood, old friend. We'll be well satisfied with this one most useful contribution."

The two men shake on it and Thomas leaves. Jackson pours himself another coffee and feels his spirits rising. Despite the dubious and risky elements of Thomas's proposal, he convinces himself that it will be a one-off, done in the British national interest, with the important added value of getting him back on his financial feet. He now considers himself well enough to go into the office to see if he can set up the interview with Khaled Mohamed.

CHAPTER 13

Jackson's return to the bureau is greeted with some surprise, not least because he appears to be a changed man.

"Well, well," says Samira, "what happened to that wreck who was here earlier in the day?"

Jackson grins. "I'm made of tough stuff. It takes more than a bit of food poisoning to hold me down for long. A hot bath, a short shut-eye on the sofa and strong coffee has fixed me."

Mack comes out of his office. "Well, Jacko, welcome back to the land of the living. You've returned just in time. I've had a tip off that there's been an incident of some sort in Ibrahim Ahmed Avenue. You and Pete had better check it out."

"Right. Will do." Jackson turns to Samira. "When you get a moment, could you give Khaled Whatsit's office a call and see if he can see me tomorrow or the next day? Feed him loads of bullshit about how much I'm looking forward to learning about his plans for the future of this country."

"I'll do my best," she says with a grin.

******

Jackson and Pete, driven by Yassin, arrive in Ibrahim Ahmed Avenue – a middle-class modern residential street -- to find firemen hosing down a burned-out BMW saloon. The badly burnt body of a man is behind the steering wheel and they flinch at the sight. Pete begins filming and Jackson walks over to talk to a group of male bystanders, most of them in traditional Arab wear.

"What happened here?" he asks in Arabic.

Most of the men shake their heads and turn away, but one man dressed in casual western clothes responds in broken English. "Ambush. Black van blocked car. Masked man shoot driver. Car set on fire. Petrol." He points to an empty can lying on the road beside the car.

Jackson calls Pete over with his camera, but the man holds his hand over the lens. "No, no. No talk to camera," he insists and walks away, hiding his face.

Omar Abbas and his Al-Jazeera camera crew arrive. Omar and Jackson confer.

"What's this about, do you think?" asks the Al-Jazeera reporter.

"Not sure, Omar, but I've just been told it was an ambush."

Omar goes to the back of the burnt-out car and checks the number plate, which is still visible. "It's a gangland job," he tells Jackson. "The car belongs to local thugs who've been feuding with a neighbouring gang. Doesn't look political. I reckon it's just a story for local TV."

Jackson murmurs agreement. "Not really our sort of story, I guess."

Both crews head back to their respective offices. Jackson gets a phone call along the way. It is Samira reporting that an interview with Khaled Mohamed has been set up for tomorrow morning. Jackson passes on the news to Pete.

"The Development Minister says we can interview him at 11am. We need to be there in good time and we need to make a good impression. I don't want you turning up in one of your stupid T-shirts. Wear a plain ordinary shirt and a tie, if you have one."

"What's wrong with this shirt?" Pete demands pointing to a cartoon Koala on his chest. "People find my T-shirts amusing."

"Sometimes they do; sometimes they think you're just being stupid."

"Well, stop going on about it, Jacko," he says with growing irritation, "I'll turn up tomorrow in something suitably boring."

"Good," says Jackson, "and I also want you to make sure you bring a still camera with you."

"Okay, but why?"

"Um, I want you to take some publicity and file photos of the minister while we have the opportunity."

"Okay, anything you say, sir," responds Pete, giving Jackson a caustic mock salute.

Jackson is too tense to be amused by this mockery.

******

123

Next morning, Jackson and Pete leave the bureau in plenty of time for the interview with Khaled Mohamed at the government offices in central Armibar. Jackson is wearing a lightweight suit and discreetly-patterned tie. Pete's concession to the occasion is a subdued, slightly faded, short-sleeved beach shirt and a rather unfashionable narrow leather tie. As Yassin drives them to their appointment, Jackson takes from a trouser pocket the "battery" bug that has been delivered to him that morning by one of Thomas Fulham's agents. "You'd better put this with your kit," he tells Pete.

Pete takes the bug, but doesn't understand why Jackson is carrying it.

"It's for the smoke alarm in my kitchen," Jackson lies, "I bought it on the way to work."

"Why give it to me?"

"Just a precaution. I don't want anything that might be seen as a bit unusual in my pockets if we get a body search. It'll be perfectly normal for you to have a battery in your kit."

Pete accepts this explanation and drops the bug into his bag.

As expected, Jackson and Pete are scanned and given a full body pat-down before being allowed to enter the government offices. Pete is instructed to switch on his camera to prove that it is not a fake and his tripod is put through the scanner. A security officer empties Pete's kit bag onto an inspection bench. He examines each item but pays no particular attention to the "battery" bug. Jackson notes that a Canon digital camera is in Pete's kit and the security officer switches it on to see that it works.

A tall man wearing an expensive western suit and tie arrives. He introduces himself as Adnan, Khaled's press and publicity officer. He shakes hands with Jackson, but ignores Pete's extended hand. Pete tries not to show his irritation. He has become used to being ignored because he is "just the cameraman".

Adnan addresses Jackson in English with a soft southern American drawl. "Good morning, Mr Dunbar, if you and your colleague will follow me, I will take you through to the Development Ministry."

No further words are exchanged as Adnan leads the two men along a long corridor and ushers them into a vast and very grand room decorated with ornate curtains, tiled Arab images and a generous use of gold leaf. Several large chandeliers hang from the ceiling. It is a room where official receptions are held and not at all what Jackson is expecting.

"Khaled Mohamed will see you here as soon as he gets a break from his duties," announces Adnan. "I suggest you set your equipment up over there," he says, pointing to a podium at the far end of the room. I think that will give you a nice backdrop for the interview."

Jackson is shaken. It would be pointless him planting the bug in a reception room and if no bug is planted, there will be no "loan" from Thomas Fulham and his colleagues.

"Oh yes," says Pete, looking around the room with approval, "this'll be perfect."

Jackson is desperate to stay calm. "Yes, it's a lovely room, Adnan, but I'm, er, not sure that it will deliver the right sort of image your minister would wish to convey."

Adnan is surprised. "Why wouldn't the minister want to be filmed here?"

Jackson's brain is in top gear as he attempts to justify his statement. "Well, as I understand it, Khaled Mohamed has built up a well-deserved reputation as an exceptionally-talented and hard-working minister. I just feel we could do him greater justice by filming him at his desk in his office."

Adnan can see that Jackson's proposal makes sense. "I see. You have judged the minister well, Mr Dunbar. I will speak to him and explain what your intentions are. He is exceptionally busy, so it may take me a little while to put your proposal to him. Meanwhile, I have taken the liberty of ordering you and your cameraman some coffee and something to eat."

"Thank you. That would be very welcome," replies Jackson.

Adnan leaves the room and a servant appears a few minutes later with coffee, dates and pastries.

Pete is baffled by Jackson's rejection of the reception room for the filming. "What's wrong with you, Jacko? This room is fucking brilliant. I could get some fabulous shots here. Better than filming in another bloody boring office."

The stress is beginning to show with Jackson. "Shut the fuck up, Pete. I want the film to be done in his office. End of fucking story! Do you fucking understand?"

Pete is taken aback by this outburst. "Christ mate, calm down will you! If you want it filmed in the fucking boring office, I will film it in the fucking boring office. Okay?"

"Yes, okay. Sorry. Let's leave it at that," says Jackson, realising that he is in danger of losing his grip.

The next hour is spent mostly in silence, waiting for Adnan to return with the minister's answer. Jackson needs to recover the bug from Pete's kit. He asks Pete if he can have a play with his still camera. "Sure," says Pete, engrossed in a game on his mobile phone, "help yourself." Jackson goes to the kit bag, takes the camera, examining it in the same way he would if he were planning to buy it, while at the same time, discreetly recovering the bug and transferring it to a pocket in his jacket.

The wait goes on and with the passing of every minute, Jackson becomes more fearful that the plan to secrete the bug will come to nothing.

The silence is finally broken with the brief return of Adnan to announce that the minister has agreed to be filmed in his office, but there will be a wait of another hour or so. "I'll send in some more coffee," he announces as he departs again.

There is a sigh of relief from Jackson and a groan of frustration from Pete. "God, I hope this bloody interview is worth the trouble!" he exclaims. "I suppose you know that the Arab high-ups always make the media wait. It's so that they can pretend they're so fucking important that they really don't need you. I bet he's not busy at all. He's probably entertaining some hot sheila on his couch."

"You're probably right, Pete," he admits, allowing himself his first smile since arriving.

"Well, there you go, Jacko. It's all part of the power game these jumped up bastards like to play."

******

Another two hours pass before Adnan calls them into the minister's spacious, ostentatious office to set up their equipment for the interview. "The minister will be along in five minutes. Will the interview be in English or Arabic?" asks Adnan.

"Mostly English, but I may repeat a few key questions in Arabic for our Arabic Service colleagues," Jackson responds.

"Good, the minister has excellent English. He was educated at Harvard, you know."

"Yes, I heard that," Jackson lies, "and I believe that he excelled as a student."

Pete completes his set-up of the camera and lighting. Adnan goes to the door and calls to an unseen person that Jackson is now ready for the minister. After an appropriate pause, Khaled Mohamed sweeps in wearing a dark blue suit with an open-necked shirt. Jackson goes to shake his hand, but the minister goes straight to his desk and sits down.

"What is it you want to ask me?" he enquires without preamble.

"Well, Minister, I thought I should concentrate on your much-praised work raising Central Arabia's commercial profile, not just in the Middle East, but in the United States and Europe."

The minister nods approval. Pete clips a microphone on the minister's suit lapel.

The interview gets under way and Jackson encourages the minister to boast about his plans for the country. He avoids asking any provocative questions and after 15 minutes wraps up the exchange with fulsome thanks to the Minister for sparing so much of his valuable time.

Khaled Mohamed gets up from his desk, takes off his clip mike, and announces that he has an important meeting to attend. Jackson hastily urges him to stay put.

"If you could spare us just a couple more minutes, Minister. My colleague, Mr Fox, needs to take some still photographs of you for our files and for publicity purposes."

"Yes, alright," agrees Khaled Mohamed, "but make it quick!"

Jackson turns to Pete. "I think a couple of quick shots of the minister at his desk, then perhaps you can take some more with him standing over there beside the national flag." He points to the flag hanging prominently in a corner of the room. He turns to Adnan. "And if you wouldn't mind, perhaps you could straighten the flag a little so that it looks exactly right for the photo." Adnan fusses with the flag, even though he thinks it is fine as it is.

Pete takes the photographs as instructed at the desk, then when the minister moves over to pose beside the flag, Jackson lifts the kit bag onto the minister's desk and ostentatiously begins to pack various bits of kit into it.

Just as Pete is about to begin shooting the photos, Jackson suggests the flag still needs a little straightening. The minister, Adnan and Pete all turn to look at the flag. Jackson fakes a loud sneeze and pushes the kit bag off the desk, causing it to crash loudly to the floor, spilling its contents.

Jackson offers profuse apologies. "Terribly sorry. Sorry, sorry, sorry. Just continue with the photographs while I tidy up," he says, taking a handkerchief from his pocket and blowing his nose unnecessarily.

Pete goes back to taking the photographs while Jackson gathers up the bits and pieces scattered on the floor around the desk. He gets down on his knees under the desk and attaches the magnetic bug to a convenient metal plate well out of sight. He then crawls out triumphantly waving a small clamp from the tripod.

"Ah got it! That's the last little bit," he announces and drops it into the kit bag.

******

Jackson and Pete stand outside the government buildings, waiting for Yassin to collect them.

"Bloody hell, Jacko, that was all a bit undignified wasn't it," says Pete, "our star correspondent crawling around a government minister's floor on his knees. You looked a right drongo! I wish I'd been able to take some pics. They'd love those back in London."

Jackson is so relieved that he had been able to plant the bug that he is no longer irritated by Pete's derision.

"Yeah. Must have looked pretty funny," he concedes. "I don't know where that sneeze came from. Just as well it didn't happen in the middle of the interview."

Yassin pulls up in the BBC car and Jackson and Pete continue their conversation as they take their seats and are driven back to the bureau.

"What did you think of the interview, Pete?"

"Why are you asking me that? You know it was bloody boring – just as I predicted. I mean, you made no attempt to try to pin him to the wall, no matter how much obvious bullshit he was shovelling."

"Yeah. I know, but I'm playing a long game with this chap."

"What the fuck does that mean, mate?"

"Sometimes you just have to think beyond the immediate moment. Anyway, we'll have some reasonable clips for the business show on BBC World. They're always desperate for stuff and have expressed interest. And in a day or so I'll phone his office and tell him how pleased everyone was with the interview."

Pete is going through the still photographs he has just taken. "What do you want me to do with these, Jacko?"

"Oh, just stick them in our library with the full uncut video in case they're needed some time."

Jackson gets out his mobile and dials Thomas Fulham. The call is picked up immediately and Jackson gets straight to the point. "Just to let you know that your delivery was made okay." He listens. "Yes, I thought you'd be pleased." He listens again. "Oh really! That's funny. I wonder if we'll be invited for farewell drinks, haha? Anyway, I'll see you soon, eh."

Pete is playing a game on his mobile while half-listening to Jackson's enigmatic call.

"Who was that?" he asks.

"Just a mate who's over here for a while. He knows people in the British Embassy and says he's been told that Stumpy Shortwood is being recalled to London."

"Ah, the tedious old bugger won't like that."

"Oh, the pain is being eased for him. He's being appointed to the House of Lords."

"What a joke! Still, the House of Ponces will be a natural home for Stumpy," says Pete as he goes back to his electronic game.

******

Jackson is in high spirits by the time he arrives back at the bureau. He excitedly tells Samira the news about Stumpy Shortwood, but she already knows.

"I've just had a call from Andrew Costello at the American Embassy," she says. "He was most amused and anxious to be the first to tell Mack the news."

"Oh right," says Jackson, disappointed that he had been scooped by the American ambassador. "Where's Mack."

"Gone to the bank, I think."

"Did Costello have anything more to say?"

"No. Nothing really. To be honest, I think he was using the call as an excuse to proposition me."

"In what way?"

"Oh, he gave me loads of nonsense about how intelligent and interesting and beautiful I was and how nice it would be if we could meet from time to time. As a starter, he suggested a game of tennis on the courts in the embassy compound."

"Aha! Did you accept?"

"Well sort of. I told him it was a wonderful idea and I suggested that when my husband got back from his contract in Lebanon we join him and Mrs Ambassador for a game of doubles."

"How did he react to that?"

Samira laughs. "For some reason, he became less enthusiastic about pursuing our friendship."

"You're a clever woman," Jackson tells her. "By the way, when am I going to meet this husband of yours?"

"Soon, I think. Nigel's contract ends in a couple of months and I'm hoping that he can then get a job with one of the engineering companies back here. I'm a bit fed up with him being away so much."

"Yes, I suppose so."

******

Pete and Farouk load the Khaled Mohamed interview onto the editing machine and Jackson goes over to see what can be extracted from it for an offer to London.

Samira's phone rings and she answers it. "BBC Armibar. Samira Lang speaking." She listens for a few moments then shouts "Where are you?!" She listens again with growing alarm. "Just stay calm. The boys will be with you shortly."

She hangs up the phone and shouts across the room: "Quick. Get down to the Old Market Square. Mack's in trouble."

"What sort of trouble?"

"I don't know. He's been hurt. There was gunfire and it was hard to hear him."

Jackson turns to Pete and Yassin. "Shit! Let's go!" Farouk offers to go with them, but is told to stay behind to prepare for a possible major story.

CHAPTER 14

The BBC car runs the red lights as it speeds towards the old part of the city and Market Square. Jackson is trying to raise Mack on his mobile, but the line keeps dropping out. The vehicle pulls up on the edge of the normally-crowded square, now empty apart from a group of soldiers exchanging gunfire with unseen people in a four-storey building above an open-fronted shop selling oranges.

Jackson finally gets Mack's mobile to answer. "What's happened? Where are you?" he shouts.

Jackson struggles to hear Mack's answer above the shooting, but he eventually establishes that Mack is lying wounded on the floor of the orange shop. Pete, who has been filming the gun battle, zooms in on the shop in the hope of seeing Mack. He can't.

"Tell Mack to wave something so that I can see where he is," Pete shouts at Jackson. Jackson relays the message and a short while later Pete triumphantly announces that he can see a blue plastic bag being waved above a low rack of oranges.

Jackson grabs the camera and takes a look for himself. "Ah yes, I can just see him." He hands his phone to Pete. "Tell Mack that I'm on my way."

"You're nuts, it's too dangerous."

"We can't leave him there!"

Pete goes to the back of the 4x4, grabs a flak jacket and offers it to Jackson.

"Sorry, too cumbersome. I'm better off without it."

By now, a couple of soldiers are lying on the ground, either dead or wounded while the rest of them have taken cover behind market stalls that were, until a short time ago, busily offering a variety of wares to eager customers. An armoured army truck arrives with reinforcements.

Jackson crouches down as he runs along the front of a parade of shops lining the square, hoping that the soldiers will be focusing their attention on the gunmen they have holed up. Then, about four doors away from the orange shop, he drops to the ground and crawls along on his belly. All the while, Pete is watching Jackson's progress though his camera and shouting the information to Mack.

The gun battle intensifies, forcing Jackson to take cover in a small coffee shop with its front door still open. Inside he sees a terrified man crouched down behind the counter.

"Can I get out the back?" Jackson asks in Arabic

The man shakes his head. "It's locked."

Jackson crawls towards the entrance and snatches a look outside. He spots a narrow gap between the coffee shop and the adjacent building. He dashes down it and is now out of sight of the soldiers. He finds himself in a narrow dusty access lane running behind the shops. He identifies the orange shop from all the empty boxes stacked behind it.

The back entrance is locked. He tries several times to force it open, finally taking a run at it and kicking it with all his strength. The door bursts open and Jackson can see Mack lying on his back on the floor in a pool of blood and among a heap of oranges. One hand is holding his mobile to one ear; the other is pressing down on his wound.

Jackson grabs Mack's phone and shouts above the noise of the continuing gunfire. "I've reached him Pete. See if you can get the car down the lane behind the shops." Jackson hands the phone back to Mack and drags him a couple of metres towards the rear exit where they can't be seen by the soldiers.

"Thanks, laddie," mumbles Mack. "I can't stop the bleeding from my fucking leg."

"I'll fix that," reassures Jackson, as he finds a knife on a nearby work bench and slashes open Mack's right trouser leg. He can now see a bullet wound through the lower part of Mack's thigh. He pulls off the tie he wore to the interview and uses it as a tourniquet around Mack's upper thigh.

"God, that hurts," moans Mack.

"Stop complaining you silly old bugger. It's either that or you bleed to death."

Jackson runs out the back door and sees the BBC 4x4 turn into the narrow access lane and ease its way towards him. He waves frantically and Yassin acknowledges him by flashing his headlights.

Jackson goes back inside the shop and tells Mack that help is on its way. He takes Mack's free hand and tries with limited success to drag him to the back door. There are two enormous explosions in quick succession in the rooms above the shop. The building shudders, and plaster and dust crash down on Mack and Jackson.

"Fuck! They must be using grenades," shouts Jackson, as he intensifies his efforts to drag his boss out the back door. There is another explosion in the room above them. This time it blows a hole in the ceiling and knocks Jackson to the ground. A timber beam crashes down and pins them both to the floor. Mack cries out in pain. Jackson, although not hurt, can't move because he is partly caught beneath Mack.

Pete and Yassin burst through the back door and scramble through the debris. They attempt to lift the beam pinning Mack and Jackson, but it is too heavy. There is another burst of gunfire and another grenade explodes in the rooms above them, showering them with more dust and plaster.

The situation is now desperate, but help arrives. Omar Abbas and Jane Kubinski with their Al-Jazeera and CNN crews, have learned of Mack's plight. Eight sets of hands raise the beam sufficiently for Jackson to scramble free, then drag Mack after him.

Pete, Yassin and Omar carry Mack out into the lane as the battle continues and the front of the building is rapidly reduced to rubble. Mack is struggling to stay conscious as he is eased into the back seat of the Range Rover.

"You'll be okay, boss" shouts Jackson as he gets into the back seat and puts the seat belt around Mack to keep him upright. Yassin revs the car, ready to get Mack to hospital. Pete decides he will stay behind with Omar and Jane and resume filming.

******

The BBC car pulls up outside the Emergencies entrance to Armibar Central Hospital. A medical team with a trolley is waiting, having been phoned ahead by Jackson.

Mack drifts in and out of consciousness as he is lifted onto the trolley. "Do you know his blood type?" a female nurse asks Jackson in Arabic.

"I've just been onto our office manager and she says he's O positive," he replies. "I'm the same group."

"It's my group, too," says Yassin.

"That's good news," declares an Asian doctor who has joined them, "we've a blood shortage after the mosque attack. A nurse will take you to our transfusion unit, while I operate on your colleague to stop the bleeding."

The doctor briefly identifies himself as Mr Than, a surgeon from Myanmar. He points at Jackson and Yassin, still covered in dirt and bits of plaster from the explosions. "The nurse will give you some sterile clothing before you go into the transfusion unit. I think you'd better have a quick shower as well."

Mack is wheeled away on the trolley while Jackson and Yassin are escorted to the transfusion unit by a nurse.

Jackson phones Pete. "We're at the hospital. Do you know your blood type?" He listens then turns to the nurse. "Type A+?" The nurse shakes her head. "Sorry, Pete, no good, I'm afraid, so you might as well return to the bureau and feed what you've got back to London. We're going to be here for a while I reckon."

Jackson gives Samira another call. "Mack's going to be okay, we think, but there is a shortage of blood. What type are you?" He listens. "Sorry, Type A is no good. What about Farouk?" He hangs on while Samira checks. She comes back on the line and tells him that Farouk is also Type A. "Bugger!" he says, "Yassin and I will just have to give a little bit extra."

******

Pete arrives back at the bureau. He is still covered in plaster dust, and gives Farouk the uncut video to transmit back to London.

Samira is ending a phone call to the Head of News, Marina Kerner, telling her what's happened.

"How was Mack?" Samira asks Pete.

"He's lost quite a bit of blood and the wound in his leg didn't look all that brilliant."

"How's Jacko?"

"Shaken and a little stirred, but he's been the hero of the day."

Further conversation is halted as they join Farouk to watch the video being fed back to London. The scenes that Pete took as he followed Jackson running and crawling to reach Mack are dramatic. "Phew," declares Samira, "that's truly awesome stuff!"

"Yep. Sure is," replies Pete, amazed by the power of the pictures on the big monitor.

The transmission continues, showing Jackson disappearing into the orange shop. Filming stops at the point where Jackson calls for help and Pete and Yassin set out to rescue him and Mack.

A male voice comes up on the intercom from London. "Hi, it's Julian here. I'm editing the Six and the Ten tonight. That's great stuff you've got there, Pete. I love the wobbly filming. It gives added value."

"Whaddya mean 'wobbly filming'?"

"Well, you know, I take it that you deliberately shot it that way for extra dramatic effect."

"Are you taking the piss, or something?" replies Pete with mounting anger.

"No, no, Pete. It was meant to be a compliment. No offence intended. Really. Anyway, when will we get your film of the gun battle? Reuters says all six terrorists were killed and also a couple of security men. Sounds a good yarn if we tie it in with Jackson's heroic rescue of Mack."

"Sorry, but I wasn't able to get that. I took cover when the soldiers began firing in my direction. All I've got is a few short shots of the gun battle when we first arrived."

"That's a pity," says Julian, "CNN has some really good stuff. They've got the soldiers blasting their way into the building and dragging out the bodies of the terrorists."

"Yeah, well," responds Pete sarcastically, "you'll just have to put it down to my 'don't give a stuff' Aussie incompetence, eh! By the way, why are you calling them terrorists? You don't know that."

"No need to get snippy, Pete. I was just asking. I'll get in touch with CNN and see if we can swap your stuff for theirs. Okay?"

"Do what you fucking like, you great fucking toad. Two of my colleagues nearly got killed today and all you worry about is whether CNN has better film than we've given you."

There is a click and the intercom goes dead.

Pete flops into a chair, his head held in his hand. Samira comes over and puts her arm around him. "Ignore, Julian. He's not really a bad man. He has a severe case of tunnel vision when editing bulletins. If he checks with newsgathering he'll find that CNN and Al-Jazeera have already offered to pool their film."

******

Two hours later at Armibar Central Hospital, Jackson and Yassin are waiting outside the operating theatre for word of Mack. Eventually, Mr Than emerges in an optimistic mood. "The bullet went straight through your colleague's thigh without hitting any bone," he tells them. "We've managed to patch him up and thanks to both of you we were able to replace some of the blood he lost. There's muscle damage and he's going to need physiotherapy. It could be a month or two before he can return to work."

"Can we see him now?" enquires Jackson.

"He's sedated and sleeping soundly. Come back in the morning. In the meantime, you should talk to your bosses about payment for my surgery and the hospital stay."

A text arrives on Jackson's mobile. It is from Felicity: "ur v brave. ru ok?" He is pleased she has enquired and replies immediately: "Am ok. don't worry. c u soon".

******

Two days later, arrangements have been made to fly Mack back home to Glasgow where he will continue his recovery. Joan is going with him. A chartered jet waits in the VIP area at Armibar International Airport as an ambulance pulls up. Mack emerges on a trolley with Joan holding his hand and accompanied by a female nurse. He is now fully alert and able to smile at the sight of Jackson, Pete, Samira and Yassin who have come to bid him farewell.

"Well, you old bugger, you'll do anything to swing an extra holiday back home, eh!" jokes Jackson.

Mack laughs then turns to Samira. "Keep a sharp eye on Jacko's expenses while I'm away, won't you," he grins, then adds "But you can allow him a tenner to replace that stupid tie he used to stop me bleeding to death."

Everyone laughs and a mobile elevator comes over to lift Mack up to the aircraft door. Mack waves Yassin over. "Got any spare fags on you? I'm dying for a ciggie. The bastards at the hospital wouldn't let me smoke."

Yassin reaches into a jacket pocket and hands over an almost-full packet of Gauloises. He reaches into his trouser pocket and produces a cigarette lighter. "You'd better take this. The cigarettes won't be much use without it."

"Thanks, Yassin, you're a fine gent. It'll make the flight back home a little more pleasant."

"Oh no it won't," interjects Joan, "it's a no smoking flight. You can have one before you get on the plane, then that's it until you get to Glasgow."

Mack turns to the others in mock anger. "See what I have to put up with! She's worse than those bampots at Broadcasting House."

Everyone laughs as he lights a cigarette and sucks the smoke and nicotine deep into his lungs with a look of deep contentment. "Ah, that's better."

Joan pats him affectionately on the shoulder. "You really are a silly old man, you know, but I suppose I'd miss you not being shrouded in a cloud of smoke."

******

There is upsetting news awaiting the team when it arrives back at the bureau. An email from Human Resources in London announces that Mack's stand-in as bureau chief is to be Dick Passick.

"Fuck me," says Jackson, "why does it have to be Psycho Passick?"

"What's the problem?" asks Samira, "we can't do without someone senior to run the bureau."

"Believe me, Psycho is a major arsehole. Broadcasting House will be cheering that they are shot of him for a while and dumped him on some other poor buggers."

Samira goes to her computer and finds a profile of Dick Passick. "I must say, he's quite handsome."

"Boy, and does he know it!" says Jackson. "He can't walk down the street without checking his reflection in shop windows. He never knowingly walks past a mirror without combing his hair and pausing to admire himself."

"Oh well, we'll just have to see, won't we Jacko. He'll be a change, if nothing else."

Jackson suddenly feels overcome by the traumas of the past few days and announces that he is going back to his apartment to have a shower and a nap. He arrives there as his maid is finishing for the day. She addresses him in broken English. "I stop now, Mr Jackson. All clean now."

"That's good. It looks nice and tidy."

"Yes, nice tidy, Mr Jackson. Can I have money now, please?"

"Oh yes, of course." Jackson takes out his wallet and finds it empty. He fumbles in his pocket and takes out some coins.

"Sorry. Forgot to go to bank. Here's five dollars for now. I'll give you the rest when you come next."

The maid is upset, but has no choice but to accept the down payment. She leaves and Jackson opens a new bottle of whisky and pours himself a stiff drink. He switches on his electric keyboard and sooths himself further by playing *Moonlight Sonata*, one of his favourite piano pieces in times of stress. He is interrupted by his phone. As usual, he puts it on the speaker. "Jackson Dunbar."

"Hi. It's Thomas. Just a quick call to tell you that your delivery the other day has been a wonderful success. We're getting very useful information. We've even learned what the gentleman concerned thought of you."

"Oh really? What did that self-important prick say?"

"To be honest, he thought you were a pushover."

Jackson laughs. "That's no surprise. I sucked up to him shamelessly. Now, about your side of the arrangement. I could really do with that going through without delay."

"It's all in hand," Thomas assures him. "The account has been set up and you'll be able to access it with a debit card. A courier will deliver the card to you at the bureau and you can use it immediately. Is that okay?"

"Yes. That'll be fine."

"By the way," adds Thomas, "we're very impressed at my workplace at your bravery in rescuing your boss. I didn't know you had it in you."

"To be honest, Thomas, I surprised myself."

"I understand. It's a bit like the times when I went into battle in Afghanistan. Something in my brain would shut down and wouldn't recognise the extent of the danger until after it was over."

The call ends and almost immediately the phone rings again. This time it is Jackson's mother.

"I've just watched you on the news, Roger," Lady Dunbar announces without preamble. "That was a very stupid thing you did. You could have been killed."

"But I wasn't, Mother. I'm still very much alive, apart from a few scratches and some clothes that need dry cleaning."

"Well, think what would have happened if you'd been killed. Now that your father has passed on, I would have been left with no-one to help me in my old age."

Jackson is aghast. "My God, do you ever listen to yourself? Do you ever, ever think of anyone but yourself? Do you?"

"There's no need to be so unkind, Roger. One day you'll be old, and by the looks of it, you won't have any children to care for you. I might as well have been childless, for all the help you've been. We privately educated you, put you through university and I even breast-fed you."

Lady Dunbar bursts into tears. "Please stop that, Mother," Jackson pleads, "crying won't resolve anything. You're not old. You know that. You're just 65 and Father left you in a very comfortable financial situation. Try to widen your circle of friends. Why not work as a volunteer for a charity or join a club? That would get you out of the house a bit more and encourage you to think of others."

Jackson's words do nothing to stem the flow of tears. "I can't stand this, Mother. If you don't discuss your worries in a sensible way, I'm hanging up on you."

The sobbing goes on and Jackson carries out his threat. He thumps the bench in frustration and pours himself a large whisky. He goes back to his keyboard – this time assaulting, rather than playing, it.

CHAPTER 15

Jackson rises the next morning in good spirits. It's a pleasant spring day -- sunny and not too hot. What really matters is that his finances are about to be sorted, thanks to his adventure on behalf of Thomas Fulham and his associates. Yassin phones to offer him a lift to the bureau, but he decides that a brisk walk would be good.

His raised spirits take an unexpected blow on reaching the bureau. Two "heavies", block his path. He knows he has seen them before, but can't remember where. They are wearing Western suits, bushy beards, over-sized sun glasses and exude aggression. Each take an arm and firmly guide him towards a white BMW parked on the kerb. There is a moment of panic as he fears that he is about to be abducted again. Instead, he sees Archibald sitting in the back seat in his usual white suit. "Good morning, Mr Dunbar," says the gambling den owner, "I was just passing and thought I'd remind you that your loan expires tomorrow."

"Yes, I know that," Jackson replies. "I'll definitely have the money for you tomorrow evening."

"Good. My boys get very bad tempered when a debt isn't paid on time and I'm sure you wouldn't want your bosses in London to know the sort of places you frequent in Armibar."

"It's okay," emphasises Jackson, "I'll have the money tomorrow. It's a promise."

"Excellent. I'll see you tomorrow, then."

The Arab heavies get into Archibald's car and it drives away, leaving Jackson shaken. He takes a few deep calming breaths before going into the bureau.

Upstairs, his mood takes another blow when he sees that Dick Passick has arrived from London and is in the process of clearing a space among the assorted papers and other detritus on Mack's desk. Samira, Pete, Farouk and Yassin are in the main work area, uncertain about what lies ahead. Samira rolls her eyes at Jackson as he takes another deep breath before stepping into the office to speak to the unwelcome colleague.

The Mortal Maze

The two men shake hands without enthusiasm. Dick is in his mid-forties and has a well-deserved reputation as a dandy. Today he is wearing a lightweight beige suit, a neat off-white shirt with cuffs, and a discreet tie.

"Welcome to Armibar, Dick," mutters Jackson. "You're quick off the mark. I hadn't expected you for a day or so."

"Hello, Jackson. I came straight away. I'm sure there's lots to be done here, so the sooner I get started the better. I've already spoken to London and said you'll provide them with a package for this evening's outlets."

Jackson frowns. "On what subject?"

"I'm sure a bright and ambitious young man like you can think of something."

Dick looks around the office and sighs. "Is it always like this?" he asks. "How does Galbraith work in such filth?"

"Oh, there's more to life than being tidy," Jackson tells him. "Mack's a great operator and boss and no-one has ever complained about the way he runs the bureau."

"That may be the case, but things are going to have to change while I'm here."

Dick screws up his face as he picks up Mack's ashtray and empties it into a bin. "For a start, this is now a no-smoking office in line with corporation policy. I've already informed your driver – Yassin, is it? – of this ruling. If he wants to smoke, he'll have to go out into the street and if he spends too much time out there, I'll dock his pay."

Dick puts on his jacket and goes into the main work area. "I'm off back to my hotel to finish unpacking and have lunch," he tells Samira, "please give my office a good clean before I get back. If you need any help, ask Farouk."

Samira is affronted. "I'm the office manager, Dick, not the cleaner. Nor is Farouk."

"Well, get a cleaner from somewhere and see that the office is respectable before I get back. I refuse to work in that pigsty."

143

Just as he is about to walk out, he points to the "I love Kylie" T-shirt being worn by Pete and orders him to change it. "I hope that's not the sort of thing you usually wear to work, Peter. You're not on Bondi Beach, you know!"

Dick walks out, having managed to annoy everyone in the team in a matter of minutes. Jackson turns to Samira with a grin on his face. "Well, Mrs Lang, I did warn you about him, didn't I."

Samira shrugs her shoulders. "Maybe he'll be better once he gets settled in and doesn't feel he has anything to prove. It must be difficult being flown in to run a bureau with all its quirky ways."

"I admire your optimism," says Jackson.

There is a knock on the entrance door and a motorcycle courier comes in with an envelope for Jackson. He demands proof of identity and Jackson shows him his passport. He is satisfied and leaves.

Jackson's heart beats faster as he takes the envelope and sticks it in his jacket pocket. "Um, I'm going out to get a coffee," he announces, "anyone else want one?"

"Yes," they all say in chorus. "You take care, mate," adds Pete with a smirk, "you know what happened the last time!"

"There'll be no repeat of that," Jackson assures him.

Jackson walks out into the street and instead of turning left to the coffee shop, he walks to the nearby ATM, tearing open the envelope as he does so. He is delighted to see that it contains a platinum debit card and a temporary pin number. He notes with a smile that the card has been issued in the name of "Roger Smith". He inserts it in the ATM slot, punches in the pin and checks the balance. There, as agreed with Thomas Fulham, is an account with $10,000 in it. Relief and excitement surges through his body. Life is looking good.

Jackson re-sets his pin number and withdraws the maximum daily allowance, $500. He buys the promised coffees and returns to the bureau.

Samira is busy on the phone organising cleaners for Mack's office. Jackson distributes the coffees, goes to his desk and picks up today's edition of *The Voice*. There is a front page story about the gun battle in market square. It is accompanied by a photograph of six men laid neatly in a row and wearing camouflage uniforms. Their faces are battered and bloodied.

Jackson holds up the newspaper for Pete to see. "The local press has decided to run this story at last, I see. It claims the bodies were all members of a major Shia terrorist cell."

"I suppose that could be right," says Pete.

The phone rings on Samira's desk. The call is for Jackson. "It sounds like your posh friend," she announces.

"I'll take it in Mack's office," Jackson says. He picks up the call on Mack's speaker phone. "Hi Thomas. I got the card, thanks very much. It works fine."

"That's good, Jacko. It was well earned. On another matter, have you seen today's *Voice*?"

"Yep. Just been looking at it."

"Have you noticed anything odd about the photo?"

"Let me have another look."

Jackson picks up Dick's copy of the paper. "Mmm. I suppose now that I study it, the uniforms these so-called terrorists are wearing seem remarkably neat and unmarked, despite them having been blown up."

"Exactly! We're being fed a line here. It looks to be part of a campaign to generate more hostility towards the Shias. It might be worth exploring."

"Mmm. Yep, I think I'll go back to the scene and see if I can find any witnesses."

There is urgent knocking on the glass door by Samira and he waves her in. "I've just had a strange call from someone with a London accent who said to tell you 'it wasn't us' and that the clue is the bank next door. He hung up before I could find out who he was."

"Thanks. That's very interesting."

Samira leaves the room. Thomas, who hears the exchange, wants to know if the call was from Bin Hassan. Jackson agrees that it probably was.

"Well, Jacko, there you go. It looks as though there's something for both of us to investigate."

******

Jackson, accompanied by Pete and Yassin, arrives at Old Market Square, which has returned to its usual bustling self. They study the wrecked building where Mack was shot. Jackson feels a chill as the events of two days ago flash before his eyes. "Christ, Pete, we were really lucky to get out of that place alive," he declares. Pete and Yassin nod their agreement.

"Why are we back here?" asks Pete. "I filmed this yesterday and there's nothing new."

Jackson points to a bank two doors along from the wrecked building. "That's what I'm interested in. I'd forgotten that Mack comes here to go to his bank."

"What's that got to do with the story?"

"Let's try to find out."

******

A couple of hours later, back at the bureau, Jackson, Pete, Samira, Farouk and Yassin are in excellent spirits and are relaxing over coffee and cake, again bought by Jackson. The television monitors in the main work area are tuned to the BBC. The cleaners have just left after turning Mack's office into something more to Dick's taste.

Dick returns from lunch at his hotel and frowns when he sees no sign of any journalistic activity. "Have you people got nothing to do?" he demands.

"Nope," replies Jackson with a smirk on his face, "we're all done for the day."

"And what makes you think that, Jackson?"

"Well, Dick, if you'd like to make yourself comfortable in your nicely spruced up office and turn on your TV, you'll shortly discover why."

Dick is irritated by the condescending tone of Jackson's remarks, but tries not to show it. He looks into Mack's office and sees the desk has been cleared and wiped clean. The ashtrays are gone and the rubbish bins have been emptied. The book shelves have been tidied and are no longer cluttered with empty coffee cups and drinks glasses.

"Mmm, that's better, Samira," he observes grudgingly, "but I still need that battered old chair of Mack's to be replaced, preferably by a nice leather one. I also want that hideous wall map changed to one that is more up-to-date and less offensive to the eye."

"I'll do it in the next day or so, Dick," she replies with an edge.

He is about to respond, but is interrupted by Jackson who points at the TV monitors. "Right, here we go! Watch this!"

Dick goes into Mack's office and switches on the *World News*. He sees the female anchor do a back announcement to the item just ended, then begins her introduction to the next report.

> *And now to Armibar, capital of Central Arabia. You may remember that a couple of days ago, our bureau chief there, MacDonald Galbraith, was wounded when he was caught in the crossfire between soldiers and a group of armed men. The pro-government newspaper, The Voice, has belatedly reported the incident and laid the blame firmly on terrorists attempting to overthrow the regime.*

The front page of the newspaper is displayed on screen.

> *As you will see, the alleged terrorists are pictured wearing military-style camouflage uniforms. But our correspondent, Jackson Dunbar, who led the rescue of Mr Galbraith, returned to the scene today and made a discovery that contradicts the government claims.*

Jackson appears on screen with the wrecked building as a backdrop.

> *The first clue that there were questions to be asked was the state of the uniforms worn by the alleged terrorists. They seemed too neat and bore no blood stains. This didn't match the fact that the men died in a barrage of bullets and grenades fired by the security forces. On my return today, I went looking for anyone who had been here during the period immediately before the gun battle began. I found*

this man, a local resident, who told me what happened. He didn't wish to be identified for fear of retribution.

The film cuts to Jackson interviewing a man with his back to the camera.

Jackson: Where were you at the time?

Man (speaking in Arabic with an English-language voiceover): I was in the bank to pay in some money.

Jackson: So what happened?

Man: Some masked men burst in with guns and forced the tellers to empty the main safe. As they were doing that, someone set off the alarm. The men panicked, grabbed what they could and ran outside. Policemen on duty in the square opened fire on the men, who fled into the offices above the orange shop.

Jackson: What were the gunmen wearing?

Man: Ordinary clothes, just like me.

Jackson shows the man the photograph on the front page of *The Voice*.

Jackson: So they weren't dressed in these fatigues?

The man studies the photograph briefly and laughs.

Man: No, of course not! They were just criminals wearing ordinary clothes and masks.

The camera cuts back to Jackson standing alone.

I also spoke to other witnesses who told me roughly the same story. A short time ago, I phoned the Central Arabian Government Information Office, but they had no comment.

The programme anchor comes back on screen.

That report from Jackson Dunbar in Armibar. And we're pleased to tell you that MacDonald Galbraith is making a good recovery in hospital in Glasgow.

Dick mutes the TV set and goes out to the main work area. "Quite a nice story, Jackson."

"What do you mean 'quite a nice story', Dick?" shouts Pete. "It's bloody brilliant. It's a scoop. The government here will be furious."

"Yes, very good," says Dick grudgingly, "but I hope it doesn't mean the authorities will try to close us down." He goes back into his office and can be seen setting up framed family photographs on his desk. There is also a nameplate *Richard Passick* placed prominently on the desk. He takes out a small foldable mirror, sets it up alongside the photographs, checks his appearance and runs a comb through his hair.

CHAPTER 16

The next morning, on his way to work, Jackson goes to an ATM and draws another $500 from the Roger Smith account. He tells Dick he wants to see a contact and would like Yassin to drive him there, as it is a dodgy part of town. In truth, he wants to be taken to Archibald's gambling den to pay off his debt. Dick agrees.

Yassin and Jackson arrive outside the gambling den. From the outside it appears to be a poorly maintained and nondescript office block. "Wait here. I'll be back in a few minutes," Jackson tells Yassin.

Jackson enters the den and goes to Archbibald who is smoking a cigar in his glass-enclosed office. "I've brought your money," he tells the den boss as he reaches into his pocket for the cash he has drawn out over the past 48 hours.

"Good," says the den boss. "Let's see it then."

Jackson counts out $700. "Where's the rest?" demands Archibald.

"What do you mean? That's your $500 back, plus your interest."

"Don't get clever with me! That's not enough. It's not straight interest on the loan. It's compound interest, plus an administration fee. I make that out to be $1,100."

"No, no! That's not right. It's robbery!"

Archibald pushes a button on his desk and there is ringing at the entrance door where his two heavies are standing. They hurry over to Archibald's office and stand menacingly with arms crossed at the door.

"Now look here, Jackson, I'm a businessman and when I make a loan I expect it to be honoured. There is no argument to be had. You owe me $1100."

"But I don't have that much on me and I can't draw out any more from my bank account before tomorrow."

Archibald changes tack. "I'm a reasonable man, so give me what you've got and I will allow you to pay the remaining $200 tomorrow. There will, I regret, have to be a late payment fee."

"Eh? What do you propose that be?

"Oh, I think $50 is reasonable."

"That's outrageous! You're a fucking loan shark!"

"Now, don't be so offensive or I might get angry. I am merely a businessman trying to earn an honest living."

Jackson knows he is beaten. He hands over another $200. "If you or your boys can meet me at the ATM near our bureau, I'll give you the balance then. I can be there at 9am."

"Okay. My boys will meet you then, and because you are such a valued client of my establishment, I will reduce the late payment to $25 as a gesture of goodwill."

"You're all heart, Archibald," says Jackson sarcastically.

"Yes, I'm often told that," he smirks. "My boys will now see you safely outside."

The two heavies escort Jackson from the den. As he goes out into the street and approaches the BBC car, he leans against the car, gasping for breath. Yassin jumps from the car and goes to him. "What's wrong?"

"Nothing. Just short of breath. Take me home please."

Yassin opens the front passenger door and Jackson flops into the seat, still gasping for breath. They set off for Jackson's apartment. Yassin has growing concerns for his colleague. "Are you sure you okay?"

"Yes, of course." There is a pause, then he admits he does have a problem. "No, I'm not okay, to be honest. The meeting was not as I expected. My contact turned out to be rather nasty."

"How nasty?"

"It doesn't matter how. It was just nasty. It was a mistake. Normally, I would've coped, but it just hit me after all the other shit recently. I'll be okay in a few minutes."

"You need days off," suggests Yassin.

"No, no! I mustn't do that. It would involve Psycho. You mustn't tell anyone about what has just happened."

"I say nothing," Yassin promises.

The rest of the journey takes place in silence and Jackson's breathing slowly returns to normal. On reaching the apartment,

Yassin again seeks reassurance that his colleague will be alright. Jackson tells him not to worry, but to inform Dick that he will be working from his apartment for the rest of the day.

"You like me collect you in morning?" Yassin asks, as he is about to drive away.

"No, don't worry. The walk will do me good."

******

Right on 9am the next morning Jackson is at the ATM near the bureau. He draws out another maximum of $500. A short while later, Archibald's BMW glides up with the two heavies in it. Jackson hands $225 through an open window. One of the heavies checks it and nods acknowledgment. The car drives away and Jackson walks the short distance to the bureau. He is taken aback to see that he is being observed by Yassin who is having a cigarette break just outside entrance, now that Dick has banned smoking in the bureau. He fears that Yassin has seen him talking to Archibald's heavies, but Yassin makes no mention of it as they greet each other.

"Good morning, Jacko. Are you feeling better?"

"Good morning, Yassin. Much better. Thanks for your understanding yesterday. I now feel a new man."

"That's good, Jacko."

The morning's editorial meeting is coming to a close as Jackson walks into the office. "Nice of you to turn up today, Jackson," observes Dick caustically.

Before Jackson can respond, a male voice comes up on the phone speaker. "Oh, hi there Jacko, it's Harry Kingston here. I've just been congratulating Dick on the great story yesterday. It got an airing on all outlets. A good start to your time in Armibar, Dick."

"My pleasure, Harry. We're here to serve, as always."

"Yes, thank you. Talk later. Bye."

The call ends and Pete turns to Jackson. "Just as well you were late for the meeting, mate. It meant you didn't have to listen to our temporary boss taking shovel-loads of personal credit for yesterday's story."

Dick bangs the desk angrily. "I object to that. We're a team here and I accepted the credit on behalf of all of you."

"Yeah, right. Then why did you keep using the word 'I' instead of 'we'?"

Dick bangs the desk again. "I won't be spoken to like that, Peter!"

"You'll get some respect, mate, when you've fucking earned it!"

Dick is now fit to explode and for want of something better to complain about, he points at Pete's T-shirt bearing a cartoon koala. "And I told you not to wear stupid T-shirts to work!" he shouts.

Pete gives Dick a rude one finger and walks from the room, slamming the door behind him.

Dick angrily turns to Samira. "Haven't we got another cameraman we can use?"

"Sorry Dick," she replies, "he's got a two-year contract."

"And you shouldn't even think of replacing him, Dick," adds Jackson. "He's the best and bravest there is in this city."

"I'm warning you, I will not put up with this insolence," shouts Dick. "I will not! You should all remember that I have the ear of very senior people back in London, and I will feel no restraint in telling them exactly how dysfunctional this bureau has become. Now, get out of my office. All of you! And close the door behind you."

Jackson, Samira, Farouk and Yassin get up and leave, sneaking amused looks at each other. Outside in the main work area they are greeted by a still-angry Pete. "What a wanker!"

Samira is emollient. "There's no point in antagonising him unnecessarily. We all have to work together, and Mack will be back soon and life will return to its normal happy state."

The others mumble their agreement.

A short while later, Dick opens the door to his office, affecting an air of calm. It is as though the angry exchanges of the previous minutes had not happened. "Samira, would you be kind enough to arrange lunch for me with Sir Gordon Shortwood? Any day will do.

And when you get a moment, I would like to see a copy of the bureau budget."

"Certainly, Dick. I'll get onto the embassy right away. I'll give you a financial statement in an hour or so when I've added the latest expenditures."

"Thank you. Much appreciated."

He goes back into his office and the rest of the team exchange discreet smiles. "I wonder if he knows that Stumpy is yesterday's man?" Samira asks Jackson.

"I suspect not, otherwise he wouldn't bother to suck up to him. It'll be interesting to see how Stumpy spins it."

"Perhaps I should warn him," suggests Samira.

"Let the arrogant bugger discover it for himself."

******

The next few days are relatively peaceful with no further clashes between Dick and the rest of the team. As expected, *The Voice* has denounced Jackson's allegations about the Old Market Square gunfight, but no serious move has been made by the regime to close down their bureau or even to impose sanctions against it. There are some low-level gunfights and explosions in Armibar. They have made small items on World News, but don't get an outing on the main UK domestic bulletins.

Jackson has made his peace with Archibald and has again become a regular at the gambling den. Sometimes he wins; sometimes he loses. The underlying trend, however, is that he is steadily eating into the $10,000 in his special account. His long-term desire to quit gambling is eclipsed by an unquenchable delusion that sooner or later his luck will improve and riches will be his.

******

The morning's editorial chat with London is getting under way as Jackson arrives.

Dick's outfit for the day might be called 'Hack's Tropical' – the sort of safari suit that only a reporter who has never worked in the tropics would be seen dead in. The ensemble comprises a matching khaki shirt and trousers, woven leather sandals and sunglasses perched on his bouffant hair. The shirt has four pockets, one on each breast and one on each sleeve. One breast pocket carries a notebook and the others are stitched in such a way that an array of pens and pencils remain neatly upright and accessible. His trousers, too, are well supplied with pockets – two normal side ones, two at the back and two on each thigh. His thigh pockets display further pens and pencils. Jackson observes the outfit with amusement and struggles to resist delivering some sort of joke about Dick having cleaned out a stationery shop before leaving London.

Dick is keen to report that he has filmed an interview with Sir Gordon Shortwood. "It's very strong stuff," he tells Mary Dunstan on the Foreign Desk. "He really has a most interesting and well-informed perspective on the internal troubles in Central Arabia. *Newsnight* and World News will love it."

"Sorry, Dick, but they won't love it at all," says Mary with a groan. "Didn't you see the interview he did with Mack a while ago? There was a hell of a row about it."

"I must have been on leave in Tuscany."

"That could be, but I'm sorry to tell you that no-one will touch your interview with a barge pole. Didn't you know that old Stumpy was being yanked back to London where he'll do no more harm?"

"Who's Stumpy?"

"Stumpy Shortwood. It's his nickname. And didn't he tell you he was about to leave Armibar?"

"No, not at all. He just hinted that he'd soon be moving on to something terribly important."

"I'm astonished that you didn't know any of this, Dick," says an exasperated Mary. "Didn't anyone in the bureau tip the wink about him?"

Dick turns to Jackson. "Did you know about this?"

"Oh sure," says Jackson with barely-restrained delight. "I would have told you if you'd mentioned that you were going to interview him."

"And what about you, Peter?" Dick demands, "did you know?"

155

"Sorry, it's news to me, mate," he lies. "Didn't have a clue, otherwise I would definitely have said something."

Dick is humiliated and angry. "Well, Mary, I'm sorry my valuable time has been wasted. Clearly the briefings I've been given since arriving here have been seriously inadequate."

"Never mind," says Mary. "We all make dumb mistakes from time to time."

The "dumb" description hits home, adding to Dick's annoyance. "I don't care for your choice of words, Mary, but let's leave it for now." He ends the call and angrily waves the rest of the team out of the office. They exchange smirks as they close the door behind them and return to their desks.

Samira lowers her voice and calls to Pete. "You filmed the first interview, so why didn't you tell him?"

Pete shrugs his shoulders and grins. "Well, he didn't ask, so I didn't tell. I'm just the cameraman and everyone knows that a bloody cameraman is clueless and just does what he's told. Anyhow, why didn't you warn him?"

"I might've if he'd bothered to tell me he was doing it. I just got a phone call saying he wanted you to go immediately to the embassy. He didn't say what for, and I couldn't be bothered to ask."

While this exchange is going on, Jackson is checking the news agencies on his computer. His attention is caught by an Associated Press report that an unnamed Central Arabian official is missing shortly after leaving government headquarters. Jackson doubts that it is a story for him, but phones Thomas just in case. Thomas says he knows only what is being reported by AP. "Probably a routine kidnapping for ransom," he adds. "It happens often in this part of the world, as you probably know."

Jackson scans the Arabic newspapers on his desk and finds nothing of special interest. He is bored and tells Samira he is going to stretch his legs and will be back shortly. His real intention is to go to the Fouad Rehabilitation Centre, a few short blocks away, in the hope of seeing Felicity. He finds her giving physiotherapy to a young Arab boy who has lost a leg. She is surprised to see him.

"Oh, there's nothing much going on at the bureau and I thought I'd like to see where you work," he explains.

"Well, this is it," she says with a sweep of her hand. The room is large and austere and badly in need of re-decoration. There is some basic exercise equipment and rows of simple metal-framed beds, most of them occupied by sick or injured children. Felicity has her hair tied back in a ponytail and wears a neat green overall and plain flat-heeled shoes. There are five Arab nurses tending the patients. They are all wear headscarves and a variety of outfits covering both arms and legs.

Jackson studies the scene. "Sad, isn't it," he observes. "I guess this is one of the few places where these kids can get proper treatment."

"It's not really 'proper treatment'. It's very basic, but it's the best that's available unless you have the money to pay for a stay in the Armibar Central Hospital."

"Well, your physiotherapy training is certainly coming in useful."

"Yes, but we're desperately short of medical supplies. The authorities here don't give a damn about these poor kids and we have to rely on a little foreign aid and gifts from charities."

Felicity continues to give the young boy his exercises. "What happened to you?" Jackson asks him in Arabic.

"Some men blew up my house and killed my mummy and daddy," he replies.

"I'm very, very sorry," says Jackson with a sigh. He pats the boy on the shoulder sympathetically and with a sense of helplessness.

He turns back to Felicity. "What sort of twisted evil mind thinks it's okay to do these things to innocent people?" he asks rhetorically.

She shrugs uncomprehendingly and offers Jackson a coffee.

"Thanks, but I'd better get back," he replies. "I've got this creepy acting boss who'll be wanting to know where I am."

"Okay. But we must make another attempt to have you around for dinner."

"Yes. That would be enjoyable. Perhaps once Mack returns here."

Jackson instinctively leans forward to give Felicity a good-bye kiss. She gently holds him away. "Not out here, Jacko. My Muslim nurses and patients would be offended."

"Sorry," he says with a shy grin.

Jackson departs and Felicity continues with the physiotherapy. She has enjoyed the surprise visit which has triggered fond memories of past times.

A few minutes later, Jackson reappears at the door. He is carrying a large bag of oranges. "These are for the kids," he announces.

"That's lovely!" she exclaims.

"I also have something for your centre. Close your eyes and hold out your hand."

Jackson slips an envelope into her hand and instructs her to count to 10 before she opens her eyes. He makes a speedy departure from the room.

Felicity finishes the countdown and opens the envelope to find it contains a bundle of banknotes. She counts out $500. She wipes tears of gratitude from her eyes.

******

Jackson arrives back at the bureau just as Dick comes out of his office with a folder in his hand. He goes to Samira at her desk. "I don't understand these expenses. They just say who they're for and the month they were incurred. I take it that you have receipts for all of these?"

"You must be joking, Dick. This is the Middle East," she tells him.

"Well, what are they for?"

"Oh taxis, hospitality, payments to contacts and some low level bribes. That sort of thing."

"Good grief. How do you know they're not all made up?"

"Trust, Dick. It's trust."

"Well, I'm certainly not going to put my name to this sort of unsubstantiated stuff."

"Don't worry, I'll see you don't have to."

Dick turns to Jackson. "Have we anything to offer London, yet?"
"Not yet."

"Well, keep trying. I want to see at least one story a day out of this bureau while I'm here. By the way, did you get anything from that contact Yassin took you to see yesterday?"

"Sorry, nothing came out of it. It was just someone hoping to rip us off by selling a made-up yarn."

"Oh well, keep trying," says Dick as he goes back into his office.

The rest of the day is, to Dick's disappointment, uneventful and Jackson announces that he is going back to his apartment. He attempts a withdrawal from the Roger Smith account at the local ATM, having forgotten that his spontaneous gift to the Fouad Rehabilitation Centre means he has already reached his daily limit. He checks the balance and winces at the discovery that he has just $1500 left.

******

Samira is finishing for the day. Farouk and Pete have already gone. Dick comes out of his office with the expenses folder and hands it to Samira. "I've seen enough for now," he says.

He adopts a more friendly tone. "Doing anything interesting tonight?"

"No, nothing special," she replies, "I'll just have a meal at home and perhaps watch a DVD."

"Oh, you like movies? What sort?"

"Art house ones with a bit of substance mostly, but sometimes I'll watch a mindless blockbuster for some light relief."

"Ah, we seem to have the same tastes."

Samira clears her desk and locks away the expenses files. Dick heads back to his office, then changes his mind.

"Um, I don't suppose you'd like to join me in a spot of dinner somewhere nice, would you?"

159

"Tonight?"

"Well, yes. If you don't mind leaving your DVD for another time?"

"Mmm. Yes, I suppose I could."

"I notice there's a nice-looking place a few doors away from my hotel. The Candle something."

"*The Candelabra*. I've not been there, but I believe it's very nice."

"Excellent. Well, shall we meet there at eight o'clock?"

"Yes," agrees Samira, "I'll pop home and change into something more suitable."

"Excellent. I'll phone Yassin to pick you up."

Samira puts on her coat and takes her handbag from a drawer. "Well, see you soon," she says.

"Yes. See you soon."

Dick prepares to close down the office for the day. He notices that Jackson's computer has been left on. He goes to shut it down, then changes his mind. He opens the email file and scrolls down the In Box messages but finds nothing of particular interest. Most of the emails are to and from newsgathering in London discussing stories Jackson has been working on. There is a clutter of browser links on the desktop. They seem routine, but in one corner of the screen he spots a link that says simply "Treasures". He opens it and sees that it is the entry page to *Towering Treasures Inc*. He can go no further because it requires a user name and password. His curiosity is now aroused. He Google's the company name and discovers that it is an online gambling operation based in the United States. He wonders why Jackson has been logging on to this company's website.

Dick finds nothing else of interest and shuts down the computer. He tries to open the bottom drawer in the desk, but it is locked. The top one can be opened, but it mostly contains old notebooks and Arabic newspaper clippings. There is also a print of the screen grab of Ahmed Faisel Bin Hassan. He is mildly curious about this, but it is not identified in any way and he puts it back in the drawer.

CHAPTER 17

Dick is already seated at the table when Samira arrives at *The Candelabra* a few minutes after eight. Her hair is up and she wears make-up, high heels, a flowered knee-length dress, a plain green jacket and some simple gold neck chains. Dick has changed into a light linen suit, a monogrammed Ralph Lauren shirt and a club tie. He stands to greet her as a waiter shows her to a chair, lays a serviette across her lap and places a leather-bound menu in front of her.

The restaurant is spacious with tables sufficiently apart to avoid conversations being overheard. It is discreetly lit by several chandeliers and miniature candelabra on each table. Most of the diners are men, some in Western dress, most in traditional Arab outfits.

"You're looking most attractive," Dick tells Samira.

"Well, you are looking quite smart yourself, Dick," she responds.

"Thank you. I always try to look my best."

"Yes, I can tell that."

"Some people don't think it matters, but I believe that I have a duty to dress appropriately for a senior editor. Good clothes maketh the man – or should that be a good man maketh the clothes?" He laughs at his own witticism. Samira merely smiles.

Dick scans the restaurant and the other diners. "I take it that this is the place to be in Armibar?"

"Yes, it is. We are in the presence of Central Arabia's great and the good and as we sit here, million-dollar political and business deals are probably being done at the other tables."

Dick is impressed. "I always get a buzz when I'm in a place like this. I think it calls for a bottle of wine that befits the venue and the occasion. I'm very partial to a good red. Would that suit you?"

She nods agreement. Dick picks up the wine list and waves over the hovering waiter. "I see that you have the same very nice Pinot Noir that's on offer in my club in London. We'll have a bottle of that, thank you."

Dick and Samira peruse the menu. Both choose a crayfish and salad starter. For the main course, Samira selects a duck and vegetable dish, while Dick opts for a rack of lamb with baby potatoes and salad.

The Pinot Noir arrives and Dick takes a test mouthful, rolls it around his tongue pretentiously and pronounces it to be excellent. The waiter fills their glasses and Dick and Samira toast each other.

"So, you are a Muslim who doesn't mind a drink," says Dick.

"No," she replies, "I'm a Christian who doesn't mind a drink."

"Of course," he says with an embarrassed half-laugh, "I must remember that not every Arab is a Muslim."

"And not every Arab is a terrorist," she adds.

"Yes, of course."

They exchange small talk as they wait for their starters to arrive. Dick tells her that he has two sons in a private preparatory school and that their names are now down for Harrow. His ambition is that before too many years pass he will be Head of News or at least a channel controller.

He learns from Samira that she has a business degree from a red brick university in London and hopes to have children once her husband completes a contract in Lebanon and has a settled job in Armibar. Dick tells her his wife, Sandra, is a public relations executive with a firm of financiers in the City of London and volunteers the information that they have an 'open marriage'.

"Does this mean you have affairs without consequences?" Samira enquires.

"Sometimes there are consequences, but they're of little importance. We're both honest enough to recognise that neither of us is monogamous by inclination."

"Oh well," says Samira, "I suppose it's okay if your wife genuinely doesn't mind, but Nigel and I could never accept anything less than total fidelity."

Dick can see a prospective sexual affair slipping away. "Well, congratulations to both of you, anyway. Everyone to their own expectations of a marriage. Your husband is very lucky to have you.

I have to say that you are a most attractive and interesting woman and I'm flattered that you've agreed to share your evening with me. I can also see why Mack chose you as the bureau manager."

"Because of my brains?"

"Oh, I'm sure. A bit of female glamour around the office is to be welcomed too," he says with a wink.

Samira doesn't care for the tone of Dick's remarks, but the starters have just arrived and she lets the topic drop.

They eat in silence for a few minutes, then Dick asks: "Tell me. Are you happy in your employment here?"

"Oh yes. I enjoy it very much. It's an admirable organisation to work for."

"Yes, admirable certainly, but not without its flaws."

"I suppose that applies to most large organisations."

Dick finishes his starter and takes a gulp of wine before resuming the questions. "Once you have your hoped-for children, would you want to return to the corporation?"

"Yes."

Dick empties his wine glass and the waiter gives it a refill. Samira's is still two-thirds full. "Drink up, my lovely! We can always get another bottle," Dick tells her.

The waiter goes to top up her glass, but she politely waves him away. "It's very nice, but I'm not a big drinker."

"Oh well," sighs Dick as he continues his questions.

"So, how long have you been bureau manager?"

"About four years."

"So you must know where the bodies are buried?"

Samira doesn't understand. "Bodies?"

"Yes, bodies. Not actual bodies, of course, but things that Mack and Jackson and Peter don't want anyone back in London to know about."

There is a pause while the empty starter plates are removed and the main courses arrive. Dick and Samira take their first mouthfuls and nod their approval.

Samira is still baffled by Dick's 'bodies' comment.

"Well, you know, there must be some fiddling of expenses and time sheets. That sort of thing," he explains with a knowing look.

"There's no fiddling," she insists. "I know there aren't many receipts, but there's no 'fiddling', as you describe it. Everyone here works very hard and the expenses are all justified in one form or another, otherwise Mack and I wouldn't approve them."

Dick empties his glass again and waves over the waiter for a refill. His manner is becoming aggressive.

"You're just being blinded by loyalty, aren't you! I bet Jackson and Peter are 'on the make'."

"No, no. That's not true. Why do you think that?"

Dick pulls back from further questioning and suggests they should eat their meal before it gets cold. There is a strained silence as they do so. Finally Samira speaks. "Why are you so suspicious of everyone, Dick?"

"To be honest, I don't like Jackson and Peter. They're so cocky and insolent. I've dealt with their type before. And I bet Farouk and Yassin are on the fiddle. Arabs always are."

"Not true," she says with growing irritation.

"There's another thing that needs looking into: is Jackson a gambler?"

"Good grief! Why do you ask that?"

Dick empties his third glass of red and the waiter gives him a refill. The bottle is now empty. Samira is increasingly concerned about the tone and direction of the exchanges. "What makes you think he's a gambler?"

Dick doesn't want to admit that he has been into Jackson's computer, so he just taps his nose, smiles knowingly and says it is his "instinct".

"Drink up," he instructs, pointing to her glass, which is still two-thirds full.

"No, I'm okay," she insists.

The drink is having its effect on Dick and he leans forward in a confidential manner. "As I have already said, you are a very pretty woman and I hope that you feel able to join my team."

"What do you mean 'join your team'? I have no intention of moving to London at this stage."

"No, no! I don't mean that. What I mean is that if there's anything you think London needs to know, you can call me in confidence. In return, I will see that any unpleasantness that might come your colleagues' way does not attach itself to you. And as I move up in the corporation, I will need to employ someone clever and pretty like you to be my eyes and ears."

Samira studies him in disbelief. "Am I imagining it, Dick, or are you suggesting that I become your spy?"

"No, no, my lovely. Spy is much too pejorative a word. I am just suggesting that your greater loyalty is to London, rather than your colleagues here, and that loyalty should not go unrewarded, if you get my meaning."

Samira has had enough. She angrily hurls the contents of her wine glass down the front of Dick's suit and shirt.

"I'm sure there's an appropriate Arabic word to describe you, but the English 'scumbag' is more than adequate," she shouts.

Dick is mortified. His acute embarrassment is exacerbated by the waiter rushing over to wipe him down with a white serviette.

"Don't think you'll be able to put this dinner on your expenses!" she declares, as she gets up to leave. "And by the way, Dick, I'm not 'your lovely'." The other diners turn to watch the disturbance. The maitre d' is alarmed and hurries over. He asks Dick to leave and to settle the bill at the cash desk out of sight of the other diners. Dick's humiliation is total.

******

The next morning, Samira turns up early before the arrival of Jackson, Farouk or Yassin. Unlike last night, her hair is back down, her make-up has been removed and she is wearing trainers, neat jeans and a loose top. She sees Dick in his office. He is seated in the new leather chair that he demanded. He is wearing his pen-laden safari suit and scanning the British newspapers on his computer screen. She takes a deep breath and goes in to confront him.

"Morning, Dick," she says coldly.

165

"Good morning, Samira," he says, struggling to maintain a semblance of authority.

Samira pulls up a chair and points a finger at him. "Let's get some things straight: you and I have to work together for the next month or so until Mack returns, so let's do a deal. I'll make no mention of what you said last night and you'll say nothing about how I retaliated. In other words, we will have a respectful professional relationship and will act as though last night never happened. Right?!"

Dick has met his match, for now, and knows it. "Yes, let's do that," he murmurs.

Samira returns to her desk in the main work area to find that Jackson has arrived. "Hey," he whispers to her, "is it true that you and Psycho went out for dinner last night?"

"It's true," she says abruptly.

"Christ! Were you that desperate for company and a free meal?"

"No need to be rude, Jacko. He wanted to be briefed on a few things, that's all. He now understands what's what in the bureau."

Jackson raises his eyebrows at this, but says nothing and turns on his computer. He scrolls through the news agency stories and comes across further references to senior government figures being snatched off the street. He wonders if this is developing into a story that requires more of his attention. He phones Thomas. "Have you seen the latest agency reports on the disappearing government people? Reuters says six have gone missing in the past few days."

"Yes, I saw that. Very interesting."

"Mmm. Yes, it is – especially as they all seem to have been lifted within a few hundred metres of the government offices. It's almost as though the kidnappers or whatever had been tipped off."

"I suppose that's possible."

"I don't suppose this is in any way related to your lot?"

"Oh, I don't see why you would think that. You mustn't let your imagination run away with you. Anyway, must go. It's a busy, busy, busy day!"

The next few days at the bureau pass without incident. There are no major stories to cover. Dick and Samira maintain an icy, business-like relationship, but he is determined not to forgive or forget what happened in the restaurant or the attitude of Jackson and Pete.

There have been a few shooting incidents and killings caused by bombs placed under cars, and despite hearing nothing from Binnie, Jackson assumes they are gang-related. At the same time, his gambling losses have mounted. His Roger Smith account has been cleaned out and he has sold the last of his shares. He and Zareena have had a row about his gambling and she tells him their business and personal relationship is over.

******

Jackson, Pete and Yassin investigate a bombing. They arrive in a rundown part of town to find the smoking ruins of a black Jeep Cherokee SUV with two charred bodies inside. In the front seat appears to be a chauffeur, while a woman is slumped in the back seat. They are not a pretty sight. It looks a rather routine event for Armibar, but Pete films it anyway, just in case it becomes significant.

Omar Abbas of Al Jazeera and Jane Kubinski of CNN turn up simultaneously. The police have yet to arrive and cordon off the area, so Omar is able to peer into the back seat. "She's familiar and so is the car," he tells Jackson and Jane, "she's the mistress of one of the gang leaders, Abdul something-or-other."

"Is it worth a story?" asks Jackson.

"Not really," replies Omar, "Small bomb, two dead doesn't really make it for us."

"Nor us," says Jane.

"Well, if you're not doing it, we won't either," says Jackson. "Let's go and have lunch."

The others agree. As they prepare to drive away in convoy, Yassin takes a call on his mobile. "Sorry," he informs Jackson, "I've got to go. Dick wants me to meet the lunchtime flight from London for a pick-up."

167

"What sort of pick-up?"

"He said he'd give me the details when I get to the airport."

"Never mind, Jacko," says Jane, "you can come with us and we'll drop you off at the bureau after lunch."

******

The three crews travel to the *Armibar Hotel* where they have a leisurely meal. They swap gossip about past triumphs and failures and complain routinely about the way they are treated by their bosses back at headquarters. They are keen rivals, but not unfriendly ones. There is a mutual acceptance that no quarter will be given in trying to scoop each other, but when danger comes their way, a comradeship overrides this, as it did during the mosque bombing and the rescuing of Mack when he was shot.

It is mid-afternoon by the time Jackson and Pete stroll into the bureau, unaware of what awaits them.

"Anything doing?" Jackson casually asks Samira, expecting the answer to be "nothing".

"Yes, there is Jacko, and you aren't going to like it." She nods towards Mack's office where a tall, grey-haired man in a lightweight beige suit and brightly-coloured tie is chatting to Dick.

"Oh Christ!" exclaims Jackson, "what the fuck's he doing here?"

"I've no idea. I came back from my lunch to find that Yassin had brought him from the airport."

The cause of Jackson's astonishment and anger is the discovery that star roving foreign correspondent Frederick Wynter is on his patch.

Jackson goes to his desk to find that his papers have been pushed to one side and replaced by Frederick's files. The computer is on and logged into Frederick's personal area. "What's all this?" he demands.

"Dick said Fred could share your desk," Samira tells him.

"I'm not having that," he shouts.

He bursts into Mack's office to confront Frederick. "What the hell are you doing here, Fred?"

Frederick turns on his best patronising manner. "Oh hello, Jackson. I thought it was time I checked out this patch – you know, just to cast a fresh eye on what's happening here and see that nothing has been missed. Dick agreed with me, so here I am."

"It would have been a courtesy to tell me you were coming."

"Oh well, you know how fast things move in this business. *Panorama* wants an in-depth look at the situation here and I'll probably do a few special pieces for the *Ten*."

Jackson's mood darkens. "You're here now, so I can't do anything about it, but I am telling you straight that you can get your arse away from my desk. I'm not sharing it with anyone. Samira can sort out another work area for you."

Frederick is affronted. "Your hostility is not appreciated, Jacko. We are One BBC, I would remind you, and I expect some co-operation while I'm here."

"You'll get the co-operation that you deserve!" Jackson shouts.

Dick enjoys seeing Jackson so upset, but decides that it is time to intervene. "Calm down, Jackson. Your attitude towards a highly-respected colleague is quite unacceptable and will not be looked upon well by London should they get to hear about it. Go back to your desk and quieten down and I'll get Samira to set up a temporary desk here in my office. I'll enjoy Frederick's company."

Jackson realises that his behaviour is likely to be counter-productive and adopts a more emollient tone. "I'm sorry, Fred, but we've been through some difficult days here recently. A desk in here with Dick seems a good idea. I believe there is a spare one that can be brought upstairs from the storeroom."

Frederick extends his hand and Jackson shakes it without enthusiasm. He goes back to his desk and moves the unwelcome visitor's files to a shelf. He logs onto his own personal area in the computer and makes a routine check of the news agencies and Arabic websites. In particular, he is seeking news of the kidnapped Central Arabian officials, but there is none.

CHAPTER 18

Several hours later Jackson is at home, microwaving a ready-made meal and half-watching a video compilation of Rolling Stones hits on his TV. His landline phone rings and he hits the speaker button. It is Omar Abbas and he is angry. "Hey, Jacko, what are you guys playing at?!"

"I don't understand."

"That car bomb this morning. You said you weren't going to run it."

"Well, we didn't, so what's the problem?"

"Well, what's that you're now running on World News?"

Jackson grabs the TV remote and flicks over to the BBC, just in time to hear Frederick Wynter's commentary on the film taken by Pete that morning.

"Oh Christ!" shouts Jackson, "it's fucking Fred. What's he been saying?"

"He says it's terrorism and has been spouting all sorts of speculative bullshit about the political situation here."

"You're kidding?"

"No, I'm not. I didn't even know Wynter was in town."

Jackson is apologetic. "What can I say, mate. The pompous arsehole turned up unannounced while we were having lunch today. I reckon that Psycho Passick did it deliberately to stir the shit."

"Well, Jacko, I'm bloody upset. I'm now going to have to go back into the office and put together a 'matcher' of some sort, otherwise our viewers will reckon we've been doing a cover-up."

"Sorry, Omar. I really am, but Wynter is a law unto himself and the bosses in London thinks the sun shines out of his exhaust pipe."

Omar hangs up and Jackson pours himself a large whisky.

******

The next morning's editorial conference is tense. Jackson angrily challenges Frederick's assertion that yesterday's bombing was terrorism, but his protests are haughtily waved aside by the roving correspondent with the unsurprising backing of Dick. "Anyway," Frederick says, "I wasn't the only one who thought it was worth a story. Al-Jazeera ran it, even though they were a bit slow off the mark." Jackson gives a shrug, resisting the powerful desire to explain why Omar had done the story, or to point out that Al-Jazeera speculated that it was a gangland assassination.

Frederick announces that he is having his own cameraman and producer fly out from London tomorrow and that meantime he will spend the day resting back at his hotel. Jackson and Pete are pleased to know they will have him out of sight, if not entirely out of mind.

As they return to their desks, Jackson asks Pete if he knew that Frederick was doing a piece on the car bomb. "Sorry, mate, the first I knew of it was when I saw it on last night's bulletin. I transferred the pix from my camera to our archive, just in case we needed them. Fucking Wynter turned up after we'd gone and got Farouk to send the pix off to London where they edited them around his voiceover."

Jackson sighs and checks the news agencies. He sees there have been two more mysterious kidnappings of government officials in recent days. He gets out a map and discovers that all the kidnappings have been about a block or so from government headquarters. He rings the local Reuters bureau chief, Kareem. "Hi, it's Jacko. Do you have any background info on all these guys who've been kidnapped?" He listens to Kareem's thoughts. "Now that's interesting! I've also been hearing that, so it might not be the usual gangland ransom stuff."

Jackson puts the phone down and leans back in his chair, puzzling over the meaning of what he has just been told. His thoughts are interrupted by a call from Felicity. She is keen to tell him that his surprise $500 donation has been put to excellent use, buying urgently-needed medicines and second-hand exercise equipment. He feels a flush of sexual tension when she praises him as 'a good and generous man'. "I'm glad someone thinks so," he replies, adding that at some time in the near future he will see if he can do a 'good news' feature on her rehabilitation centre.

The call has to end as another one is coming in. Coincidentally, it is from Thomas responding to a text message sent earlier in the day. Although there is no reason why Jackson shouldn't mention the call from Felicity, he opts not to. He has some questions for Thomas and they agree to meet in half an hour for a coffee. He puts on his jacket and opens the door to Mack's office where Dick is busily typing on his computer. "Just going out for a short while," he says, "I need to meet an old mate who's just arrived in town." Dick looks up and frowns, but before he can say anything, Jackson closes the door and heads for the exit.

******

When Jackson arrives at the coffee shop across from the British Embassy, Thomas is already seated at the usual spot and a waiter places two Arabic coffees and water on the table. The two men shake hands and get down to business without preamble.

"I see that you have 'Wet' Wynter on your patch," says Thomas.

"How do you know his nickname?" asks Jackson.

"Oh, we like to keep tabs on high profile reporters. We probably know more about him that he does," he laughs.

"I'm sure you do," smiles Jackson, "but I can't imagine there's all that much to know, apart from the occasional extra-marital shag. He's just a tedious, self-important suit full of bugger all."

Thomas laughs. "You don't care for him much?"

"You could say that."

"So, did you give him the duff lead on yesterday's car bombing?"

"Not at all. He just made one of his notoriously-shallow assumptions. If it's a car bomb, it must be terrorism."

"Yes, well as you probably know, it was a gangland job. Nothing more. We've checked it out."

They sip their coffee and Jackson changes the subject. He wants to press Thomas about the mysterious kidnappings. "Are you sure you know nothing about them? I mean, the first one was just one day after I made that delivery for you in Khaled Mohamed's office. I've just been told that all those who've been 'lifted' are members of Khaled's faction in the government."

Thomas responds with a knowing smile. "Just a coincidence, Jacko."

172

"Really?"

"Well, that's the official line anyway. Off the record, there may be a link, but don't worry your head about it. They've just been removed from the scene where they can do no harm to Western interests."

"Removed to where?"

"Who knows, Jacko? Just 'removed' – by our American friends."

Jackson becomes worried. "Look, Thomas, I don't want this thing to get out of hand. I did that little job for you on the understanding that it was to provide you with information – not to allow kidnappings or renditions or whatever. I don't like it. I don't like it at all."

Thomas tries to calm him. "What you did has been immensely useful to us and our friends. Sometimes the information received during operations like these necessitates some adjustments to our original plans. You must understand that. There's a lot at stake here and there'll be something in it for you, professionally and personally."

Jackson is still uncomfortable, but before he can take the discussion further, Thomas slides a note across the table. "You won't regret this, Jacko."

Jackson studies the note, frowns and puts it in his back pocket.

"And one more thing," Thomas says, "we best not meet in public any more – at least not for the time being. Instead, we should communicate by phone."

"Really? Is that a good idea?"

"It's not going to be a problem. The geniuses in our technical department have successfully tested new telephone encryption software that uses a secure satellite link. It's bloody brilliant. It means that when we call from the embassy or our designated mobiles, the only people who can understand what we say are those on the phone number we've dialled. Anyone trying to monitor the calls will hear nothing but a terrible screech that will feel like rusty nails are being driven into their brains. It's truly bloody brilliant."

"Very clever," says Jackson, "but should you be telling me this?"

"Well, you're one of us now, Jacko."

Jackson is alarmed. "No, no, Thomas. I'm not. Just because I've helped you out a little, you can't suck me further into your operation."

"It's not as simple as that, Jacko – not when the national interest is at stake. Anyway, let's not fall out over this. It'll be okay in the end."

Thomas drinks the last of his coffee, gets up and leaves. Jackson reaches into his pocket for Thomas's note and studies it thoughtfully as he finishes his coffee.

******

Next morning, Frederick Wynter turns up with his producer and cameraman and dominates the morning editorial conference with his plans and thoughts on the future of Central Arabia. When Jackson is finally asked by Dick if he has anything to contribute, he shrugs his shoulders and says that he and Pete are owed some leave and will take the rest of the day off. "Perhaps, if Yassin is not needed, he can take Pete and me to see some of the tourist sights we wouldn't normally get to."

This is news to Pete, but he makes no comment, instinctively suspecting that the statement should not be taken at face value. Frederick says he has booked a chauffeured saloon for the day and won't need Yassin. The meeting breaks up.

Two hours later, the BBC car carrying Jackson and Pete is parked by Yassin in an avenue dividing Central Arabia Plaza from several hectares of bulldozed wasteland. Jackson consults the note given to him by Thomas. "This is the spot," he announces.

Pete is annoyed. "Would you like to explain why we're here?" he demands.

"I don't know myself," Jackson confesses. "All I've got is a tip-off to be at this spot at this time."

"Is that all?"

"That's all."

Pete groans and slides down in his seat.

"Stop complaining," Jackson tells him, "at least you're not bored out of your mind stacking supermarket shelves or sweeping the streets."

"True, but does it ever occur to you what a bonkers business we're in?" responds Pete.

"Quite often," admits Jackson. "People outside journalism view us with a mixture of admiration, bafflement and contempt, and who can blame them. What sane person would feel compelled to head towards danger, rather than away from it? They also can't understand why it's so competitive."

"Yeah," says Pete with a sigh. "My family in Australia think I'm nuts. They can't understand why we take such risks just to get a story ahead of our rivals. I've tried explaining, but I'm not sure I really know. Do you?"

"Well, sort of. We always want to be first with a story. There's no satisfaction in being told by someone 'that's not news. I heard that on another channel or read it in my newspaper'."

"What made you go into journalism? Was it because of your dad?"

"That's part of it," admits Jackson, "and I liked writing and the thought of doing exciting things. I also felt my reporting would help put right some of the world's wrongs."

Pete raises an eyebrow. "That's funny, Jacko. Don't you think you should sort yourself out first before you try to fix the wider world?"

Jackson laughs. "You Aussies don't do diplomacy, do you!"

Their discussion is abruptly interrupted by the sound of approaching sirens.

"Maybe this is what we're waiting for," says Jackson.

Pete jumps from the car and begins filming a convoy approaching from the south towards the plaza. As it gets closer and travels past the wasteland, he can see that a police car is in the lead, followed by an official government limousine with blacked-out windows and two military trucks with armed soldiers standing in the open backs.

The convoy sweeps past them and into the plaza. Pete is about to stop filming when there are two brilliant flashes, followed a second later by the rumble of two huge explosions. Their car is rocked by the shockwaves.

The official limousine, the police escort and one of the military trucks are hurled in the air in a cloud of smoke and dust. This, most definitely, is their story.

"Shit!" shouts Jackson. He instructs Yassin to phone Dick and tell him what has happened and that he and Pete are on the scene.

Jackson and Pete run towards the blast with Pete filming as he goes. They arrive to see a massive crater in the roadway with water spouting from a ruptured water main. There are bodies and body parts everywhere and all the shop fronts within 100 metres or so are blown in. Some shops are on fire. There are piercing screams from the wounded men, women and children. Most are lying on the ground, but some are staggering around blindly in a state of shock. A woman, stripped semi-naked by the blast, collapses onto the footpath. Two uniformed convoy guards have escaped injury, but wander aimlessly around the devastation, no longer carrying their weapons and too shaken to react in any useful way.

While Pete continues filming, Jackson pauses to take in the detail.

Back at their car, Yassin manages to get only the briefest of messages to Dick before the mobile network is shut down, as it was with the mosque bombing.

Jackson also tries to ring the bureau but sees there is no signal. He goes to Pete and instructs him to take lots of close-ups of the dead and wounded.

"Jeez, mate, are you sure?"

"Yes, I'm sure. Let's not sanitise this with too many wide shots. I want the report to reveal what it's really like when a bomb goes off."

"If you say so, mate, but just remember we're here as observers not axe-grinders, and you know London won't allow the close-ups. It'll be too upsetting for viewers."

"We'll worry about that later. For now, just do as I say!"

Jackson sees a small boy screaming and clutching the dead body of his mother, trying desperately to shake her back to life. "Quick, Pete, get that," he instructs. "And get some of the body parts scattered about."

Jackson spots the wrecked official limousine still smoking and lying in its side against a burning shop. He looks inside and sees Khaled Mohamed suspended by his seat belt in the back of the car. He can tell from the minister's wounds that he has not survived the blast. He waves Pete over to film the car and the dead minister, then he does a brief piece-to-camera describing the devastation, naming the dead minister, and expressing the view that it is not terrorism but an assassination related to a power struggle within the government.

As he finishes, he sees the CNN crew drive up and begin filming. Jane Kubinski runs over to him. "You were here quick, Jacko."

"Just luck. We were passing by just as it happened," he lies.

Jane peers into the wrecked limousine and sees the body inside. "Do you know who he is?"

Jackson shakes his head than immediately realises this denial is taking professional rivalry too far. "Well, actually, it's Khaled Mohamed, the Development Minister. I did a very boring interview with him a few weeks ago."

"Was he important?"

"Important enough to assassinate, I guess."

"So, it's not a gang thing this time?"

"No, definitely more important than that."

"Thanks, Jacko."

"My pleasure, Jane. We'd better get back to the bureau to do the feed. It looks like we've beaten you to this story," he says triumphantly.

Jane grins. "Sorry to disabuse you of that, Jacko, but we brought our satellite link and we'll be on air before you get down the end of the street."

"Bugger! Oh well, at least we'll have the best film," he shrugs.

Jackson and Pete run back to their car and accelerate down the road against a flow of police vehicles and ambulances heading towards the bombing with their sirens screaming and lights flashing. In the midst of these oncoming vehicles is a taxi that suddenly swerves across their path and screeches to a halt. Yassin slams on the brakes and attempts to go around the taxi, but there isn't room. He fears they are being ambushed. Instead, Frederick Wynter emerges from the taxi and walks over to them in a deliberately-languid manner intended to convey a message that he has seen it all and done it all during his long career covering conflicts of every sort.

Jackson is furious. "What the fuck are you up to, Fred? Do you have to drive about as though you're in a crap Hollywood movie?"

Frederick is dismissive. "C'mon, Jackson. I don't have time to mess about. What's the story?"

"It's just along the road, if you want to see for yourself."

"No, I'll use your film. London will want me to do a report, seeing I'm on the spot."

Frederick returns to his taxi which moves out of the way to allow the BBC car through. Yassin shouts to the taxi driver in Arabic. Jackson bursts out laughing. "Nice one, Yassin," he says.

"What's so funny?" Pete wants to know.

"I told the taxi driver to take Mr Wynter the long way back and not to drive too fast," Yassin replies.

"Brilliant!" declares Pete.

Fifteen minutes later they rush upstairs into the bureau to see Dick and Farouk watching Jane Kubinski doing a live report from the scene.

"Look, you've been scooped," Dick shouts to Jackson, "and why haven't you been answering your mobiles?"

"Get stuffed. This is a biggie and we've some stunning film that Jane would die for."

Farouk has already set up a link to London and Pete immediately starts a direct transfer from his camera. Dick goes back into his office to watch the transfer on his monitor. Jackson grabs a chair and jams it under the lock of the bureau entrance door. He tells Samira that no-one – absolutely no-one -- should be allowed in without his say so. He goes to his computer and types some quick notes for a live piece from the bureau studio.

Dick comes out of his office. "Some of that stuff you've just sent back is bloody hard on the eyes and stomach, Jackson. Did you need all those close-ups?"

"We shot it as it was, Dick. It's a nasty business and the public ought to be able to see it."

"They won't use the close-ups, you know. Far too graphic. Casualty porn. By the way, did you see anything of Frederick when you were there?"

"Oh yeah," replies Jackson, "he was pissing about as usual and he told us that he'd meet us back here. I don't know where he's got to."

Pete grins broadly and gives Samira a wink. It dawns on her that Frederick is being maliciously outsmarted.

Jackson does a live crossover to London, explaining what happened and claiming it was a total coincidence that he and Pete were on the scene, neatly skipping over the obvious question about how Pete's camera was running when the explosions were detonated. Jackson repeats his view that the assassination was brought about by a power struggle within the government. As Dick and Pete had predicted, London does not run the gruesome close-ups, relying instead on Pete's wide scenes and slow motion shots of the explosions and the convoy vehicles flying through the air.

Dick comes out of his office again. "Are you sure about the people behind the explosion, Jackson? I'd have thought it would have been the work of this *Soldiers of Allah* group."

"Very much doubt it, Dick, but I should have confirmation one way or the other in the next few hours."

"How will you get that?"

Jackson taps his nose, knowingly. "I have my ways and my contacts."

"I hope you're right. I don't want us getting on the wrong side of the government again."

Dick checks his watch and turns to Samira. "Any word from Frederick yet?"

"No, not a thing," she replies. "I can't contact him because the government has shut down the mobile network again."

Dick goes back into his office and closes the door behind him, just as the bureau entrance door handle begins turning back and forth furiously. There is sharp knocking on the door and Samira hears Frederick's muffled demands to be let in. Pete also hears it and drowns it out by running some bombing tape with the volume turned up high.

On the other side of the door, Frederick can hear the sounds of victims yelling and screaming. He bangs again on the door then puts his shoulder to it. To no avail. He gets out his mobile to ring the bureau, but the network is still down. He realises that his way into the bureau is being deliberately blocked.

CHAPTER 19

Dick is mystified at next morning's editorial meeting about the failure of Frederick to show, but he gets his answer when Mary Dunstan comes on the line from the Foreign Desk in London. "I've just had word that there's been a change of plans by Fred Wynter. He thinks Afghanistan is about to blow up and that he should get there straight away. I hope that won't mess up your coverage arrangements."

Everyone except Dick breaks into broad grins. "It'll be okay, Mary," says Jackson, trying not to sound too pleased, "we'll just have to manage without him."

"I thought that might be your answer," replies Mary, "but I should alert you to the strong possibility that Sally Singer will fly out to replace Fred on your patch."

There are groans all round, even from Dick. "Oh Christ! What have we done to deserve this!?" exclaims Jackson.

"Just joking," laughs Mary, "she's on leave and doing lectures on a cruise ship in the Caribbean. Honest." Mary has enjoyed winding up the Armibar team and has a fit of the giggles as she ends the call.

Dick suggests that Jackson and Pete return to Central Arabia Plaza – this time with the satellite link – and do a live update from the explosion scene. Jackson agrees.

On the way, the mobile network comes back on. Jackson sends a brief text to Thomas, asking him to call. He fears that the assassination of Khaled Mohamed was somehow linked to the bug he placed in the minister's office. He also wonders why the assassination took place in a crowded shopping centre, causing so many innocents to be injured or killed. A few minutes later he gets a reply text from Thomas: "2 busy 2 talk. Will call 2morrow".

******

Jackson and Pete are exhausted and are drinking a refreshing beer back at Jackson's flat. It has been a triumphant day. Pete's film is in great demand by broadcasters around the globe. Dick has had to admit that Jackson and Pete have done the bureau proud and he is not slow to bathe in the reflected glory. Although CNN was first on the air with the story, its film didn't match the jaw-dropping spectacle of Pete's shots of the convoy being blown up. Al-Jazeera was caught completely flat-footed and could show only aftermath film, having arrived on the scene nearly an hour after the assassination. At the same time, Jackson has modified his explanation of how they got film of the convoy being blown up, claiming they had pulled up to get a coffee and that when Pete heard the approaching sirens, he automatically grabbed his camera and began filming.

"Would you like me to knock up something to eat?" Jackson asks Pete.

"Depends what you have in mind," he replies cautiously.

"Let's see," says Jackson as he goes to the refrigerator and finds it almost empty. He takes out the remains of a large meat pie. He sniffs it, winces and tips it into the rubbish bin. He opens a cupboard and studies a row of cans.

"I could do you baked beans on toast," he tells Pete with a smile.

Pete screws up his face. "Thanks, but no thanks, mate. I gave up that sort of food in my early 'teens. I'll go back to my apartment. There's a nice chilli dish awaiting my attention."

He gulps down the last of his beer and goes to the front door. "See you in the morning, Jacko." He leaves and Jackson empties a tin of baked bins into a saucepan on the stove. He puts sliced bread in his toaster and flips the top off another bottle of beer.

The landline phone rings and Jackson hits the speaker button. "It wasn't us," announces the voice of Ahmed Faisel 'Binnie' Bin Hassan, without any preamble.

"I guessed that," responds Jackson, "but who was it?"

"It was your lot and the Americans, with the approval of the presidential palace. They wanted the traitorous prick Khaled Mohamed out of the way."

The line goes dead, to the immense frustration of Jackson, but he knows that Binnie will always keep his calls brief to stop his location being traced.

Jackson eats his baked beans, washed down with beer, and reflects on Binnie's claim. It fits his suspicions that the British were involved in the assassination. He feels a growing anger about the number of innocent people who were killed or maimed. He decides that he needs something stronger than a beer and pours himself a large whisky. He dials Thomas Fulham.

The call is immediately picked up and answered abruptly. "Yes, Jacko, want do you want?"

"I need to talk to you about what happened today."

Thomas is irritated. "Look, I'm far too busy. All I can say is that there was a bit of a stuff-up."

"In what way?"

"It shouldn't have happened where it did."

"Christ!" exclaims Jackson.

"A shame, but at least that bastard Khaled Mohamed won't be causing any more trouble."

Before Jackson can respond further, Thomas cuts him short. "I'll ring you tomorrow as promised." The line goes dead.

Jackson finishes his whisky and is about to have a shower when the phone rings. It is his mother. For a change, she greets him in a positive and uncritical manner: "Hello, darling, I just thought I'd phone to congratulate you on the wonderful reports you did on today's news."

"Thank you, Mother. That's nice. No complaints about how I looked?"

"No, darling, you looked lovely. I was very impressed and so were all my friends at the Bridge Club."

"Oh, so you're playing Bridge now, are you?"

"Yes, darling, I'm not very good at it yet, but I took your advice to get out a bit more."

"Excellent, Mother. I'm really pleased about that."

"Yes, it's good and I think they're flattered that they now have a member of the aristocracy among their members. But there's one thing I wanted to…"

Jackson angrily interrupts her flow. "What do you mean 'aristocracy'?"

"Well, you know, I'm 'Lady Dunbar' and the Bridge Club likes that."

"That may just about make you a fringe part of the establishment, but it certainly doesn't elevate you to the aristocracy. Honestly, Mother, you're such a terrible snob. You really are!"

His mother brushes this aside. "As I was about to tell you, everyone is so impressed with your bravery on the television lately, and I decided on the spur of the moment to write to the Director-General to make a suggestion."

Jackson is immediately suspicious: "What sort of suggestion?"

"Well, darling, I explained how old I am and that you are the only family I have. I told him that I thought that it wasn't right for them to keep you in such a dangerous place and that you would make an excellent senior manager back here in London where you could also keep a closer eye on my welfare."

Jackson groans. "Oh Mother! I hope you haven't posted that letter."

"I just managed to catch today's last collection. I sent it First Class, so that he should get it tomorrow."

Jackson groans again. "Mother! I just can't believe that you did that. You have no right to interfere in my career."

"But, darling, I need you back here. I'm lonely and my health isn't good. What if you got killed? I would have no-one to look after me." She begins sobbing.

"So, this is what this call is all about, eh?! More self-centred pity. More interference in my life and my career."

His mother's crying increases.

"Look, Mother, I'm in no mood for this. I've had a hard day, and you know that if you really do need me back in London, I can be there in a few hours. Just leave me in peace."

Jackson ends the call, pours himself another large whisky, has a shower and collapses onto his bed, naked and inebriated. He doesn't sleep well, being frequently disturbed by flashbacks to the casualties in the Central Arabia Plaza.

******

Jackson awakes with a severe headache and washes down two paracetamol with a black coffee. By the time he reaches the office, he is feeling a little better. His spirits are boosted by the avalanche of praise arriving from around the world for his Central Arabia Plaza scoop. He and Pete are kept busy providing follow-ups.

Dick is enjoying the reflected glory. Additionally, he has made friends with an attractive female company executive staying at his hotel and they have a lunch date.

While Dick is out lunching, Jackson gets his promised call from Thomas. He goes into Mack's office and closes the door behind him. "Right then, tell me more about the stuff-up."

"I can tell you only if you give me a rock solid assurance that you won't report what I'm going to say," insists Thomas.

"I'm not happy with that."

"Take it or leave it, Jacko."

Jackson takes a minute to think about it.

"Are you still there, Jacko?" Thomas calls out.

"Yes, I'm still here… Okay, tell me."

"Well, the guys who set up the situation apparently placed the explosives in the wrong part of the sewer. It should have been in the section where the road passes the wasteland near where you were parked. That was intended to keep collateral casualties to the minimum."

"Oh fuck," exclaims Jackson, "how did that screw-up happen?"

"Dunno. The sewer charts were probably wrong, I guess. You know what it's like in this country."

"But hang on, Thomas! That doesn't figure. If the explosives were in the wrong spot, how was it that they still blew up under the convoy?"

There is a pause before Thomas replies. "The explosives were fitted with a magnetic trigger, and a matching magnet was clamped to the underside of the minister's limo. So, it didn't really matter

185

where the explosives were, just so long as the limo passed over them."

"Fucking hell, Thomas. You guys think of everything."

"Not quite everything. Our chaps obviously didn't check the sewer charts properly."

"Obviously not," agrees Jackson.

"Well, you just can't get the staff these days," Thomas jokes.

Jackson isn't amused. "You don't seem too bothered about all the casualties."

"To quote America's Donald Rumsfeld 'stuff happens'," responds Thomas, "and looking at the bigger picture, our main objective was achieved. So job done!"

Jackson is angered by this comment, but restrains himself. "Yes, I guess that's how people in your business see it, but could you pop around here for a few minutes after everyone else has gone tonight? I'd like to show you something."

"I've got a lot on my plate."

"It's important, Thomas. I'll text you as soon as the coast is clear."

"Okay, but it'd better be worth my while."

The call ends and Jackson goes back to his desk and is cheered by a further string of congratulatory emails.

******

That evening, as arranged, Thomas turns up at the bureau. He is in a hurry and has no time for pleasantries. "So what do you want to show me?"

Jackson goes to the video machine. "I take it that you saw my reports on the assassination?" he asks.

"Not an assassination, Jacko, a neutralisation, if you don't mind. But, yes, of course I saw your reports and I was impressed, as always."

"Right, Thomas, I now want you to see some of the scenes that my bosses felt were too dreadful to show."

Jackson pushes the 'play' button and immediately the monitor shows a series of graphic close-ups of wounds and body parts. He winds up the volume, filling the room with piercing blood-curdling screams. Thomas flinches.

Jackson spools through to another section of the video. It shows wounded and terrified children howling at the top of their voices. Thomas angrily hits the 'stop' button, unwittingly causing the video to freeze on a close-up of the little boy trying to shake his dead mother alive.

Thomas is furious. "What the fuck is this all about?" he shouts.

"I thought it was just possible that you might feel some shame. I wanted to show you the full, brutal, unadorned result of the actions of you and your ilk. What would you say if those kids had been Sophie and Sam?"

Thomas's fury now has no limits. "We're at war. The death of a few innocent women and children is the price that sometimes has to be paid for the higher good of democracy."

It is now Jackson's turn to lose control. "I'm out of this, Thomas. No more of your dirty games."

"Sorry, Jacko, that's not an option for you – at least not yet."

Thomas leaves, slamming the door behind him. Jackson switches off the video editor and slumps into a chair behind his desk. He takes several large breaths to try to calm himself. After a few minutes, he goes into Mack's office and hunts through the cupboards until he finds a half-empty bottle of Mack's single malt Glenfiddich whisky. He flops into Dick's new chair and drinks straight from the bottle.

******

Eight hours later, Jackson comes to, finding that he is still in Dick's chair. He looks at the wall clock and is shocked to discover that the normal working day will soon begin. The empty whisky bottle is at his feet and he hastily returns it to its hiding place, vaguely thinking that when Mack returns from London he will blame Dick for emptying it. He turns off his computer and grabs his jacket.

187

As he heads for the exit, Pete comes in with his camera kit. "Hey, so there you are, Jacko! I knocked on your door at the apartments, but got no answer."

"No, um, I had to come here early to answer an urgent enquiry from some silly prat at Broadcasting House," he lies.

"Well, you don't look too flash mate. Is everything okay?"

"Yeah, yeah! Of course," he replies tetchily. "Tell Dick and Samira that I'll be back in an hour or so after I've had a shower and some breakfast."

"No worries, mate. Take your time. I'll let you know if there's anything important from the morning conference."

******

Jackson catches a taxi home and feels a growing sense of anger – partly at his inability once again to control his drinking, but mostly at how he has allowed himself to be sucked into the brutal and apparently uncaring world inhabited by Thomas.

Once inside the apartment, he vows to restart the day in a more civilised manner with a hot bath, brewed coffee and a proper breakfast of porridge, toast and a Spanish omelette. He opens the refrigerator and is pleased to find that his maid has replenished it.

An hour later, he is finishing his second coffee when the phone rings. It is Felicity.

"Hi Jacko," she says with false cheer.

"Hi Felicity. This is an early time of the day to be calling. Is everything okay?"

"I'm not sure. Did something happen between you and Thomas last night?"

"Er, why do you ask?"

"He arrived home drunk and in a foul temper. I tried to find out why, but he wouldn't tell me. I then raised the matter of having you around for dinner and he angrily told me to forget it. He said you were a self-important, know-nothing hypocritical shit. I was shocked. He poured himself a large drink and when the TV news came on with more on that dreadful bombing in Central Arabia Plaza, he became very agitated. I told him how terrible it was and that some of the victims were now trying to recover in my rehabilitation centre. I said I couldn't understand how people would do such terrible things and then he completely lost it. He started screaming at me that I was as bad as you and talked rubbish about 'stuff happens' and that it was for 'the higher good of democracy' etc, etc, etc, blah, blah. I've ever seen him like that before."

Jackson is taken aback, but adopts a soothing voice. "I'm really sorry to hear about that. Were you frightened?"

"No, not frightened really, just horrified. And he woke up Sophie and Sam. By the time I came back into the room after settling them down, I found him curled up in a foetal position and snoring away on the floor in the corner. I went to bed and locked the door behind me. When I got up this morning, he was lying on top of the bed in the spare room, still in his work clothes."

"Is he still there?"

"No, he got up a little while later, had a shower, got dressed and went off immediately to the embassy."

"Did he not say anything?"

"No. Well, not much anyway. He swallowed a couple of paracetamols and muttered some weak apologies for coming home drunk. He said he'd had a very rough day. That was it. To be honest, I think he was so pissed last night that he didn't fully remember what happened."

"Perhaps that's just as well."

"Maybe, Jacko, but I still don't see what set him off like that. After all, the assassination wasn't his fault, was it."

"Yes, well something seems to have hit a raw nerve with him," says Jackson, evasively. "We had the same sort of argument when we were talking about the killings last night, but he was quite sober when he left me."

"I hope he's calmed down by the time he comes home this evening."

"Yes, I hope so, too, for your sake, and for the kids."

"Sorry to bother you with this Jacko. I'd better get back to work. I'm at the rehab centre and it's heart-breaking seeing what's happened to those kids. Some will never fully recover. But thanks to your kind donation, we're fairly well off for bandages and other medical stuff."

"I'm really pleased about that," says Jackson.

The call ends and Jackson brews another coffee. He consults his address book and dials a number. A woman answers: "Hello, Smith Charles and Brownlow, solicitors. Jillian Charles speaking. How can I help?"

"Hi Jillian! It's Jackson Dunbar."

Hello, Mr Dunbar. Very nice to hear from you again. We've been watching your adventures on television. We hope that you're okay."

"Yes, I'm okay."

"Excellent! How can I help?"

"I'd like to make some anonymous donations to a charity that I've an interest in. I'm proposing that I transfer money from my main bank account to you every few months and that you then pass it on to the charity, simply stating that it's come from an anonymous well wisher."

"Why do you want it to be anonymous? There are tax benefits for you if you declare it."

"No, it's personal. I don't want the charity to know where the money's coming from."

"I think we could do that, just as long as it's clear there's no money laundering involved."

Jackson laughs. "No problem there, Jillian. It'll come from my salary account and is for a legitimate charity, the Fouad Rehabilitation Centre in Armibar. I'll email you the contact details and 250 pounds will be transferred by bank standing order to you every three months, starting next month."

"Excellent. We'll process it for you with pleasure. Meantime, you take care, Mr Dunbar."

CHAPTER 20

In London, Mack Galbraith arrives by taxi at New Broadcasting House. He has flown down from Glasgow where he has been making a steady recovery from his wounds. Although he still needs a walking stick, he has been declared fit enough to return to Armibar in the next week or two. But first his bosses in the news department want to talk to him. He is not looking forward to the experience. While he admires some of those who have worked their way up through the ranks, they are far outnumbered by those he regards as overpaid and with little genuine talent. He is under orders from wife Joan not to allow himself to be provoked. He has promised to do his best.

Thanks to the sartorial attentions of Joan, Mack is looking as neat and tidy as he ever will be. He wears a smart dark grey off-the-rack suit and bright multi-coloured tie. He pauses near a bin for a few minutes to draw heavily on a cigarette. He studies the glitzy glass-fronted entrance to the headquarters building and mutters under his breath about the extraordinary cost of it all.

He stubs out the cigarette in a sand tray beside the bin and ventures into the entrance, waving his security pass at the guards scrutinising the steady flow of staff and visitors negotiating the revolving doors. He goes to reception and is told that someone will be down to collect him shortly. He grumbles as he is informed that he must display his security pass at all times while in the building.

Mack is recognised and greeted by several colleagues. His hand is shaken with friendly enthusiasm and sympathy is offered about having been wounded. He goes to the viewing area to peer down on the vast newsroom. It reminds him of an ant nest and he vows that he will never agree to work in such a clinical, smoke-free environment. After several minutes, a smartly-dressed woman in her mid-thirties appears at his side and identifies herself as Louise, personal assistant to Marina Kerner, the head of news. She asks him to follow her upstairs.

Mack is ushered into a conference room that doubles as an executive dining area. A large wooden table is set for 10 diners.

191

Marina is standing in the corner of the room surrounded by other news executives, a mix of men and women that includes representatives of the personnel and publicity departments. A waiter is serving water, juices and wine from a tray, while another makes sure all the table settings are correct.

Marina, who is wearing a trouser suit, sees Mack and goes to him to exchange air kisses. "It's wonderful to see you looking so well again, Mack," she enthuses with a gentle Belfast accent.

"Thank you, Marina. I should be fine by the time I get back to Armibar."

Mack leans his walking stick against the wall and shakes hands with the rest of the party, most of whom he knows, if only through phone calls and emails. The drinks waiter offers him red or white wine, but he thinks it is wise in this situation to take a mineral water.

Marina claps her hands for attention. "Well, ladies and gentleman, shall we take our seats and begin the meal," she says more as an order than a question.

The assembled party sit at their designated places with Marina at the head of the table and Mack to her right. There are two empty seats at the far end of the table, but these are explained when Mary Dunstan and Harry Kingston arrive breathless. "Sorry we're late ," says Mary, "but we had to sort out a problem with one of our stories."

"Anything I should be told?" asks Marina.

"No, nothing to bother you about," replies Mary. "It was just a small things arising from a misunderstanding."

"Good," says Marina, "but make sure I'm told if your misunderstanding develops into anything serious."

Marina turns to Mack. "We consulted your wife and she suggested a sardine salad starter and a green salad with your filet steak."

Mack shrugs. "Ah yes, salad! Joan knows what's good for me, even if I sometimes don't."

As the starter is served, Marina proposes a toast. "It's an honour to have in our midst Mack Galbraith, one of the finest foreign correspondents in the history of the corporation. On behalf of everyone, let me say how pleased we are that you, Mack, will soon be putting your considerable skills to use in the field once again."

"Hear, hear," the others respond in chorus as they bang the table with approval and raise their glasses to their guest.

"Well, thank you very much for those flattering words," responds Mack, knowing full well that they are just that: flattery. He does not delude himself that over the past couple of decades there haven't been better foreign correspondents. Further, he knows he is often viewed as an irritant and loose cannon by his masters. Still, he does know that his position is reasonably secure, for the time being at least, there being few others with his depth of knowledge and reputation for delivering good and accurate stories from the Arab world.

Marina announces that she will take the opportunity during the meal to brief everyone present about how she sees news developing over the next few years. The others murmur their approval, knowing full well that they have no choice but to listen.

For the next 45 minutes, Marina hardly touches her food as she delivers a vision splattered with current management speak. There is much talk of "delivery", "platforms", "programme silos", "outward facing social media", "customer orientated websites" and "stakeholder involvement". Mack fails to stifle a yawn.

As the coffee and tea trolley is wheeled in, Marina summarises what she asserts are not just her views but those of everyone at the very top of the corporation. "Finally, let me say this to you: We must future-proof our multi-platform digital operations and greenlight more imaginative customer content. We must take affirmative action to ensure that our audiences are constantly replenished. We must dust down and remove our ladders of ambition from the garden shed. By that, I mean we should not just be happy with the low hanging, easy-to-pick fruit. We must eagerly clamber to the very top of the trees to seize the prized ripening apples and pears before they fall into the ever-open grasping baskets of our commercial competitors. So… That is how I – we – see life over the horizon of opportunity. I sincerely hope you share these most essential visionary ambitions."

Those around the table clap their hands and murmur their approval, some more enthusiastically than others. Mack takes the opportunity to blow his nose.

Marina turns to Mack and asks if there is anything he would like to add. Despite his promise to Joan to behave himself, he is unable to hide his disdain. "Well, thank you for that briefing, Marina. I wish I understood it. Back when we were both news trainees, you from Belfast and me from Glasgow, we talked to each other in plain English. Clearly, I have been left behind when it comes to inter-personal high-level management newspeak. But never mind. Those of us out in the field will continue to do our best to inform and entertain what you call "our customers" in language that they'll understand."

There is nervous tittering among the Marina loyalists while Mary and Harry exchange amused glances.

Marina is offended and not at all apologetic. "Well, Mack, your contempt for headquarters management is well known, but you must understand that broadcasting in all its forms is moving forward at a terrifyingly fast pace and new language is required to keep up with it."

"Oh well, Marina, I don't much care what tortured language is used in your plush boardrooms, provided those who use it genuinely understand what they are saying and what they need to achieve."

"There is clearly a gulf here between us," she says with an icy smile, "so let's move on to other matters: your assessment of the situation in Central Arabia. Are the current troubles there a passing issue or long term?"

"Oh, I think they'll be around for some time. First of all, there is the fierce power struggle going on in the government between those who want to strengthen ties with the West and others who want the country to be a conservative Muslim one. The recent assassination of the Khaled Mohamed, the Development Minister, is part of that struggle. Then there is another matter, the importance of which is not yet entirely clear – the terrorist group *Soldiers of Allah*. They seem to be lurking in the wings planning major attacks on western interests. But Jackson Dunbar is well across that angle."

"Yes, I was going to raise the matter of Jackson," says Marina. "Is there anything you should be telling us about him?"

"What do you mean?"

"Matters that we should know about."

Mack is getting tetchy. "As far as I'm concerned, he's a well-informed, talented, enthusiastic and brave correspondent. He saved my life. What more is there to say?"

The deputy head of news, Robert Horsfeld, who is sitting quietly across the table from Mack, chips in. "What Marina is alluding to, I'm sure, are a couple of matters that have been the subject of rumours recently."

"What rumours?"

"Um, there are two issues that have come to our attention, but let's first deal with his, um, gambling."

Mack is astonished. "What gambling?" I've heard nothing. He's often a bit short of cash, but I believe that's due to some property deal in which he was ripped off. That could happen to any of us."

"Of course, Mack, but even so, there does seem to be some substance to the rumours. We have, er, reason to believe that he has an online gambling account that he accesses from his work computer. For obvious reasons we don't approve of that."

Marina interrupts. "Mack, if, as you say, you don't know anything about that, then I think you should look into it as soon as you get back to Armibar. You know, just to be on the safe side – and discreetly, of course. We don't want any interface problems with the National Union of Journalists."

"Yes, of course I'll investigate, Marina, but I'm confident the rumour-mongers are going to be disappointed."

"I hope so, Mack." She turns back to her deputy. "Now tell us about the second rumour."

"Um, yes," agrees Robert with some further hesitation. "Um, as you, er, have told us, Jackson is very well informed – unusually so, to be honest."

"Yes, he is," confirms Mack. "He's a very bright lad with good Arabic and an excellent understanding of the region way beyond his years."

"But not a team player, I believe," states Robert.

"No, not a particularly good team player, I admit, but I put that down to ambition and enthusiasm, or over-enthusiasm sometimes. I did have some early problems with him, but those were happily resolved. And to be truthful, I'd prefer to have someone who occasionally needs to be brought to heel rather than some dull character who just sits on his arse waiting for stories to land on the desk."

"Quite right," interjects Marina, "but please continue, Robert."

"I accept that Jackson is ambitious and enthusiastic – that's to be applauded – but I do have some reservations about how he seems to be so well informed after just a few months on the patch. Do you know where I'm going with this?"

"No, Robert, I don't know. Tell me without resorting to riddles! Get to the fucking point!"

Marina frowns at Mack's angry swearing and interjects. "Calm down, Mack, just let Robert explain."

"Yes, um, Jackson has an impressive number of scoops and I wonder what, um, price has had to be paid for these?"

"Price?" asks Mack. "What do you mean by 'price'? Are you suggesting that he gets them through bribery?"

"That's, er, possible, of course, but I'm, er, thinking of something else."

Mack angrily turns to Marina. "Will you please order your stuttering, incoherent deputy to explain in single syllable words what he is on about," he demands.

Marina decides to take over. "Yes, we should explain there are concerns that Jackson could have two masters. You know, he could be a kind of, er, double agent. So you can see why Robert is having some justified difficulty with such a sensitive matter."

Mack erupts in fury and begins shouting. "So that's what this lunch is all about, eh? It's all about rumours some prick has put into circulation about Jackson. Some arsehole who's out to destroy Jackson's career."

"Calm down, Mack," pleads Marina, "as head of the news department I cannot ignore such rumours. They must be looked into."

Mack knows this is true, although he remains angry about the manner in which the rumours were raised. He says that if that is all they have to discuss with him, he would like to get back to Heathrow to catch his shuttle flight to Glasgow.

"Umm, there is a third thing I've just remembered, Mack," announces Robert. That girl you've got working in the bureau… Sonia."

"Samira," corrects Mack, "what about her?"

"Is she right for the job, do you think?"

"In what way?"

"You know, efficiency-wise, trustworthy-wise – and personality-wise?"

"For God's sake, you're talking in riddles again, Robert?"

"Um, what I'm getting at is she okay with checking the expenses properly and is she – shall I say – a little unnecessarily aggressive? Does she get a little above herself?"

Mack again explodes. "Samira is brilliant. She does her job with great care and dedication, and if she's occasionally a little bossy, I would remind you that she is, after all, the bureau manager. You wouldn't be raising her 'bossiness' if she were a man, would you Robert!"

Mack turns to Marina. "I'd like to say that this has been a pleasurable experience, but that would be a grotesque distortion of the truth."

"I'm sorry you feel that way," she responds, "but sometimes there are tricky situations that must be addressed. I will get Louise to escort you back to main reception. Have a good flight back to Glasgow and we look forward to hearing from you again from Armibar. And give my best wishes to your wife, Janie."

"It's Joan," he says crossly.

"Yes, Joan. I remember now. She writes very good history books, I seem to remember."

Mack picks up his stick and goes to Mary and Harry. "Well, it was nice to see you two, anyway," he says before leaving the room with Louise.

******

At the British Embassy in Armibar, Thomas Fulham has asked for a private chat with his boss, Bartholomew "Bart" Watson, whose cover title at the British Embassy is Anglo-Arab Cultural Liaison. It is proving to be a difficult meeting.

"Are you really serious about this?" Bart asks Thomas.

"Yes sir," replies Thomas, "I really would like to be transferred back to London."

"Good God, man! Why would you want to do that?"

"It's a personal matter."

"What sort of personal matter?"

"Just personal, sir!"

Bart is getting angry. "That's just not good enough, Thomas. You're an officer of Her Majesty's security services and this doesn't mean you can move in and out of postings whenever you feel like it. We're potentially facing a serious situation in this region and we desperately need well-informed people with excellent Arabic."

"I'm really sorry, sir, if you feel that I'm letting you down."

"Well, you are bloody letting me down," Bart shouts. "You are in Armibar because I personally recommended you as someone who'd be able to hack it, even in the toughest of situations. Now look at you! You come up with some weak and unspecified 'personal reasons'. That's pathetic!"

Thomas is crushed and does not reply. Bart studies him for a while before resuming his questioning. "Are you having trouble on the home front?"

"No, Flip – Felicity – and I are okay. We have our occasional ups and downs, like most married couples, but we're fine."

"What does she think of your wish to go back to HQ?"

"I haven't mentioned it to her," Thomas admits. "I thought maybe that I would be able to tell her I was being sent back to London because I was needed there to work on some sort of important commercial development project. I mean, she doesn't know what my real job is. She really does believe that I'm the commercial attaché."

"She must have her suspicions that you're not all you seem."

"I don't think so, sir. I keep a good secret and it's best that she's not troubled by my work."

"You have a point, but marriages can be put under stress if a wife discovers such a secret. They begin to wonder if there are other secrets to be uncovered."

Thomas nods agreement. A servant comes in with coffees and water and while these are being distributed, it gives Bart pause to reflect on what he has just heard. The servant bows and leaves and the conversation resumes.

"Look, there's no reasonable possibility that I can allow you to leave this post at this time. We need you here to deal with this Bin Hassan fellow and his *Soldiers of Allah*. Their involvement in that demo recently was very nasty. They seem to be lying low for the moment, but I suspect they're planning something big. And there's also the matter of your mate, Jackson. You know what our strategy is for him, and if you were to go back to London, we would lose that vital link."

Thomas goes to interrupt, but Bart presses on. "Let's do a deal. You stay here and get on with your most important mission and I promise you that once you – we – have dealt with Bin Hassan and neutralised his *Soldiers of Allah* you can go back to London with a useful promotion. I think that's reasonable, is it not?"

Thomas knows that this is the best his boss can offer and nods his agreement. He then goes on to raise consequential issues: "There are just two things I would like to mention, sir. Jackson Dunbar and

I were never close friends, but even so, I feel bad that we are using his weakness for gambling to screw him around quite so mercilessly. Once I've completed my mission, can you give me an assurance that we let him go to resume his normal life, whatever that is?

"Yes, we can do that, Thomas. I suspect that his usefulness will have expired by then anyway."

"Thank you."

"And what was the second thing?" Bart enquires.

"Um, I know we and our American friends have to play hardball with the terrorists and the Islamist-leaning faction in the regime, but that mess-up the other day with the assassination of Khaled Mohamed had some dreadful consequences."

"Agreed. It was not nice, but these things happen."

"I know, sir, but I also saw some of the film that wasn't transmitted. It was shocking what happened to those people – particularly the kids. What if those kids had been ours walking along that street?"

"Well, luckily they weren't, eh," Bart says without showing any real sympathy.

Thomas feels tears welling up in his eyes. There is a pause before Bart speaks again. "Are your 'personal reasons' the impact that matter had on you? Are you finding this side of your job emotionally difficult?"

Thomas nods agreement, and wipes away more tears.

"Look, Thomas, we have to meet nastiness with nastiness in our game, you know that, but I do understand your situation. I've been there, too. It's very hard, but someone must do it. I suggest you have a chat with Dr Blackstone in the embassy clinic. He's very understanding and will help restore your equilibrium. And if it makes you feel any better, I can tell you privately that the freelance lads who messed up the other day have been told they won't be paid for the job and have been shipped back home.

CHAPTER 21

Jackson is having a night in and in need of some female company. He rings the *Zing Zing Club*. "Hi Leila. It's Jackson here. Is Zareena there?"

"Sorry, Mr Jackson, she's not available," replies Leila without any warmth.

"That's the third time in the past week. What's going on?"

"She's just not available. I've got other nice girls you could see. There's Maggie. You'd like Maggie. She's very pretty and has just joined me from Wales."

"Wales? What's she doing out here, then?"

"Family problems back home, I think. But you'd like her. You really would."

Jackson is exasperated. "Sorry, Leila, Maggie would be too risky. Once she discovered I was on television and moderately well known, she would flog the story to some crappy tabloid newspaper back home."

Leila is becoming equally frustrated. "I'm sorry Mr Jackson. It's either Maggie or a couple of Russian girls who don't speak English or Arabic and only do bondage."

"Shit! Well, when will Zareena be available?"

"I honestly don't know. When she tells me, I suppose. She's part time because of her studies, and anyway, my girls have a right to choose who they want to see."

"Are you telling me that she's 'not available' in the sense that she doesn't want to see me?"

Leila pauses before replying. "Look Mr Jackson, I think you have to accept that you may not see Zareena again. You really should meet Maggie. You'd get on well with her, and as she's new on my books, I can offer a special introductory rate."

"No, no, no! It's Zareena or no-one." declares Jackson as he angrily ends the call.

******

Next morning, Jackson phones Samira to say he will be in a little late because he needs to meet a contact. In truth, he goes to Armibar

University and waits around the main entrance scanning the students as they turn up for their lectures. He sees Zareena arrive on a bus with a group of male and female students. He waves, hoping to catch her eye, but she appears not to see him. In desperation, he runs over to her. "Zareena, we need to talk," he tells her, as he takes her arm.

She angrily shakes him off. Get away from me," she shouts in Arabic. "I'm not Zareena. Who are you?"

Before Jackson can answer, she turns to her fellow students. "Does anyone know this man?" They all shake their head. She turns back to Jackson. "I don't know who you are, but if you don't go away now I'll call Security."

Jackson realises that he is out of order. "Sorry, sorry," he says, "I mistook you for an old friend."

Zareena and her group hurry on their way, muttering among themselves about the incident. The university grounds clear as the students enter the lecture rooms.

Jackson sits on a bench seat and reflects on his behaviour. He rings Samira and says nothing came out of the meeting with his contact and that he will be in as soon as he can find a taxi. She tells him that there is nothing important from the morning editorial meeting with London and not to rush.

Jackson downloads his latest emails onto his phone and while he is checking them, he discovers that Zareena has returned. She is furious. "What are you trying to do to me, Jacko? Ruin my reputation at the university?"

Jackson is full of remorse. "I'm so sorry. I just wanted to talk to you about why you won't see me."

Zareena looks around to ensure they aren't being watched. "Well, we're talking now. We've been friends as well as having a business arrangement, and it's because we've been friends that I don't want to see you any more. You're never going to stop gambling, are you!"

"But I will. I will. I just need that big win to set myself up again financially, then I'll quit."

Zareena is exasperated. "Listen to yourself, Jackson! You are, as you English like to say 'living in Cloud Cuckoo Land'. Gambling addicts are all the same."

"I'm <u>not</u> an addict," he stresses, "I can give up any time I like. I just need that big win. It's only a matter of time, then I'll stop."

She shakes her head. "And what about your drinking?"

"That's just because of the stresses I'm under – the explosion at the mosque, rescuing Mack, and my money worries. Once I set myself up financially again, I won't need to drink. I know I can be a better man."

Zareena studies Jackson despairingly and again shakes her head. "Well, until you do become a better man, I'm not interested in seeing you. Now, I must go or I'll miss my lecture. Good bye, my friend." She walks back towards the university complex and Jackson wearily hails a passing taxi.

******

Jackson is shaken by Zareena's character assessment and her ending of their relationship, but such is his state of mind that he comes to the conclusion that the best solution to his problem is to accelerate his ambition to score the Big Win with his gambling. All he needs is a suitable stake. His shares have been cashed in and his flat in London would take too long to sell. Then he remembers Granny Dunbar's jewellery.

Two hours later, Jackson is in a shabby pawn shop in a deprived part of the city. He is wearing a floppy sun hat and large dark glasses to minimise the chances of him being recognised. He had lied to Samira that he is chasing another lead on *Soldiers of Allah*. In fact, he caught a taxi back to his apartment where he went through his wardrobes to find the small carved wooden box containing the jewellery inherited from his grandmother.

He empties the contents of the box onto the shop counter. There is an assortment of rings and cheap necklaces. The pawnbroker, a North African, wears a shabby Western suit and an equally-shabby keffiyeh. He dismissively pushes the rings and necklaces to one side. "Twenty-five dollar for those," he says in broken English.

203

His eye is caught by a small velvet bag. He empties it into his hand and sees a small diamond-encrusted brooch. He studies it through a jeweller's magnifying eyeglass and nods that he is interested. "I give you a thousand."

"You must be joking," declares Jackson, "that's Cartier!"

The pawnbroker shrugs. "One thousand," he repeats.

Jackson scoops up the jewellery into its box. "That's a rip-off. I'll find somewhere else for a better price."

He heads for the exit, but the pawnbroker calls him back. "My friend," he says, "let me see brooch again."

Jackson returns to the counter and the pawnbroker affects to study the brooch more carefully. "Okay, friend. Very nice. Brooch 2000. Rest 500."

Jackson knows this is still a rip-off, but he accepts that it will probably be all he can get in his current circumstances. "Okay," he says, "but in American dollars and it's a loan, not a sale. I'll return to collect the items within a week."

The pawnbroker nods agreement and goes to a safe from which he takes a tin containing bundles of American dollars. He counts out the loan in 50 and 100 dollars notes and gives Jackson a scribbled receipt. "Interest for week 10%," he adds, "if you not return in week I sell."

"I'll be back," Jackson assures him.

As the pawnbroker is about to return the jewels to their box, he notices a small black-and-white photograph lying on the bottom. It is of an elderly grey-haired woman.

"You want?" the pawnbroker asks Jackson.

"Oh, thanks," says Jackson. It's a photo of his granny and he slips it carefully into his shirt pocket.

******

Back at his apartment, Jackson puts the pawnbroker's loan in a drawer and decides that he will investigate what he might get for his flat in London, should he decide to put it on the market. He rings his estate agency and is put through to Roderick Turner. "Hi Roderick. It's Jackson Dunbar. I'm the chap who bought that flat in

Willoughby Road last year. You know, the one you rent out for me."

"Ah yes, Mr Dunbar, of course. I see on the telly you've been leading an exciting life in Arabia. I hope you're now safe and well."

"Yes, I'm fine," replies Jackson. "I'm calling to explore whether I should sell the flat."

"You mean now?"

"Yes, well as soon as possible."

Roderick hesitates. "Umm, is that a good idea just now?" he asks.

"Why do you ask that?"

"Only that the market is a bit flat at the moment and as a new tenant has just moved in, it might have a negative impact on the price we can get."

"What's a realistic figure?"

"Well, Mr Dunbar, taking all things into consideration, I would reckon £350,000.

"Bloody hell!" explodes Jackson, "that's what I paid for it."

"Yes, well, as I've said, the market is a bit flat at the moment, and as you took out private mortgages totalling 90% of the selling price, the rent you're getting is only just covering the repayments. To be honest, Mr Dunbar, I would stick with the flat for a few more years until the market picks up."

"So much for your assurances that the flat would be a nice little earner."

"Situations sometimes change, Mr Dunbar, and just for the moment, we're going through a bit of an unexpected dip in the market."

"Thanks for nothing, Roderick," says Jackson as he ends the call.

******

Jackson returns to the bureau in ill temper, but explains this away to the team as frustration that his prospective "lead" on the *Soldiers of Allah* had come to nothing, causing him to waste most of

205

his morning. He goes to his desk and notices a *Post It* sticker on his screen. "Call your mother," it says.

He waves the sticker at Samira. "What's she want this time?"

Samira shrugs her shoulders. "Sorry, Jacko, I don't know, but she sounded very angry. She said something about the DG refusing to discuss your career. She seemed particularly cross that his letter to her hadn't even been signed by him."

"Oh fuck!" Jackson exclaims. "That woman is driving me nuts!"

Pete overhears the exchange and wants to know what is going on. "Should I take it, mate, that your mum has been trying to suck up to the DG to your career advantage?"

"Get stuffed, Pete! I've got enough on my mind without extra needle from you."

Samira intervenes before a row gets out of hand. "Stop it, boys, please!" She checks to see that Dick is busy at his desk and that the door to the office is closed, then calls Jackson and Pete over to her desk. "I've just had some very good news," she whispers.

"What's that," Pete asks.

"I'm not telling," she teases, "I want it to be a surprise."

"Well, when will we get that surprise?" Jackson wants to know.

"Just be here on time for tomorrow morning's editorial meeting," she instructs.

The rest of the day goes quietly and Jackson returns to his apartment with the intention of trying his chances at the roulette tables at Archibald's gambling den. But his luck is out. Archibald is hosting an invitation-only night and won't be able to accommodate him until later in the week. Jackson logs on to *Towering Treasures Inc* but his credit has expired. He decides instead on a shower, a beer, a bit of undemanding television and an early night, wanting to be ready and fresh for Samira's promised surprise tomorrow morning.

******

The next morning Jackson, Pete, Yassin, Farouk and Samira assemble on time for the morning editorial conference. Unusually, Dick is not at his desk. "Where's Psycho?" asks Pete.

"Ah," replies Samira, "that's Part One of your surprise. He flew back to London last night and won't be returning any time soon."

There is spontaneous applause from the rest of the team. "So what's Part Two?" enquires Jackson.

Samira gives a broad grin and goes to the bureau entrance. "Here's Part Two," she says as she opens the door. There is a pause, then Mack Galbraith appears in his usual scruffy clothes and waves his walking stick in greeting. There is another burst of applause and cheering.

Mack joins the team in the office, still walking with a slight limp, grinning from ear to ear and thrilled to be back at work. He looks around at his tidy and squeaky-clean office. "What's happened here?!" No answer is necessary as the team laugh loudly. He sniffs the air. "What's that smell?" Samira informs him that it is Dick's air freshener. "Christ!" is his only response.

Mack goes to the new leather chair bought by Dick and eases himself into it. "I like this chair anyway," he declares, "but where are my ash trays?"

"They're here, Mack," says Samira as she retrieves two from a cupboard and puts them on his desk.

"That's better," he says. He points his walking stick at the bright "No Smoking" signs Dick had stuck to the walls. "And you can take those down right now." There is more laughter as he offers a cigarette to Yassin and lights one up himself."

Samira winces. "If you don't mind me saying so, Mack, we did rather enjoy this place being a 'no smoking' area."

"Okay, I'll see what I can do to cut it down."

Pete chips in. "Let's do a deal, Mack: you cut down the smoking and I'll stop wearing stupid T-shirts to work."

"I see you're still a cheeky young bugger!" Mack responds with a resigned smile. He points to Pete's T-shirt displaying a grotesque cartoon of the Queen disporting herself in a most unladylike manner. "I take it you're just trying to wind me up with that one."

"No, not really," replies Pete, "it was intended to wind up 'Psycho'. I thought he'd still be here. But you can relax. As of today

I'll be a model of sartorial propriety. The T-shirt joke has run its course."

Mack nods approvingly and claps his hands. "Well, we'd better talk to London." He dials the Foreign Desk and Mary Dunstan answers. "Good morning, Mack. Very pleased to hear you back on base."

"Yes, Mary, wonderful to be here again with the team, although I doubt that I'll be able to find anything now that Psycho has tidied everything away." Mary laughs. "I understand, Mack. I've seen your office and I also know what Dick's is like. I think a surgeon could carry out a major operation on top of his desk without the risk of the patient catching an infection. Anyway, down to business... We have a packed diary of local and foreign stories today, so unless you've got something really outstanding, we won't need anything from you. It'll be a good day for you to settle back in and return your desk and ashtray to their usual overflowing state."

Mack and the rest of the team laugh. "Thanks, Mary. Talk again tomorrow."

"Indeed, Mack, but when you get a moment I think we should have a private chat about some of the things that were raised when you were here for that embarrassing lunch."

Mack shifts uncomfortably in his chair and the rest of the team exchange enquiring glances. "Will do," he says as he ends the call.

"What was that about, boss?" asks Pete.

"Oh, just a little bit of shitty point-scoring by some of the bampot bosses with nothing better to do with their dreary lives. Nothing for you to worry about."

The meeting breaks up and Mack is left alone to make the requested call to Mary. She tips him off that the rumours about Jackson and Samira appear to be coming from Dick Passick. He agrees that this is most likely and thanks her for the warning.

Samira enters his office with a folder of expenses claims. "Why didn't Psycho do these?" he asks.

"He was concerned that there were so few receipts and we agreed it was best to leave them for you to approve," she explains.

Mack raises an eyebrow. "Receipts? Obviously someone who's never worked in the Developing World," he observes.

Samira gets up to leave, but he motions her to stay. "How did Psycho behave while he was here?" he asks. "Any conflicts?"

"Oh, we established a working relationship with him, eventually. He's not a man you naturally admire or like, but there was nothing we couldn't handle."

Mack wants to know more. "Were there any incidents that I should be aware of? Anything that might have provoked him to raise matters with our bosses?"

"As I said, Mack, there was nothing we couldn't handle and he's returned home basking in the reflected glory of how we handled the coverage of the assassination of Khaled Mohamed. He should have no reason to bad-mouth us."

"I'm pleased to hear that," says Mack.

It's now Samira's turn to ask questions. "Is there something you should be telling me?"

Mack lights a cigarette while he considers an answer. "Umm. Well, there's something that we should keep between the two of us… Someone has told London that Jackson has a gambling problem and that he's even using his computer here to access a website."

Samira is surprised. "That's news to me. He's always short of cash, but I've just accepted that he isn't very good with money and that he's still having problems with some bad property purchase back home."

"What about his computer? Have you seen anything that would suggest he's an online gambler?"

"No, Mack. Nothing. The only way to find out would be if he goes away from his computer with it still logged on. His browsing history would tell us which sites he visits, but I would never want to do that."

"No, no, we mustn't do that," agrees Mack. "I think we can assume that this is some story concocted by Psycho. I'll tell London that I've investigated and found that it's all bull manure."

CHAPTER 22

That evening, Jackson is back at his apartment for a snack meal and a shower in preparation for a few hours at Archibald's gambling den. He makes an upsetting discovery: He finds his photograph of Granny Dunbar in a tattered state on the kitchen bench. It is attached by a paper clip to a note scribbled in Arabic. The note is from his maid and it tells him that she found the photograph in a shirt pocket after putting his clothes through the washing machine and drier. He thumps the bench in anger, but he knows it is mostly his fault. He tries to smooth the photograph, but it is beyond salvaging and he eventually drops it in the rubbish bin with a sigh.

A couple of hours later, Jackson is refreshed and aiming to make his fortune at Archibald's roulette tables, using the loan raised by his granny's jewellery. Archibald tells him he can stay just an hour because he has a group of high-rollers who are taking over the den for another late-night invitation-only event. At the end of the hour, Jackson is on a winning streak and has more than tripled his money, but Archibald tells him his time is up.

"Oh c'mon," shouts Jackson, "that's not fair. You're sending me away because I'm winning."

"You'd be most welcome to stay here to allow me to take my losses back from you," assures Archibald, "but my establishment has been booked by a group of very wealthy clients who would regard your bets as pocket money. You have your winnings, so go away quietly or I will have you forcibly removed."

Jackson has no choice, so leaves quietly and hails a taxi to take him to his apartment. He is both frustrated and elated. On the one hand, he is annoyed that his time at the gambling tables has been interrupted; on the other, he deludes himself that his winnings tonight are merely a forerunner to the big money that will allow him to escape all his debts and return to a gambling-free life. Meantime, it will allow him to recover Granny Dunbar's jewellery from the pawnbroker. He vows to do that tomorrow.

******

At the next morning's editorial meeting, the team notes that Mack's desk is rapidly returning to its pre-Dick Passick state, but in a concession to his colleagues, Mack stubs out his cigarette and doesn't light another while the meeting progresses.

Pete has news from his girlfriend, Kelly. She has told him that she saw a document marked "Confidential" that was accidentally left on the office photocopier. It lays out provisional plans for her bank to pull out of Central Arabia if the bombings and other terrorist acts don't end soon.

"Any chance of her sneaking a copy of the document to you?" Mack asks.

"Fair go!" exclaims Pete. "I'm not going to ask her to do that. She could be fired, especially as some of her workmates know we're friends."

"Understood, laddie. Still, it's very useful to be aware that at least one bank is getting nervous about the situation here. No doubt you'll let us know if these provisional plans harden."

"Sure, boss."

Mack sees a new Reuters message on his computer screen. It reports that a new Development Minister has been appointed. He is Hadeed Hussam, said to be pro-Western and a supporter of President Hasani.

"Have either of you heard of him?" Mack asks Farouk and Yassin.

They both shake their heads.

"Oh well. I'll see what I can find out and do a radio piece for World Service," says Mack. "As for Jackson, I suggest you spend the day touring the foreign embassies here to see if they have something we might be missing. Perhaps Pete could see if there's any film of this guy Hussam."

The meeting breaks up. Pete goes to his locker and changes into a plain T-shirt without any provocative illustrations. Jackson goes back to his desk and discreetly phones Thomas to discuss the news of the Development Minister appointment. He is told that Hussam is a political lightweight – a technocrat who does not have the

Machiavellian skills or network support to present President Hasani with a challenge.

Jackson wants to know if the bug he planted in the minister's office is still active. He is told that it is, but because of Hussam's low status, is unlikely to provide any useful information. Anyway, the battery is beginning to run down. "To be honest," he tells Jackson, "our priority has to be the mysterious silence of your terrorist buddy, Bin Hassan. Have you heard anything from him lately?" Jackson assures him that he hasn't.

Jackson spends most of the day visiting as many embassies as will see him, but gains no new information, or at least no new information that is credible. His impression is that most European diplomats in the city see the American Embassy in Armibar as the only major player in the city. Even the Russian Embassy thinks that.

His last task for the day is to call at the pawnshop to recover Granny Dunbar's jewellery. He is in for a shock. He hands the pawnbroker his receipt and begins counting out the payment from yesterday's roulette winnings. "You're $2500 back, plus interest of $250. Right?" he declares.

The pawnbroker shakes his head. "No, $500 and $50 interest."

"Eh? But that's just for the rings and necklaces! What about the brooch?"

"I keep brooch to sell. $10,000," he says.

Jackson is dismayed. "No, no, no! The brooch is mine. Give it back!"

"No, it Cartier. I sell it for much dollar."

"You can't do that," shouts Jackson, "that was my grandmother's. It has to stay in my family."

There is a pause, then the pawnbroker announces "Okay. You can have for $8,000."

"That's robbery," says Jackson, still shouting.

"You insult me," says the pawnbroker, "it $8,000."

"I don't have $8,000."

"How much you have? You show me. Empty your pockets!"

The pawnbroker rings a bell beneath the counter and is promptly joined by two men in traditional wear and oversize dark glasses. Jackson has no option but to empty his pockets onto the counter. The pawnbroker pushes Jackson's key ring, pens and notebook to one side and takes Jackson's large roll of dollars. He expertly counts the banknotes. They total $6,500. He shrugs and tells Jackson that he will accept that sum for the jewels.

Jackson returns his personal items to his pockets while the pawnbroker unlocks his safe and places Granny Dunbar's box of jewellery on the counter. Jackson is furious, but there is nothing he can do about it. He takes the jewellery and goes to leave, but the pawnbroker waves him back and hands him $10. "For taxi home," says the pawnbroker with a smirk.

Back at his apartment, with just $1 left after paying for his taxi, Jackson pours himself a large whisky. He is rattled, but not yet prepared to accept that his latest misfortune is largely due to his own foolish behaviour.

******

Next morning at the bureau, Jackson is recovering from a hangover and still deeply upset about what happened over Granny Dunbar's jewellery, but he affects a cheerful air. Mack returns to the subject of the local troubles. Now that President Hasani's rival, Khaled Mohamed, has been removed from the scene, the only recent violence in Armibar has been some low-level clashes between criminal gangs. He wonders why nothing has been heard of the *Soldiers of Allah* or Bin Hassan.

"Is there any way you can get in touch with him?" Mack asks.

Jackson shakes his head. "Sorry, he just makes very brief calls from a mobile whenever he wants to tell me something."

Mack thinks about this for a bit before coming up with an answer. "Tell you what… Why don't I write a general piece about the security situation here and suggest in passing that *Soldiers of Allah* might no longer exist? Do you reckon that might flush out Bin Hassan, if he's still active?"

"It could, Mack. It's worth a try, anyway. Just don't show me the piece before you send it so that I have an element of denial."

"Right then," Mack announces, "I'll knock together something now and put it over before lunch."

"Righto," replies Jackson, "I'll make myself scarce while you do it. I've been thinking of doing a package on the Fouad Rehabilitation Centre."

"Oh, what's that?"

"It's a charity that helps the victims of terrorism and violence in Central Arabia. Mostly looks after kids who've been injured."

"It sounds a bit marginal. I'm not sure we could successfully pitch it to London. Is there a British angle?"

"Yes, it's run by this English woman who's married to some guy at the British Embassy."

"Do I know her?"

"Possibly. Felicity Fulham."

"Mmm. I remember her. An interesting woman. I met her a few months ago at an embassy cocktail party. Her husband is commercial attaché or somesuch. He's a bit of a smooth-talking bastard, I thought, but I guess you have to be in that sort of job."

"Yes, I guess so," agrees Jackson. "Anyway, I think I'll pop round to the centre now and see if they'd be interested in me doing a TV piece. By the way, I've just given Samira my latest expenses and would appreciate it if you could sign them off today."

"Short again, Jacko?"

"Sorry, but I've had some unexpected costs that have left me a bit tight until my salary comes through tomorrow."

Mack shrugs his shoulders, reminded of what was suggested in London about Jackson's constant financial shortfalls.

******

Felicity is hard at work with her patients when Jackson turns up at the Fouad Centre. She is replacing the bandages on the stump of an arm of a young girl. She is pleased to see Jackson. "This is a nice surprise. What brings you here?"

"Officially, I'm here to explore the possibility of doing that TV report I mentioned before, but I also thought it would be nice to catch up with you."

"Thank you," she says, giving him a broad smile.

Jackson points to the young girl being bandaged. "What happened to her? Another plaza bomb victim?"

"No, she was messing about with some unexploded stuff lying on a bit of wasteland. She's lucky to be alive."

Felicity completes the bandaging. The little girl is quietly weeping. Felicity gives her a reassuring hug and turns back to Jackson. "Have you time for a coffee?"

"Sure. It's a quiet day so far."

They move to the kitchen where Felicity lights a portable gas stove under a kettle. She goes to a large cupboard and points to the contents. "There you are, Jacko: all the medicines and bandages we bought with your money."

He nods approvingly. "Well, money very well spent. It's my pleasure to have helped out."

The kettle is now boiled and Felicity makes two cups of instant coffee. She and Jackson sit down in a couple of battered leather seats.

"How are things with Thomas? Any more drunken episodes?" Jackson asks.

"No, nothing like that. He seems a little less stressed and was very embarrassed about how he behaved that night."

"Are the kids okay?"

"Oh yes, they're fine, but a little cautious when he's around because of his drunken outburst the other night."

There is a pause while they sip their coffees, then it is Felicity's turn to ask questions. "So, how have things been with you, Jacko?"

He hesitates before answering. "Umm, a mix of good and bad, I suppose. The best bit is that Mack is back running the bureau instead of that nasty bag of shit, Dick Passick."

"And the bad?"

"Just a few temporary financial problems that need sorting out."

Felicity studies him intently. "You've been gambling again, haven't you!"

"Just occasionally – as a distraction really."

"A distraction from what?"

"Well, you know, the mosque bombing and that sort of thing. But, you know, I'll have things sorted soon."

Felicity knows Jackson too well and is sure there is more to it than that. "Just how much gambling? And how much drinking?"

"It's okay. It's manageable," he insists.

"I've heard that before, Jacko. I hope you're not going back to the bad old days."

Jackson is irritated. "Leave off, will you! The 'bad old days' as you so tactlessly put them, are behind me."

"Sorry, Jacko," she says, "it's not my business anymore, but I still do worry about you."

They finish their coffee in an uneasy silence, broken only when Felicity says she must get back to her patients. He promises that he will be in touch again if he gets the go-ahead for the TV feature.

******

Jackson returns to the bureau to collect his expenses – mostly hospitality and a few taxi fares totalling $120 – and checks his computer to see if there is anything that needs his attention. All is quiet and Mack tells him that his promised story raising questions about *Soldiers of Allah* has been written and delivered to London. He also reports that one of the TV magazine programmes is interested in taking a feature on Felicity's rehab centre.

With Mack's agreement, Jackson says he will spend the rest of the day on call back at his apartment. When Yassin delivers him there, he is immediately greeted by the sight of a partly-consumed bottle of whisky on the kitchen bench. He is unsettled by Felicity's reference to the "bad old days" and empties the bottle into the sink. He feels better for this positive act and wishes Felicity could see him doing it. He makes a cup of coffee, and ponders the dire financial situation he once again finds himself in.

He switches on his electric keyboard, but before he can play anything, the telephone rings. It is Bin Hassan – the call he was hoping for. "What's this nonsense I've heard about my group disbanding?" his old school friend demands.

"Where did you hear that?" replies Jackson, affecting not to know.

"Mack Galbraith on your news just now."

"Oh, I see."

"It's rubbish, Roger – and we're about to prove it. It's pay-back time for the Americans. Just you wait!"

"Binnie, please!" implores Jackson. Please stop this before it's too late. It's crazy. Please, Binnie!"

The line goes dead.

******

Half an hour later, Jackson makes a surprise return to the bureau. He goes straight into Mack's office and breathlessly tells him about the call from Bin Hassan. They are immediately faced with a serious dilemma. Do they tell the Americans and risk losing an important contact, or do they say nothing and hope that it is an empty boast? It quickly becomes clear that they must alert the American Embassy, even though the warning is in such vague terms.

As they consider how best to do this, Samira pokes her head in the door. "Mack, have you seen the service message from Reuters?" Mack turns to his computer and sees. "URGENT: Unexplained tightening of security around US Embassy, Armibar. More later."

Mack turns back to Jackson. "You'd better get down there fast and find out what's going on. Pick up Pete on the way. We're going to have to disturb his 'quality time' with his Aussie lady friend. I'll phone him now to make sure he has time to get his trousers back on!"

By the time Yassin and Jackson reach Independence Avenue, Pete is already waiting outside girlfriend Kelly's gated apartment block. He is annoyed as he gets into the car. "Christ! A guy can't even have a shag without being ordered out on a story. What the hell's this one about, Jacko?"

217

"Not sure, but there's something going on at the American Embassy. It might be big."

As they approach the embassy compound, they find the neighbouring streets barricaded by American marines in armoured vehicles. They wave their press passes and are allowed through to the wide avenue where the embassy – once the grand palace of an Arab dignitary – is situated in spacious grounds surrounded by high iron railings and razor wire. Concrete slabs have been placed strategically around the compound with the specific intention of stopping car and truck bombs from reaching the grounds. There are more armed marines in armoured vehicles, and a body scanner has been set up at the entrance to the building.

Their car is ordered to park on the opposite of the avenue, about 100 metres from the embassy building. Pete jumps from the car and starts filming. Jackson phones Mack to report his arrival and is told that there has been nothing new from Reuters or any of the other agencies. He hurries towards the embassy gates and is surprised to see Thomas Fulham leaving.

"Hey, Thomas, what are you doing here?" he demands.

"I'm here for the same reason as you – the tip off from your old friend Binnie."

Jackson is taken aback. "What do you mean?"

"Oh for Christ's sake, Jackson! Stop making out you don't know any Binnie. Of course you do! You went to school with him – Ahmed Faisel Bin Hassan. That was easy to find out."

Jackson knows that he can no longer deny the connection. "So, you've also been monitoring his calls to me?"

"Of course, we are. That's our fucking job. We hear the lot: your calls to the Zing Zing Club, your rows with your mother and your calls from your old school mate, Binnie. And I guess from the tone of your phone discussions with my wife, there's more to your one-time relationship than you'd be prepared to admit."

Jackson is shaken by this last revelation. "You're wrong," he protests, "we're just good friends, no more than that."

Thomas laughs. "Yes, I know that. She'd be mad to be involved with someone as screwed up as you."

Jackson doesn't respond.

"Anyway, get on with doing your story, dear boy," Thomas tells him. "Binnie is just trying to put the frighteners on us, I reckon. He would guess that we're listening to his calls, which is why they're so brief and why he uses a different mobile from a different part of the city whenever he phones you. But it's inevitable that one of these days he'll slip up and we'll get him."

"Don't underestimate him, Thomas. He's a very clever chap committed to his cause, which seems to be largely aimed at the Americans."

"Maybe, but the Yanks have their security well in hand. They know their stuff."

"I'm not so sure. It's an old building and doesn't look as though it'd withstand a well-placed rocket or bomb."

"Don't worry about that, Jacko. It may look like a vulnerable building, but in truth, it's been turned into a bunker."

"Well, I hope they're checking their drains. They don't want a repeat of what happened with Khaled Mohamed."

"Their drains are good. I checked that. There are super-strong grilles across them and they're inspected every day for anything suspicious. If the *Soldiers of Allah* do try anything, it will be with a truck bomb or something like that, but they won't be able to get past the barriers."

"I hope you're right," says Jackson as Thomas goes to his waiting embassy car and it is waved on its way.

CHAPTER 23

Jackson and Pete are joined by their CNN and Al-Jazeera rivals, along with the news agencies and a couple of reporters from the state-run media. Only Jackson knows why there is this tightened security. After a while, press officer Randy Abrahams comes out of the embassy to give a briefing to the assembled journalists. He plays down the significance of the extra security, claiming it is primarily an exercise to demonstrate to potential attackers that they cannot succeed. He denies there have been any specific threats. Most of the journalists take this statement at face value and go back to their offices.

The CNN and Al-Jazeera crews also want to leave, but are reluctant to do so while Jackson and Pete remain on the spot. Mack instructs his team to stay put until at least the evening. All three crews send satellite reports back to their bases, but these get only the briefest of showings in view of the downbeat and reassuring statement by Randy Abrahams.

Finally, as the sun goes down, Mack allows the team to leave. Yassin drops Pete off at Kelly's address and returns Jackson to his apartment. Once inside, Jackson finds a message waiting on his answering machine. It is from Binnie and it is brief and to the point: "It's noon tomorrow, Roger. Exactly at noon. Be there, but don't get too close."

Jackson is baffled why the message is so specific. Binnie must know the line is likely to be monitored by the security services, so why also tip them off? Is it an attempt to frighten or deliberately mislead them? Is he just playing games?

Jackson decides to go back to the bureau so that he can talk privately to Mack. They go into a huddle, but they get no nearer to coming to any plausible conclusions about the purpose of Binnie's message.

Mack decides that the time has come when he must tell Marina Kerner about the source of Jackson's information. He rings her office and the call is taken by the deputy head of news.

"Good evening, Robert, I need to speak to Marina," says Mack.

"She's very busy at the moment. Perhaps I can deal with your call."

"Sorry, but I must speak to Marina."

"Well, it can't be so important that I can't deal with it."

Mack is getting angry. "Don't piss me about, Robert, just put me onto Marina."

There is a pause and some clicks on the line before the call is picked up by Marina: "Yes, Mack, what's the problem? Not a complaint, I hope."

"No, it's not a complaint; it's something you need to know about the scoops that Jackson has been getting."

Mack explains in broad terms that Jackson has been getting direct messages from the leader of the *Soldiers of Allah* and that this has become known to the British and American security services. He also mentions the mystery about the latest specific threat.

"Why didn't you tell me about Jackson's source when you were here?" she demands.

"I decided that it was best you didn't know, but the situation has now changed because I'm not sure where this is taking us."

"Yes, I can see that, Mack. Make sure we're not being taken for suckers as a mouthpiece for a two-bit terrorist group with high, unrealised ambitions. I don't want any blowback over this. The government is still breathing fire over our recent revelations about the minister who was caught in a pants-down situation with an opposition spokeswoman."

"I understand. It's very sensitive, but I think it'll be okay. I'll send our team to the embassy tomorrow even though it seems highly likely to be a total waste of time. All the evidence is that the embassy security is rock solid."

There is a pause while Marina considers the situation, then she gives the go-ahead, adding "Make sure those guys of yours are wearing flak jackets and helmets. I don't want families complaining that we don't observe a duty of care with our staff. Is that understood, Mack?"

"Yes, it is very well understood, Marina," he replies, exchanging resigned smiles with Jackson, who is still sitting beside him.

******

Next morning, Yassin drives Jackson and Pete back to the American Embassy and they park at the same spot as yesterday. There is no sign of other news teams.

The extra barriers set up the previous day are still in place, but there is a more relaxed atmosphere among the marines on guard duty. Jackson assumes that Binnie's call to him yesterday was monitored, but if that was the case, it isn't obvious that it is being taken too seriously.

Pete is having another ill-tempered day. "Surely Mack doesn't expect us to waste another boring 12 hours here."

"Just shut up, Pete!" orders Jackson, "the boss wants us here, and here is where we'll stay as long as he wants us to. Why don't you get out of the car and make yourself useful by getting some shots around the embassy?"

Pete grumpily agrees. Yassin hands him a flak jacket and steel helmet. "Bugger that, Yassin. I'll look like a poseur and a wimp."

Jackson checks his watch. "It's now 11.30. Make sure that you're back here before noon," he instructs Pete.

"Why so time-specific, mate?"

"Don't ask! Just make bloody sure that you're back here before noon."

"Jesus, mate! Lighten up!" he tells Jackson as he picks up his camera and walks off down the street.

******

It is five minutes before noon and Jackson is feeling the tension, worried that Pete has not returned to the car as ordered. He sees his cameraman nonchalantly making his way back and waves to him to hurry up.

It is now two minutes to noon, and Jackson's gut tightens as he and Yassin intently study their surroundings. Pete reaches the vehicle and sits on the bonnet, his camera beside him.

"Better get the camera ready, Pete," says Jackson. Pete shrugs irritably and switches it on. "Christ, mate! You're really getting on my tits!"

Jackson ignores the complaint and studies his watch intently as the seconds and minutes tick by. It is now five minutes past the hour. Nothing has happened and he begins to feel a mixture of disappointment and relief.

He dials Mack on his mobile, but before the call can be picked up, there is a loud rumble. The road beneath them vibrates, then shakes violently. Pete is toppled from the bonnet onto the road. He jumps up and begins filming wildly, not understanding what is happening or what will happen next.

Jackson and Yassin, still in their car, watch stunned as the embassy is jerked from its foundations and splits apart. Flames, smoke, rocks and earth shoot high into the sky. Pete steadies himself against the car as he continues filming the surreal scene unfolding before him.

Debris begins raining down on Pete and the car. Pete is knocked to the ground. The windscreen of the car is shattered.

Yassin scrambles into the back seat, forces a door open and drags Pete and his camera inside. He is bleeding from dozens of cuts on his head, arms and hands. Despite this, he thrusts the camera out the window and resumes filming.

There is another, different rumble as the shattered embassy building sinks into the ground in slow motion. It comes to rest a couple of metres below the level it was just seconds before. A brief chilling silence follows, broken only by the sound of debris falling back to the ground. Then there are screams from the injured and the terrified.

"Fuck me!" exclaims Jackson to himself, "that's pay-back – big time!"

******

At the bureau, Mack, Samira and Farouk hear the sound of the explosion as it bounces back and forth across the city. "Boy, that's a really big one, Mack!" shouts Samira. "And I bet it's the American Embassy," Mack shouts back.

He runs to his phone and tries to raise Jackson, but Jackson is simultaneously trying to phone him. Then the mobile network is shut down.

"Did they take the satellite kit with them?" Mack calls to Farouk.

"Yes, boss, they have all they need."

"Thank God for that!"

"I hope the boys are all okay," says Samira.

"Oh, they'll be alright," replies Mack as he dials the Foreign News Desk in London to tell them to clear the decks for a big story.

******

There is chaos at the wrecked American Embassy. As Pete and Yassin line up their portable transmitter with a satellite, Jackson tries to assemble some coherent thoughts for a live report. Bewildered residents and workers in the neighbourhood emerge into the streets to survey the wreckage. Part of the embassy is on fire and some of the wounded are desperately clambering from the wreckage of what had, until a short time ago, been widely considered to be a terrorist-proof fortress.

The satellite link with London is operational and Pete connects his camera, ready to transmit his pictures uncut and live into World News. Yassin is concerned about Pete's injuries, but he insists they are nothing to worry about. Blood is running down his face, but he wipes it away on his shirt sleeve.

There is a crossover from the World News and Pete turns his camera on Jackson for a breathless live introduction to the startling film taken as the embassy is destroyed. Pete then transmits further live pictures back as Jackson runs to the twisted embassy railings to look into the wreckage. He can see a number of bodies. The sirens of the emergency services can be heard approaching.

Mack is astonished as he watches the World News output on the monitors in his office. He is frustrated that his leg wound stops him from joining his team on the scene. Samira volunteers to go instead.

Mack agrees and says Farouk should go with her to provide technical back-up.

Samira and Farouk's trip by taxi to the embassy is a difficult one because many roads are choked or closed to allow ambulances and security vehicles unrestricted movement. They are forced to make the final few blocks by foot.

Samira is horrified to discover Pete in shock and near collapse from his injuries. She orders him to give his camera to Farouk and to lie down in the back seat of their vehicle where she can clean him up and bandage his wounds using the car's First Aid kit. She remonstrates with him about his failure to wear his flak jacket and helmet.

The CNN crew arrive on foot, having been unable to negotiate the traffic in their car. They have a camera, but no satellite equipment which had to be left in their vehicle. Almost at the same time, the Al-Jazeera team arrives, also on foot and breathless.

Jackson is in the middle of a live report with Farouk operating the camera. The moment he finishes he is approached by Jane Kubinski and Omar Abbas, both demanding to know how he came to be on the scene at such a fortuitous time.

"Just a coincidence," he insists. "Nothing else was happening, so Mack sent us here to do a possible follow-up to yesterday's story. We just got lucky again."

"Bullshit!" shouts Jane.

"I agree," says Omar. "Something fishy is going on with your tip offs, Jacko."

Jackson shrugs dismissively. "I can't stand around arguing with you about this. I've got another 'live' to do. If you stop your sour-grapes whingeing, I'll try to find you both a couple of five-minute slots on our satellite." He goes back in front of his camera and prepares for another cross-over.

Samira concludes that none of Pete's injuries requires urgent hospital attention. She does what she can to make him comfortable and goes to the wreckage of the embassy. A couple of marines are doing their best, without much success, to hose down the fire raging at the back of the building. A string of stretchers bring out the casualties. Among the walking wounded is press attaché Randy Abrahams who is escorting a stretcher about to be loaded into an ambulance. Samira runs to him. "Are you okay?" He nods. "Yes. Just minor cuts, I think, but he's not too good." Samira turns to see Ambassador Costello lying motionless on the stretcher in a blood-covered ripped shirt and boxer shorts.

"Oh my God!"

"The ceiling of his office collapsed on him," explains Randy. "I doubt he'll make it to the hospital alive."

Samira runs back towards Jackson, who is in the middle of another live report and having to shout to be heard above the noise. She stands by the camera, waving her hands frantically to indicate that she has important news. Jackson motions her over to join him in front of the camera.

My colleague Samira Lang has been over to the ruins to watch the rescue operation. What can you tell us?

> *Well, the most important news, Jackson, is that among the many casualties being brought out from the wreckage is the American ambassador, Andrew Costello. I saw that he was very badly wounded.*

Are you quite sure it is Ambassador Costello?

> *It's definitely him. Our bureau chief, Mack Galbraith, and I had lunch with him, here at the embassy, only recently.*

Thanks for that, Samira. The news about Ambassador Costello will certainly raise the anger here and in Washington to a much higher level – and I predict, a much more dangerous one. I believe the ambassador has a family connection to the White House. Is that correct, Samira?

> *Yes, it is. He's a cousin of President Benson and I believe they're quite close.*

Thank you for that, Samira. That certainly adds another important element to the story... Now back to Bill Smythe in our studio in London.

"Don't go just yet, Jackson," Bill calls out. "Perhaps you can answer a question that's already doing the rounds here: how did the terrorists manage to get so much high explosive beneath the embassy? Would they have used the drains, like they did during the recent assassination of the Central Arabian Development Minister, Khaled Mohamed?"

That's a very good question, Bill, but I have no answer to it – at least not just yet. Only yesterday, when I was reporting on the security exercise here, I asked the embassy people about the drains. They assured me that they had made them secure. The only other possibility that comes to mind is that the terrorists dug tunnels under the building and filled them with explosives. But that would be a hell of an exercise for a small group of people. And there's another mystery: if you look behind me, you will see that the embassy appears to have dropped into a large hole. That's quite baffling. Who dug that hole?

"Baffling indeed, Jackson," agrees the anchor. "We'll let you go for now and look forward sometime soon to the answers to those questions."

Yassin has been listening to Jackson's comments and goes over to him. "I know answer: catacombs," he says in his halting English.

"Catacombs? What catacombs?"

"Catacombs under us."

"Here in a Muslim country? Here in Central Arabia? Are you sure?"

"Long time ago many Christians here, before it Central Arabia. They put dead in catacombs," Yassin explains.

"How do you know this?"

"I tourist guide before BBC. I take Christian groups there sometimes. Entrance in next street."

"Fuck me, Yassin! Do many people know about the catacombs?"

"Many Armibar people know."

"But not the Americans, it seems," observes Jackson wryly.

227

Jackson tries to contact Mack with the news, but the mobile network is still down. He turns back to Yassin. "Could you take me to the catacombs entrance? Now?"

"Okay."

Jackson has a problem. He is due to do another live report to London as soon as CNN and Al-Jazeera have finished borrowing his satellite link. Also, he doesn't want his absence from the scene to raise any suspicions among his rivals. He goes to Samira and tells her that he and Yassin are popping into a nearby street to find some food and a toilet.

"What about your next 'live'?" she asks.

"If I'm not back, you can do it."

"Me?"

"Yes you!" he insists. "You'll be fine. Just tell them what you've seen and any other information you have. You'll be fine. I know you will. Just talk to the camera as though you're telling a friend what you've seen."

Samira is pleased but equally nervous at suddenly finding herself thrust into the limelight on such a big story.

Jackson and Yassin go to their car and find Pete now sitting up but still rather numb. Jackson tells him they are off to check something out, without specifying what it is. They borrow Pete's still camera and a torch from his box of kit.

Ten minutes later, Yassin is leading Jackson down a narrow *cul de sac* lined with stone buildings several centuries old. At the end, is a steel grilled gate across a tunnel entrance about two metres high and a metre wide. They see light smoke drifting from the tunnel and there is a strong smell of burning.

The gate is locked and Yassin knocks on a nearby door. It is occupied by the gate keeper, a man he knows from his time as a tour guide. He asks in Arabic for the key and enquires if there have been any other visitors to the catacombs in recent times. "Yes," the gatekeeper replies in Arabic, "some workmen were here a few days ago to carry out repairs."

"What sort of repairs?" Jackson asks in Arabic.

"The gate keeper shrugs. "I don't know. But they had lots of cement."

"Cement?"

"Yes, bags of cement. There was a truckload and they took it into the catacombs on a trolley."

"Are you sure it was cement?"

"I didn't check. It was none of my business."

"Did you recognise the men?" Yassin asks.

"No, they were just workmen. They said they were from the government, so I gave them the key and they returned it later in the day."

Yassin unlocks the gate and he and Jackson enter the tunnel. Although it is now two hours since the embassy explosion, there is still a strong smell of smoke. Dust also hangs in the air. The torch is required to see their way through about 200 metres of winding tunnel, which is strewn with rubble from the explosion.

At the opening to the main cavern where the Christians used to place the bodies of their dead, they are confronted with an astonishing sight. There is a shaft of daylight cutting through the dust. It comes from a hole blasted in the roof. A large section of the embassy building has collapsed into the cavern. Bone fragments from bodies interred many centuries ago are scattered everywhere. The shouts of the rescue workers and their equipment can be heard from above, punctuated by occasional screams and calls for help from the injured.

Back on the surface, at the shattered embassy, Samira has been called upon to do a live report. She begins nervously, but in seconds forgets that she is being watched intently around the world by millions of TV viewers. She is swept along by a determination to report the latest developments to the best of her ability. Her report includes the news that the number of casualties could be as high as 300.

Mack is increasingly frustrated and tense as he sits powerless back at the bureau. His ashtray is overflowing as he lights one cigarette after the other. The mobile network is still down, so he is amazed to see Samira standing in for Jackson without explanation. He sits back and spontaneously begins clapping. "That's my girl," he shouts at the monitor.

The other monitors in Mack's office show that CNN and Al-Jazeera have managed to get pictures from the scene, but they are brief and confined to the aftermath. It is obvious that those crews were not at the embassy at the time of the explosions. He is elated that his decision to act on the tip from Bin Hassan has paid off so spectacularly.

A flash comes up on his computer screen telling him that Ambassador Costello died from his wounds on his way to hospital.

Jackson and Yassin are finding it hard to take in the scale of what they are witnessing in the catacombs. Jackson takes a series of still photographs and curses the absence of Pete and his video camera. Yassin has a possible answer. "Give me camera," he instructs Jackson. He examines the camera briefly then declares: "It can video. I point camera. You talk".

Jackson hastily assembles some thoughts and delivers a piece-to-camera. He and Yassin run back to the others outside the embassy entrance. Pete has recovered sufficiently to take over the filming from Farouk and is busy capturing the rescue operation. Samira asks Jackson if he found any food. "Never mind food, we have something much, much better than that," Jackson tells her as he takes the memory card from the still camera and gives it to Farouk. "Get that back to London straight away."

Jackson sees that CNN and Al-Jazeera are doing live reports a short distance away and Farouk reports that they have managed to get their own satellite equipment to the location.

At the bureau, Mack lights up yet another cigarette and notes that all the television channels and news agencies are doing catch-up, while the World News anchor, Margaret Mathieson, is boasting that the BBC team were the only ones on the scene to catch the actual explosion.

Mack decides it is time for a calming whisky. He goes to the cupboard and finds the bottle that had been drunk dry by Jackson.

He blames Dick Passick, but his irritation is temporary when he hears the World News anchor introducing the video made by Yassin and Jackson in the catacombs.

"Jings!" shouts Mack as he watches in astonishment as Jackson does his piece-to-camera. The video has an unsteady "amateur cameraman" look, adding to its visual impact. "Wow, wow, wow!" exclaims Mack. When the catacombs video ends, the screen cuts back to Samira confidently interviewing Jackson and Yassin about how they found the catacombs. Mack's day is made all over again!

Jackson and Samira finish their 'live' and she warns him that the CNN and Al-Jazeera crews are "steaming mad" about being scooped.

"Just sour grapes," replies Jackson with a shrug.

"It's more than that," she says. "They think there's something very questionable about how you get advance information about these terrorist stories. To be honest, I think there's something odd going on as well."

"Don't worry about it, Samira. One day I'll be able to explain. Meanwhile, I'd better go and see our competitors and sort something out with them. I don't want to piss them off unnecessarily."

A Central Arabian Army truck arrives with headlights flashing and horn tooting. The back is packed with men and women wearing flak jackets emblazoned with the word "Press" in English and Arabic and protected by four soldiers ostentatiously waving their automatic weapons.

The crews from CBS, ABC and Fox and an assortment of journalists and producers jump down from the truck, anxious to catch up with events while one of their number hands over a fistful of dollar notes to the driver.

"Ah, I see the big boys have just flown in from Jordan and Israel and paid their way to the scene," observes Jackson with a smile.

"You'd better go over and make 'friendly' with them," Jackson tells Samira. "Keep them distracted while I pacify Jane and Omar. If they want to know what's going on, tell them to tune into the BBC," he laughs.

Jackson waves over Yassin and they both go to where CNN and Al-Jazeera are set up, side-by-side. Jane and Omar have just heard about the catacombs film and are in no mood for civil conversation.

"Calm down, guys," Jackson instructs them. "You know the score. I beat you on the past few stories, but don't forget you walked all over me with your film of that violent demo a while back. I nearly lost my job over that."

"Fuck you!" shouts Omar. "Something doesn't add up, Jacko."

"Hey look," he replies. "Let's talk about this over a drink in the next day or so, but first I'm about to make you an offer: It was Yassin who tipped me off about the catacombs and he'll take you there and explain their history. That'll leave you ahead of the lot who've just flown in. Okay? "

Jane and Omar are grudgingly grateful. They and their crews follow Yassin back to the catacombs entrance. Jackson goes over to Samira who is being keenly questioned by the new arrivals.

CHAPTER 24

Nightfall and the city's mobile phone network has been switched back on. Mack heaps praise on the team, particularly on Samira for standing in for Jackson with such skill. He seeks assurances that Pete will not need urgent medical treatment, then instructs Yassin to take everyone home just as soon as a local freelance cameraman arrives to provide emergency overnight coverage for the bureau.

Mack wants Jackson dropped off first. "Check your answering machine immediately and let me known if there is anything interesting," he tells him. Jackson understands the significance.

******

As Jackson enters his apartment, he sees the red "message" light blinking on his answering machine. There are 10 messages awaiting his attention. He pushes the "Play" button and pours himself a beer as he listens to the messages. There are four from his mother, all weepingly appealing for him to return to the safety and comfort of London, a congratulatory call from the Foreign News Desk, praise from the office of the Director-General, two messages from Thomas Fulham demanding an urgent call-back, and finally two from Binnie.

"Yes, it was us this time, Roger," Binnie announces, "and there's more payback to come." There is a click as the call ends.

Then there is a second brief message: "Congratulations on finding the catacombs. If the Yanks had bothered to learn this country's history, they'd also have known they were there – right under them."

Jackson switches on his computer and goes to the *Soldiers of Allah* website. It also proudly proclaims responsibility for the destruction of the American Embassy and announces that more attacks are being planned in Central Arabia and elsewhere.

Jackson phones Mack at the office. "As you guessed, there were messages from Bin Hassan. He says the wrecking of the embassy was the work of *Soldiers of Allah.* Want me to come in to do something on this?"

"No, no," replies Mack, "you've done more than enough for today. I'm putting together overnight packages using Pete's film and your pieces-to-camera. You get a good night's rest, laddie. Tomorrow will be another very busy day."

Jackson phones Thomas and finds him extremely agitated. "Well, the gloves are really off now!" he declares. "The White House and 10 Downing Street have been in touch with each other and are about to go on television to declare their determination to neutralise *Soldiers of Allah*. But they want your mate Binnie to be captured alive so they can extract from him, by any means necessary, the sources of his funding and his links to any other groups. His type seek death so they can go to paradise, but we'll give him hell on earth instead.

"He won't be easy to catch."

"I agree, Jacko, so we'll probably need your help with this."

"Oh no!" Jackson shouts. "I've told you, I'm finished with your lot."

"That's not for you to decide," responds Thomas. "I'll be in touch when we come up with a plan."

Jackson pours himself another beer and reflects on how quickly a triumphant day can end so distressingly.

******

Next morning, Jackson and Pete meet outside the wrecked American embassy to do a filmed update. Neither is in good shape. Pete has many bandaged cuts and bruises from yesterday's falling debris, while Jackson is recovering from an unsettling night, his brain whirling from his conversation with Thomas, from Binnie's threats of more terrorist acts and from nightmares that relived yesterday's shocking bloodshed. Yassin is at a garage getting a new windscreen fitted for the car. The freelance cameraman who was on duty overnight hands over his film of the rescue operations to Pete and goes off duty.

"Sorry to say it, but you still look a bit of a mess," Jackson tells Pete.

"I'm a bit ratshit, to be honest, mate, but I'll be okay. There are plenty of others worse than me. I just couldn't get some of those images out of my mind last night."

"Me too," confirms Jackson. "I see on the news wires that the ambassador's wife lost both her legs."

"Shit! That'll piss off the White House even more."

"It certainly will!"

Jackson turns to study the wrecked embassy. There is disbelief that this fortress of a building was reduced to rubble in less than a minute. It reminds him of when he was once sent to report on an earthquake in southern Italy. It is as though the embassy building had been hit by a giant sledge hammer.

As he contemplates the totality of the destruction, Pete films the rescue operations, mostly carried out by marines using heavy lifting equipment. There is a shout as more bodies are discovered.

"Let's do a piece-to-camera and get back to the bureau," says Jackson.

******

On their return, both Mack and Samira express their concern about Pete's injuries. Yassin is back with a new windscreen in the car and is ordered to take Pete to the Armibar Central Hospital for a check-up, no matter how long he has to remain in a queue behind the other bombing casualties.

Samira tells Jackson that his mother has been phoning, wanting to talk to him urgently. As though on cue, she phones again. Samira insists he take the call.

"Yes Mother," he says without warmth. "What's the problem?" He listens. "You know damned well that I wasn't injured because you can see that I'm okay by looking at your television set." He listens again. "What do you mean 'what should you do about your headache'? Do what the rest of the bloody world does and take an aspirin! He listens further, then begins bellowing into the phone. "How dare you accuse me of not caring about you! When did you ever care about me, eh? When!? You left Granny Dunbar to bring me up while you and Dad ponced around the world doing suck-up

235

interviews with the rich, the famous and the glamorous. And where were you when I fell sick? Eh? In Monaco? In St Moritz? In Washington? Or in Timbuktu? Who bloody knows! There wasn't even a phone call. Not even a second-class postcard! And where were you when I got expelled from school? Who bloody knows?! You left it to poor Granny to rescue me from myself. <u>She</u> was my mother. You never were. And did you ever say 'thank you' or 'sorry' to Granny? Of course not! You didn't even turn up at her funeral. I'll give you a chance to say sorry. 10, 9, 8, 7, 6 ... Go on, Mother, say it … 5, 4, 3, 2, 1, zero... See! You can't! Never apologise; never explain. That's you all over!"

Jackson slams the phone down with such force that it shatters. "Oh fuck," he mutters and begins sobbing uncontrollably. Samira goes to Jackson and puts a supportive arm around his shoulders. He responds with an arm around her waist. "That woman drives me mad," he says as tears run down his face. Samira nods sympathetically but says nothing.

Farouk is embarrassed by this unchecked display of emotion. Mack comes out of his office and decides to take him for a coffee next door while Samira helps Jackson through his distress.

Samira and Jackson sit quietly holding each other for 10 minutes as the tears subside. Finally, he turns to her with a gentle smile. "You're a gem. I'm really sorry about my screaming match. I really lost it. Sorry."

"We've all been under a lot of stress," she replies. "You've seen some terrible things and you've coped with them remarkably well. Sometimes it takes just one extra unexpected problem to tip you over the edge. I feel the same sometimes. At times like that I really miss Nigel."

"Did he see you on television yesterday?"

"Yes. He rang this morning to tell me how proud it made it him."

"That's good. He has every right to be."

Mack, Farouk and Yassin return with coffees for Samira and Jackson. "Thanks, guys. I feel a lot better now," Jackson tells them, wiping away the last of his tears.

"It's okay," says Mack. "Anyone who tells you they don't react emotionally to what you've seen is a terrible liar."

Mack picks up the broken phone and says with a wry smile: "I'd appreciate it if you didn't break any more of these or I might have to dock your pay."

"Sorry about that, boss. I'll drink my coffee then pop down to the phone shop for a replacement. I won't even put it on my expenses," he grins.

Pete and Yassin return from the hospital. Pete has a few extra bandages on his forehead and arms, but assures everyone that none of his wounds is serious or require stitches.

Yassin interjects. "Doctor say you must rest!"

"Oh I'm okay. Really nothing wrong." He changes the subject. "I did a bit of sniffing around while I was there and I was told that a lot of shit was flying about among the casualties over how the embassy didn't know about the catacombs. More importantly, I also learned that my sex life is taking a serious turn for the worse. My Aussie friend, Kelly, phoned to say that she and many of her colleagues at the bank are being flown home tomorrow and that the bank may be permanently moved out of Armibar."

"Sorry about your sex life," says Mack, "but I'll chase up the bank angle. It won't go down too well with the government here."

******

The next three days are extremely busy with follow-ups to the embassy explosion, and an extra producer is flown in from London to help. Pete has continued working and there are fewer bandages on display as his wounds heal. His film of the embassy explosion has been seen on just about every TV news outlet in the world and the acclaim has been pouring in.

There has been another avalanche of praise for Jackson's reporting. He is now much calmer and has managed to have some alcohol and gambling-free days. He has encountered his CNN and

Al-Jazeera rivals while out filming. Their reaction has been professional, if not exactly friendly, and there has been no further mention of their complaints about his scoops.

Samira's *ad hoc* reporting has attracted the attention of the Head of News. Marina Kerner offers to fly her to London for some intensive TV training, so that she can provide back-up for Jackson. Samira is flattered, but says she would prefer to stick with her job as bureau manager for the time being – at least until her husband finishes his current contract and rejoins her.

******

It is the fourth day after the embassy explosion and the morning editorial meeting is breaking up without having produced any significant story ideas. Mack's phone rings and he takes the call. "Hello, BBC Armibar."

The call is from a man with a strong Arabic accent. "Yes, BBC, I have story for you…"

"Thank you," says Mack, "what is it?"

"Many soldiers in Hasini Square. Much trouble."

"What sort of trouble?"

There is a click and the line goes dead. Mack turns to his wall map and sees that Hasini Square is about four kilometres away. He turns back to the team. "Mmmm. You'd better get over there to check it out," he tells Jackson, Pete and Yassin.

******

The BBC car pulls into Hasini Square a short while later, but there is no sign of noteworthy activity, military or otherwise. There is just the usual smattering of locals going about their daily business.

Yassin parks the car while Jackson decides what to do next. He is about to phone Mack, when two black Mercedes cars appear from nowhere and block their vehicle front and back.

Two men leap from the front car, an estate, and they wave hand guns at nearby groups of pedestrians who flee into the side streets. Jackson immediately recognises the men as the ones who took him to see Binnie.

238

"Shit," mutters Pete, "it's an ambush!"

As the gunmen approach, Jackson tells Yassin and Pete to relax. "We'll be okay. Just do as they say." Jackson winds down his window and is told: "Come with us, Mr Dunbar."

Pete is also told to get out of the vehicle. He automatically picks up his camera, but is instructed to leave it behind. Yassin is ordered to stay with the car.

Jackson, Pete and Yassin are frisked. Their mobile phones are removed from their pockets, switched off and taken away by one of the men. The back seat in the Mercedes estate is folded down and they are made to lie on the floor and are covered with blankets. Pete begins shaking and Jackson whispers assurances to him that they will come to no harm.

One of the gunmen goes to Yassin and tells him that he must stay where he is until Jackson and Pete are returned – probably in about an hour. He is also warned that they will be killed if he calls for help.

Jackson and Pete are driven away and about 15 minutes later the car is parked and they are led, still with their heads covered by blankets, into a building. The blankets are removed and they see they are in a sparsely-furnished medium-sized room with the curtains drawn. There are two straight-back chairs facing each other and a small, modern video camera set up on a tripod. They appear to be in a different building from the one where Jackson first met Binnie.

A few minutes pass. A door is thrown open and Ahmed Faisel Bin Hassan strides in. He is unsmiling as he shakes Jackson's hand. Pete is astonished and alarmed to find himself in the presence of a man who has just propelled himself into being one of the world's most wanted terrorists. Bin Hassan extends his hand to Pete who shakes it with nervous hesitation.

Binnie adopts a business-like manner and gives no indication that he and Jackson know each other. "You can interview me about the embassy. I'm sure your colleague will know how to work our camera. You have a maximum of 10 minutes. Just tell me where to sit and we can begin," he tells Jackson.

Jackson takes the seat on the left and motions to Binnie to take the other. Pete explains that he will need to quickly familiarise himself with the camera and to take some set-up shots before the interview can begin. This gives Jackson time to put his thoughts in some sort of order. Several minutes pass, during which Jackson and Bin Hassan face each other in silence, then Pete announces that the interview can begin.

"Please begin by telling me your name," says Jackson.

"I am Ahmed Faisel Bin Hassan, leader of *Soldiers of Allah*."

"You have an English accent. How is that?"

"The answer is simple. I was born in England and went to school in London."

"What school was that?"

"You know what school. It's been widely reported by you and others. We were friends there. You know that!"

This disclosure catches Jackson off-guard. He calls a halt to the interview, but Pete keeps the camera rolling.

"Shit, Binnie," Jackson explodes, "Are you trying to stitch me up? I didn't want anyone to know."

"It's better that they do, Roger, so you can then tell your audiences what you remember of me and why I have embarked on this course of action. I'm hoping that this interview will demonstrate that you have an understanding of why I've been set on this course of action. I still regard you as a very good friend."

"I hope you're not expecting me to become your mouthpiece because I'm not. I also don't think it's a good idea – not yet at least – for it to become known that we were school friends. You may have a serious grievance, but that doesn't justify you killing people who weren't in any way involved in the slaughter of your family. Just because they're American doesn't mean they're guilty of anything!"

"Let's not argue over this, my old friend," says Binnie with a resigned sigh. "Ask your questions and you can be on your way."

The interview resumes where it left off.

******

As promised, Jackson and Pete are being driven back to Hasani Square. Pete has the interview on a memory card from Bin Hassan's camera. Again, Jackson and Pete are made to lie on the floor and covered in blankets.

Yassin is waiting in their car, as ordered, and being watched by the men in the second Mercedes. Jackson and Pete are told they can go, and as they return to their car, Pete's camera kit and their three mobile phones are handed back to them.

The two Mercedes drive away and Jackson and his two colleagues switch on their mobiles. They immediately burst into life with anxious messages from Mack and Samira. Jackson reports that they are all okay and will explain what happened as soon as they get back.

They head for the bureau and Yassin wants to know what happened.

"Wait until we get to the office and I'll tell everyone at the one time," Jackson replies.

"You sure have a fucking lot of explaining to do, Jacko," shouts Pete. "I nearly shit myself when we got lifted, but no wonder you didn't seem too bothered. You're a fucking mate of that bastard!"

"Correction, Pete, I was a mate – many years ago."

"Maybe, but you could've fucking told me how you were getting all these tip-offs!"

Pete turns to Yassin. "Did Jacko tell you?"

Yassin shakes his head. "No. I told nothing. Very frightened."

"You're a real prick sometimes, Jacko. A real prick!" Pete shouts. "You're putting our lives at risk because you don't seem willing or able to communicate basic essential information with your closest colleagues."

Jackson knows his cameraman's angry reaction is justified. "I'm really sorry. I know how you feel. One of these days I hope that I can explain it all to you. Believe me, I had no idea this was going to happen. Bin Hassan is paranoid about being tracked down and both

241

times I've been lifted there's been no advance notice. I was terrified the first time it happened to me."

Pete and Yassin grudgingly accept Jackson's apologetic explanation.

CHAPTER 25

Back at the bureau, there is much talk between Mack, Jackson, Pete and Samira about the sensitivity of the interview. They have watched a replay. Jackson is annoyed to discover that Pete left his camera rolling during the private chat when the formal interview was suspended. "Why did you do that?" he demands.

"Sorry mate, but you should know that a good cameraman always keeps a recording running, just in case something unexpected happens."

Mack intervenes. "Pete's right, but we mustn't let this bit leave our office. The fewer people who know about Jacko's links with Bin Hassan the better – at this stage anyway."

The formal part of the recording is strong stuff with a potential to be political and military dynamite. Binnie tells the story about what happened with his family in Iraq then goes on to make an impassioned justification of the destruction of the American Embassy. He says he is at war with America and its allies and other attacks are in various stages of planning. He warns that his war will continue until the Americans punish the soldiers who murdered his family and stop interfering in the Muslim world. Jackson challenges Binnie's motives – two wrongs don't make a right, he asserts – but these are swiftly and angrily swept aside. When Jackson tells him that he cannot hope to survive his war, he replies that he doesn't care, so long as the destruction of his family has been avenged.

Mack wants to talk to Marina Kerner before the interview is sent back to London. He tells Pete to help Farouk prepare the interview for transmission while he and Jackson talk to her.

******

Marina's immediate reaction is enthusiastic, but when Mack informs her there are very sensitive matters to be discussed, she insists that Robert Horsfield be called into her office.

"Do you have to?" Mack asks.

"Yes I do. He's my deputy, for God's sake, and he must be kept in the loop about delicate policy issues."

Marina calls out to Robert to join her and she puts the conversation on speaker.

"Well Mack, it seems to me that Jacko has another hell of a scoop, so what's the problem?" she asks.

"There's an awkward reason why he gets some of these scoops. He went to school with Bin Hassan and they were great mates."

"Ooooh, I see! How come no-one has discovered this?"

"Back then I was known as Roger, so no-one made a connection with my broadcasting name," Jackson explains.

"Is there any mention in the interview of you and this chap having been to school together?"

"No, not in the actual interview."

"Are you still mates?"

"Hell no!" exclaims Jackson.

Mack intervenes. "Jacko has tried more than once to convince Bin Hassan to quit terrorism before it's too late and in the interview his questions are quite aggressive."

"How urgent is it that we use this interview?" Marina asks.

"It could be held a day or so, I suppose."

"Good. Get an encrypted version sent direct to me straight away so that Robert and I can view it before transmission."

Robert comes on the line. "We have to think this through very carefully, Mack. It will also need to be seen by the Editorial Policy and Legal departments – perhaps even the DG."

"Okay, but don't let too many people see it until transmission."

"Of course not," assures Robert, "but we must go through certain processes so that our backs are well covered."

******

Two days pass before a carefully-edited version of the interview goes out as a headline on all major corporation outlets, with an extended version leading *Newsnight*. There is much emphasis on Jackson's aggressive questioning to avoid any perception that the corporation is condoning terrorism. The presenter explains that Jackson and Pete were given no warning they were about to be snatched off the street by armed men and offered an interview with

Bin Hassan. No mention is made that Jackson and Bin Hassan were once friends.

The story gains traction around the world and Jackson's rivals in Armibar are once again irate. Jane Kubinski and Omar Abbas complain bitterly that their bosses are furious that they have been scooped yet again. They want to know why he didn't, at least, give them a nod and a wink that the interview was about to be broadcast. They want to know how they can contact Bin Hassan for an interview and are disinclined to believe him when he insists that he has no way of making contact.

Another angry person is Thomas Fulham. He accuses Jackson of betrayal by not telling him about the interview. Jackson explains how it came about, but Thomas cannot be pacified. He replies that Bin Hassan must be caught before he carries out any more terrorism and that, like it or not, Jackson should be on standby to help when called upon.

That night, a stressed-out Jackson buys a bottle of whisky on his way home and pours himself a large one immediately he gets in the front door. As the alcohol takes hold, he goes into his bank account and sees that his monthly salary is there. He transfers $1,000 into his *Towering Treasures Inc* account and begins gambling. Three hours later his losses have mounted and his whisky bottle is half empty. He falls drunkenly into bed, still fully clothed and without setting his alarm.

******

Jackson is woken next morning by his phone. It is Samira wondering why he isn't at the morning editorial meeting. "Sorry, my alarm didn't go off," he mumbles. "The battery must need changing. I'll just have a bite of breakfast and be in as soon as I can."

"Skip breakfast, Jacko. Get yourself in here right away. There's a crisis that needs dealing with urgently."

Jackson is now wide awake. "What sort of crisis?"

"We'll explain when you get in. Make sure you're looking presentable as you'll have to go on air to defend yourself."

"Christ! Defend myself against what?" he demands.

"I'm not going to discuss it with you on the phone. Just get your backside in here as soon as possible. Yassin is on his way to pick you up."

She ends the call. Jackson puts on the kettle to make an instant coffee and takes a couple of paracetamol. He goes to the bathroom to splash cold water on his face and to shave. He has a thumping headache and is full of self-loathing at getting so drunk and losing so much money on the gambling site.

Jackson's hand shakes as he shaves, but he manages not to nick his face. He gets dressed, gulps down his coffee and goes downstairs. Yassin is waiting for him as he emerges from the apartment block. "What's going on, Yassin?"

Yassin shrugs. "Big trouble. I told nothing."

******

On his arrival at the bureau, Jackson finds Mack in his office furiously sucking on a cigarette and in a huddle with Pete and Samira. He hurries in. "What's this about?" he demands.

"This is what it's about," says Mack angrily as he turns his computer screen towards Jackson.

Jackson sees the front page of the *London Daily Mail*. There is a headline in large type: "BBC man friend of top terrorist".

"Oh shit!" exclaims Jackson.

"Yes, shit indeed, laddie! And there's a full page inside on your friendship with Binnie, or whatever you call him. They've really gone to town on you. They now know you were at school with Bin Hassan and they've been talking to some of the others who were in your class. No doubt the quotes are selective, but most are rather unflattering. They've also talked to your former headmaster who is lukewarm about your academic record and very upset that his school is the subject of scandal. Put bluntly, it's a classic full-frontal *Daily Mail* assault on its hated BBC."

"But how can they do that?" I made it clear in my interview that I didn't accept Binnie's views, and anyway, how did the *Mail* know we used to be friends?"

246

"Well, Jacko, that's the Number One question: how <u>did</u> they hear about it? They've got direct quotes from the private chat you had in the middle of the recording."

Mack turns to Pete. "Are you absolutely 100% sure you cut that private bit out of the interview recording?"

"Most definitely, boss, and I made a final check before sending it off to Marina Kerner."

"Shouldn't we get Farouk in on this?" suggests Samira. "He did the editing?"

"Yes, he should be here," agrees Mack.

Samira calls Farouk into the room. "Farouk, have you any idea how someone in London got to see the private part of the Bin Hassan recording?"

Farouk is surprised by the question. "Well, I sent it to Dick Passick."

Mack explodes. "You fucking what? You sent it to Psycho? Are you fucking mad?"

Farouk can't see what the problem is. "Why are you shouting at me? He phoned me just as I was about to finish work and said he'd been asked to review Jacko's interview. He said there seemed to be an edit in it and I told him that there was. He asked me to send him the full uncut interview, which I did. What's the problem?"

"The fucking problem, my useless friend, is that no-one – absolutely no-one – outside the bureau was meant to see that bit of the interview," shouts Jackson.

Farouk is growing angry. "I'm not your 'useless friend'," he shouts. "I did what I was told by one of the big bosses in London. If no-one was supposed to see it, why didn't anyone tell me?"

Mack bangs his hand on his forehead. "Didn't you know no-one outside this bureau was supposed to see it?"

"No, boss. No-one said anything."

"Oh fuck!" declares Jackson. "Didn't Pete mention it?"

"No," says Farouk, still unable to comprehend the gravity of the situation.

"Sorry, but I didn't think to," admits Pete. "I just thought everyone knew how sensitive it was."

Mack lights another cigarette. "What a mega fuck-up!"

******

Mack sends everyone out of his room and calls Marina, who had been on the phone first thing in the morning with some blistering, career-endangering observations on the problems she now faces with the *Daily Mail* story.

Marina is awaiting his call and has been discussing the crisis with Robert Horsfield and the Head of Press Relations, Tristan O'Mahoney. Mack tells her that he wants Dick Passick to be present.

"Why's that?" Marina asks.

"I'll explain when you get him in."

Marina can be heard calling for Dick to come from his office down the hallway.

While Mack waits for Dick's arrival, he lights yet another cigarette and taps the desk in frustration.

Marina comes back on the line and reports that Dick has arrived and everyone is listening on the speaker.

Mack goes on the attack. "Before I explain anything, perhaps Dick can tell us all why he called my technician and demanded the uncut interview of Bin Hassan. And why the fuck did he go over my head to do this?"

This is news to Marina. "Did you, Dick? Did you ask for the raw video? And if so, why didn't you raise this with me first?"

Dick is caught off guard. "Well, um, as you know, I was one of those on the panel asked to review the interview before it was broadcast. Knowing certain things about the Armibar operation from my recent time there, my instincts told me there was something missing from it. It just didn't flow smoothly."

"What do you mean 'knowing certain things' about my bureau?" Mack bellows.

"Yes," interjects Marina, "what do you mean, Dick?"

"Oh, there were just things that worried me, but I don't want to say any more in this forum."

Mack is rapidly losing control of his temper. "Look, you creepy prick, just let me tell you…"

Marina interjects again. "Stop it! Let's get back to how this embarrassing business got into the press. I hope that it was nothing to do with you, Dick."

"Hell, no! Course not, Marina. I'm sorry that I was slightly out of order in asking for the uncut video, but I wasn't the only person to see it. Farouk put it up on the open circuit, so it could have been seen by any number of people who wanted to make a quid out of selling the story to the *Mail*."

Tristan O'Mahoney joins in. "Marina's right. Our first priority is to decide how to deal with this matter. My press office is inundated with calls from hacks here and abroad wanting to know why a well-known BBC reporter is friends with a terrorist."

Mack interjects. "Let's make this very clear, Tristan. Jacko is not – repeat not – a friend of a terrorist. He's a brave and honourable journalist who once had a friend who's turned to terrorism. He strongly opposes what Bin Hassan stands for and made that very clear in the interview. Can we really be responsible for the behaviour of school friends who have turned bad? Of course not!"

"Well, how do you propose we deal with this?" Marina asks.

"The best way is for Jacko to offer himself for interview and explain the situation as it really was, and is. I'm sure that sensible people will quickly appreciate that the *Mail* is an axe-grinding anti-BBC rag that has misrepresented the true situation. If Jacko handles these interviews well, I'm sure the story will blow over in a few days and it may even add to his status as a source of reliable news about Bin Hassan and *Soldiers of Allah*."

"That seems to be the best way forward," agrees Tristan. "We'll arrange the interviews with some supportive hacks if you brief Jackson on how to handle them."

"Well, that's it," says Marina, "but I will say to Dick that while I accept that he would not lower himself to leak stories to the press, his behaviour in this affair does not meet with my approval."

"I understand that, Marina, but I hope that you'll come to accept that my actions were carried out with the very best of honourable intentions."

The conference call ends and Mack calls Jackson and the rest of the team into his office to explain the plan of action. They all agree with what has been decided, although Jackson is still not over his hangover. Mack also suggests that the CNN and Al Jazeera crews, along with the local newsagency reporters, be invited around for peace-making drinks and snacks and the offer of some previously unknown titbits about Bin Hassan and his schoolboy friendship with Jackson. Again, they agree.

What follows is an exhausting series of back-to-back live interviews for Jackson with BBC and rival outfits explaining how the Bin Hassan interviews came about and how sad he is that his former school friend has turned against western society. Tristan O'Mahoney is pleased with the way Jackson handles them and reports that early feedback indicates the *Daily Mail* attack is being neutralised.

As Jackson takes a break and returns to his desk, Samira tells him that his mother has been on the phone. "I can't talk to her today," he replies grumpily.

"You won't have to," says Samira, "her call was to me this time. She was very upset about the newspaper stories and insisted that I pass on the message that she thinks you are a disgrace. She was so embarrassed that she had to resign from the Bridge Club."

Jackson thinks this is very funny, but Samira warns that his mother had vowed never to have any contact of any sort with him ever again.

"Oh well, every downside has an upside, I suppose," he says grimly. "The less I hear from that self-centred destructive woman the better."

******

Mack is chain-smoking again as he makes calls to his mates in London, trying to establish who leaked the story to the *Daily Mail*. None has any useful information. Then he gets a call from Mary on the Foreign Desk confirming his suspicions about Dick Passick.

"I thought you should know that I overheard Psycho boasting to a couple of others in the pub that he had settled a few scores by letting a journo cousin on the *Mail* listen to the private bit of the Jacko recording. He was well pleased with himself."

"Fuck! Thanks, Mary. He's an unconscionable shit!"

"He is indeed. I'm wondering whether I should tell Marina."

"I wouldn't do that. It might backfire on you. Psycho will deny it and Marina won't want to risk keeping the story going by holding a disciplinary hearing. We'll just have to let this one go, but at least we know he's an enemy within."

CHAPTER 26

A week goes by and although the international anger about the destruction of the American Embassy remains high, Jackson hears nothing more from Thomas Fulham. He is hoping against hope that any plan to capture Binnie will now not include him. To avoid drawing attention to himself, he decides not to do the television feature on the Foaud Rehabilitation Centre for the time being. The postponement gives him a chance to visit Felicity to explain why, but more importantly to see her again. He arrives at the centre with a large bag of oranges for the patients and apologises to Felicity for not having any spare cash for another donation. She and the patients are grateful for the oranges.

"Sorry that I'm postponing the feature," he says, "but there's a lot on at the moment and I don't want to rock the boat further with Thomas."

"Are you and Thomas back in contact? He's not mentioned you recently."

"I bumped into him at the American Embassy the day before it was blown up, but otherwise we don't see each other."

"Well, I don't see that much of him, either," Felicity admits, "and when I do, he seems totally pre-occupied – probably by what happened to the Americans. I'm worried that the next attack will be on the British Embassy. He says the *Soldiers of Allah* are not thought to be targeting the Brits, but I think they're asking for trouble by providing temporary accommodation for those diplomats who survived the embassy attack."

"I'm sure he'll be okay," assures Jackson without really believing it.

"I get the feeling that he wants to move back to London," she says, "but the children are happy and doing well in the International School here and I don't want to abandon the kids at my rehab centre until I've had a chance to train my assistants."

"What makes you think Thomas wants to leave?"

"Nothing concrete, just little things like him being embarrassed when I spotted him browsing real estate websites for family properties in London's commuter belt. He says he was just checking the housing market out of idle curiosity."

Felicity's comments intrigue Jackson, but he chooses not to press the subject. They go into the centre's kitchen and Felicity makes coffee and raises the controversy over the *Daily Mail* article. "Is it really true you went to school with this terrorist who blew up the embassy?"

"Yes, it is, but it's nothing like the *Mail* presented it. They tried to make out that I was being the mouthpiece for his jihadi campaign. Absolutely not true."

"Embarrassing, though, isn't it?"

"Yes, it was tricky for a bit," Jackson admits.

"Did Thomas know about your friendship?"

"Well, he does now," says Jackson, neatly avoiding the question.

He finishes his coffee and announces that he must go. He checks that no-one can see them and gives Felicity a brief kiss on the lips. She smiles, but says nothing.

******

Two more weeks pass by without any calls from Thomas or Binnie. Jackson is beginning to feel more relaxed. News from the patch has gone quiet and he tells Mack that he and Pete might do the feature on the Fouad Rehabilitation Centre. As the three of them discuss what form the feature might take, Samira comes in, grinning from ear to ear. "Have a look at the email that's just gone out from Marina's office," she says excitedly.

Mack goes into his email folder and within seconds he also breaks into a broad smile. "How fucking wonderful," he shouts. "Listen to this: 'Departure of Richard Passick. A brief note to let you all know that Dick has decided to leave us to pursue new opportunities outside broadcasting. His resignation will take effect at the end of the month, but meanwhile, he will be using up the leave that is owing to him. I take this opportunity to thank him for his valuable contribution to our operations over two decades. I am sure he will be in contact with his many friends should he wish to arrange a farewell party. Signed on behalf of Marina Kerner, Head of News."

"Wow!" exclaims Jackson, "what's behind that I wonder?"

"Let's find out," says Mack as he dials the Foreign Desk. The call is taken by Mary.

"Hi Mary, it's Mack. We've just seen Marina's email about Dick."

Mary laughs. "I didn't think it would take you long to call. The whole place is buzzing with the news. The creepy bastard came in as usual this morning and soon after was called to an urgent meeting with Marina and the Human Resources bosses. After about an hour, he returned to his office, gathered up his things and left without saying a word to anyone. Extraordinary!"

"Well, c'mon, Mary. Tell us why he was fired?" demands Mack impatiently.

"There's been nothing official, of course, but he recently had a very beautiful intern, just out of university, begin working for him. Within a few days Dick tried it on with her. She brushed him aside, thinking he was an opportunistic old groper, but later on, he invited her out to dinner. She said no, but he didn't give up. She recorded him on her smartphone just as he began telling her that if she wanted to have a television career she needed to adopt what he called 'a more positive approach to the social opportunities' offered her. When she continued to reject his advances, he got angry and told her he was going to terminate her internship."

"So what happened next?"

"She went straight home and played the recording to her very important father, who went nuts."

"And her father is?"

"Sir Ivan Biddlestone, a High Court judge."

"Holy shit!" roars Jackson as the office erupts in gleeful laughter. "This is magnificent!"

"So what happened next, Mary?" asks Mack.

"Well, I believe Biddlestone got straight onto the DG who's a member of his club in Pall Mall, and the rest is history, as they say. Bye, bye Psycho Passick!"

Samira chips in. "I guess the creep will still walk away with a big pay-off and a confidentiality agreement, so no-one outside the organisation will get to hear what happened."

"I doubt it, Samira, as one of his many enemies here has apparently leaked it to the *Daily Mail*, so he won't be able to hawk himself around as someone who just got bored with the BBC and is looking for new challenges. And he is too young to start drawing his staff pension."

"I know it's not nice of me to say this, Mary, but revenge is so sweet."

"Indeed it is."

The call ends and Mack, Jackson and Pete return to planning the feature on the Fouad Centre.

******

Jackson and Pete arrive at the Fouad Centre and are greeted by Felicity and her staff. Neither she nor Jackson indicate to Pete that they were once in a relationship. The filming takes a couple of hours as they talk to Felicity, the Arab nurse being trained as her deputy, and several of the child patients. They have the makings of a compelling feature – a mix of sadness and kindness and an inspirational determination by the injured victims to make the best of their lives.

Felicity offers Jackson and Pete a coffee. They are excitedly regaling her with news of the downfall of Psycho Passick when Yassin bursts in saying that Samira has been trying to get in touch.

"Sorry!" mutters Jackson, "our phones have been switched off while we were filming. I'll call her back as soon as we've finished our coffee."

"No, she say you come back now. She say it important," Yassin insists.

Jackson switches on his mobile. "Okay. I'll give her a call."

"No, no call. You come with me – now!"

255

Jackson turns to Felicity. "Sorry about this. I'd better do as I'm told. It could be a development with the *Soldiers of Allah* lot."

******

As soon as Jackson and Pete arrive back at the bureau, Samira ushers Jackson in to see Mack in his office. They close the door behind them.

"What's all this about?" asks Jackson with a frown.

"Take a seat, Jacko," says Mack, "we've some sad news for you."

"Like?"

"I'm afraid your mother's died."

"Oh, God! When?"

"About 10 days ago, apparently."

Jackson is shocked and instantly angry. "Why am I being told only now?"

Samira replies. "I had a call from her solicitor an hour or so ago and she said that your mother gave instructions that in the event of her death you weren't to be notified until after the funeral and cremation had taken place."

Tears begin to roll down Jackson's face. "How did she die?"

"The solicitor said she had a couple of severe strokes, the second one being fatal."

"Oh God," says Jackson, "they must have been something to do with the headaches she was complaining about when we had that terrible row a few weeks ago."

"That's possible, I suppose," replies Samira, "but you never know with strokes."

Jackson slumps forward, his head in his hands. Samira goes out to the work area to tell Pete, Farouk and Yassin what's happened. Mack gets his whisky bottle from a drawer in his desk and pours himself and Jackson stiff drinks. Mack fidgets uncomfortably, not quite sure how to handle the situation. Eventually, he suggests that Jackson let Pete and Farouk put together the rehabilitation centre feature and that he leave the voice track until tomorrow.

Jackson, now red-eyed, agrees and goes back to his desk. Pete, Farouk and Yassin all tell him how sorry they are. Pete gives him an embarrassed hug and decides that he should take Farouk and Yassin out for a coffee, leaving Samira to help soothe their colleague's grief.

Jackson unlocks the bottom drawer on his desk and takes out a folder. It contains photographs and stories about his mother and father. He picks out a large black-and-white studio portrait of a pretty girl in her late teens or early twenties and holds it up for everyone to see. "This is her. This is Mother as she was in the 1960s."

Samira comes over for a look. "Oh, Jacko, she's so beautiful."

Jackson picks out a yellowing newspaper clipping with the headline *Nixon Must Go*. The byline is *Roger Dunbar, Washington Correspondent*, alongside a portrait of a distinguished grey-haired man wearing a jacket and tie. "Mmm. Your father was so handsome," says Samira. "I can see something of him in you."

"I've never really thought about it," Jackson replies as he continues to go through the file. He shows Samira a photograph of his mother standing alongside President John Kennedy in the Oval Office.

Samira is impressed. "Fancy your mother knowing Kennedy!"

"Oh, I don't think she knew him at all, but she sure knew how to get herself into celebrity photos," he replies.

Samira remembers there is something else she needs to tell him. "Um, the solicitor also said that you should look out for an email from his firm because they would be sending you a copy of the will."

Jackson checks his emails and finds the message. He stares at the screen for a minute, summoning the courage to open the attachment. He takes a deep breath and clicks on it. He studies the contents and tears run down his cheeks.

He turns to Samira. "It's all gone to animal welfare organisations."

"Really? Nothing for you?

He shakes his head. "Doesn't look like it. See for yourself."

Samira comes over and reads from the will as Jackson scrolls through it. "Mmm. Battersea Dogs Home, the Cats Protection League, The Horse Trust, The League Against Cruel Sports, and even some swan and owl sanctuaries. Mmm. Your mother obviously loved animals."

"More than people, I'm afraid," he shrugs.

Jackson continues to scroll down the page. Towards the end, he sees a sentence that refers to him. It begins: "I have chosen not to provide for my only son Roger Jonathan Dunbar known professionally as Jackson Dunbar and currently a foreign correspondent with the BBC for the following reasons: 1) As I have approached old age, he has failed to behave as a son should towards his mother and…"

Jackson scrolls further down the page to read the rest. Samira continues to look over his shoulder.

"2) I know that if I leave anything to my said son he will use it to feed his gambling addiction."

Jackson kills the screen, but it is too late. Samira has seen it. "Gambling! Oh, Jacko, so that's why you're so short of money all the time!"

Jackson is acutely embarrassed. "She exaggerates. I'm not addicted. I just like the occasional harmless flutter. Anyway, I'm giving it up."

"Are you sure? Absolutely sure?"

"I'm sure."

Samira remains unconvinced. "Well, just promise me that if it's anything more than a 'harmless flutter', you will seek professional help."

"No need to worry about me, Samira. It's just Mother giving me a farewell kicking. You won't tell anyone will you?"

"No, of course not – just as long as it doesn't interfere with your work."

"Thanks. You're a gem."

Jackson closes the file on his mother with a sigh and wipes away his tears. Pete and Farouk return and ask him if he is okay, not knowing what else to say. He assures them that he is alright, so they get to work editing the interviews shot at the rehab centre. "Thanks for doing that, guys," he tells them. "I'll put down the voice track in the morning."

******

Back at his apartment, Jackson pours himself a whisky and studies the file of photographs and newspaper clippings. He finds a photograph of his mother as an older woman and is overcome with sadness. He closes the file and makes a sandwich while he runs a bath.

CHAPTER 27

Jackson wakes up next morning with another hangover and a vague memory that he lost more of this month's salary on *Towering Treasures Inc*. He studies himself in the mirror and hates what he sees. He rubs shaving gel into his whiskers and begins shaving himself. As his face reappears through the shaving gel, he feels a flash of anger and smashes his fist into his reflection. The mirror shatters and gashes his hand.

"Fuck!" he screams. He runs to the kitchen and wraps kitchen towels around the injured hand. He returns to the bathroom, cursing his anger and stupidity and rummages through a First Aid kit to find a suitable bandage for the wound. He washes the blood away and fixes the bandage into place, then gets dressed.

On arrival at the bureau he finds the team gleefully studying a computer print-out of a page from the *Daily Mail*. There is a bold headline *Exclusive: Beeb boss and the judge's daughter*. It goes into detail about what Dick Passick is alleged to have said to his intern and there is a snatched photograph of him looking uncharacteristically dishevelled as he collects his milk from the doorstep of his Islington apartment. He is quoted as threatening to sue anyone who suggests he has ever done anything improper.

Jackson is pleased to see Psycho get his comeuppance, but is too pre-occupied by his own troubles to spend time gloating. Mack notices the bandage on Jackson's hand and is told that it was an accident with a kitchen knife and is nothing serious. He goes through the edited package on the rehab centre with Farouk and puts down the voice track, making sure that there is a reference to where donations can be sent. He is pleased with the finished feature and asks Farouk to send it to London. Farouk burns a courtesy DVD of the feature for Felicity. Jackson takes it to her, along with news of his mother's death.

Felicity is full of sympathy, having had her own ups and downs with Lady Dunbar when she and Jackson were lovers. "You really shouldn't feel bad about your mother," she tells him as they share coffee in the rehab centre kitchen. "She was attracted to the rich and famous like bees to honey, and she was very upset when she was forced by her parents to marry your father."

"What do you mean 'forced to'? Was it a kind of arranged marriage?"

"No, nothing like that. It was a 'shotgun marriage', if you'll excuse that crude term. Surely you knew that?"

"I had no absolutely no idea," says Jackson, astonished by this revelation.

"Oh dear, I seem to have let the cat out of the bag. I'm so sorry."

"Don't be sorry, Felicity. Tell me more. I need to know."

"Well, your mother let it all pour out one day over a few sherries, and she told me she was six months pregnant when she married your father. Her parents were pillars of Roman Catholic society. They were upset about the shameful possibility that they would have an illegitimate grandchild. An abortion was out of the question, so they pushed her into getting married."

Jackson goes silent while he takes in this information, then he poses another question: "Do you think she was in love with my father?"

"I don't know," Felicity admits. "They were certainly much attracted to each other, but I don't think parenthood was ever on their agenda. They were party people. He was bewitched by her great beauty and she enjoyed having her social insecurities endlessly indulged by a man who could open doors to a new and glamourous world."

"So, Mother can't have been pleased to have me come along and disrupt this life?"

"Well, she didn't put it quite like that – at least not to me -- but you'll have to accept that she was not one of life's natural mothers. I gathered that she didn't object when your father's mother – Granny Dunbar – volunteered to bring you up."

Jackson is dumbfounded by what he has learned, and he and Felicity sit quietly as they finish their coffee.

"Must get back to the grindstone," Jackson says finally. "Thank you for what you've just told me. It explains a lot."

261

He gives Felicity a chaste kiss and goes back to the bureau. Further contemplation of what he has just learned about his mother is swept away when he finds Mack keenly watching the CNN monitor which has just announced some breaking news: the *Soldiers of Allah* website is stating that Bin Hassan has been "martyred" in a drone attack on a building on the outskirts of Armibar.

"Wow, that's a turn-up!" declares Mack as he calls up the website on his screen. Jackson and Pete gather around to study it. "That might be why everything's gone quiet," says Jackson.

The three of them study the screen which displays what appears to be the badly scarred body of Bin Hassan lying on a makeshift stretcher. Beneath the "martyr" announcement is a bold-lettered declaration in Arabic with an English translation: "Allah Will Have His Revenge".

"Boy, that sure changes the game!" exclaims Jackson. "We'd better do a holding piece for London, then I'll investigate further."

"I'll look after the holding piece," says Mack. "You check around our contacts for anything more."

Pete has been studying the website intently. "Hold on guys, there's something odd about this," he warns. He enlarges the picture of Bin Hassan, studies it further then declares: "It's been Photoshopped! Look closely and you can see that the head doesn't join up properly with the body. It's been faked, guys!"

"Shit! But that makes no sense," says Jackson. Why use a Photoshopped picture instead of the real thing?"

"Maybe his face was too messed up to show," speculates Mack.

"That's possible," says Jackson.

"There's another thing," says Pete. "I reckon the head is a frame grabbed from my video of the Bin Hassan interview. It's from my set-up shots when I filmed him side-on and in close-up. Whoever has done this has snatched a frame with his eyes closed during a blink."

As they sit thinking about the reasons for the fakery, they see Al-Jazeera is now also running the story of Bin Hassan's "death" as a fact. Jackson suggests that they should tip off Omar that Al-

Jazeera should be cautious about going hard on the death and Samira says she will give him a discreet call..

Mack's phone rings. It is Harry Kingston on the Foreign Desk in London wanting a 'matcher' on the story.

"I'll do something for you shortly," Mack tells him, "but we're going to do a rather careful piece, at least to start with."

"Why the caution, Mack? It's as clear as a bell. The official *Soldiers of Allah* website shows Bin Hassan's body. The guy's dead. Why would they claim that he's been martyred if he's still alive?"

"That's what we're trying to figure out. There's a smell about it we don't like. I can't say any more over the phone."

"Okay, Mack. But let's have something very soon. The news desks are already on my back and are chasing the White House and the Pentagon for comments."

The call ends. Mack starts work on a piece for London. Jackson decides he should pay a quick visit to his apartment on the off-chance that there is something on his answering machine.

******

On entering the apartment, he sees there is a single message. As he had hoped, it is from Binnie. As always, there are no wasted words. "Someone has hacked our website and locked us out of it. Stay around and I'll call you back."

Jackson immediately phones Mack with the news.

"Do you think it really was your mate?" he asks.

"It sounded like him, but I have to admit that his voice isn't particularly distinctive and also the line was a bit crackly. He's going to call again."

"Right. I've done a careful piece for London. They still can't see why we don't go hard on it, especially as the Americans say they believe it and claim to have carried out the drone attack with the agreement of President Hasani. Maybe the photograph has been faked because Bin Hassan was blown to bits and your call was from someone else trying to seed confusion."

"Maybe, but the caller used my first name 'Roger'. Very few people know that."

"Well, let's see what you can learn when this person calls back."

Jackson ends the call, but another one comes in almost immediately. This time it is Thomas.

"Right, Jacko, it's action stations for you!"

"What the hell do you mean?"

"It means that you are now working primarily for us, with the bonus of getting more brilliant scoops for your other masters."

"I'm not! I'm not! I'm not working for you!" roars Jackson.

"Yes! Yes! Yes! You are," replies Thomas coldly. "Your old mate, Binnie, must be stopped at all costs and you have an obligation to play your part. You owe it to civilised society. And there's plenty in it for you."

"Like what?"

"Like two million US dollars."

"How much?"

"Two million US dollars, Jacko – a gift from a grateful White House. And if you don't believe me, check your Roger Smith account and you'll see there is a down payment of $250,000. This is your big opportunity. You'll become an international hero and you'll have the chance of your lifetime to give yourself your much-desired new start in life. You can shake yourself free of any need to gamble. Don't you see that?"

Jackson is staggered by the offer and although he doesn't wish to admit it, Thomas's argument is attractive. "So what exactly have you in mind for me?"

"Well, here's the situation: There was no drone attack, of course. We don't have drones here. We made that story up. We hacked the *Soldiers of Allah* website to spook Bin Hassan and his boys by declaring him to be dead. We are confident this is causing all sorts of confusion and panic in his group and among those who are funding and co-operating with him. The website was used as a route for coded messages, but we've stopped that. It's now under our control. He can't get into the website, nor can he remove it. Above all, he'll need to re-establish his authority by being seen to be alive and well."

"I can see that's a rational assumption, but I still don't get where I'm supposed to come into it."

"You come into it because we want you to be 'lifted' again for another interview."

"Forgive me for being obtuse, Thomas, but I still don't get it. How will that help?"

"It'll help us track down his location."

"I don't see how. I haven't the faintest clue where he takes me. You know that. As I've said in my broadcasts, we couldn't see where we were and our phones were taken away and switched off. No-one except Binnie and his boys know where we are taken."

"Ah, but we will because when you're lifted you'll have a tracking device on you. You can hide it in your cameraman's kit, like you did with the bug you planted for us in Khaled Mohamed's office."

"There's just one flaw with that proposal, Thomas. Pete was made to leave his kit behind with our driver. The interview was filmed with Binnie's own camera."

"Hell! I didn't realise that. Never mind, I'm sure our technical guys will have another solution."

"Maybe, but you have to keep in mind that I never know when these interviews are going to take place. Only Binnie knows that."

"Yes, we're working on that problem."

The call ends and Jackson rings Mack to suggest that any stories about the reported death of Bin Hassan should not go into detail about why there are suspicions about the website. He says he will explain later and tells his boss that he is going to stick around at the apartment in case Binnie calls again.

Jackson leaves the phone off the hook for a few minutes while he goes downstairs to the nearby ATM. He accesses the Roger Smith account and sees that the promised $250,000 is there, although when he tries to make a withdrawal, he gets a message that the money is "not yet available".

265

On his return to the apartment, Jackson pours himself a beer and waits for Binnie's next call. He has now convinced himself that he will be acting in the best interests of western society by helping to capture Binnie, and that the American money is no more than a fair reward for the risks he is taking. Two million dollars is a lot of money, but he rationalises that it is quite modest when compared with the \$25m offered for Osama Bin Laden.

There is a knock on the door and he finds Samira there with a man he has never seen before. "Hello Jacko, this is my husband, Nigel," she explains. "We were just passing and I thought you'd like to meet him. We've also come to offer our condolences."

Jackson and Nigel shake hands. "Very sorry to hear about your mother, Jackson," says Nigel. "It must have been an enormous shock."

"Yes it was a bit, but it's very nice to meet you at last," says Jackson, "I know that Samira has been missing you. I'd invite you to stay for a cup of tea, but I'm expecting an important phone call any moment."

"That's okay, Jacko, we weren't planning to stay," Samira assures him. "Nigel urgently needs to sort out a few things and I must return to the bureau to do the monthly accounts."

Jackson and Nigel shake hands again. "Well, now you're back, we must have a proper chat over a meal somewhere," says Jackson.

"Yes, indeed," says Nigel.

The phone rings. "That's my expected call, so I'd better take it," Jackson says as he hastily ushers them out the door.

It is Binnie again. "Those lies about my death are taking hold," he reveals, "so we'll have to do another interview. We'll do it in two days from now." The line goes dead.

A couple of minutes pass and the phone rings again. It is Thomas. "We've just heard your mate's call. As always, it is too quick for us to get to him. But our plan is working, so we'll ratchet up the claims that he really is dead and that *Soldiers of Allah* is disintegrating without his leadership. By the way, the tracking problem has been solved. Our boys tell us they have a device that can't be detected.

"How come?"

"Because you stick it up your arse."

"Oh Christ! You are joking, I hope."

"No, it's not a joke. It's plastic and flexible and about the size of a small tampon. It even looks like one with a cord you use to remove it."

"Are you really suggesting that I go around with a tampon up my arse all day long?"

"No, of course not. You only have to insert it when you go anywhere your terrorist mate might lift you."

Jackson is still unable to get his head around this proposal. "Okay, so let's imagine that I do have this thing stuck up my bum. Does it mean that you'll be tracking me all the time while I wait to be lifted?"

"No, that's not it. The battery might run flat. What you do is when you've finished your interview, you make an excuse to go to the toilet, where you remove the tracker, switch it on and stick it somewhere out of sight. We'll have armed snatch teams scattered about the city and they'll give you 10 minutes to get clear before grabbing Bin Hassan and anyone with him. Then Bingo! You'll be the speedy recipient of the rest of your reward and have yet another brilliant scoop. What's not to like about that, eh!"

"It might work. When am I going to get this 'tampon' thing?"

"It's just been delivered to my apartment, but unfortunately I'm about to leave town for a few days."

"Where 'out of town', may I ask?"

"You don't need to know. Let's just say that I'm off the coast and among friends."

"So how do I get the device?"

"I've phoned Flip and told her that it's a microphone you accidentally left at the embassy during one of your interviews and I've stressed that she should take it to her centre in the morning for you to collect first thing."

"I'll do that."

"Okay Jacko. Let me know as soon as you have any contact of any sort with Bin Hassan. I can only guess how he's going to set up the interview without alerting us. I'm sure he knows we monitor his calls to you."

"Yes, he does, but he'll come up with something I'm sure. He's a smart bugger."

******

Jackson's maid turns up with a supply of fresh food and spends an hour tidying the apartment. He explains away the broken bathroom mirror and the cut on his hand as a "silly accident".

As the afternoon wears on with no further call from Binnie, Jackson decides to treat himself to a meal at *The Cedar Tree*. Jamil agrees, reluctantly, to charge it to Jackson's account. When Jackson returns to the apartment, he finds messages from Binnie and Thomas.

Binnie's message is in code: "You and your cameraman must be outside the headmaster's office near your bureau immediately after the metalwork class finishes."

Jackson is baffled at first, then understands the message. He calls Thomas with his interpretation. "I've worked out when it's going to happen."

"Excellent," says Thomas. "I had no idea what he was talking about when we monitored his call."

"It's simple really. I'll be picked up at midday outside the café called *Room 10* about a block away from the bureau."

"How did you figure that out?"

"It's code from our days together at school. Everyone knew the headmaster's office because of the large polished brass numbers on the door. Anyone who got into trouble would be told 'go to Room 10'."

"What about the day and time?"

"That's also easy. Binnie and I hated metalwork classes, which were always on a Wednesday – that's tomorrow – and they always finished at midday in time for the canteen lunch."

"That looks sorted then, Jacko. You'll have plenty of time to collect the tracker from Flip before being picked up, and if all goes well, by the end of the day Ahmed Faisel Bin Hassan will be ours and no threat to anyone, anymore."

******

Jackson phones Mack with the news. It is agreed that no mention will be made to London of the advance warning given by Bin Hassan. "The interview will be a nice surprise for them and two fingers to the *Daily Mail* and their lot," says Mack. "Yassin can pick you and Pete up first thing and we can then discuss exactly how you should conduct the interview. Meanwhile, have a good night's sleep. Tomorrow will be another big day for you."

"Thanks, Mack, but before you go, one more thought: How about I alert CNN and Al-Jazeera that there will be another interview and promise them a few clips that they can broadcast immediately after us? They're good guys and I don't want to drop them in it again with their bosses."

"Mmm," ponders Mack, "good idea. I'll have a private chat with them in the morning."

Jackson pours himself a modest whisky and phones Pete to inform him of the proposed interview. He will see him downstairs at 9am. Pete is excited by the prospect of another meeting with a now-notorious terrorist.

Jackson phones Felicity to make sure that she will have the "microphone" with her when she goes to the centre in the morning. She tells him that it is already in her bag, so that she won't forget it.

Felicity sounds unhappy and Jackson wants to know why. "Things are getting difficult at home," she admits, "I really don't know what's…"

Jackson interrupts. "Before you go any further, whose phone are you using?"

"My own, of course! Why?"

"Hang up and ring me again from the landline phone in Thomas's study."

"Okay," she says, baffled. A couple of minutes later she calls again, using Thomas's phone.

"It's a security issue," he explains. "My phone is probably bugged, but as Thomas is a diplomat dealing with commercial matters, calls from his phones are encrypted and can't easily be unscrambled.

"Oh, I see. That makes sense."

"You can now speak freely," he tells her. "What's your problem?"

"Thomas is my problem, to be honest. He's very stressed out and getting more and more secretive and difficult to deal with. Even the kids have noticed that he's changed. And another thing: I believe he's a spook."

"What makes you think that?"

"He accidentally left some documents lying about in the study a few days ago and they were all about snatch squads and military reports and that sort of thing. When I asked him about them he flew into a rage and told me to keep my nose out of his business. He's now gone off somewhere, but wouldn't say where. He said he'd be back later this week, but would be out of touch until he returned."

"I wouldn't get too alarmed," Jackson tells her. "There's no doubt a simple explanation – linked to the pressures arising from the American Embassy bombing."

"Maybe, but there's more to it. Because of my suspicions about what he's really doing here, I've been going through his study. I found where he'd hidden the keys to his desk and in one of the drawers were several photographs of a pretty young woman. On one of them there was a handwritten message: 'I'll remember last night for the rest of my life. Thank you'. It was signed by someone called Katherine."

"What's she look like?" he asks.

"Dark hair and aged about 30. Quite good looking, I have to admit. Do you know a Katherine?"

Jackson realises that the girl is probably the receptionist at the British Embassy, but he chooses not to say so.

The Mortal Maze

"Maybe it's someone from his past, before his marriage to you," Jackson suggests.

"Absolutely not," she replies, "it has a date stamp on it from a few months ago."

"What are you going to do about it?"

"Nothing for the moment. I need to think it through."

"Would you leave Thomas?"

"If the affair's still going, I may have to, especially as he's been lying to me all this time about his job. There's no trust left in our relationship."

Jackson says nothing for a few moments, then poses a question. "Is there any chance we might get together again?"

"No, Jackson," she says firmly. "You know that. I can't cope with the constant worry about your addiction."

"I'm not addicted," he insists, "in fact I've already given up gambling. I won't need it any more. I've had the big win that I always knew I'd get. I'm sure, that given a chance, I can prove it to you."

Felicity gives a big sigh. "No, Jacko, I'd be jumping from the frying pan into the fire. I still love you dearly, but I don't believe you can give up gambling. There's such a need in you. I hope that we'll always be friends but that magic required for an intimate relationship has gone. And now I have the kids to think of. They love their dad despite his faults."

"Let me prove myself. Stick with Thomas as best you can, and we can talk again in six months. If I haven't gambled between now and then, maybe you'll give me another chance."

"Sorry, Jacko, but I'm too tired and too stressed to give you such an assurance."

271

CHAPTER 28

Jackson wakes early the next morning, having had a restless night worrying that something might go wrong with the Binnie interview. He has a light breakfast – a couple of pieces of toast washed down with coffee – then goes downstairs at the appointed time. Pete is already waiting, and so is Yassin.

"Another exciting day ahead of us, Jacko," declares a grinning Pete.

"Mmm, it looks promising," replies Jackson, trying his best to appear totally at ease. "I will, at least, have time to give some proper thought to my line of questioning."

"Yep, it's looking good," says Pete as he and Jackson get into the Range Rover.

Jackson tells Yassin that they need to call by the Fouad Rehabilitation Centre to collect a microphone.

"What microphone?" asks Pete. "Does Felicity Fulham think it's one of ours?"

"Not sure," replies Jackson, anxious to drop the subject.

"I'm not missing one, so it must be someone else's. I'd definitely know if I were missing one. Give her a call and tell her, so we can go straight to the bureau."

"No," snaps Jackson, "her husband, who works at the British Embassy, says it definitely has our label on it, so maybe it was left there some time ago by a visiting crew. It'll take only a few minutes to collect."

Yassin starts the car and drives away. He gets barely a couple of hundred metres along the almost-deserted street when his path is blocked by a Mercedes estate that pulls out of a side street and forces the car into the kerb. A second Mercedes pulls in behind them. They are the same cars and the same men who lifted them in Hasini Square. Two of the men jump from the estate car, waving hand guns, and run to the BBC vehicle.

Jackson and Pete know the routine. They give up their phones and are quickly frisked before getting into the estate and lying down on the rear floor. Yassin also hands over his phone and is told to remain where he is until Jackson and Pete return, and not to make contact with anyone in the meantime.

The car speeds away and Jackson and Pete are told to pull a blanket over their heads. This time Pete is relaxed and looking forward to an adventure. Not so, Jackson. He realises that Binnie has outsmarted everyone and that the grand plan to capture him is rapidly coming apart at the seams.

The car speeds through the streets of Armibar for about half an hour. "This is great," whispers Pete to Jackson, "just great!" Jackson doesn't reply. All he can see ahead is trouble. He may get another scoop, but at a very high personal price. There is unlikely to be the chance of another similar operation to capture Binnie, and Jackson's dream of riches is rapidly turning into the darkest of nightmares.

The car turns off the road and parks up a gravel driveway. Jackson and Pete, still with their heads covered by blankets, are led by the two men into a building of unknown type and taken to a room where the blankets are removed.

The room is different from the one where they did the previous interview. Again, there are two chairs facing each other and a video camera set up on a tripod. Pete is told to prepare the camera for filming. He notices that Jackson is agitated, but doesn't remark on this because of the presence of the Arab guards. In any case, he assumes that it is no more than pre-interview nerves.

******

Mack is growing concerned that Yassin has yet to deliver Jackson and Pete to the bureau. They have missed the morning editorial conference and his concern turns to alarm when he discovers their phones appear to be turned off. He calls out to Samira: "Have you heard from Jacko or Pete this morning?" She shakes her head. "Perhaps they've been held up in heavy traffic."

"Possibly," admits Mack, "but why have they switched off their mobiles?"

"Do you think they've been snatched again by Bin Hassan?"

"That wasn't the plan."

"What plan?" she asks.

Mack realises that Samira hasn't been told about the interview. "It's just that they're supposed to be here by now to talk about a possible feature," he lies.

"I'll call their home numbers. If there's no answer, they may have been lifted again and are on their way to do another scoop interview with Bin Hassan. I wouldn't worry too much. They'll probably turn up before long.

******

As usual, Felicity drives Thomas's embassy Jaguar to the rehab centre, dropping Sophie and Sam off at the International School on the way. She has her bag with her and is so pre-occupied by her marital concerns that she has all but forgotten that Jackson is due to collect his "microphone". Immediately she enters the centre she is immersed in various problems that have arisen overnight with some of her more seriously injured child patients.

******

Jackson is increasingly tense as he and Pete wait for the interview to begin. When Bin Hassan finally enters the room, there are no friendly handshakes and he abruptly announces: "If you are wondering why the plans were changed, it's simply an extra security precaution."

"I can't see why that was necessary," says Jackson, trying not to display too much irritation.

"I don't trust anyone," replies Bin Hassan, "and that's why I'll remain a free man."

Jackson makes no further comment.

"Let's get this done," instructs Bin Hassan. "I'll make a statement and will not answer any questions, but your viewers will be able to see that I'm very much alive and as determined as ever to carry out my mission."

Jackson is unhappy about this. "I think there should be questions, otherwise it might appear that we have become your mouthpiece. My bosses in London might even choose not to run the statement."

"I don't believe that. They'd be mad not to."

"You're probably right," admits Jackson, "but we'll have to accompany your statement with a declaration that you refused to answer questions."

"So be it, Roger."

Jackson has another idea. "Let's compromise. I'll ask you a question that will allow you to make your statement, then when you finish, you must allow me to ask at least one question for my own professional credibility. Whether you choose to answer it is up to you. As you well know, I'm in no position to force you."

Bin Hassan thinks about this for a few moments, then agrees. "Okay, but let's do this standing up and let's make it quick." The guards remove the chairs and Bin Hassan orders them to stand each side of him, but a pace behind. "I want you to make sure my guards are in the frame," he instructs Pete. "I want your viewers to see that I'm not alone."

Everyone gets in position and Pete starts filming.

Jackson begins his introduction:

> *My cameraman, Peter Fox, and I were snatched off the streets of Armibar this morning by members of the Soldiers of Allah terrorist group...*

Bin Hassan angrily cuts the introduction short:

> *No, no. I won't allow you to describe us as terrorists. We are soldiers fighting a just war. Now, start your introduction again...*

Jackson does as ordered:

> *My cameraman, Peter Fox, and I were snatched off the streets of Armibar this morning by members of the group calling itself Soldiers of Allah. They did so because they wanted us to see that their leader, Ahmed Faisel Bin Hassan, is still alive, contrary to the claims on the group's official website which appears to have been hacked. As is now widely known, Ahmed and I went to school together in London and we were, at that time, good friends. We have since taken very different paths and Ahmed knows that I do not approve of the way he and his group is waging their*

war. He wishes to make a short statement before allowing my cameraman and me to go free.

Bin Hassan responds:

First let me repeat to you in the strongest of terms: We are not terrorists. We are freedom fighters – fighting to shake off the yoke of the callous, imperialistic American military machine and to avenge what their own terrorists did by destroying my entire peace-loving family in Iraq. Let me tell you that our fight will go on until we have achieved victory. Our destruction of the United States Embassy in Armibar is just the first of many such operations, not just here, but in other parts of the world. Clearly, the Americans now know that we are a serious challenge to them, which is why they have carried out a cyberattack on our website and are manipulating it to spread lies about my death and the alleged collapse of Soldiers of Allah. That is the end of my statement.

As arranged, Jackson attempts to ask a question:

Do you have any regrets about the innocent people who died in the embassy attack and might die in future attacks by your organisation?

Bin Hassan responds:

I will not answer any questions. It would be pointless.

Jackson persists:

You may think it pointless, but our viewers would surely like to know if you have any qualms about your operations. Is the killing of innocent people ever on your conscience?

Bin Hassan is annoyed:

I told you! No questions! Now switch off the camera. Now!

The two guards produce their hand guns and wave them at Jackson and Pete and there are no further attempts to pursue the questioning.

******

On the way back to Yassin, Jackson's mind is in turmoil, but Pete is elated. "Another great scoop we've got, Jacko," he whispers.

276

"I even got those thugs waving the guns at us before I switched off the camera. Fucking brilliant!" Jackson is too emotionally drained to respond.

On their arrival back at their car, their phones are returned, but they are ordered not to move or call anyone for five minutes, so that the two Mercedes have a chance to get clear of the area. As they wait impatiently for the time to elapse, Jackson sags in the front seat, struggling vainly to plot a way out of his predicament. He now knows that the $2m promised by the Americans will never be his and that the $250,000 deposit will probably be withdrawn from the Roger Smith account. Then there is also the problem of having to deal with Thomas and any future demands he may decide to make. Pete, on the other hand, remains hyperactive with excitement and keeps repeating "Brilliant! Bloody brilliant!" until Jackson can stand it no more and tells him to "shut the fuck up!"

The five minutes waiting time expires and Jackson phones Mack to tell him about the surprise change of plans and to report that Yassin is driving him and Pete to the bureau. Mack is relieved to know that they are safe and is keen to view the fruits of their latest adventure.

******

When Thomas told Felicity that he was "off the coast and among friends", the bald truth was that he was on the American aircraft carrier *Advance,* anchored in the Mediterranean. It is here that the top-level survivors of the attack on the Armibar Embassy were taken for their safety.

Thomas is seated in front of a computer on a small bench in one of the carrier's battle rooms. Alongside him is a bespectacled and uniformed US Navy commander, Todd Chilton, aged about 50 and with greying hair, close-cropped in the accepted American military style. As a member of the armed forces since he was a teenager, he has the air of a man who has seen it all and done it all.

The room has all the appearances of a NASA installation. There is a wall full of video screens, one larger than the rest, and all operated by lower rank male and female officers seated at computers on a bench immediately in front of Thomas and Todd.

It is 11am and Thomas and Todd have been in the battle room since breakfast, preparing for the moment when Jackson will complete his mission by planting the tracking device. Both are getting tense.

Thomas points to the main screen showing an aerial map of Armibar with a series of flashing lights evenly spread about the city. "All our snatch squads seem to be getting into position. Once Jackson Dunbar's tracker shows up, they'll be ready to pounce."

"My guess is that Bin Hassan will be somewhere in the north west of the city, hiding in the slums," speculates Todd.

Thomas disagrees. "Sorry, but he's from a well-off middle class family and I reckon he'd be more comfortable in one of the reasonably affluent areas in the south-eastern suburbs."

"Want a bet?" asks Todd with a grin.

"Righto. I'll put 100 dollars on that. Will you match me?"

"Sure," says Todd, reaching for his wallet and depositing a $100 note on the bench.

******

At the bureau, Mack and the rest of the team view the Bin Hassan recording. Mack is impressed, but says he will clear it with Marina Kerner before anyone else outside the bureau sees it. He also remembers that he promised to offer it to CNN and Al-Jazeera. He says he will do that once Marina has approved the video for broadcast.

Mack notices that Jackson has gone to his desk and is staring anxiously into the middle distance. "Hey, why so morose? This Bin Hassan stuff is great."

"Thanks," replies Jackson without enthusiasm, "glad you like it."

"Yeah, mate, what's got into you?" Pete asks him. "You've been acting funny ever since we got lifted."

"Sorry about that, but I don't feel very well."

Mack estimates that it will be two or three hours before the video is cleared to go and suggests that in the meantime Jackson go upstairs to his apartment where Joan will show him to the spare room for a nap. "We'll get the interview ready for transmission and will call you down when we're ready to go. All being well, you'll be feeling better by then." Jackson agrees.

Joan greets Jackson at the apartment door. "Mack tells me that you are feeling a bit 'off'."

"Yes, not too sparkling," he agrees. "I just need to rest a little, then I'll probably be okay," he says without conviction.

Joan shows him to the guest bedroom. "Make yourself comfortable here. I'll be working in my study next door and I'll knock on the door when they want you downstairs."

"Thanks, Joan," says Jackson. "How's your book coming along?"

"Quite well, I think. My publishers like the idea of my imagining what it'll be like for the royal family a hundred years from now."

"Good luck with it, Joan. I hope it's as successful as your other books."

"Me too," she says holding up a hand with her fingers crossed.

Jackson goes into the guest bedroom and closes the door behind him. He lies down on the double bed, but is in no mental state to sleep. He stares bleakly at the ceiling, hating himself for getting into such a fix with no easy way out.

******

It is now 1.30pm – 90 minutes after Jackson and Pete were due to be lifted – and Thomas and Todd are anxiously scanning the main screen for any sign of *BH1*, the identity given to Jackson's tracking device. "We should have something by now," worries Thomas. "I hope nothing's gone wrong."

"Maybe your device isn't working," suggests Todd with a frown.

"No, I'm sure it's not that. We made tests from all parts of the city and it never failed."

"It'd better not," says Todd with growing irritation. "And your mate Jackson had better not let us down either. There's too much at stake here. We're being keenly monitored by the White House and the Pentagon."

"Jackson won't let us down, Todd. He now agrees that Bin Hassan cannot be allowed to remain free. And two million dollars is a financial carrot that he's in no position to ignore."

******

It is a half day at the International School and Felicity leaves her assistants in charge of the rehabilitation centre while she takes Sam and Sophie out for the afternoon. She throws her bag on the back seat, having completely forgotten that it still contains the "microphone" that Jackson had failed to collect.

Sam and Sophie come running out of the school to greet their mother. They are in the school's neat grey and green uniform. Sophie gets in the front seat, Sam in the back. They drive away.

"Have you got anything to eat, Mummy?" Sam asks.

"Haven't you just had lunch?" Felicity wants to know.

"Yes, but I'm still hungry," he says.

"There are some mints in my bag. Have one of those," she tells him.

Sam rummages around in Felicity's bag and finds a bag of sweets. He takes a couple and pops them in his mouth. He also finds Jackson's "microphone" in its small cardboard box.

"What this, Mummy?" he asks, holding it up for her to see in the rear view mirror.

"Oh Heavens, that's Uncle Jackson's microphone! He was supposed to collect it this morning. Just put it back in my bag and he can get it some other time."

Being a curious child, Sam ignores his mother's order and opens the box to see what is in it. He takes out the tracker and sees that it has a toggle switch at the top. He flicks the switch and a tiny red light is illuminated. After a few seconds he switches it off, then on again. His mother sees him playing with the device and shouts at him: "Put that away immediately! Uncle Jackson will be cross if he knows that you're messing about with it."

Sam reluctantly switches it off, puts it back in its box and drops it onto the seat beside him. "Where are we going?" he asks.

"To the park for some fresh air."

Sam groans. "The park is boring. Why can't we go home so that I can play games on the computer?"

"You can play games after we've been to the park and you've done your homework," she tells him.

"I don't want to go to the park," he moans.

"Well, you're going, so that's it!"

"Just shut up, Sam," shouts Sophie. "I like the park. I want to play with my friends there."

CHAPTER 29

On the aircraft carrier *Advance*, Thomas and Todd are relieved, then baffled, when the tracker *BH1* pops up on the screen, then disappears, then returns, then disappears. "What in damnation is going on?" asks Todd.

"I don't know," replies Thomas. "It's almost as though he's trying to send us a message. The tracker is not in either of the places we thought it might be and it seems to be moving."

Todd shouts to the row of officers in front of him. "Give us a satellite shot of where that signal came from."

A picture comes up on one of the screens and it shows a street not far from the centre of Armibar. The road is busy with cars and other vehicles. "Well, that doesn't help, does it," says Thomas. "The signal could have come from any of those vehicles. At least we know that the tracker seems to be working, so we'll have to sit here patiently and see what happens."

"I don't like this," says Todd tetchily. "Why is the tracker moving? It should be in a fixed position."

"Let's see what happens next. I'm sure that Jackson won't let us down. Relax."

"Is there any way we can make contact with him?" asks Todd.

"Impossible, at least not until he is released by Bin Hassan's lot, but let's see what they say when I ring his office."

There is no mobile phone signal on the ship, so Thomas uses a control room phone to dial the BBC. The call is answered by Samira.

"Good afternoon," Thomas says, "I wonder if I could speak to Mr Jackson Dunbar?"

"I'm sorry," Samira replies, "but Mr Dunbar is not in the office at present."

"That's a pity. When will he be available?"

"Not for a few more hours, at least. I can pass on a message if you give me your name."

"No, it's okay. It's not urgent. I will try again later this afternoon."

"Tomorrow would be better," advises Samira. "Mr Dunbar will be very busy for the rest of today."

The call ends and Thomas turns to Todd. "See! It all looks okay. We just have to be patient."

******

Felicity drives into the park through an avenue of palms and heads for the playground. She pulls up in the shade of a large tree next to a refreshments hut. She and the children get out of the car and she buys them each an ice cream. Sam is still complaining about being taken to the park. "Stop being difficult," she tells him. "Be quiet and eat your ice cream!"

The three of them walk the 100 metres or so to the playground with its swings, roundabouts, slides and climbing frames. They finish their ice creams and the two children join in playing with a number of other children. Sam grudgingly begins to enjoy himself, first on the swings, then on the slides. Sophie prefers the climbing frames.

Felicity takes a seat on a park bench and engages in small talk in English with a well-to-do Western-dressed Arab woman, the mother of some of the other children. She takes no particular notice when Sam runs to join Sophie on a rope climbing frame.

Several minutes pass then she hears a dull thud and screaming from Sam. She sees him sitting on the ground and crying. She goes to him and picks him up. "What happened?" she asks.

"Sophie pushed me off the frame," Sam asserts, wiping away tears.

"No, I didn't," insists Sophie, "he fell when he tried to pull me off the frame."

"She's lying!" Sam shouts.

"No I'm not," insists Sophie, "he was definitely trying to make me fall, Mummy. He's a very nasty boy."

Felicity, faced with two conflicting accounts, is inclined to believe Sophie, in view of Sam's previous ill temper. She helps him off the ground and sees that his knees are scraped and his shirt torn.

"Now look what you've done," Felicity shouts. "That shirt will have to be replaced. I'm really fed up with you today, Sam. Go back to the car. Stay there until Sophie and I return."

He sulkily returns to the car and climbs into the back seat, while Sophie, proud of her victory over her irritating brother, returns to the climbing frame and Felicity resumes her chat with the Arab mother.

Sam is angry and immediately bored. He helps himself to another mint and for want of something more interesting to do. He returns his attention to Jackson's "microphone". He swings it around by its cord, then switches it on and off a couple of times, then on again. The device generates little further interest and he drops it back on the seat. He goes to the car window and looks dejectedly at his sister in the playground.

******

Upstairs in Mack and Joan's apartment, Jackson summons the courage to phone Thomas to explain how the plan to capture Bin Hassan has spectacularly failed, but Thomas's phone appears to be switched off or out of range. He then remembers that he was to have collected the tracking device from Felicity. He dials her mobile and is surprised to have it answered by a boy's voice.

"Hello, who is that?" asks Jackson.

"It's Sam."

"Oh hello Sam, it's Uncle Jackson. Why are you answering your mother's phone?"

"She left it in the car."

"Where's she gone?"

"She's in the playground with my nasty sister. Sophie told lies about me and I've been made to stay in the car."

"Oh, I see. What playground?"

"At the park we usually go to. I don't know its name."

"Oh yes. I know the one: Malik Malouf. Well, when your mother comes back, tell her that I'll pick up my microphone another time."

"It's here in the car, Uncle Jackson. I've just been looking at it."

Jackson is alarmed. "You haven't been playing with it, have you?"

Sam senses the sudden change of tone in Jackson's voice. "No, Uncle Jackson, it just fell out of Mummy's bag, but I put it straight back again," he lies.

Jackson is relieved. "Well, it's important you don't play with it, Sam, as it could, er, break very easily."

"Yes, Uncle Jackson," he says, then asking "when are you going to visit us again to read some more *Hairy Maclary*?

"I don't know, Sam. I may have to go away for a while. I don't know. But I can't talk any more just now. Please tell your mother I phoned."

"Okay," confirms Sam and the call ends.

******

On the aircraft carrier *Advance*, there is huge relief in the battle control room when the *BH1* signal comes up steadily on the main screen.

"At last!" shouts Todd. He turns to the row of operators in front of him and calls for a satellite view of the area. A clear live picture comes up on the screen, showing that the source of the signal is a car partly obscured by a tree.

"That's really odd," observes Thomas. "Why the hell would Jackson be taken to a park? That makes no sense. We sometimes take our kids there. Why didn't they go to one of Bin Hassan's safe houses?"

"Well, Thomas, ours is not to reason why, but it appears that we've both lost our bet. The evil cocksucker has tried to outsmart us by doing the interview in a completely unexpected spot. How long will it take your snatch squads to get there?"

Thomas checks the screen and sees that there are two armed teams in the area. "About five minutes," he estimates.

"Good," says Todd. "We'll send instructions that they block off all Bin Hassan's possible escape routes, but to stay well away from the target."

Thomas doesn't understand. "What do you mean they should stay away from the target? That's not the agreed plan. They should go straight in and grab him, just as soon as Jackson is clear."

"There's been a change of plan," reveals Todd.

"What are you talking about?" Thomas demands.

Todd doesn't reply and instead calls to an officer at the end of the row in front of them. "Are you locked onto the signal yet?"

"Yes, sir, all set to go," comes the reply.

Todd pushes an intercom button and shouts into it. "Fire both, five seconds apart." Thomas is stunned and after about 10 seconds, a voice comes up on speaker: "Both launches confirmed, sir."

The colonel turns back to Thomas. "Sorry, Buddy. Orders from the Pentagon. We can't risk missing this guy. Two Tomahawks are now on their way to blast him to Paradise. Your job is to make sure that your snatch squads don't let him leave before the rockets reach him in about 10 minutes. If he tries to move, they must open fire and force him back into the target area."

Thomas is furious. "You guys have stitched us up. Killing him may make you look good on the news bulletins, but it's a short term policy. There's much more to be gained from capturing and interrogating guys like Bin Hassan. You don't seem to understand that being martyred is a plus not a minus for them. But they hate being locked up for the rest of their miserable lives."

Todd shrugs his shoulders. "Let's talk about this later. Our job isn't yet done." He turns his attention back to the screen with the satellite picture. "Let's get a closer look at the target."

The operator zooms in and Felicity's car can be partly seen protruding from under the tree. But there is no sign of any movement.

"Has anyone seen Jackson and his cameraman leaving?" asks Thomas.

The satellite operator turns to them. "Well, I saw a car leaving the park about the time *BH1* first showed on the screen. Maybe they were in that."

"Did the car come from the same part of the park?" Thomas asks.

"Sorry, I don't know," replies the operator, "I only saw it going out the main gate."

The British snatch squads have arrived and are spreading out across the park boundary.

"Your boys are in place," notes Todd. "They've been told not to take any pre-emptive action, so they'll be safe."

The location being targeted still baffles Thomas. "I really don't get it. Why would Bin Hassan choose that area? And why did we have those brief signals from the tracker? That was never meant to happen."

"Stop worrying, buddy, there must have been a reason and that's definitely the right tracker giving us a 100% strong signal," says Todd, who goes back to watching the satellite view.

"There's a playground very near the target. Can we see that, please? Thomas asks.

The operator zooms out to show a dozen or so children and adults there. "Won't they be hit by the blast?" Thomas asks.

"The Tomahawks have pinpoint accuracy," replies Todd. "There shouldn't be too much collateral damage. Can't be helped if some of them are hurt, though."

"Five minutes to impact time," announces an operator in the front row. At the same time, a woman and a child can be seen leaving the playground and walking towards the target area.

"Shit!" declares Thomas, "they're walking straight into the blast."

Todd shrugs his shoulders. "They probably won't feel a thing when it happens."

The satellite operator zooms in for a closer look and the two figures can now be seen more clearly. "Oh Christ, it's Felicity and Sophie," screams Thomas.

"Do you know them?" asks Todd.

"It's my wife and our daughter, Todd. Christ! Something terrible has gone wrong. They must have the tracker. Quick. Cancel the strike before it's too late!"

"Hell, buddy, that's not possible. They're on a pre-set route. Does your wife have a mobile?"

"Yes, of course."

"Well, ring her and tell her to get to hell back to the playground as fast as she can."

Thomas dials Felicity's mobile from a phone on the bench. It rings out for what seems an eternity. Finally, it is answered by Sam. "Is that you again, Uncle Jackson?"

"No," shouts Thomas, "it's Daddy. Where are you?"

"I'm in our car."

"At the park?"

"Yes, Daddy."

"Quick! Get out of the car as fast as you can and tell Mummy and Sophie you must all run as far away as you can."

"Why, Daddy?"

"Just do as you're told, Sam!"

"But I can't Daddy. I was naughty and Mummy told me I must stay in the car until she returns."

"You must get out of the car, Sam. Now! Please. You must!"

"I can see Mummy coming back now. I'll tell her what you said." Sam ends the call.

There is an announcement over the battle room speaker on the carrier *Advance*: "One minute to impact."

Thomas buries his head in his hands, unable to watch the screen, but Todd is transfixed by the image of Felicity and Sophie continuing to walk briskly towards the car. Then there is a flash as the first Tomahawk makes a direct hit on the car, followed seconds later by another direct hit. Todd flinches, but there is a triumphant roar from the operators sitting along the bench in front of him and Thomas.

The screen blinks, then through the cloud of black smoke it is briefly possible to see the upturned and unrecognisable wreck of

Felicity's car. The tree it was under has been reduced to a shredded stump and the adjacent refreshment hut has been obliterated. Over in the playground, the image is clearer with several children and adults seen lying on the ground, either wounded or dead.

Thomas's body shakes and he begins to weep, his head in his hands. Todd, too, is shocked and puts a hand on Thomas's shoulder. "Sorry buddy," he says. "Sorry." He knows there is nothing more that he can say.

CHAPTER 30

Jackson has been called downstairs to the bureau where Jackson and Farouk have finished editing the Bin Hassan interview. Mack says London has cleared it for broadcast and it will go out at the top of the next hour – just 10 minutes away – and will be followed by a live Q&A. "Will you be okay for the Q&A, Jacko?"

Jackson nods a little uncertainly. "Yes, I should be okay. I'll just make myself a strong coffee first."

Mack goes to Samira. "Give CNN and Al-Jazeera a call and tell them we've got this interview and they can have as much of it as they like, provided they give us a full credit."

She picks up her phone and begins dialling as Jackson goes onto the broadcast stand where Farouk fits him with a lapel microphone.

Jackson's brain remains in turmoil and he is finding it difficult to think clearly. The Bin Hassan interview is now being simulcast on World News and the domestic News Channel. Farouk gives Jackson a one-minute warning that the video is about to end.

Samira calls out to Mack: "I've told CNN and Al-Jazeera and they're going to record it off air. They want to know if we heard the two explosions a short time ago. I told them we hadn't."

"We'll look into it as soon as Jacko comes off air," he replies.

Samira's phone rings and she takes the call from someone with a news tip. "Oh, it's just happened has it?" she asks. "Well, thank you very much for that. We'll get a reporter there right away."

She puts the phone down and calls to Mack. "Those explosions were missiles of some sort hitting Malik Malouf Park."

Jackson overhears her. "Where did you say?"

"Malik Malouf Park," she repeats.

"Oh my God!" he shouts. "Oh my God! Oh shit! Felicity and the kids are there."

Jackson rips off his microphone and runs to Yassin. "Let's go. Take me to the park as fast as you can!"

Mack is gobsmacked. "You can't go now, they're crossing over to you from London."

"Fuck London!" shouts Jackson.

The Mortal Maze

Mack looks up at the monitor to see presenter Margaret Mathieson announcing that she is about to talk live to Jackson. But all that comes up is a shot of the empty broadcast platform. "Oh dear," she says, "we seem to be having some technical problems there, so let me summarise what emerged in that exclusive statement made to us by the terrorist leader Ahmed Faisel Bin Hassan…"

Jackson and Yassin go out the door. Pete grabs his camera and goes after them. "Hey, guys, wait for me!"

"What's that all about?" Mack asks Samira.

"Sorry, but I haven't the faintest idea."

"Well, who's Felicity?"

"I don't know. I've never heard him mention anyone by that name."

As they talk, the phone rings and Samira hits the speaker button.

"BBC Armibar. Can I help?"

"Um, I hope so," says a male voice with an educated East Coast American accent. "Is your reporter Mr Dunbar there by any chance?"

"Not at the moment. He's just gone out on a story."

"I see. Has he gone to investigate the explosions?"

"Who is this speaking?" Samira asks.

"My name doesn't matter, ma'am," says the American voice. "I am calling on behalf of one of Mr Dunbar's friends."

"Do you know something about these explosions?"

"Oh no. Not at all, but it's urgent that I speak to Mr Dunbar. I think my friend has his mobile number, so we'll call that."

"You can try if it's really urgent, but it's not a good time," she tells him.

"Well, thank you for your help anyway. Goodbye."

The call ends. "What was that all about?" Mack asks Samira. "There seem to be things going on that I know nothing about."

Samira draws Mack's attention to a flash that's just appeared on her computer screen. "The agencies are already onto the park explosions," she says. "There are reports of two cruise-type missiles

291

seen coming in very low from the Mediterranean just before the blasts."

"I'll get onto London and warn them that it looks like another 'biggie' is heading their way," says Mack. "Grab a taxi and get your backside to the park pronto. I'm worried that Jacko is imploding, so we might need your back-up. Take the satellite kit with you and Farouk and I'll get everything else set up."

Samira grabs the satellite kit and runs down into the street where she hails a passing taxi.

******

Yassin is breaking the speed limits and running red lights to get Jackson and Pete to Malik Malouf Park. Jackson is in shock and Pete can't understand why. "What's going on with you, mate? We've done this sort of story before. What's so special about this one?"

"There's been a terrible, terrible fuck-up. I think a friend and her kids are at that park."

"Shit, man, that's serious," says Pete, "but why blame yourself? It's just bad luck. Anyway, we'll probably find they're okay."

As the Range Rover approaches the park, black smoke can be seen rising high into the sky. Soldiers, wearing camouflage outfits of an unidentified army are blocking the main entrance, but Jackson orders Yassin not to stop. He flashes his headlights and furiously toots the horn.

The soldiers, seeing it is a non-threatening media vehicle, jump aside and the car heads down the palm tree avenue at speed towards the playground. It skids to a halt just metres from the blast scene. Pete jumps out and begins filming while Jackson desperately seeks Felicity and the children. He runs to the playground as the first ambulances arrive. They are not there, but there are a number of children and adults lying on the ground, some dead, but most crying from wounds. He returns to the blast scene and sees body parts and shredded clothes lying in the blast crater. He realises instantly that they are the remains of Felicity, Sam and Sophie.

******

In the battle control room of the carrier *Advance*, Todd puts down the phone after his anonymous call to the BBC and tells Thomas that Jackson is alive and apparently on his way to Malik Malouf Park. He hands Thomas the phone and urges him to try Jackson's mobile. He nods agreement. As he dials the number, Todd's attention is drawn to a screen showing BBC News with Jackson interviewing Bin Hassan.

Jackson takes Thomas's call as he stares in dismay at the overturned remains of Felicity's car.

"Yes!" he says abruptly.

"Jacko, it's Thomas. Where are you?"

"I'm at Malik Malouf Park."

"Have you found Felicity and the children?"

"Yes. I have."

"That's good?"

"It isn't good, Thomas. They didn't survive."

"Oh Christ," says Thomas, beginning to sob, "what've we done?"

"What have you done, Thomas? Don't fucking try to fucking implicate me in responsibility for this fucking disaster!"

Thomas begins to shout. "If you'd done what we agreed, this wouldn't have happened. Did you lose your nerve?"

"No, I didn't lose my nerve, Thomas. Binnie just outsmarted us and lifted me before I had a chance to collect the tracker from Felicity. It's as simple as that. So the brutal truth is that your target is still alive while your wife and children are dead. You betrayed me and you betrayed your own family by trying to kill him. It's your fault, Thomas. You have to face up to the fact that you're a treacherous bastard." Thomas begins sobbing into the phone and Jackson angrily cuts him off.

Samira has arrived in her taxi and successfully talked her way through the barriers set up by the security forces. She looks in astonishment at the devastation left by the missiles and runs to Jackson, now sitting on the edge of a blast crater and staring blankly into space as tears stream down his face.

"Are you okay, Jacko?" she asks.

He shakes his head. "No, I'm not. I'm not at all okay."

Pete takes a break from filming and goes to Jackson and Samira. "I've just been called by Mack saying that London wants an immediate 'live' using the satellite kit. Can you be ready in a couple of minutes?"

Jackson shakes his head again. "Samira will do it." He turns to her. "Just describe what you can see and explain that all this has been caused by American missiles fired during a stuffed up attempt to kill the terrorist Ahmed Faisel Bin Hassan. That'll be enough for now."

He walks off towards the BBC car, a crushed man.

Pete watches him go. "Jeez! Jacko sure is a mess. Anyway, are you okay to do the live, Samira?" She nods agreement, still distracted by the emotional unravelling of a colleague. "Okay," Pete says, "I'll set up the satellite link while you put your thoughts in order."

CHAPTER 31

Thomas is in a dark suit and tie and standing with a group of about 20 mourners beside an open grave in the grounds of a parish church in a genteel suburb of West London. The sky is overcast and there is a slight chill in the air.

Thomas face is grey and drawn. He appears to have aged more than a decade.

The mourners include a man and three women standing together, but apart from the others. They are Felicity's elderly parents and her two sisters, Beverley and Nina. All are in a state of shock.

Three coffins – one adult size and two smaller ones – are wheeled from the church on funeral biers. The mourners are acutely aware that the coffins are almost empty because so little of the bodies could be recovered from the blast scene.

The coffins are lowered into the grave by the assistant funeral directors – first the one for Felicity, then those for Sam and Sophie.

The elderly vicar steps forward in his black cassock, sprinkles a handful of earth on the coffins and intones the traditional words.

> *We have entrusted Felicity, Sam and Sophie to God's*
> *mercy,*
> *and we now commit their bodies to the ground:*
> *earth to earth, ashes to ashes, dust to dust:*
> *in sure and certain hope of the resurrection to eternal life*
> *through our Lord Jesus Christ,*
> *who will transform our frail bodies*
> *that they may be conformed to his glorious body,*
> *who died, was buried, and rose again for us.*
> *To him be glory for ever.*

The vicar and the mourners murmur *Amen.*

Thomas is handed a red rose by the funeral director and he lets it drop into the open grave.

Felicity's family move away without speaking and leave the church grounds in a chauffeur-driven saloon car. They have made it known that whatever the truth of the events leading to the deaths in Malik Malouf Park, they hold Thomas responsible.

295

Thomas steps away from the grave and accepts softly-spoken condolences from a line of male and female mourners. Last to speak to him is Bart Watson, his MI6 boss in Armibar. There is a protracted, rather embarrassed handshake. "I wish I'd taken better notice of your worries," Bart admits. "No words, no matter how heartfelt, can bring back your wife and children. But I can assure you that despite this dreadful and regrettable event, our determination to bring Bin Hassam and his like to justice will continue undiminished."

Thomas mutters a "thank you" and Bart departs. Thomas returns to the grave, takes one more look at the coffins and wipes away his tears. "Forgive me, Flip; forgive me, kids; forgive me, Lord," he murmurs. He nods to the two grave diggers and they step forward with their shovels to complete their task.

In a different part of London, Jackson sits in a semi-circle of about 30 men and women of all age groups. The room is functional and austere, and a variety of signs and posters on the wall make it clear that it is in a community hall. A meeting is about to begin, chaired by Barbara, a woman in her forties with a warm smile, no-nonsense greying hair and wearing neat informal clothes.

"Welcome back," she says. "I'm delighted to see that there are no drop-outs this week. Additionally, we have a new member who wishes to be known as Roger. Some of you may recognise him from the television news, but I know that there will be no breaches of our firm bond of confidentiality." She signals to Jackson to stand up. "Right, Roger, perhaps you could introduce yourself and tell us a little about why you have joined our group."

Jackson stands and begins speaking. "I am… I have… Umm. Let me start again: Hello. I'm here because I have finally recognised that I need help. I have an addiction – a gambling addiction and I drink too much. For a long while I have denied this. I have become a chronic liar to myself and to my colleagues and friends. I deluded myself that once I got the 'big win', I would walk away from gambling, but I can't. And I'm not sure why. To be honest, this addiction is ruining my life. Worse, it has ruined – destroyed, even –

the lives of others I loved. I am overwhelmed by shame and remorse. That is why I'm here."

Jackson resumes his seat with tears running down his face. There is a ripple of sympathetic applause from others in the group. "Thank you for being so honest about your situation," says Barbara. "Honesty is the first important step towards recovery. Your story is far from unique. Everyone with us today has a tale to tell about gambling as a compulsion, but you're among friends now. Over the years, our little group has been very successful in helping addicts regain control of their lives. I feel confident that your honesty, with our support, will lead you back to a normal life. Please take heart, Roger."

The meeting ends after an hour and Jackson shakes hands with his new friends. He is invited to join them for a coffee, but says he has someone waiting for him in the lobby. That someone is Zareena, now wearing an elegant business suit. They exchange kisses. "How did it go?" she asks.

"It'll be a long haul," he replies. "It's not just the gambling problem; it's the guilt that I'll always feel about the deaths of Felicity and the children."

"That'll always be difficult," she agrees, "but I'm pleased that you're making a serious attempt to re-start your life."

"Thank you, Zareena. It's good to have the support of a good friend."

"It's Maya, my real name, from now on, Jacko," she says with a gentle smile. "Zareena is my past; Maya is my present and my future."

"Sorry, yes it's Maya," he agrees with a warm smile.

They are joined by a tall fair-haired Middle Eastern woman also wearing smart Western clothes and, like Maya, in her mid-twenties. She is introduced to Jackson. "I'd like you to meet my university friend, Luna. She also has a six-month study visa and we've taken a flat together to see how our relationship develops."

"Very nice to meet you, Luna," Jackson says.

"Yes, and you, too," she replies. "I used to watch you on the television in Armibar. You're a very brave reporter and Maya spoke of you as a good friend."

"That's very nice," he says. He turns back to Maya. "What's the situation with your mother?"

"Oh, I've saved up enough money for her to join us on a tourist visa," she explains, "then we'll have to see what happens. It's looking good, though, as Luna and I have been told we have a very good chance of getting long-term jobs here as court and hospital translators. My mother will probably be allowed to stay here, as long as we can support her."

Jackson checks his watch. "Well, I'd better get back to the newsroom. I'm working part time for a few months as a respite from the stresses and dangers of Armibar and while I try to sort myself out."

He and Maya exchange kisses and he shakes Luna's hand. "See you both again, soon, I hope." He walks off and Maya and Luna go into a nearby coffee shop, hand-in-hand.

END NOTES

JACKSON DUNBAR

With a combination of one-to-one psychiatric counselling and membership of the gambling addicts' group, Jackson gradually comes to terms with the deep rejection he felt as a child when his parents took little interest in his life. He has successfully stopped gambling, accepting that he must view his addiction in much the same way as an alcoholic recognises that there is no such thing as "just a little drink". He is grateful that circumstances prevented him from selling his apartment in London as this has given him a base from which to steadily re-establish his finances. The BBC has given him a new job as a London-based Middle East analyst, a post he enjoys. He knows that the images of what happened to Felicity, Sam and Sophie will be with him forever.

MACK GALBRAITH / SAMIRA LANG / PETER FOX

Mack, Samira and Pete have remained in Armibar reporting on the country's struggle to avoid becoming another Egypt, Libya, Yemen or Iraq. Mack has given up smoking at long last after an old school friend died of lung cancer. He is feeling better for it. He is enjoying what will be his final 10 years stationed in the Middle East.

After an intensive training session in London, Samira is doing most of the TV reporting from the Armibar bureau. She is pregnant with her first child. Her engineer husband, Nigel, now has a permanent job in Central Arabia.

Pete continues to be the best television cameraman in Armibar and is settling down with a local woman he met on a reporting job. He is hoping that one day the gangland death threats against him will be lifted and he will be able to return to Australia.

THOMAS FULHAM

Thomas has been transferred back to London where he now works for MI5, Britain's domestic security agency.

Because of his Arabic language skills and his experience of the Middle East, he is given a desk job monitoring the activities of local jihadis. He plans to retire in a year so that he can devote himself full time to the Felicity Fulham Trust, a charity he has established to raise funds to equip hospitals around the world treating child victims of war.

Although he has women friends, the circumstances surrounding the deaths of Felicity, Sam and Sophie are still too raw for him to consider another serious relationship.

AHMED FAISEL BIN HASSAN

The United States Defence Department announces a $5m reward for information leading to the capture or death of Ahmed Faisel Bin Ahmed. His movements are consequently betrayed by a member of *Soldiers of Allah*. He is captured by an undercover American squad on his way to Armibar International Airport to catch a London-bound flight, posing as a prosperous businessman. He had a false British passport in the name of Jeremy Carlisle, his bushy beard was gone and his hair was short and neat. In place of an ankle-length Arab thawb and his keffiyeh headwear was a dark Paul Smith suit with a discreet striped tie.

The Americans smuggle him out of Central Arabia and fly him to a prison in a remote part of Texas where he is interrogated by a joint Anglo-American team. He is later reported to have been "shot dead while attempting to escape." Despite the ferocity of the cross-examinations, Bin Hassan never revealed why he was trying to return to Britain.